The Beach Escape

RACHEL
MAGEE

The Beach Escape

Cover design by Michael Rehder

Print 978-1-952210-65-5
eBook 978-1-952210-66-2

www.hallmarkpublishing.com

Chapter One

TODAY WAS NOT SUPPOSED TO be the first day of Molly Lawrence's new life.

Molly 2.0, the updated, cooler, more glamourous version, was scheduled to start at eight a.m. on Monday morning. She'd written it that way on her calendar and had arranged the rest of her plans accordingly. Today, for example, she was supposed to be unpacking her moving boxes. Tomorrow? Laundry and grocery shopping. But one unexpected call in the middle of the night had changed all of that. So, here she was, launching the revamped version of her life three days early.

She brushed cat hair off her shirt, left over from her last client—a gorgeous twelve-year-old Ragdoll cat named Cupcake in for her yearly checkup—and pulled up her schedule.

Truth be told, she hadn't expected to need this new life at all. Up until four months ago, she'd been convinced that Molly the Original was pretty perfect, going exactly according to the plan she'd drawn up in her junior high diary with those colorful sparkle gel pens. And yet the entire thing had unraveled in the course of one day.

One really bad day.

But how she'd gotten here wasn't the point. The point was she was getting the rare chance to reimagine her life. She could go on adventures she'd never even considered before. Take her new gig, for example. Instead of a normal vet who showed up to the same neighborhood clinic day in and day out, she was transitioning to a career as a traveling vet who bounced around from city to interesting city, filling in for those out on short-term leave. And she couldn't be more excited that her first assignment was a three-month stay in the beautiful Florida panhandle beach town of Emerald Cove.

Of course, that assignment was supposed to start on Monday, but the vet she was replacing had a baby who'd decided to make an early appearance. Maybe that was a good sign. Along with adventure, Molly 2.0 was going to embrace spontaneity. She was going to be one of those people who rolled with the punches and could go with the flow. At least, that was her goal as soon as she got more used to how this whole spontaneity thing worked. At the moment, she wouldn't have hated having a little more of a heads up so she could've washed her brand-new puppy-paw print scrubs before she had to wear them.

But all in all, scratchy scrubs aside, it'd been a pretty great spontaneous first day of her adventurous job. The clients at Gulfview Animal Clinic had a lot to do with that. Putting it simply, they were amazing. Every single one of them had been sweet, accepting, and more than welcoming. Their humans weren't so bad, either.

Molly pulled up her final appointment of the day and clicked on the name, Chompers. Normally—or what she was calling normal from the vast experience of her eight-hour shift—that double-tap should've taken her to the screen where she could access all of the animal's charts and information. However, this one didn't go anywhere. The only information connected with this client were the letters ECTRR. Odd.

She jabbed at the screen, trying a couple more tricks she'd picked up during the day, but nothing worked. That was the problem with spontaneity. Things didn't always go as well as they did when they were carefully planned out. Learning how to navigate an unfamiliar system on the fly without anyone to show her the ropes was a perfect example. Hopefully, Chompers' owner could fill in the missing details she needed to complete today's appointment.

She walked from her office through the back entrance of exam room two to make sure it was ready for the patient, then headed out the door on the opposite side that led to the lobby.

"Chompers." She always used a sing-song voice when she talked to animals. In her experience, it seemed to put the nervous creatures more at ease, even from the very first time she said their name.

Only this time, there weren't any animals hanging out in the waiting room, nervous or otherwise.

She craned her neck, looking all around the small spaces where fur babies could hide. "Chompers?" she called again, checking her tablet to make sure she had the right name.

"That's me." The only other living being in the room stood from his chair and strode toward her.

The first thing she noticed about this particular creature was that he wasn't a furry, four-legged friend. He was a man. One with warm chestnut eyes and the kind of authentic smile that was contagious. The stubble covering his chiseled jaw seemed to be more a product of his lifestyle than any sort of deliberate fashion choice, which somehow made it more attractive. He looked like someone who'd stopped by after wrapping up some epic adventure. Or maybe he was on his way to start an epic adventure. Or maybe both.

"You're Chompers?"

He extended his hand. "Actually, it's pronounced Grant Torres." His grin widened, producing a set of charming dimples. Of course he had dimples. He was like the poster child for ruggedly handsome. He probably free-climbed rocky cliffs, then stopped traffic at the top to help little old ladies cross the street, too. "It's a pleasure to meet you..."

"Molly. Dr. Molly Lawrence." She grasped his hand. Molly had never thought to classify someone's grip as friendly, but his was. It caused a bubbly feeling in her chest.

"Ahh, the locum vet. Dr. Lacey tells me you'll be filling in for her while she's out on maternity leave."

Molly took her hand back and clutched the tablet against her chest. "That's right."

"Welcome to Emerald Cove, the most charming town on 30A." He leaned closer as if sharing a secret. "At least, that's the claim according to our visitor information."

Molly couldn't help but smile. He had the kind of charm that drew her in. She tucked a fly-away lock of recently highlighted hair that had freed itself from her ponytail behind her ear. "Thanks. I'm looking forward to getting to explore it." She'd been in town for less than twenty-four hours and so far had seen the inside of the furnished condo and the inside of the vet clinic, but she had big plans for a beach stroll after work to explore her new town.

"You should check out Rock Bluff. They have great food, amazing views, and live music on the weekends." He grinned again, showing off his dimples and causing another round of bubbles in her chest.

"Sounds great. Thanks for the suggestion." She made a mental note of it. "But I'm guessing you didn't come in just to give me dinner recommendations. How can I help you this afternoon?"

Grant slid his hands into his pockets. "Is Dr. Lacey around? I have an appointment with her."

Molly flashed her best apologetic expression. "No, sorry. She had to start her leave a little early. It's only me here today."

A look of compassionate concern crossed his handsome face. "Is she okay?"

"Dr. Lacey gave birth to a healthy baby girl yesterday, and both mom and baby are doing well." Molly recited the official update she'd been given to pass on to clients, her mind flickering to the adorable image of the scrunchy-faced newborn Dr. Lacey's husband had texted over that morning. "Is there something I can help you with?"

"Maybe." Grant's mouth twisted to the side in consideration. “Dr. Lacey tells me you have some experience with turtles.”

“Some,” Molly agreed. “I did a year-long internship at a zoo, where I worked with several different breeds. Plus, I saw the occasional pet turtle at the neighborhood practice I was with.”

“Great.” Relief seemed to wash over him. “We have a final exam today and I’d hate to put it off. Would you be willing to help us out this one time?”

As far as Molly knew, a final exam was a memory from college that still gave her nightmares, and she had no idea what any of this had to do with Chompers, but it was her job to help them out. “I’m happy to assist any way I can.”

“Unfortunately”—Grant jerked his thumb toward the doorway—“the big guy was in a mood today, so we’re going to have to go for a ride. I hope you don’t mind.”

Molly stared at the doorway. “Go for a ride? Like a house call?”

Grant bobbed his head from side to side as if considering the term. “Sure, I guess you could call it that.”

“I didn’t know Dr. Lacey did house calls.”

“She does when a hundred fifty-pound loggerhead turtle doesn’t want to go for a ride.”

Molly was all for trying to embrace spontaneity, but this conversation had taken a turn into the bizarre zone. “You have a loggerhead turtle? At your house?”

Grant chuckled. “That would be a sight, wouldn’t it? How about we start over.” He held out his hand again. “I’m Grant Torres, director of Emerald Cove Turtle Rescue and Rehabilitation Center.”

ECTRR. All the pieces were starting to come together. “That makes a lot more sense.” She shook his hand for a second time. “I’m the still-learning-the-ropes substitute vet.”

His eyes twinkled. “Looks to me like you’re killing it.”

She took her hand back, trying to push the sparkly feelings away. She wasn’t the kind of girl who fell for handsome strangers at first sight, like some sort of leading lady in a romcom. At least, not anymore. Although, if she were being totally honest, the fact that this one spent his days caring for sea turtles wasn’t helping. “What exactly does Dr. Lacey do for you?”

“She’s our staff veterinarian. A facility our size doesn’t need a full-time vet. Most rehab centers have a turtle expert come two to three times a month and schedule the turtles around the visit. But since we have our own expert living right in our backyard, she allows us to schedule her whenever we need her.” He shrugged. “We’re a little spoiled.”

“That’s fascinating. I had no idea she did that.” It was starting to make more sense why there wasn’t a chart for Chompers. He wasn’t a Gulfview patient. The appointment on her schedule was probably a placeholder so she wouldn’t get double booked. “I’m sorry she’s not going to be able to make today’s appointment. She’d planned on being here today, but the baby had other ideas.”

“I hear babies have a way of doing that.” His eyes twinkled. “How about you?”

She pointed at herself. “Me? You want me to come examine your loggerhead turtle?”

“I know your job here doesn’t include working with us. But you do have sea turtle experience, and it would really help us out.” One corner of Grant’s mouth pulled up in a lopsided grin that shouldn’t have been as charming as it was.

Nervousness twisted in her gut. The good news was she’d finally gotten rid of the bubbly feeling in her chest. The bad news was it had been replaced with a sort of jittery energy that seeped through her whole body. It’d been more than five years since she’d worked with a sea turtle, and even then, she’d always had another, more qualified vet with her. This was way outside her area of expertise. “It’s been a while since I’ve done anything like that, and I’m far from being an expert. I don’t know that I’m your best candidate.”

“At the moment, you’re our only candidate.” He shoved his hands into his pockets and his tone shifted to one steeped in compassion. “The thing is, this is Chompers’ final exam. He’s met all of his recovery goals and is doing great. The only thing standing between him and the open waters of the ocean is being cleared by a vet. We could get on one of the other specialists’ schedules, but it’ll mean Chompers is stuck in a tank for at least another month.”

That tugged on her heart. Molly didn’t want any creature to have to spend one minute more than absolutely necessary in a hospital, especially a giant sea turtle who could swim hundreds of miles in a day. “I…” She wanted to protest again. Maybe if she’d known ahead of time, she could’ve had a chance to plan for this. She could've reviewed her notes, done some preparation work to get herself ready...

But then she stopped herself. Wasn't her goal to be more adventurous and spontaneous?

She nibbled on her lip, considering the possibilities. "What kind of exam are we doing?"

"Just a basic exam. Nothing fancy."

"It's been a while since I've done even a basic exam." She absent-mindedly traced the perimeter of her tablet with her finger, trying to mentally pull up what she knew about sea turtles. "I mean a long while."

"I happen to know that working with sea turtles is like riding a bike. Once you hop on, it'll all come back to you." And there was that grin again. "I'll even give you a ride to the rehab center in the turtle ambo."

"A turtle ambulance, huh?"

Everything in her wanted to pass. Showing up three days early to a job she knew she was starting was one thing. But examining sea turtles at a rescue and rehabilitation center? That was a whole different level of unexpected.

But what kind of effort was she making on her new goal if she passed on the first spontaneous adventure that came her way? Plus, she'd never been in a turtle ambulance before.

She drew in a deep breath, hoping she didn't regret what she was about to say. "All right. Let's do this."

Chapter Two

GRANT LED THE NEW LOCUM vet to the turtle ambo he'd parked in Gulfview Veterinary Clinic's tiny parking lot. It was a good thing it was late in the day and there weren't any other Gulfview clients there, because the large green truck took up almost half the lot.

"Huh. I guess a turtle ambulance is just like a people ambulance." She paused and propped her hands on her hips, her head tilting to the side as she took it in.

"Except for the turtle painted on the side and a slightly modified cabin, it's one and the same."

Dr. Lacey had given him a quick background on the substitute vet who'd be replacing her for the next few months. She'd graduated top of her class, had an impressive, well-versed work history, was very involved in several charities, and had come highly recommended. Grant had imagined such an accomplished vet to be older, serious and, though he was embarrassed to admit it, maybe slightly stuffy.

But Dr. Molly Lawrence was as far from stuffy as she was from old. She had to be close to his age, probably around thirty, and her brightly colored cartoon scrubs and high, swingy, blond ponytail showed a playful side he found intriguing. But what really caught his attention was her eyes. There was a kindness there that resonated with him, and he found himself wanting to know more about Gulfview's substitute vet.

"You even have lights. Do they really work?" Molly asked.

"Of course. Climb aboard, and I'll let you turn them on." He opened the passenger side door for her.

She eyed him skeptically. "On the road? Like this is an emergency?"

"It is an emergency to Chompers. The sooner we get this over with, the sooner he can get back in his tank and relax. Doctor visits make him nervous."

"I feel his pain. Turtle visits make me nervous."

Grant chuckled. Impressive resume, playful spirit, and obvious passion for animals. She was by far the most interesting vet he'd met in a long time, even if she did seem a little on the cautious side. So far, he approved of Dr. Lacey's choice for her replacement. He walked around to the other side and climbed into the driver's seat, sticking his key in the ignition. "To be clear, that was a no to the lights and siren?"

"Wait a second. You didn't say anything about a siren." She paused and pursed her lips together, reconsidering the question. "Nope. Still a pass."

He shrugged. "Okay, but your loss." He shifted into drive and slowly pulled the big old ambo out of the parking lot and onto the busy two-lane highway that ran through the middle of town.

Molly settled in her seat, keeping her gaze on the

scene in front of them. "Tell me more about our friend Chompers and what we'll be doing today."

"It's a standard comprehensive exam. Think of it like a checkup to make sure everything's running the way it should before we release him into the wild."

"We did a couple of those with the turtles when I was at the zoo." She snagged her bottom lip with her teeth, as if replaying the exams in her mind. "Except for the release part, of course."

"Well, sure," Grant agreed. "The zoo must've been fascinating. What was your favorite animal to work with?"

Molly lit up, her passion for animals evident. "There were so many amazing animals, it's hard to narrow it down to a favorite." She tapped her chin while she thought. "They had a pretty great tower of giraffes. Although the fact that they had three calves while I was there might've swayed my opinion a bit."

"A tower of giraffes? Is that what you call a group?"

She nodded, taking her eyes off her surroundings and focusing her attention on her driver. "We also had an active *crash* of rhinos and a lively *flamboyance* of flamingos."

Grant shook his head in mock disbelief. "And to think, in the marine world we only have boring old schools and pods."

Molly grinned, and it seemed to brighten the entire ambo. "Yeah, but marine animals are pretty fascinating, which makes up for it."

Yep, he liked this Dr. Lawrence already.

He pulled into the parking lot of the plain, square cinderblock building, which felt like his second home. "And that brings us to our final destination. Welcome to Emerald Cove Turtle Rescue and Rehabilitation Center, or as we like to call it, Turtle Rehab."

"Already?" Molly sat rigid in her seat, the same look of nervousness she'd had when he'd first proposed the idea of the exam washing over her. "I thought I'd have more time to...mentally prepare."

"Small-town problems. When there's only one main road and two stoplights, everything is close." He opened his driver-side door and waved for her to follow. "Come on. I'll show you to the veterinarian suite."

"Oh, okay." Although it was an affirming response, she didn't make a move to get out of the ambo.

So, examining a turtle at a rescue and rehab center was a little outside of her comfort zone. He got that. This was a new experience for her. But he'd seen her resume and had read her recommendations. She was more than qualified to be here. Plus, he really needed a vet to sign off on this turtle so Chompers could get back in the ocean, where he belonged.

He made the first move, climbing out of the ambo and walking around to her side. She followed his lead by at least getting out of the truck. She stood in the parking lot staring up at the building.

"We have a pretty cool new state-of-the-art X-ray machine," Grant coaxed. "We got it last year thanks to a generous private donation, and we're not past the point of showing it off."

"An X-ray machine, huh?" Molly shifted her gaze from the building to him, looking amused. "What did you do before?"

"It was tricky." He walked past her and opened one of the double glass doors, holding it to clear the way for her to walk inside. "We had a very ancient, very small one that was usable for about half of our guests. And even then, it only worked about half the time. To be fair, it did a better job of making us good friends with the repair man. Two months ago, I was a groomsman in his wedding to one of my rehab techs, so..." He gave a nonchalant shrug.

"That didn't happen."

Grant nodded at the door he was holding open for her. "Want to see a picture? I have one in my office."

Hesitantly, she started toward the open door. "You said it worked on half of your guests. What did you do the other times?"

"We took them to the hospital, of course."

She paused, as if caught off guard. "The hospital? Like, the people hospital?"

"That's the one. They're the only ones locally who had a machine big enough for some of our larger turtles."

"So you just put them on a gurney and wheeled them through the waiting room with the other patients?" She laughed. It was a deep, happy, authentic sound that left a hint of joy lingering in the air. "I bet that got you some weird looks."

Some of the lingering joy seeped in to his soul, making the world seem a little brighter. "You have no idea."

"Man, would I have loved to see that." Looking more encouraged, she marched past him into the building.

Grant followed her in. "This is our education center and gift shop. We offer tours of our facility several times a day and host a variety of educational opportunities, most geared toward kids, but you're welcome to join any of them."

She had only taken a few steps inside before she paused again. Her head swiveled as she took in the entire space. Grant scanned the room too, trying to look at it through her eyes. He was proud of this space. They'd worked hard on it, and it was, in his opinion, the perfect combination of interactive displays that provided education and shelves of sea-turtle-inspired merch that helped keep this place operational. Plus, if he did say so himself, there was a pretty impressive saltwater fish tank along the far wall he'd helped to install.

"Wow." Molly strode over to the closest display, the one that introduced the five different sea turtle species found in Florida, and tapped on the touchscreen. A picture of one of his all-time favorite loggerheads filled the screen. "This place is way cooler than it looks from the outside."

Grant chuckled, leading her down the center aisle toward the counter that ran along the far wall. "We get that a lot. Apparently, it has something to do with the entrance being understated." He shrugged, as if the lack of any sort of signage in front of their already plain building was a problem he didn't understand. "Maybe we should put a big picture of our new X-ray machine out there to impress people."

Molly scoffed and followed along behind him. "Yeah, that'd probably do it."

He let out a sigh, thinking through the most common criticism their little rehab facility got. "I guess I've never been inspired to spend money out there when the real magic happens in here." Truth be told, when push came to shove, he'd spend ten thousand dollars to better the experience for every living thing that graced those doors long before he sank even a penny into making an already functional exterior prettier. Which was probably why they had a new state-of-the-art X-ray machine and not new signage out front.

"Understandable," she said, which only boosted his already high opinion of her. Professional opinion, of course, as a fellow animal caretaker.

"This is Kya, our fearless gift shop manager." He paused at the counter and made a deliberate effort to refocus on the rehab center instead of Dr. Molly Lawrence. After all, his job was to get his final exam, not become best buds with the new temporary vet.

"It's nice to meet you," Molly said to Kya. "This place is truly amazing."

"Thank you," Kya, an energetic lady with a blue-frosted Carol Danvers haircut and a perma-grin, beamed. "But you have to see the turtles. They're the real stars of the show."

"Exactly." After all, that was the very reason she was here, wasn't it? Grant jerked his thumb at the door behind them with the big Employees Only sign. "Speaking of which, you ready to meet Chompers?"

Once again, nervousness flared in her gut. "Ready" wasn't quite the word she would've used, but it was probably time to get started before she talked herself out of it. "Lead the way."

Molly stepped through to a space that caught her off guard. Not only was the front of the building a bit on the understated side, it didn't look all that large. After walking through the expansive education center, she was expecting this area to be small. However, the hallway on this side of the door was the exact opposite. It was almost as if they'd stepped into Mary Poppins' magic carpet bag.

"Through that door is the bathroom and kitchen, in case you need either, along with the offices." He motioned to the single door on the left side of the long, wide hallway they were standing in. "Our tanks are out there." He pointed toward the automatic sliding glass doors at the end of the hall before turning his attention to the double swinging doors on their right. "And our vet suite is over here. You ready?"

No, she wasn't ready, but she followed him through the doors anyway, hoping her smile didn't look too forced.

The vet suite was a large, open, brightly lit room that rivaled any procedure room she'd worked in. The major difference was the huge metal table in the middle and the giant sea turtle on top of it. A guy and a gal, both dressed in khaki shorts and matching green Turtle Rehab logoed shirts, stood on either side of him.

"This is Dr. Lawrence. She's filling in for Dr. Lacey while she's out," Grant said as they approached the trio. "Apparently she had her baby last night. No one thought to mention that to me?"

The gal who had the same bright eyes and dark lashes as Grant clasped her hands together, looking delighted. "The baby came? I've been so busy today I haven't even looked at my phone, but as soon as we finish up here, I'm pulling up Insta to see some pictures." She stepped forward and extended her hand. "It's nice to meet you, Dr. Lawrence. I'm Claire."

"Claire is one of our rehab technicians and Chompers' primary caretaker." He slung his arm around her shoulders. "She also has the great privilege of being my little sister."

Claire rolled her eyes and flipped her long, dark hair. "No one ever accused my brother of being humble."

The other guy stepped forward, offering his hand. "And I'm Mateo Torres, head of rehab. I also happen to be his cousin, but don't let that taint your opinion of me." He was slightly shorter than Grant and stockier, but had enough of the same features that you could tell they were related.

"Please, call me Molly." She shook their hands and tried to push back the feeling of being wildly underqualified to be here. She had nowhere near the experience of the people standing in this room.

But she was good with animals. Working with critters of all kinds wasn't just her job, it was her passion. This task might not be in her comfort zone, but it didn't mean she couldn't do it, especially if it'd help the turtle get back into the ocean sooner.

Drawing in a calming breath, she focused on the patient in the middle of the room. "And this must be Chompers." She slowly inched closer to the loggerhead turtle, careful to stay in his line of vision. When she got close enough, she squatted down so she wouldn't seem so large and overwhelming.

Part of her responsibility was making sure the patient felt as calm and comfortable as possible during the process. And since most animals could sense fear and anxiousness, it was time for her to take control of the situation.

"Hello, sweetie. Aren't you one big, handsome fella." Talking to the animal she was about to treat in a calm sing-song voice was her standard approach. She found it usually put the animal at ease, especially when she followed it up with well-deserved pets and cuddles.

Chompers, however, was having none of it. He looked right at Molly, lunged his head forward, and snapped his strong triangular jaws at her. The cracking sound echoed through the sterile room. Molly's pulse kicked into the same gear as a track star in the middle of the hundred-meter dash. Even though she wasn't in the vicinity of his reach, she instinctively took a step back anyway. She hadn't even started working with the turtle yet, and already things weren't going well.

"Sorry about that. We should've warned you. Chompers is a bit feisty," Mateo said.

Claire, standing well out of the way of his jaw, rubbed his shell. "We think he means well. He just needs to work on his people skills."

"Right." Molly refreshed her smile, although this one was quite a bit more forced than what she'd managed last time. She squatted down in front of Chompers to try again, making sure to leave plenty of space between her and the turtle. "Understandable, pal. Somedays I don't want to people, either." Chompers still looked rather annoyed, but didn't snap at her again, which she took as a good sign. "I hear we're doing a final exam? Something about springing you out of here."

"That's right," Claire answered in a cheerful voice. "He's met all of his recovery goals and is doing great. As long as you verify that he has a clean bill of health, he'll be released on Tuesday."

Chompers acknowledged the woman's voice with a nod in her direction, a gesture that Molly found endearing. She'd only known the turtle for a handful of minutes and already she was falling in love with his feisty but loyal personality. So, examining him was out of her comfort zone. Being here was out of his comfort zone. If she pushed her own issues aside, she actually had the power to do something about his situation.

She laid her hand on the giant shell, careful to stay clear of his strong jaw. "Then what do you say we get this over with?"

She stood, looking at the three sets of eyes that were watching her interact with the turtle. She wouldn't say she was feeling confident. At least, not yet. But she was feeling determined, and she could work with determined. Determined got things done.

"Do you mind if I take a minute to read through his chart before we start? I want to make sure I don't miss anything."

"Absolutely." Grant grinned as he handed her a small laptop computer. "Welcome to Chompers' care team."

Forty-five minutes later, the exam was complete. Chompers was being wheeled out to his tank, and Molly was floating on a cloud of euphoria.

Grant had been right. Working with turtles was

like riding a bike. She might've been a little wobbly at first and quite a bit slower than an expert, but the second she'd emersed herself in the exam, it had all come flooding back. Loggerhead turtles were an amazing breed, but Chompers' unique personality made him especially cool. She'd enjoyed examining him. It seemed like a fitting conclusion to her unexpected day.

She stood next to the counter in the now-empty vet suite to finish writing in his chart. It was taking longer than it probably should've. Her step-by-micro-step notes were detailed even for her, and she had earned herself the nickname Tolstoy at her previous clinic. But in this case, she wanted to make extra sure she didn't miss anything or leave something out.

"I duck out for a minute to take a phone call, and everybody disappears?"

Molly looked up from her work to see Grant stroll into the room with his signature grin and deep dimples. "Guess you really know how to clear a room."

He made his way over to her and leaned against the counter, casually crossing his arms in front of his chest. "So what's the verdict, doc?"

Molly typed in one last note and saved the information. "He appears to be in great health. But, if you don't mind, I'd love to have Dr. Lacey take a look at his chart when I meet with her next week before we officially clear him. I'd like a second pair of eyes to make sure I didn't miss anything."

"No problem. He's tentatively scheduled for release next Tuesday. But since it's not a public release, it won't be hard to shift it a day or two if needed."

"A public release?"

"Right, sorry. I forget we sometimes talk in a code that not everyone knows." He shifted, his normally casual tone turning more formal. "As often as we can, we announce the release of our rehabbed friends to the public so the community can come and cheer them on with us."

Molly had once watched a YouTube video of a rehabbed turtle being released. Even the video had the kind of feel-good encouragement that hit deep in the soul. She couldn't imagine what it'd be like to witness it in person. "I can see why. That has to be inspiring for everyone involved."

"Release days are one of my favorite parts of the job." He gestured to the pictures of turtles being returned to the ocean that hung around the room. "But occasionally, when it's better for the turtle, we keep the release restricted to rehab staff only for a quieter send-off."

"Makes sense. I'd hate for Chompers' spirited personality to cause any problems on his homecoming day."

"Exactly right."

Molly glanced around the room, taking in the uniqueness of a clinic designed specifically for sea turtles. "This is all so fascinating." Pushing her fears aside and being spontaneous had paid off.

"I might be a little biased, but I'd say it's hard to not fall in love with this place." He motioned to the chart in front of Molly. "Thanks for stepping in today, by the way. We appreciate it more than you know."

"My pleasure. Chompers seems like a special turtle. I wish him all the best as he returns to exploring the deep blue sea."

"As do I. And we're all grateful that'll happen sooner rather than later." Grant paused for a second. His playful demeanor faded away and his mouth twisted to the side as if he was considering something. "I know this is a big ask, but would you consider being our resident vet while Dr. Lacey is on leave?"

The heaviness of the question landed on Molly like a weight, forcing her down from the euphoric cloud. "You want me to treat all the turtles?"

"With Dr. Lacey out and the surge of new turtles we've admitted lately, we really could use the help. Plus, you were great with Chompers today. You have a way with animals."

Molly raised a questioning eyebrow. "He almost took my finger off. Twice."

Grant shrugged as if losing a digit was a mere inconvenience. "He tried to take a chunk out of the boat when he was being rescued. We think it's his love language."

Molly's mind raced through the magnitude of what he was asking.

As if he knew exactly what she was thinking, he straightened and slid his hands into his pockets. "The truth is, we don't have a lot to offer you. The stipend we pay our vets is offensively low, and it would be in addition to all the work you're doing at Dr. Lacey's clinic. I understand it's a big ask."

"I..." She fumbled over the words. On the one hand, she was passionate about animals and always wanted to help. But on the other hand, she was far from qualified for what they were asking. Filling in once for a simple exam of a healthy turtle when someone else could review her work was one thing.

Being the primary person in charge of all the turtles was something else entirely. "I mean…"

Grant held up a hand to stop her. "Before you answer, why don't I give you a tour of the facility? It's important to have all the facts before you make a decision."

Molly propped her hands on her hips and gave him a pointed look. "Are you trying to use your adorable turtles to get me to say yes?"

A sly grin pulled at his mouth. "They seem to be far more persuasive than I am."

"Fine." Molly screwed her resolve to its sticking place. "I'm agreeing to the tour because I'm curious about every aspect of what you do here. But know there's a good chance my answer will be the same at the end as it is right now. I just don't think I'm the person you're looking for."

"Fair enough."

She followed him out of the vet suite and down the hall. Automatic sliding doors opened, and they stepped outside, where they were greeted by a gentle blast of coastal humidity from the warm summer day and the whirr of multiple electric pumps.

"Welcome to the Turtle Zone."

"It's so big." She paused on the sidewalk to take in the massive outdoor area. Large tanks and what appeared to be an impressive aquarium stretched all the way from the back of the building to the water's edge. Blue shade sails strung overhead softened the intense Florida sun, while tall palm trees flanked the perimeter of the property. She'd said it before, and she felt confident she'd say it again: this place was amazing. "Seriously, y'all need better signage out front."

Grant seemed amused at her reaction. "Top of my list as soon as we get another big donation check." He strolled down the wide sidewalk that ran through the middle of the vast rehab space all the way to the dock at the other end. "But first, how about that tour I promised you?"

Molly scurried to keep up, her gazed focused on the first group of tanks. "I hope this is an interactive tour, because I have a lot of questions. Starting with, how many turtles do you have?"

"It varies. Our facility is divided into three different zones. This is the Care Floor. It's our version of an ICU. It has a capacity of up to twenty. Right now, we have thirteen." He stopped among a sea of blue-and-white circular tanks that stretched out in neat rows on either side of the sidewalk. "Each time we admit a new patient, this is where they stay while they're healing." He stepped off the sidewalk and led her over to one of the tanks that was roughly the size of a small above-ground swimming pool. "Each tank is filled with water that has been taken straight from the gulf, purified to remove any harmful toxins that could cause additional problems, and temperature regulated to provide the ideal environment."

Molly peered over the edge, where a medium-sized green turtle was happily paddling around. "I wouldn't mind swimming in a pool like that."

Grant chuckled. "Right? Only the best for our patients."

The turtle swam over to where Molly was standing and popped his head up for a breath, as if coming to greet her. "And who is this guy?"

"This is Teddy. He came to us about six months

ago with a condition called Fibropapillomatosis. It causes benign tumors, but occasionally they have to be removed if they're impairing the turtle's function. Like Teddy here, who had a few growing over his eyes, blocking his vision."

Molly watched the turtle as he took a lap around his tank, his bright curious eyes looking up at her. "He looks pretty healthy now, though."

Grant nodded. "Yep. His surgeries were successful and he's healing nicely. A couple more weeks, and he'll be headed home." He moved to the next tank. The water in this one was only filled to about half of the level. "Shelley, on the other hand, is at the beginning of her stay. She came to us about a week ago with the same condition. The tumors on her flippers keep her from getting full range of motion, making it hard for her to swim."

Molly's heart lurched and she wanted to reach out and touch the sweet creature. Instead, she rested her hands on the side of the tank and watched. "Is that why her water is lower?"

"Yeah. We were letting her get her strength up. But she's doing great and ready for her surgery. We're waiting for a vet who can do it."

Grant had been right. The turtles were a lot more persuasive than he was. Who wouldn't want to help out these sweet babies? They were amazing creatures who deserved to be in the ocean where they belonged. But she just wasn't qualified. An exam of a healthy turtle was one thing, but a surgery she'd never done before was way outside of her comfort zone. "I'm not trained for that. And since I'm only in town for three months, I'll hardly have time to get up to speed before I leave again."

"Understandable. But it's my job as director to ask. You know how it is."

"I'm sorry. I wish I could, but..." She let her words trail off and watched Shelley's slow-moving flippers make splashes as she made her way around the tank.

"Hey, you made it out to the Turtle Zone." Claire's bright voice broke the tension. She strolled up, pushing a cart full of stainless-steel bowls. "And it's the best part of the day—feeding time! Want to help?"

Molly tossed an accusatory look in Grant's direction that she hoped was on par with a cranky librarian. "You planned this, didn't you?"

Grant chuckled, holding up both hands in surrender. "I promise you this is a total coincidence. I'm not nearly that crafty."

Claire's gazed bounced between the two of them. "I have a feeling I walked into the middle of something."

The conflict building up inside Molly came out in a sigh. "Your brother was just asking if I'd be interested in filling in while your vet is out." There was no doubt this place was amazing, and what they did here was inspiring. If circumstances were different, she'd be all in. "I wish I could, but the timing isn't right."

"Completely understandable. You just rolled into town and you'll have plenty to keep you busy at Gulfview." Claire's words might've been bright, but it wasn't helping Molly feel any better about her decision. She was doing the right thing, wasn't she? Claire picked up one of the bowls and handed it to Molly. "But, you can still feed the turtles before you leave. Take it from me, it's therapeutic." She led her to a nearby tank with the name Taylor Swifty written on the board on the side. Plucking a piece of frozen crab from the bowl in Molly's hands, she gently dropped it several inches in front of the turtle's face. "Isn't that right, Swifty? You're looking good today, girl."

Molly followed suit, dropping a piece of what appeared to be lobster in the tank. Taylor Swifty paddled over and gobbled it up in one big bite. "You're right. This is therapeutic." She selected another piece and dropped it in the tank, letting the good vibes of a happy turtle snacking on her favorite foods filter through her. "You said there were three parts of the Turtle Zone? If the Care Floor is one, what are the other two?" She was equal parts curious about the rest of the facility and hoping the change in subject would divert attention from the debate going on in her mind.

Grant stepped closer to her and pointed at the areas between them and the water. His enthusiasm and passion for this place radiated off of him. He pointed at the areas between them and the water. "That area in the middle with the square tanks is dedicated to the work we do with hatchlings. We currently have two one-year-old Kemp Ridley turtles hanging out there. And past that is the Discovery Lagoon." Grant rubbed his hands together like an eight-year-old boy about to dive into a brimming bag full of Halloween candy. "The Discovery Lagoon, in case you were wondering, is the greatest addition we've made to Turtle Rehab since it opened and, I don't want to be braggy here, possibly the coolest thing in all of Emerald Cove."

Claire rolled her eyes and grabbed the next bowl

off the cart. “It also happens to be my humble brother’s pet project.”

Grant shrugged with a sort of mock humbleness. “I’m just stating facts. Visiting the Discovery Lagoon is ranked the number one thing to do in Emerald Cove on Trip Advisor. If I’m allowed to quote the official review: ‘It’s the perfect combination of natural habitat for the residents and prime observation opportunity for community education programs.’”

Molly raised an eyebrow. “Perfect, huh? Well, this I have to see.”

“Then, by all means…” Grant bowed slightly, extending his arm in the direction of the large tank in question.

Molly set the empty bowl on the cart and stepped onto the central sidewalk, headed that way with Grant following along next to her.

“Grant, you have a visitor.”

He paused and turned to the voice coming from the building. Molly turned as well.

Kya, the lady from the front desk, was standing next to a man who appeared to be around their age. The man was dressed in khakis and a slightly wrinkled button-down shirt with a worn leather satchel hanging over one shoulder.

Grant’s animation faded, and Molly could’ve sworn he turned serious—or was it nervous?—for a fraction of a second. But as soon as the expression flickered across his face, it was gone, and his easy grin returned. “I’m so sorry, but I gotta take care of this.” He glanced over to where his sister was tossing greens into Teddy’s tank. “Claire, can you finish the tour?”

Molly didn’t miss the crease of concern that

formed above the bridge of her nose when Claire glanced at the newcomer.

"Sure." She set the bowl on the cart and wiped her hands on the towel hanging over her shoulder.

"Thanks." He turned back to Molly. "Her tour might not be as detailed as mine, but you're still in good hands. I'll catch up with you in a few." There was a hint of concern lingering under his lighthearted banter, and before either of them could say anything, he jogged up the path to where Kya and the stranger were waiting.

Claire watched him, her mouth twisted to the side.

"Who's that?" Molly was well aware it was none of her business, but the unease that filled the air piqued her interest.

"An old friend from grad school, I think," Claire said, not taking her eyes off her brother. "I have no idea why he's here, though."

Molly watched Grant greet the newcomer and lead him inside. This time, she was certain there was a look of unease when he glanced back at them just before they disappeared through the sliding doors.

"Huh," Claire said, more to herself than to Molly. She shook her head, as if shaking away whatever thought was inside, and turned to Molly. "You ready to check out the Discovery Lagoon?"

"I'd love to."

They continued down the concrete steps, past the rows of smaller square tanks toward a huge amoeba-shaped pool outlined with large stones. The path continued on its downward slope, heading to what Molly assumed was the front of the pool, but Claire stepped onto one of the boulders on the pool's edge and motioned for Molly to join her.

Molly followed and looked over into the pool. "This isn't just kind of cool. This is one of the most amazing aquariums I've ever seen." From this angle, she could see several sea turtles swimming among natural-looking coral formations and live sea plants above a white sandy bottom. Schools of colorful fish weaved in and out of the stone structures.

Claire giggled, seeming to relax. "We like to downplay it in front of Grant so it doesn't go to his head, but this pool is spectacular."

They walked along the rocks on the side to where a small stone bridge crossed over the corner of the pool. From up there, they could look down on top of the water to get a better view of the action, and it was fascinating. Molly could've stood there and watched for hours.

"Two hundred thousand gallons, six different coral structures, and I don't even know how many tons of rock. It makes our old one-hundred-thousand-gallon rectangular pool look pathetic," Claire said.

"It's enough to make most aquariums in any zoo jealous. We had a pretty big tank at the zoo I worked at, but it was nowhere near this gorgeous."

"We use this mainly for our permanent residents." Claire turned her attention to Molly as she explained, "Our goal is to return every turtle to the ocean, but the reality is some face damage that makes it impossible to survive in the wild. They turn into ambassadors either here or at other zoos and aquariums around the country who teach the public about their amazing species."

"How many permanent residents do you have?" Molly asked, trying to count the turtles that were in constant motion in the tank.

"Right now we have five who will live here with us forever. But there are three who are waiting to get transported to their forever homes and one who's hanging out with us while his display undergoes renovations at his aquarium." She pointed to the far side, where a giant net sectioned off a small part of the pool. "And, of course, Chompers is in our solo pool. We were hoping maybe a more authentic environment would help him calm down."

"Has it?" Molly asked, watching the giant loggerhead meander through the rocks in his space.

"As far as we can tell, he's as crotchety as the day we brought him in." She smiled lovingly at the animal. "But I like the ones with the big personalities. They always leave the most lasting impressions."

Molly nodded in agreement. She had the same thought with the animals she worked with. "How long have you worked here?"

"Officially, I've been on the payroll since I graduated from college last year. But I've been up here working with turtles since I was old enough to walk. Same with Grant. I guess that's the way it goes when your family started the rehab center."

"Your family started this place?" The turtles seemed to notice who was standing on the bridge and slowly started making their way over to them.

Claire nodded. "To be specific, my dad did when he was a teenager. Of course, he had no idea then of what it would become."

Molly pulled her focus off the turtles and looked at

her tour guide with a whole new interest. "How did he decide to start something like this?"

Claire pulled a handful of what Molly could only assume were turtle treats and handed a few to Molly before she tossed some into the water. "My dad came from a family of commercial fisherman, and they'd find injured sea turtles from time to time. Back then, forty years ago, there weren't a lot of options for places to take them. He started bringing them here, to what was his family home, and researched ways to help them. Over time he realized that what was a side project had turned into his passion, and little by little this place grew into what it is today." She held her hands out as if putting it on display. "The largest nonprofit turtle rescue and rehab center along the Florida Panhandle, committed to rescuing, rehabilitating, and releasing sea turtles."

Molly tossed a few of her treats in the water and watched the turtles scoop them up. "That is quite a legacy."

"My parents were amazing people." An expression crossed her face that was part wistful, part heartache. "That turtle over there, our largest resident, is named after my dad. Bart."

Molly laid a sympathetic hand on Claire's arm. "Thanks for sharing the story with me. This place seems very special."

They were both quiet for a moment while Molly watched the turtles glide elegantly through the water.

"Sorry about that," Grant said as he joined them on the bridge. "What'd I miss?"

"Your sister was just telling me the background of this place."

"Ahh." He grinned. "Did she include that before I came in with the Discovery Lagoon project, this was a regular ol' rectangular pool with a few boulders at the bottom?"

Claire rolled her eyes. "You're hopeless."

"I think the word you're looking for is 'inspired.' Or 'amazingly talented.' Either works."

"'Arrogant' was actually what came to mind. Or 'big-headed.' I could go on." She gave him the taunting look only a sibling could pull off.

Grant ignored it and turned his attention to Molly. "So now that you've seen the whole thing, what do you think?"

"It really is spectacular," Molly said, trying to take in all the different colors and shapes of the fish, turtles, and plant life living in the lagoon. "The entire facility is amazing." She rotated slowly to take in the entire view. The Hope Floor above, the Discovery Lagoon in front of her, and the dock that led out to the sparkling Gulf of Mexico. It was as great a facility as any she'd seen. "You've thought of everything, even down to the picturesque sailboat at the end of your dock."

"Technically, that's not part of the facility," Claire said, looking amused. "It's Grant's home."

Molly's eyes had widened so many times during her tour that there was a strong likelihood they'd stick that way and she'd live out the rest of her life like a surprised cartoon character. "You live on a sailboat?"

"Guilty."

"For real? Like, permanently?"

Grant studied the boat with a look of pride. "As permanently as I lived anywhere, I suppose."

"We tried to talk him into getting a place that was a little less volatile during storms, but it didn't work," Claire said.

Grant shrugged. "I kinda like the commute here. Plus, I can always crash on your couch if there's a big storm."

"I've never met anyone who lived on a boat before." She considered that for a second. "I've never even been on a sailboat before."

"Never?" There was a hint of shock in Claire's voice.

Molly took in the white boat gleaming against the cobalt sky. It was so perfect, it almost looked like a picture on a postcard. "I'm from a small town in Kansas. There aren't a lot of sailboats there."

Claire clapped her hands together, looking delighted. "Then you should let us take you out!"

"Like take the boat out in the ocean?" A cold trickle of fear rolled down her spine. She'd never been on a boat of any kind in the ocean, either. A lake, sure, but the ocean? It seemed bigger and scarier and, well... "Is it safe?"

"I've sailed that boat all around the Gulf. She's perfectly safe." Grant gave her a reassuring smile. "Tomorrow is supposed to be a perfect day for sailing. You should come."

"You have to say yes. It'll be a sort of thank you for filling in today." Claire bounced on her toes.

Sailing on the ocean was way outside of her comfort zone, but then again, the vast majority of today had been outside of her comfort zone. Next time she made a goal of adding more adventure to her life, maybe she needed to be more specific that she didn't have to do it all in one day.

"Okay," she said before she could talk herself out of it. "I'd love to."

Chapter Three

After Grant made plans with Molly for tomorrow's sail and convinced her to wait until then to give her final answer about working for them, he returned her to the vet clinic. As soon as he was alone in the turtle ambo, he switched his focus from finding a new vet for Turtle Care to his buddy, who was waiting for him at The Burger Shack. Today had been full of surprises.

He turned onto the main road and inched through summer traffic on the way to his next meeting. On the bright side, this one was taking place at his favorite restaurant.

The Burger Shack was one of those locally owned places that was small and friendly with an ocean view and more seating outside than in. Half of the patio was covered, and the other half had red umbrellas over tables that went right up to the sand. It was always filled with good food, warm coastal breezes, and laughter, making it the perfect place to meet up with an old friend on a Friday night. And better yet, it was the perfect cover to make this meet-up look like a social visit instead of what it was.

Judging by the crowds, Grant wasn't the only one who'd thought this restaurant was a good choice. The place was packed. It was only early summer, but tourist season was already in full swing. He wove through the carefree vacationers to a high-top table on the far edge of the uncovered deck. "Hey, Jonathan. Sorry to rush you out earlier." Grant shook his buddy's hand before sliding into the seat opposite of him. "I haven't mentioned the job offer to anyone at Turtle Rehab and I wasn't quite ready to let that cat out of the bag."

Jonathan nodded. "Understandable."

"Here we can talk without a bunch of eavesdroppers listening in." He glanced around at the couple of tables nearby to make sure there wasn't anyone seated there who might be interested in their conversation.

Jonathan chuckled. "After years of working at the university, I know how that goes." He motioned out at the beach, where the powdery sand melted into the waves. "Plus, you can't beat the scenery."

"You think the view's great? You should try the fried pickles. They're out of this world." Grant caught the waiter's attention and put in an order for his favorite appetizer, along with a couple of drinks. When the waiter walked away, he turned his attention to his old college buddy and possible future employer. "So, how are things at the old alma mater?" Yes, Grant was aware the question was avoiding the elephant in the room, but he wasn't in the mood to wrestle with elephants quite yet.

Jonathan settled in his chair, seeming content to take the long road to why they were really there. "Other than missing you, not a whole lot has changed. Dr.

Ford is still running the department. He still looks as old as he did the day we started undergrad and still wears the same 1970s pineapple shorty swim trunks anytime we do field work."

Grant scoffed. "It's surprising those things haven't disintegrated."

"Isn't that the truth."

"Is Dr. Brett still terrorizing the masters' students?"

Jonathan nodded. "She's still requiring a ten-page scientific paper with perfect APA citation by the end of the first week. Newbs still walk out of her first class with the same dazed expression."

The memories of being one of those newbs pulled at the corner of his mouth. Those were good days.

Jonathan continued. "And the undergrads still show up thinking a major in marine biology means they'll be hanging out at the beach and drinking mai tais for the next four years."

"You mean that's not what we do all day?" Grant joked. Memory after memory of the seven years he'd spent at what could arguably be considered his favorite place paraded through his mind. "It's good to know some things never change."

The server slid a basket of steaming fried pickles between them, and Grant thanked him before grabbing one and popping it in his mouth.

"Jennifer left," Jonathan said, his voice a little quieter, a little more serious. "She took a job with the EPA down in Miami."

"A government job, huh?" He popped another fried pickle in his mouth and chewed slowly, savoring the tangy taste as his memories shifted to his ex-girlfriend.

"She's heading up a research team. We were sad to see her go, but she's a great choice for the job." Jonathan took a sip of his drink. "You know she and her husband had a baby last year. A little girl."

"Good for her." It was a statement he meant from the deepest part of his soul. Jennifer was a great person and one amazing marine biologist. Maybe things hadn't worked out between them the way they'd thought they might, but life had a way of changing even the best-laid plans. Although, it had all worked out for the better, hadn't it? She'd gotten to marry the true love of her life and start the family she'd always wanted. Not to mention she'd snagged a job that sounded like it was designed for her. And he'd gotten...

Well, he'd gotten to come home at a time when he needed to be here and the chance to take care of what needed to be taken care of. Plus, he'd built a pretty cool pool for the turtles, so there was that.

Which brought him back to the reason he was sitting here, across from his old buddy. "I've considered your job offer. I gotta say, it's tempting. Really tempting. But coming back to the university as an adjunct professor isn't what's best for me at the moment."

There. He'd said it. Of course, it was a conversation he'd assumed they'd have over the phone and he wouldn't have to look his friend in the eye as he delivered the news, which was making him second-guess his decision. Maybe it would be...

But no. This was the right choice. He nodded once, hoping the decisive movement would trigger the decisive parts of his brain. Of course there was the familiar tug pulling him to the place he loved, especially after reminiscing with an old friend. It'd be ridiculous to think there wouldn't be. They were offering him a chance to return to doing what he was passionate about, like research and creating positive change, not to mention finally finishing what he'd started before life had gotten in the way.

But that had been a long time ago, and like he'd said, life had caused his priorities to shift. He was ninety-nine percent sure he was making the right call.

Okay, fine, maybe the percentage wasn't quite that high. But it was at least in the seventy percent range, which made it statistically significant.

Jonathan stared at his hands as if he was considering his next move. "I had a feeling you'd say that."

Silence fell over the table. Grant shifted in his chair, not quite sure what else he needed to say. He'd addressed the elephant, hadn't he? Why was it still standing there?

"But Jennifer wasn't the only one to leave this year." Jonathan's words were soft, but he looked up with the sort of confident expression of a man throwing down all four aces. "Stan also left."

"The director of research?"

It'd been a while since Grant had been involved in all that was going on at the university, and plenty had changed, even if it wasn't Professor Ford's choice in swimwear. But Stan used to be the head of grant-funded research projects. Grant knew the position well, because it also happened to be his dream job.

Of course, now that things had changed, it was a lot more dream than any sort of real-life possibility.

Jonathan picked up a couple of pickles and casually dragged them through the sauce. "Not only that, he was three months from starting a five-year study we worked forever to secure the grant for. One we're calling the Intricacies of Ocean Habitats."

The announcement caught Grant off guard. That was his project. He'd come up with the idea while working on his master's degree and the project he'd wanted to focus on for his doctorate before...well, before a lot of things. "You're finally doing it."

The hint of wonder in his voice didn't even come close to describing the wonder welling up inside him. And, if he was being completely honest, there was a tinge of jealousy creeping in as well, but who'd blame him? He'd been dreaming about that particular research project for a decade. Still, the project wasn't about him. It was about marine animals everywhere, and whether or not he was part of it, he was thrilled it was getting done. "Good for y'all. But will losing your head researcher put you in a bind?"

Jonathan nodded. "But we've got a replacement in mind."

"Who are you looking at?" Grant flipped through the Rolodex in his mind of biologists he knew could handle that kind of job. Biologists he trusted with his project.

Jonathan folded his hands in front of him and looked straight at Grant. "You."

Grant froze, mouth hanging open and hand hovering midair above the pickle basket. "Me?" Surely he hadn't heard him right. Grant was nowhere near qualified enough for that job. Since he'd never finished his doctorate, he didn't have his PhD. And that was only the first reason on a very long list.

Jonathan shrugged. "Dr. Ford thinks, and I agree, that you have a unique set of skills that make up for not having a PhD. No one else knows the background of this study the way you do."

"I..." Grant was at a complete loss for words. Him? The Director of Research?

"Not exactly why you thought I was here today, huh?"

It wasn't even in the same ballpark of where he'd thought this conversation was going. "Let me get this straight. You want me—" he pointed at himself, "—to be the Director of Research at your university." He pointed at Jonathan.

"First of all, it's *our* university. And yes, that's the general idea." He took another sip of his drink. "Although, to be fully transparent, there are two other people on our short list. Obviously, you're at the top, but the decision is not completely up to us. The board of directors also has a say."

Grant nodded, still trying to wrap his mind around what was happening. "Sure. Makes total sense."

"If you're interested, and we hope you're interested, we can move you to the next step of the interview process."

Grant nodded again, feeling somewhat like a bobble-head doll. He should probably have thoughts about this offer, or at least some emotions pulling him one way or the other, but he was too stunned to think. So he went with the next best question he could come up with. "What exactly would that entail?"

"Good question." Jonathan ticked off the list on his fingers as casually as if he were naming things he needed to pick up at the grocery store. "Interview with me and Dr. Ford. A meeting with the research team, who you pretty much know. And an interview with the chancellor. He told me to tell you hi, by the way." Jonathan dropped his hands to his lap and got more serious. "The main thing you'll have to worry about is an interview with the board. But, things will move quickly. We're hoping to have someone in the position by the end of the summer at the latest."

Conflicting thoughts pulled at him, physically causing his shoulders to slouch. He'd come here with every intention of saying no, but this was different. This was his dream job. When people asked what he wanted to be when he grew up and he could give an imaginary, in-an-ideal-world answer, this was it. This job was the perfect combination of the field work to satisfy his need for adventure and the office work that kept him grounded. And if that wasn't enough, he'd also get the chance to work directly with the people who could make a difference in the lives of marine animals living in the wild and in captivity. How could he walk away from this?

On the other hand, taking the job would mean leaving here, along with everything he'd come home for. Was he prepared to do that?

"Do you mind if I think about it?"

"Not at all. You're going to be at Dr. Simmons' symposium next weekend, right? You can give me your answer then."

"I wouldn't miss it."

"Great." Jonathan picked up the menu in front of

him. "In the meantime, let's order some burgers. You say this place is the best?"

"Nothing on that menu will disappoint you." Grant stared at his own menu, although he had a feeling that with everything else weighing on his mind, he'd hardly be able to taste whatever he happened to order.

Saturday morning, Molly woke up ready to take on day two of her new life. It was time for her to *carpe diem* and adopt an *hakuna matata* attitude and whatever other catch phrase she'd missed out on in her previous perfectly planned-out existence. This was her opportunity to do whatever she wanted and live her best life.

Although, that best life needed to include unpacking so she wasn't living out of suitcases for the next three months. It wouldn't hurt to hit up a grocery store, either. It was hard to *carpe diem* with only half a bag of pretzels left over from her drive down.

But first, she needed coffee.

She popped one of the coffee pods she'd brought with her—thank goodness for that forethought—into her single-serve coffee machine and waited for it to fill the "Beach Hair, Don't Care" mug she'd found in the cabinet. When it was finished, she clutched the warm mug between her hands and turned, surveying her apartment.

It was small but comfortable. Light spilled in from the giant sliding glass doors, making it feel bright and inviting, and even from where she was standing, she could see the ocean. Which reminded her, she hadn't taken the time to enjoy her ocean view from her ocean view apartment yet. That problem would get rectified right now.

She pulled open the sliding door and stepped onto the fourth-floor balcony. It was incredible. The sand glistened in the morning sun, and the emerald water sparkled like it was full of jewels. She could smell the salt in the air and hear the faint rhythm of the waves rolling into shore, mixed with the distant cry of a seagull. Sipping her coffee, she let the scene settle over her. So maybe life hadn't worked out the way she imagined it would, but waking up to this for the next three months didn't stink.

She walked over to the railing and closed her eyes, breathing in the warm, coastal air and the fresh, new beginning.

"It's a great view, huh?"

The unexpected voice caused Molly to jump. That was when she realized the ocean-induced tunnel vision had caused her to miss two important things about her balcony. First, her balcony was actually connected to the balconies of the condos on either side of her, divided only by large metal partitions that sloped down as they got closer to the railing.

The second was there were people standing on each of those balconies. To be more specific, there were two women—probably around her age—each standing on her own balcony on either side of Molly's.

"You must be the new girl," the bubbly lady on her right said. She had blond hair pulled up in a messy bun on top of her head. "I'm Ellyn. Welcome to the building."

"Oh, hi," Molly said, still slightly flustered.

"And that's Hadley." Ellyn motioned to the woman on Molly's left with the long brown hair and the sundress, clutching a large cappuccino style coffee mug.

"It's nice to meet you both. I'm Molly." She flashed them an awkward closed-lip smile because...had she even brushed her teeth yet? "Sorry, I didn't notice you were out here."

"We're out here every morning. It's the perfect place to enjoy your morning cup of coffee." Hadley took a sip from her mug.

"Or two. We're not judging if you need two cups," Ellyn added. "In fact, you should start joining us."

"Oh, I don't know..." Molly let her voice trail off, because how could she say she wasn't sure if she wanted to hang out and make a bunch of new BFFs? In fact, her number-one goal of her new life, even in front of the adventure thing, was to not make any deep connections. She'd had a bunch of those in her previous life, including what she'd thought were the bestest of friends, and it hadn't worked out so well. The familiar wound throbbed in her chest.

Molly pushed the painful memories out of her mind and gave them the politest excuse she could think of. "I'm, uh, not going to be here long. I'm only on a three-month assignment."

Ellyn brightened. "Hey! That's Hadley's story too." She had the kind of peppy enthusiasm that made Molly wonder if she was always this excited or if she'd already downed her two cups of coffee and was working on number three. Although, Molly had to admit her attitude was a bit contagious. “At least, it was supposed to be, but she keeps hanging around.”

Hadley nodded in agreement. “I’m a project manager for new construction projects, and I moved here for a nine-month assignment. When that wrapped up, I took another six-month job. But, the longer I stay, the less sure I get about leaving.”

“I can see how that would happen. It’s beautiful here.” The parts she’d seen in the short time she’d been there, anyway.

“And it’s not just the scenery. The people in this town are amazing too. If you’re not careful, this place will cast its spell over you.” Hadley took a sip of her latte.

Molly turned to the neighbor on her other side. “Are you here on a temporary assignment too?”

Ellyn shook her head, a few blond strands freeing themselves from her bun. “Nope, I’ve lived here forever. There’s no place else I’d rather be. I own an art gallery just up the road.” She motioned in the direction she was talking about and took a sip from her mug. “But enough about us. Tell us about you. What brings you to Emerald Cove for three months?”

“I’m a locum veterinarian, basically a traveling vet who fills in for people who are out on short-term leave. I’m here for Dr. Lacey at Gulfview Animal Hospital.”

“Oh, right. While she’s at home with baby Ellison.” Ellyn beamed. “I saw a picture, and she is adorable. I’d want to stay home and cuddle with her all day too.”

“You know Dr. Lacey?”

Hadley waved an airy hand. "It's a small town. Everyone knows everyone here."

"Ugh." Molly's spirit began to take a dip. "I came from a small town in Kansas. I know all about the rumor mill and how everyone can get caught up in everyone else's business." In fact, it was the main reason she'd left Kansas. Her eyes flickered to the now-bare finger on her left hand.

One horrifying day, everything she'd thought was going so right had gone terribly wrong, and she'd become the subject of all the "have you heard" conversations. And if her life falling apart and having to bear all the whispers and stares wasn't bad enough, there was also being stopped almost everywhere she'd gone by someone offering her a wide range of super-not-helpful advice. She had no intention of putting herself in that kind of situation again.

"It's a town full of humans, which means there's the occasional drama, but I think you'll find that Emerald Cove is full of good people with big hearts." Hadley blew on her coffee.

Ellyn's head animatedly bobbed up and down. "Agreed."

"Big hearts, huh?" Molly's mind drifted back to the sea turtle rehab center. The place had impressed her, and a large part of that was due to the people who ran it. "I got a chance to tour Emerald Cove Sea Turtle Rescue and Rehabilitation Center. Do you know Grant Torres, the director?"

"I know Grant," Ellyn offered. "He's part of one of the big families in Emerald Cove that has lived here forever. Good people. Why do you ask?"

"He offered to take me out on his boat today. I

wanted to make sure I wasn't headed out to sea with a wanted felon or something."

"Ohhh." There was a knowing glint in Hadley's eyes. "Well, I also know he's single and an all-around great guy. Quite the catch. I approve of your date."

Molly waved her hand in the air as if to erase the words before they landed somewhere and became a serious thought. She was not looking to go on any sort of date. Not now, and quite possibly not ever.

And even if, for some weird reason, she could be talked into a date again far, far into the future, it certainly wouldn't be with a guy from a big family in a small town. No matter how charming his dimples were.

"Absolutely not a date. In fact, his sister Claire is coming too. It's a kind of thank you for helping them out yesterday."

Hadley studied her for a second as if she was trying to weigh the truth in Molly's denial. "In that case, he's a master sailor. Plus, I adore his sister. You're in good hands."

"Good to know." Molly sipped her coffee as she searched for a new topic that wouldn't involve Grant Torres. "So, you two have coffee out here every morning?"

"Every day at seven," Ellyn said. "Join us! It's a great way to start the day."

Molly stared at the mug in her hand and reconsidered the offer. Sure, she wasn't looking to lay down roots in this new town, but maybe coffee with the neighbors was more about being amiable than making lasting connections. Plus, she wanted to take full advantage of this view while she could. "I'm going to have to invest in some better coffee. This plasticky quick-serve stuff kind of dampens the vibe."

"I can help you out with that." Hadley held up the fancy mug as an example. "I have an espresso machine and am happy to whip up whatever you like. Playing barista is a bit of a hobby."

"Actually, you joining us would be a big help. We've rigged up a system for her to be able to pass me my daily vanilla latte. But if you were here to pass it, that would make life so much easier."

Molly sized up the space between them. Her balcony wasn't large, but it would still be a challenge to pass a hot coffee back and forth between them. "You have a coffee passing system? This I have to see."

Ellyn giggled. "Join us tomorrow, and we'll show you. Of course, it'll be the last time we use it, since you'll be our new delivery system."

"Your new delivery system, huh? In that case, how can I say no?"

"You can't," Hadley said. "But so I'm prepared, what do you like?"

"Can you make a mocha?"

"One steaming-hot mocha will be ready for you at seven a.m. tomorrow."

Maybe a daily coffee date with her neighbors wasn't exactly in the plan for her new life, but so far, nothing about Molly 2.0 had gone according to the way she'd thought it would.

But who didn't like coffee?

"I'll be here."

Chapter Four

Saturday was the perfect day for sailing. There were clear skies and a steady breeze. It was the kind of morning that begged to be spent on the open water, and Grant was itching to feel the wind in his sails. He just had to wait for Dr. Molly Lawrence to get there.

If he were being totally honest with himself, his excitement about today's sail wasn't entirely due to the perfect weather. There might've been a tiny part of him that was looking forward to seeing Emerald Cove's newest vet again. To put it simply, she intrigued him.

He wanted to blame it on the fact that she was a fellow animal lover or that she had a natural way with animals that was inspiring to watch. But, if he dug deep down, there was more to it than that. There was something about her that he couldn't quite put into words.

It had to do with the way she was willing to step out of her comfort zone, even when she didn't have to. She had this sort of courage and determination that sparked something inside him.

But Grant had never been one to dig down deep. He was more of a live-in-the-moment kind of guy, and today's moment was focused on taking a slightly intriguing new friend out on his boat to thank her for her help. If he got really lucky, he might even convince her to do more work for them—which, for the record, was a hundred percent about the turtles and had absolutely nothing to do with the fact that he wouldn't mind seeing her again.

"I'm not sure about this."

Grant looked up and saw Molly walking down the dock toward him. At least, he assumed it was Molly. It was hard to see her face with all the stuff she had on.

She wore a long, yellow raincoat under a tightly cinched and slightly too large red lifejacket. White rubber shrimp boots stuck out the bottom, while an oversized khaki rainhat covered her face. And if that wasn't enough protection, she also had a giant inflatable float under one arm and a pool noodle in her other hand.

He tried not to laugh as he walked over to greet her. "Good morning, sailor. What's with the outfit?"

"Precaution," she said. "I want to be prepared."

"Prepared for what? A pool party in the rain?"

She looked up at him from under her hat, worry swirling in her marine-blue eyes. "I don't know. Things could go wrong. There could be a rogue wave that knocks us over or a giant, really angry shark that attacks our boat. We might fall overboard in the middle of the ocean and have to float there until someone finds us."

Grant chuckled. "You clearly watch too many old movies."

She shrugged, nibbling on her lip. “Maybe a few.”

“If it’s any consolation, no megalodons have ever been spotted off the Emerald Coast. Plus, we’re not going far. We’ll only be out for a couple of hours.” He held his hand out to help her aboard.

She somehow managed to prop her hands on her hips while still holding onto the floats and gave him a pointed look, ignoring his outstretched hand. “Gilligan was only out for three hours, and you saw how that turned out.”

“Gilligan?”

She shrugged. “I used to spend the night at my grandma’s when I was little. We also watched a lot of old TV shows.”

“Don’t worry, Mary Ann. The radar is completely clear. It should be smooth sailing without any issues today.”

She pushed her lips out in a cute little contemplative grin. “So the rain hat is overkill?”

He held up his thumb and forefinger. “Little bit.”

She pulled the hat off and her arms dropped limply to her side, the floats dangling from her hands. “I can’t help it. I’ve never been on a boat in the ocean before. Where I come from, if we take a boat out, it’s on a lake. There are no waves, or animals that eat you. And if something goes wrong, we can swim to shore. This all seems so...” She paused, apparently searching for the right word.

“Scary?”

She glanced up at him from under her lashes. “Yeah.” She nibbled on her bottom lip again. Then, as if she gathered up all her resolve, she squared her shoulders and jutted out her chin. “But I’m committed to following through with my new-adventure resolution, which is why I'm still standing here and not waving to you from the safety of solid ground."

And there it was again. That little spark flared, causing a puff of warmth to spread through him. As someone who was a big believer in adventure, he admired her commitment to try something new. Which, he quickly reminded himself, was very different than admiring her. "How about this. You promise to remind yourself that those are movies and not real life. And I promise to keep us close enough to the shore that you can see land."

She seemed to brighten, which he took as a good sign. "I think I can handle that."

"Then let's get this new adventure started." He held his hand out to her again. "Do you trust me?"

She stared at his hand for a second before her gaze flickered up to his eyes. And then she grinned. To anyone else, it would've been a normal grin, but something about it caused a flutter that caught him off guard. What was that about?

She tucked the pool noodle under her other arm and took his hand, stepping onto the boat.

"Welcome to *Dream Catcher*," he said, taking the floats from her. "You've now officially been on a boat in the ocean."

Molly shot him a questioning look. "We haven't even left the dock yet."

Grant shrugged. "Maybe not. But you're standing on a boat and it's floating in the ocean, so I'm pretty sure that counts. And now that you've conquered that fear, the rest will be a walk in the park."

She gave him a pointed look.

"Okay, so maybe that was a bad choice of words. I meant to say, it'll be no big deal."

"I hope you're right."

"You can put your things in here." He led her through the sliding door to his small salon. "Also, my sister sends her deepest apologies, but she won't be able to join us today. She wanted me to tell you that she, and I quote, doesn't usually 'flake out' on her friends."

"I hope everything's okay."

Grant tossed the floats onto the built-in banquette. "Physically, she's fine. It was a 'wedding emergency.'" He made air quotes when he said the last two words. He had no idea what kind of emergency there could be with a wedding that was still two months away, but he'd learned that when it came to wedding stuff, it was better to nod and act sympathetic than ask a bunch of questions.

"Oh, no! That's awful. What kind of emergency?"

It wasn't that she cared that caught him off guard. Most people reacted with some level of sympathy when someone had an issue. But Molly's voice had the same distress his sister's had had when she'd called him an hour ago. "Something to do with the dress. They ordered the wrong size or something."

Molly pulled a face that could best be described as yikes. "Seriously, I'm okay with rescheduling if you need to help her."

Grant could feel his eyebrows knit together in confusion. He loved his sister, but what on earth was he going to do about a wedding dress problem? He didn't even understand the issue. When he ordered pants in the wrong size, he simply returned them and got ones that fit. But judging by how Claire had sounded when he'd suggested that, it was an absurd thought. "She and her maid of honor are meeting with the dress shop and a tailor. I was told I wasn't needed. Plus, I'm not letting you out of your first sail that easily."

She set her bag and rain hat on the couch next to the floats. "Fair enough. But you know the dress is a big deal, right? A problem with the dress can be pretty upsetting."

Grant considered that for a second. Claire had seemed pretty upset when he'd talked to her. He should probably text her to see how it was going. "Honestly, this whole wedding thing is new territory for me. I'm trying to be supportive, but I don't understand most of it." He shrugged, grabbing two bottles of water from his fridge before handing one to her. "I can analyze scientific data without a problem, but analyzing the nuances of the different wedding cakes is beyond me. I mean, don't you just pick the one that tastes the best?"

Molly shook her head and tsked in playful disbelief. "Typical."

"That's pretty much what Claire said when I went with her to the cake tasting." The discussion had flown past him about five minutes after they'd walked in, when they'd started discussing the different frosting options for the look they were trying to achieve. Although, all things considered, it wasn't an awful wedding task. Seashell Bakery made some delicious cakes. "Do you have a lot of experience with weddings?"

As soon as the question left his lips, Molly's mood seemed to shift. Her playful grin faded away and her gaze settled on an imaginary spot on the floor. He couldn't be sure, but he could've sworn a hint of sadness flickered in her eyes. "Some." As if she suddenly realized her expression had changed, she looked back at him and slapped on a smile that was much more forced than anything he'd seen on her before. "You're a good brother to be so involved in the planning aspect. I mean, your whole underestimating the seriousness of the dress is a problem, but she's still lucky to have you."

"Since we lost both of our parents some years ago, I'm trying to fill in by being the most awesome brother of the bride there ever was." The forced smile and conversation pivot wasn't lost on him, but he let it go. He barely knew her, which meant it was none of his business why "some" wedding experience seemed to steal her joy. But that didn't mean he wasn't curious. "I think we all agree that wedding planning isn't my strength. I don't even know the difference between the style and the theme. Or why you need either one."

Molly laughed. It was a legit laugh that brought back her authentic smile, and the sight of it caused that fluttery thing again.

"Luckily for you," he said, doing his best to push the fluttery feeling away, "I am really good at sailing. What do you say we untie and get out there? The ocean is calling."

"I guess there's no time like the present."

He led her outside and up the four steps to the helm. It wasn't as spacious as the seating area on the aft deck or in the salon, but there was more than enough room for the two of them. "Make yourself comfortable. Just give me a second to untie us, and we'll be off." He checked a couple of things on the control panel before he went along the side of the boat and untied it from the dock. When the last rope was thrown aboard, he shoved off and jogged up to where Molly was waiting at the helm.

He stepped around her and flipped the switch to start the engines. "We have to use the motor to get us off shore, but as soon as we're out in the open water, we'll switch over to the sails. You ready?"

"Not even a little bit." She tightened her already white-knuckled grip on the rail. "But let's do it anyway."

"A girl after my own heart." He put the boat into gear and they pulled away from the dock.

They motored about four hundred yards offshore before he killed the engine. He loved this moment. As soon as the rough mechanical noise from the engine died, the harshness of the world seemed to fade away. Out here, with only the sound of the wind and the waves and nothing between him and the horizon, he found a sort of peace outlined in possibility. Out here, it felt like he could breathe.

"Welcome to the open water."

Molly clutched the railing but twisted in her seat, taking in the full panoramic view. "I'm not going to lie, my blood pressure might be well past the healthy range at the moment. But it is breathtaking."

He stared out at the water that slowly melted from clear jade to a deep emerald, and let the calm beauty seep into his core. "That it is, but I didn't bring you out here to bob in the ocean all day. I promised to take you sailing, so let me raise the sails."

"Oh, right. Do you need help?"

"No, I got it. You sit tight for a few."

"Sitting tight isn't a problem at all." She adjusted her position, wrapping more of her arm around the railing, causing the bottom of her long raincoat to flutter in the sea breeze.

It only took a few minutes for him to hoist the sails, and almost instantly the wind caught. Grant settled behind the wheel as the boat sliced through the water.

"Wow," Molly said as they glided through the waves, parallel to the shore. "It's so quiet. Very different than the boats we take out on the lake."

Grant draped his hand over the wheel. It was a gorgeous day with little traffic out on the water. "I love it out here. It's relaxing and peaceful."

Molly wrinkled her nose. "I'm still working on the relaxing part. But it is peaceful. As long as we don't shipwreck or capsize or whatever."

Regardless of what her words said, he could tell by her grip that she was starting to loosen up. Maybe she wasn't completely comfortable yet, but she was moving in the right direction.

"The great thing about catamarans is that their design is naturally buoyant. It's almost impossible for them to not float. Plus, the water is calm today. We're completely safe, but if it gets to be too much, say the word, and we'll head in."

Molly shook her head. "Thanks. But I have to say, I'm not hating it."

"I'll take that as high praise," Grant said.

"In fact, I guess I don't need this." She unbuckled her lifejacket and did some sort of Houdini-style stunt to slip off her raincoat without removing the lifejacket.

"That's a nifty trick."

"Safety first." Her eyes sparkled as she refastened the lifejacket and gave the straps a firm tug.

"You look like you're getting more comfortable already. We might make a sea lover out of you, after all."

She chuckled. "I've always loved the ocean. It's floating in the middle of it on a piece of wood that makes me nervous."

"*Dream Catcher* here is made out of fiberglass, which is five times stronger than wood."

"I'll keep that in mind." Molly readjusted her grip on the rail, looking less than convinced.

"In fact, why don't you sail her?"

"Who, me?" Molly pointed to herself as if there was someone else on the boat to whom he could be referring.

"Yes, you," he said. "It's empowering. Come on." He waved her over.

Reluctantly, she stood and took the two steps to where he was.

Her shoulder ever so slightly grazed his arm as she steadied herself at the helm. It was only the whisper of a touch, but it echoed all the way through him, leaving him feeling slightly off balance. "The ship's wheel works a lot like a car's steering wheel. Just keep her headed in the same direction." He pointed to the gage on the panel. "This little readout here shows you which direction we're going in relation to the wind. You want to keep that line pointed to the top."

Molly snagged her bottom lip with her teeth and studied the panel. "What if I tip us over?"

"We're not going to tip over. You'll be fine." He lifted

his left hand from the wheel to allow her to grip that side. She took a half step closer to him, close enough that he could now report that she smelled like a field of flowers on a summer day mixed with coconutty sunscreen.

Slowly, she wrapped her hand around the wheel in the same spot he'd just vacated. "Are you sure about this?" Her voice was thick with hesitation.

"I have complete confidence in you." He let go with his other hand and held it up in the air.

She quickly grabbed the other side of the wheel as if it was the string of a balloon about to escape. "Now what?" She stood as rigid as a mannequin, lips pressed together in a thin line and her wide gaze superglued to some spot in front of them. Her grip was so tight around the wheel, he thought it might leave permanent indentations in her hands.

Grant leaned against the side railing, casually draping his arms in front of his chest. "That's it. You're sailing."

"Wait, I am?" She stared at him with a slightly horrified look.

"Yep. Looking good, captain. Just keep it between the lines." He tapped on the display on the control panel again.

"I'm sailing." Her gaze flickered between the control panel, the ship's wheel, and the water in front of them. "On the ocean." Wonder flooded her voice, and her grip relaxed enough that some of the color started to return to her knuckles.

Grant knew that wonder. It was what he'd felt the first time he'd sailed a boat, what launched his love affair with the ocean. "It's a powerful feeling, huh?"

Molly took a second before answering. “Totally powerful.”

“Be careful. It can be addictive. Once you get bitten by the bug, it’s almost impossible to go back to being a land-dweller.”

“That might be a problem. I have no idea where my next assignment will be, but I feel fairly certain it’ll be on the land and not at sea.”

Grant propped his arm on the rail next to him, keeping an eye on things. “A traveling vet is an interesting job. I bet it takes you to some pretty interesting places.”

Molly kept her gaze glued to the water in front of them, clearly concentrating on captaining the boat. “This is actually my first assignment. But so far I approve of the destination.” She let go of the wheel with one hand long enough to tuck a strand of her golden hair behind her ear. “My last job was in a neighborhood veterinarian office. The kind who sees mainly dogs and cats with the occasional pet turtle or pig to keep things interesting.”

“Pet pigs, huh?”

Her animation returned, giving her a spark that made her come alive. It was the same phenomenon that happened when she’d told him about the zoo animals in the ambo. “You’d be surprised how common they are. They can be really sweet, although they require a lot of attention.”

Watching her light up when she talked about animals resonated somewhere deep in his soul. He also had that spark. “So, what prompted the change from neighborhood vet to traveling vet?” Grant paused.

"Unless that's a personal question, in which case, don't feel like you have to answer."

"You're letting me drive your sailboat in the middle of the ocean. The least I can do is answer a few semi-personal questions."

"Technically, you're *sailing* my boat."

"See? I don't even know the correct term, and you're still letting me do it." She glanced over at him long enough to flash a cheeky grin.

Then, something strange happened. Just as it had during the wedding conversation, a hint of pain flashed in her eyes. It was the kind of hurt that made Grant want to wrap his arms around her and pull her into him. But since they were barely the kind of friends who answered personal questions, he shoved his hands in his pockets instead.

"My, uh, life took some unexpected turns, and I found myself needing a change." Her shoulders sagged a bit. "One of my friends from school is a locum vet. I decided to give her a call to see how she liked it, and about a month later, I ended up here."

He knew a thing or two about unexpected turns. It was also the reason he'd ended up back here, not that he was complaining. Here wasn't a bad place to be. *But the project Jonathan had talked about, there...*

He pushed the thought out of his mind. He didn't need the raging debate of should-he-stay or should-he-go hijacking his perfectly peaceful day of sailing. "I'm sorry about the unexpected turns. But we—Chompers, especially—are glad you landed here."

She seemed to brighten. "Chompers was a great example of how good things can come out of the unexpected."

Grant had to agree. *This moment would be another example*, but he kept that thought to himself. "And thanks to you, this time next week he'll be halfway to the Caribbean."

"Aww. I love being part of a happy ending."

"Speaking of which, have you given any more thought to helping us out on a more regular basis? We have plenty of happy endings you could be part of." He knew it was a long shot. She'd already said no, and he realized there was little reason for her to change her mind, but he owed it to every turtle they worked with to ask again.

"It's tempting."

"Which part?" He tried to keep the conversation light, kind of like gently approaching an animal in the wild to not scare it off. "The long hours, or the low compensation?"

"I'm going to go with the charming patients." Then, once again, she snagged her lip with her teeth, the way she did when she was nervous. "But like I said before, the timing just isn't right."

"Fair enough." He wasn't sure where the flash of disappointment came from. Saying no was completely understandable. "But that doesn't mean you have to be a stranger. I speak from experience when I say visiting the turtles can be good for the soul."

Molly turned, taking her eyes off the water in front of her for the first time, and locked her gentle gaze with his. "I might take you up on that."

But before he could respond to the warm feeling rising up in his chest, their conversation was interrupted by a shrilling alarm. The high-pitched sound sliced through the peaceful afternoon air.

Molly jumped, her eyes widening with panic. "What's that? What's happening? Are we sinking?"

The sound sent a shot of adrenaline racing through Grant as well, but for a different reason than what Molly was thinking. "Everything's fine with the boat. The alarm's coming from my phone." He pulled the cell phone out of his pocket and silenced the screeching sound while his own concern grew. "It's a notification from Turtle Rehab. It means there's some sort of turtle emergency."

Panic rose in Molly and, since she wasn't sure what else to do with all of the jittery energy, she gripped the ship's wheel tighter. It was highly possible that she'd leave fingerprints in the steering wheel from the amount of time she'd spent squeezing it since taking control of the helm. "Which turtle?" She pushed away all the other emotions she'd brought on board, harnessed the inner calm she needed for these kinds of situations, and focused all her energy on the facts. "What kind of emergency?"

"Not an emergency with one of our turtles." Grant studied his screen, worry lines cutting into his brow. "There's a turtle in distress spotted in the wild."

Molly couldn't deny the concern in Grant's voice. Whatever was going on was something to be taken seriously. But there was something else there too. He had this sense of steady strength that she found comforting.

Before she could ask another question, he had already typed a message on his phone and was dialing a number.

"Hey, it's Grant," she heard him say. "I'm out on *Dream Catcher* and I'm only about fifteen minutes away from those coordinates."

She kept her focus on steering the boat as she strained to hear what was being said on the other end of the phone. But between the wind, the waves, and her own thumping heartbeat, she couldn't make out any of the words.

"I have Dr. Lawrence with me. We can make the extraction. But we'll be closer to the marina. It'll be faster if you meet us there with the turtle ambo." He paused again to listen then said, "Copy that. We're changing course now, and I'll radio the other boat. Tell them I'll be on channel six." He punched off and slipped the phone into his pocket. He turned to her with an expression full of sympathy. "I'm so sorry about this, but do you mind if I hijack this trip to rescue an injured turtle?"

"Of course not. What's going on?"

"A boat not far from here spotted a turtle in an entanglement, which means some sort of something is wrapped around it, and it's having trouble swimming."

"Is it serious?"

"It's hard to know until we see the turtle. Could be as simple as cutting off whatever it is and treating the scratches. Could be a lot more serious."

"How can I help?"

"This expedition will put us out of eyesight of the shoreline. Are you okay with that?"

"Yes, whatever it takes." Her answer didn't surprise her, because of course she was willing to be a little uncomfortable to rescue an animal. What did surprise her was the sense of confidence she had about it.

Their short sailing excursion slightly offshore hadn't made her feel comfortable on the open water. She wasn't rushing out to buy her own boat to cross the Atlantic or anything. But she trusted Grant and she felt safe—well, as safe as one could feel when floating on a piece of fiberglass in the giant ocean—when she was standing next to him.

"What can I do?"

"Hang out here and keep the wheel steady while I take down the sails. Then we'll switch to using the motors to get out there faster." He was already headed down the steps to the deck.

"Got it." She adjusted her grip on the wheel as he climbed up to the sails. A few minutes later, he was back at the helm, flipping switches on the control panel and starting the engines.

"We're going to go a little faster than we did before, so hold on. It might get bumpy."

Molly widened her stance to steady herself. With all of the nervous energy jittering around inside her, she couldn't sit. So she stood next to him and clutched the side rail with all the grip strength she had.

He turned the boat in a wide arc so they were pointing almost directly out to sea and picked up the boat's radio. "*Dream Catcher* for *Lucky Day*. Come in, *Lucky Day*."

"This is *Lucky Day*."

"This is Grant Torres from Emerald Cove Turtle Rehab. Who am I talking to?"

"Bret." The voice on the other end sounded young—Molly would've guessed a teenager—and she could hear his nervousness over the radio waves.

"Hey, Bret, thanks for calling us. Do you still have eyes on the turtle?"

"Yeah. He's off the bow. What should we do?"

"We're on our way to you. Make sure you keep an eye on the turtle, but don't let your boat get too close. We don't want to risk an impact injury."

"Right," the voice said.

"I'm about ten minutes away. Give me your coordinates again."

They spent a few minutes talking about the exact longitude and latitude as the catamaran bounced over the waves. Wind rushed past, and the ocean spray misted her skin as they sped out toward the horizon.

The ride seemed to take forever, each minute crawling by. Neither of them spoke a word. There was nothing around them except endless water and uninterrupted sky. Molly stood tense and alert, like a racer waiting for the signal that would launch her from the starting line. Finally, Grant slowed to a putter, causing the boat to sink slightly into the water.

"Keep your eyes out. I don't want to hit it," he said to her before he picked up the radio. "Hey, Bret, we're here. Do you still see the turtle?"

"It's off our bow at ten o'clock," the young voice said.

Grant inched closer, and Molly franticly scanned the reflective surface of the sea. There was so much water, so much area to cover. The enormity of the situation started to set in, causing a big, hollow pit in the middle of her stomach.

"Ahhh. There you are, sweetheart." Grant's voice was calm, offering her a sense of easiness she hadn't felt a moment ago. He steered the boat in a wide arc around the smaller fishing boat and jutted his chin out in the direction of where he was looking. Between the waves and the reflective surface of the water, it was hard to see anything, and Molly could barely make out the form of the turtle.

"I'm going to try to get in front of her." They slowly inched forward. "The best way to load her on this boat is using the steps on the back of the hull."

Molly kept her eyes on the sea turtle the entire time. It was hard to tell from their distance what was wrapped around the turtle's middle. A rope, maybe? What she could tell was that the turtle was definitely stressed. Her movements were slow and labored and she floated on the surface, sticking only her head underwater.

"So, I'm going to need your help." Grant tossed the words out casually, as if he were about to ask her to hold a door for him or pick up a pen he'd dropped.

"Okay." The word drawled out because she, on the other hand, was a lot more hesitant. Being on the boat in the middle of the ocean and rescuing a wild sea turtle weren't just outside of her comfort zone. They were in a completely different galaxy. But she wasn't one to sit on the sidelines when it came to animals, no matter what galaxy she was in.

"How do you feel about getting in the water?"

"Umm..." Molly stared at the deep emerald water surrounding them. She swallowed hard. He wanted her to get in that? Like she said, this was a whole other galaxy.

Sure, she didn't mind "swimming" in the ocean when she was at the beach and only went waist deep, but that was different. She could see the bottom there. Big fish didn't usually hang out in the shallow water near the shore. Out here, though? This was their stomping ground, so to speak. And the water they were in was so deep that there was no way she could see the bottom, no matter how clear it was.

"Or you can steer the boat and I can get in," Grant suggested.

"You want me to steer your boat?"

He shrugged. "Sure. There's nothing to it." He motioned to the wheel and the controls next to it. "All you do is keep it pointed the right direction and use the throttle to ease the boat forward or backward to keep it from knocking into the turtle. Or, you know, me."

Molly glanced from the ship's wheel to the turtle in the water, fear sloshing around in her belly like a couple of rogue waves.

Since she didn't like option A or B, she wanted to choose C. She wasn't sure what that would be, but she was confident it didn't have anything to do with taking a dip in Jaws' backyard or figuring out how to control this huge boat when there were lives at stake.

But since there were two jobs that had to be done and only two people there to do them, she was stuck choosing between a bad idea and a worse idea. "Guess I'm going swimming." She stared at the waves slapping against the side of the boat and hoped she was making the right call.

"You're going to be great." Grant smiled. It was the authentic, encouraging kind that was almost as tangible as if he'd wrapped his arms around her, calming some of her jitters. "Plus, you'll get to put that life jacket to good use."

Molly gave the straps another firm tug. "Not really something I wanted to put to use, but I'm willing to go to extreme measures for a sea turtle."

"A woman after my own heart." There was a twinkle in his eye that gave her a dash of courage.

She followed Grant down to the aft deck and slipped out of her shorts and flip-flops, setting them on the bench. At least she'd thought to wear a swimsuit.

Grant opened one of the storage boxes and pulled out what looked like two hefty pool noodles with blue mesh connecting them. She'd used something similar as a soft stretcher when they'd had to move one of the larger marine animals at the zoo. "Swim out to the turtle, load her on the stretcher, then I'll come down to the steps and help you lift her aboard. There's nothing to it."

Molly took the stretcher and stared out at the water in front of her. "Right. Nothing to it."

"I'll get you as close as I can. When I cut the engine, jump in. You've got this."

She tucked the stretcher under one arm and braced herself against the side of the ship as she walked down the wide stairs that were built into the starboard hull. *Dream Catcher* slowly inched closer to the turtle. The waves splashed up over the last step, and she clutched the railing.

She wasn't sure she had this. She was way out

of her depths, no pun intended. Her heart raced and her palms were so clammy that her grip was slipping. But there was a turtle who needed help, and the only way she was going to get that help was if Molly pushed aside her fears and did what had to be done.

The motor stopped, and Grant yelled down, "All clear."

That was her cue. With a deep breath, she lowered herself so she was sitting on the step with her legs dangling in the cool gulf waters. "Here goes nothing," she whispered as she pushed herself off the safety of the boat and into the middle of the ocean.

Her first surprise was that the water felt nice. If she wasn't on a rescue mission, she might've even gone as far as to say it was refreshing.

"Hey, baby." She spoke in a calm voice as she did her best to stroke out toward the turtle. "I'm here to help you. You're going to be fine. *We're* going to be fine."

The turtle lifted its head as if to acknowledge her and then dunked it back underwater. Molly didn't blame her. She wasn't buying the words she was saying, either.

As she got closer to the turtle, she could tell the thing wrapped around the shell was some sort of buoy. The floating part had lodged itself under the turtle, making it hard to not list to the side and impossible to dive under the water. The sight pulled at Molly's heart and caused her to kick harder to reach the turtle quicker.

"Oh, you poor thing." She tried to maneuver closer to the turtle, but moving in the water while wearing a lifejacket and carrying a floating stretcher wasn't as easy as it sounded. "We're going to get this off and get you all fixed up. But first I have to load you on this stretcher so my friend Grant can put you on his boat."

"You're doing great, Molly," Grant called from the helm.

"Great" seemed like a strong word. She had no doubt her "swimming" through the ocean roughly mimicked an uncoordinated walrus on land. Lots of effort, but not a lot of progress. She was thankful no one was recording this to be able to laugh at her for all of eternity.

Still, she appreciated his encouragement.

She stopped a few feet away from the turtle with the stretcher floating next to her. "Any suggestions on the best way to get this thing under her?" While she had experience with transporting marine animals, she'd never loaded one onto the stretcher before. That job usually fell to the animal keeper. And even then, she'd only ever seen them do it in a tank where they were standing on the bottom. Floating in an ocean added a level of complication to everything.

"I find that from behind works the best. Make sure to fully submerge it before you open the sides, and it will naturally kind of scoop her up." Grant pantomimed the action from the boat.

It sounded easy enough. "Hang in there, baby. I'm a first timer at this rescue thing too," Molly cooed as she positioned the stretcher in front of her. "You relax, and I promise I'll figure things out on my end." Hopefully sooner rather than later.

Just like Grant had instructed her, she inched closer to the turtle and put the two floating sides of the stretcher together, pushing down to submerge the structure.

It didn't work. The entire thing went less than an inch under the surface before it popped back up. Molly let out a sigh. This was going to be harder than she'd thought.

She tried again. This time she leaned on the noodles with all the weight she had. Unfortunately, between the life jacket and the buoyancy of the salt water, it wasn't much. The part closest to her submerged to the level she needed, but the front half stayed entirely out of the water.

Frustration stacked up inside her and she wiped away some of the water that had splashed on her face. "This is not as easy as it looks," she said to the turtle. "Third time's the charm. Here we go."

She tried one last time, gripping the floating sides about halfway up their length. Then she did a giant scissor kick, propelling herself upward before plunging her entire body weight down on the floats.

It worked. Enough, anyway, to get the stretcher deep enough to clear the animal. Quickly, she thrust it forward, underneath the turtle, as she opened the floats on either side.

It wasn't perfect. The turtle's front flippers were still hanging off, and the float on the far side didn't quite make it all the way around, but she could work with it. And luckily, the turtle seemed to understand that help was on the way, and relaxed instead of fighting it.

"See? I told you we could do this." Triumph flooded through her like a waterfall of shiny, golden rays, brightening her whole outlook. “Let’s get you on the boat.”

“Good work!” Grant pumped his fists in the air in celebration.

Maintaining a firm grip on the stretcher, she kicked toward the boat. It seemed to not take as long to return to the boat, and when she looked up, Grant was already standing on the steps waiting for her. Together, they lifted the turtle out of the water and carried her up to the deck.

“This is the most secure spot where she won’t slide around too much.” Grant led them to the far corner of the deck and set the turtle on the floor. “Do you mind putting some towels around her to protect her from bumping into anything? Towels are in there.” He pointed to a bench behind the turtle that doubled as a storage bin.

“No problem. I’ll stay down here with her while you drive us home.” Water dripped off her and formed a puddle on the deck around her, but Molly ignored it. She kneeled down next to the turtle, examining the rope wrapped around her. She couldn’t tell if it was the same long rope or multiple pieces tangled together, but the thick cords twisted all over the turtle, squeezing against her shell and cutting into her flippers. The Styrofoam buoy ball was lodged so tightly against her that her front flipper was sitting at an awkward angle. She laid a gentle hand on the turtle’s shell. “Oh, sweet thing, you really got tangled up in this mess, didn’t you?” She looked up to find Grant. “Do you have a knife? I’d like to get the rope off her as soon as possible.”

“Already on it.” He pulled a large fishing knife out

of the same storage bin the stretcher had been in and handed it to her before he scurried up the steps to the helm. She hardly noticed the engines start or the cool breeze that left goose bumps on her skin as the boat sped across the water. Her entire focus was on the turtle.

She tucked towels around the animal to keep her secure before she started sawing through the thick rope closest to the buoy ball. Once she broke through, there was enough give to move the ball out of the way. She gingerly set the turtle's flipper on a soft pillow of towels. "The good news is it doesn't seem like your flipper is broken. It looks like most of your injuries are soft tissue damage. But we'll get a quick picture of your insides just to make sure." Molly kept a running commentary as she worked on the turtle. She was a firm believer that animals deserved to know what was going on, even if they didn't understand all the words.

Water continued to drip off her ponytail, but she brushed the drops off her face and kept working, sawing through another tight section of rope. "But judging by how weak you are, what you could really use is a good meal and some rest. We'll make sure you get plenty of that too."

She broke through the rope and slid it from under the turtle, tossing it out of the way. "You're going to be just fine, baby. Help is on the way."

Chapter Five

TWO HOURS LATER, GRANT WAS sitting at his desk filling out the admission paperwork when Molly walked into his office. Her hair was still damp from her impromptu swim and she looked a little wind-blown, but she'd swapped out her dripping wet T-shirt and life jacket for a dry Turtle Rehab logo T-shirt he recognized from the gift shop. For the first time all day, she looked relaxed, which Grant took as a good sign.

"So what's the prognosis, doc?"

"Good. The prognosis is very, very good." Molly dropped into the chair in front of him, letting out a contented sigh. "Her injuries—and we did confirm the turtle's a she—were mostly cuts and minor soft tissue damage. We cleaned them, I gave her an antibiotic shot, and Claire told me to cover them with... honey?" She arched her eyebrows at the last word, an intrigued look lighting up her face.

"Yeah, it sounds weird, but we use it a lot in the turtle world. It's a natural antiseptic and poses no risk to the turtle if they happen to ingest it. Win-win."

"It's brilliant. I totally learned a new trick today

that is about to become one of my go-to treatments." Molly shifted in her chair. "Anyway, we're keeping the water low in the tank for now to give her a chance to rest and get her strength up, but she gobbled up the shrimp and squid she was fed, which is a great sign."

"Good. How about the X-rays?"

"Everything looks normal. I'll have Dr. Lacey take a second look when I talk to her this week, but I don't see any reason why this turtle won't be able to make a full recovery."

The news brightened the already sunny day. "That's good to hear." Grant knew the turtle wasn't out of the woods yet, but it sounded like this story was on its way to a happy ending.

"I know. This turtle is such a sweetheart. She deserves the best."

"Agreed. But in the meantime, she needs a name. Usually we let the people who found her name her. The kids from the boat wanted to name her Lucky after their boat, *Lucky Day*."

"Cute."

"It would be, but that name is a little superstitious for those of us in the turtle rehab world. In our experience, turtles named Lucky tend to not live up to their name."

"We don't want that. Are you going to call them back and ask for a second choice?"

"Actually, I thought you could have the honor. After all, you played a key part in her rescue."

"Me?" Molly looked surprised.

"Sure. You're the hero of the day."

"Heroes wear capes and, in case you didn't notice, I was wearing a lifejacket. I'm pretty sure that's the opposite of a cape." There was a hint of joking in her voice as she dismissed the compliment.

"I happen to see it a different way. For starters, you sailed the boat that we used to rescue her." He held up a finger as if ticking off his detailed list.

Molly rolled her eyes. "For about five minutes before we even knew about the rescue."

"Yes. But you were headed in the right direction, so it still counts." He held up a second finger. "Two, you physically got into the water to rescue her."

Molly nodded. "I did do that. Clearly, sea turtles make me do things that defy all logic."

Grant chuckled and held up a third finger. "And you sped up her recovery by doing her initial exam and coming up with a treatment plan instead of us having to wait for an out-of-town expert to come in. Plus, you saved me a lot of paperwork. Because of you, I don't have to spend as much time in this office, which makes you a pretty big deal in my book."

That coaxed a grin out of her. "I still have to run the treatment plan by Dr. Lacey. At the moment, it's only a suggestion based on my limited knowledge."

"But it has helped us out more than you know. So thank you."

Molly's playful grin faded away and she stared at her hands. "About that." She paused, her teeth snagging her lower lip in that cute way she did when she was unsure about something. Finally, she drew in a deep breath and looked up to meet his gaze. "I'm in."

"In?" A rush of excitement blew through him. Was she saying what he thought she was saying? "For the sake of being on the same page, what exactly are you in for?" And he really hoped her answer was working with him.

Them. He meant them. He hoped she was saying she'd be the center's new resident vet. For the sake of the turtles, of course.

"I'll take over the vet contract while I'm in town. I mean, I can't do everything an expert could do, but I'm willing to do whatever I can. If that will help you."

"Absolutely. We'll take whatever help we can get."

She held a hand up to stop him. "But it comes with two conditions."

He leaned back in his chair, intrigued. "Two conditions, huh?"

She gave him the kind of serious look of a teenager with a well-prepared presentation on why she should stay out past curfew. He half expected her to pull out a PowerPoint presentation. "First, don't expect me to jump in the middle of the ocean for any more rescues. If there's literally anyone else around, I'm staying on the boat."

Grant couldn't help the side of his mouth curling up. "Fair enough. But you have to admit, it's pretty empowering."

The serious teenager-look faded a bit as wonder lit her eyes. "Totally empowering. Which brings me to my second thing. I want to make you a deal."

"What kind of deal?"

"I'll come in every Tuesday and Thursday evening. And in exchange, instead of financial compensation, I'd like for you to take me on excursions. Ocean-related outings that are similar to going out on your boat today." She paused, some of her confidence waning. "Unless you're too busy, which I understand. I know you have family and commitments outside of all the work you do here." Instead of stopping, she charged ahead like a snowball pointed downhill, her words picking up speed as they went. "Or if you're not interested, that's cool too. I know it's a big ask. I thought I'd, you know, throw it out there to see what you thought. No big deal if it doesn't work out. You know, it never hurts to ask, right? But if you'd rather—"

"I'd love to," he interrupted.

She looked up, a little surprised. "You'd love to?"

"You're asking me to do all the things I love and call it work. Of course I'm going to say yes."

She let out a relieved sigh, her negotiating face returning. "To be clear, I'm not asking you to be my personal cruise director for the entirety of my time in Emerald Cove. I was thinking maybe once or twice a month."

"I'm guessing this has something to do with your commitment to try new things?"

She nodded sheepishly. "Yeah. I figure that since you're from here, you might have a few ideas."

"A few," he agreed, his mind racing with possibilities. "In fact, I have an idea already. Do scientific symposiums classify as excursions?"

Molly laughed. "Not exactly what I was thinking, but it's like you know me."

Grant held up his hand to stop her. "First of all, it requires a road trip, which I think we can agree is an adventure in itself. And second, it's a seminar by some of the leading turtle experts in the country on new procedures."

Molly's eyes got wide. "That sounds amazing. Are you sure it's okay if I tag along?"

"I know the presenters, so getting you in won't be hard. Plus, I'd enjoy the company. It gets awfully lonely in the big ol' turtle ambo on my own."

Molly raised an eyebrow. "You're driving the turtle ambo?"

Grant had always meant to buy a new car when he'd moved back home six years ago. But in a town where a bike was often more convenient than fighting traffic and it never hurt to have the turtle ambo close in case of an emergency, he'd never gotten around to it. "You got a problem with my luxury ride?"

"Nope." She shook her head. "Nothing says road trip like a giant green ambulance."

Grant didn't miss the sarcasm in her voice. She wasn't wrong, though. While driving the ambulance around town was convenient, it wasn't the most comfortable on long trips.

"How about I drive?" she offered.

"I mean, you're missing out, but if you insist."

She laughed again, which made him even more confident about this plan. This wasn't at all how he'd seen this conversation going, but he couldn't have been more delighted about the new plan.

Of course, being this delighted about spending time with a woman gave him a slight hesitation. The last time he'd felt like this—and it had been a while—things hadn't turned out the way he'd expected.

But almost as quickly as the thought popped into his mind, he pushed it away. This whole adventure agreement with Molly wasn't personal. It was professional, which made it a completely different ballgame. Besides, didn't enjoying spending time with one's colleagues make a more pleasant workplace? And from what he'd seen, Molly was going to make a great addition to their team.

"I have to ask, what made you change your mind about working here?"

"The turtle we rescued today." Molly glanced in the direction of where the tanks were. "She deserves the best chance at a full recovery. I'm not going to be in town long, but it can be my mission to get her the best care possible and back in the ocean before I leave. And maybe a few of the others while I'm at it."

Grant nodded. "I know the feeling. Which reminds me, you still have to give our newest turtle a name."

Molly thought about it for a second. "Hope," she said eventually. "Because we all need a little hope in our lives."

"You've been in town less than a week and you've already gotten yourself a side hustle," Hadley said Monday morning after Molly had finished telling them about her decision to help out at Turtle Rehab.

"Not a side hustle. I'd say it's more of a pet project." She giggled after hearing how it sounded. "Or you know what I mean." She took a sip of the latte Hadley had made for her. "This is great, by the way."

"A good view and conversation with friends are enough to make even the most basic coffee amazing." Ellyn took a sip of her own coffee. "Although, I'm glad you're here, because it makes it easier to get Hadley's caffeine creations."

"Yet there's a small part of me that's a little sad

I'm the reason you retired the coffee-box-delivery system." A picture of the small wooden box they'd rigged to a pully system that strung between their two balconies floated to the front of her mind. "That was some A-plus science fair stuff if ever I've seen any."

"It was all Hadley's idea," Ellyn said, sipping her coffee.

Hadley gave a nonchalant shrug, even as a proud grin tugged at her mouth. "Apparently there's no limit to what I'll do to be lazy."

"Well, it was brilliant," Molly said. "And so is this coffee. For real, if you ever get tired of the whole project-management thing, you should open a coffee shop."

Ellyn's eyes got wide. "Right? That's what I'm always telling her."

Hadley waved a dismissive hand in the air. "Okay, we get it. Coffee's great; the delivery box was inspired. But what I want to hear about is the rest of Molly's story."

"That's it. That's the whole story." Molly shrugged. "We rescued the turtle, and I agreed to be their resident vet while I'm in town. In exchange, they're going to take me on a few excursions to show off the best of what the Florida panhandle has to offer."

"Which is why you're going out of town with Grant next weekend?" Hadley clarified.

"I'm not sure it qualifies as going out of town if it's a day trip. But yes, that's why I'm going."

"Hmm." Ellyn flashed her a knowing look over the rim of her coffee mug as she took another sip. "Sounds chummy."

Sure, Molly knew what it sounded like. She'd been

afraid of that when she'd proposed the plan to Grant. Asking someone to be her personal excursion guide had the potential to be taken the wrong way. But their agreement was nothing more than a business deal. He needed a vet, and she needed someone to help her navigate through a new town and check a couple of boxes off her personal growth list. "Nope. Not chummy," Molly said quickly. "Simply a work thing. Purely professional. There's definitely no chumminess whatsoever. Just, you know, a couple of colleagues."

"To be clear..." Hadley blew on her coffee, her expression falling somewhere between facetious and teasing. "That's a no to things being chummy?"

Ellyn giggled on her other side.

Molly rolled her eyes. So maybe she'd been a little too emphatic in her denial, but the truth behind the statement stood. "It's as chummy as things can get at a scientific symposium."

The truth was, a business relationship was as far as it could go. Grant was a great guy, and maybe in a different time or a different place, it'd be a different story. But as it was, Molly was actively avoiding anything of the sort, chummy or otherwise. Anything more than professional would be a direct violation of the first and most important rule of Molly 2.0—no relationships.

She glanced down at the finger where the two-and-a-half carat, emerald-cut, diamond engagement ring had been until three months ago. As it turned out, relationships were not the sure thing she'd once thought them to be. They were risky. The kind of risk that could bankrupt a person, in fact, which was how she ended up here.

One day life had been humming along and she'd thought everything was great. Fine, maybe great was a stretch. But it was good, and good was good enough, wasn't it? She and her dreamy fiancé had been headed toward picket fences and rocking chairs on the front porch. As far as she'd been concerned, all was right with the world.

Then one day it had all come crashing down. She'd thought they were meeting up at the wedding venue to talk about the best location for the cakes and the dance floor, maybe where to put the favors. But that conversation had gone a very different direction. Apparently, he was in love with someone else.

And to make it even worse, that someone else also happened to be her maid of honor.

"The thing is, relationships and I aren't exactly on speaking terms at the moment."

"Ahhh." Hadley nodded as if she knew what that felt like. "I've been there before."

"I'm sorry, honey." Ellyn leaned as far over as she could and squeezed Molly's hand, offering her a sympathetic smile. "And we promise not to try to set you up with anyone else in Emerald Cove, don't we, Hadley?"

Hadley held up a hand, defensively. "It is never my intention to set anyone up. I can't help it if I naturally see connections everyone else misses."

Hadley and Molly looked at each other and giggled, breaking some of the tension.

"Luckily for you, Ms. Matchmaker, there's no connection between me and Grant other than working at the same place." And as far as she was concerned, there wouldn't be any connections ever. She was officially out of the game.

It was strange to compare her situation to a turtle's, but she and Hope actually had a lot in common. They'd both shown up in this town with broken pieces and a life that'd taken a strange detour.

If only broken hearts were like turtle shells, and all it took to heal them was a little bit of honey.

Chapter Six

IT WAS STILL DARK WHEN Molly pulled up to Turtle Rehab early Saturday morning, but she didn't care. Her insulated coffee cup was full, the address of where they were going was typed into her navigation app, and her fully charged laptop was ready for note-taking. She hadn't been this excited about something since... Well, it'd been a while.

Grant must've been waiting for her inside the gift shop, because she'd barely shifted the car into park before he walked through the glass doors. He paused under the dim light of the porchlight to lock up before he strolled toward her.

For the first time since she'd met him, he wasn't wearing his standard shorts and flip-flops with his polarized sunglasses hanging around his neck. Instead, he was dressed professionally, with a ECTRR logoed polo tucked into black chinos and actual lace-up shoes. He even had a backpack slung over one shoulder. She had to admit that while his ruggedly handsome, seafarer vibe looked good on him, he wore professional well. Really well, in fact.

He climbed into the front passenger seat of her

midsized black SUV, which had seemed sensible when she'd bought it for a life of frosty Kansas winters counterbalanced with hot, sticky summers. Now that she was down here in the sunny panhandle of Florida with the gorgeous weather and sea breezes, she wished she'd at least sprung for the sunroof.

"People in Emerald Cove do own closed-toe shoes. I was starting to think there was a city mandate against them," she teased.

"We only wear them when absolutely necessary. And it doesn't mean we like it." He stared down at his suede dressy sneakers as if talking directly to them.

"Well, you look nice."

"Thanks." He fastened his seatbelt. "I have to admit, I'm a little surprised you're not wearing a full NASCAR flame-retardant driving suit with a helmet for our little trek east."

"You're making fun of me, aren't you?"

Grant grinned. "Maybe a little bit."

"Everyone laughs until they need something from my emergency preparedness kit." She threw a sidelong glance in his direction. "Don't come crying to me when you get something stuck in your teeth at lunch and you need some floss."

"I'm already preparing my heartfelt apology and retraction for such an occasion." He shrugged. "I'm not saying it's good, but you're going to want to have that floss ready."

His playfulness caused a flurry somewhere deep in her chest, which she promptly ignored. There was no flurrying allowed. Hadn't she made that clear enough when she'd been talking to Hadley and Ellyn earlier this week?

Just to prove it to herself, she changed the subject to something more professional. "I have to admit, I was so excited about today's lecture I had a hard time sleeping last night. I'm totally nerding out over these new surgery techniques for sea turtles." She pulled out of the parking lot and onto the main road. Normally, there was quite a bit of traffic, but at this predawn hour, they appeared to be the only ones out.

"Then you're in for a treat. Dr. Simmons is one of the best."

"And you said he's a close friend of yours? How did you come to be such good buddies with the leading turtle expert in the country?"

"He was part of an eight-person research team I was on that spent three months at sea. You get to know someone pretty well when you all live on the same sixty-foot boat for ninety days."

"Three months? I thought you said working with sea turtles wasn't all sailing and hanging out on the ocean."

Grant chuckled. "So maybe there's a little more of that than I let on. But that was my longest one."

"You did others?" If he was trying to make it sound less dramatic, he was failing. How much time had this man spent at sea? No wonder he liked living on a boat.

"I did two others while I was at the university. One as a research assistant and one when I was working on my doctorate."

"I didn't realize you had your PhD." Over the past week, Molly had spent more time working and talking with Grant at Turtle Rehab, but clearly there was a lot she didn't know about the mysterious man of adventure riding in her car, starting with his education. "What's it in?"

"I studied marine biology." There was a pause, and Grant shifted in his seat, looking the most uncomfortable he had since she'd met him. "But I don't have my PhD. I left the university before I finished my dissertation."

"Oh." She did her best to keep her voice neutral although the news surprised her. She knew from friends who'd gotten their PhDs that the dissertation was a hard and sometimes frustrating process, but Grant didn't seem like the type to give up when things got difficult. In fact, she would've said the opposite. What would've caused him to walk away from something he was obviously passionate about, especially so close to the finish line?

Molly considered asking him about it, but Grant changed the subject.

"I have to admit, I have an ulterior motive for wanting to leave so early this morning." He had that sly Wile E. Coyote look that told her there was a better-than-good chance whatever he had in mind was going to be out of her comfort zone.

"You mean, you weren't trying to pad our three-hour drive time by two hours in case we ran into summer traffic?"

"Summer traffic is nothing to joke about. Wait until the height of tourist season. You'll avoid driving at all costs." His eyes got wide with a look of mock horror. "But in this case, I wasn't too worried about the tourists. As per our agreement, I'm taking you on your first excursion."

"I thought the symposium was the excursion."

"What kind of adventure tour guide would I be if the best thing I could come up with was a scientific symposium at a moderately fancy hotel?"

"An awesome one who cares about learning." Seriously, Molly didn't see the problem. They had to drive outside of the city limits. That seemed adventurous.

"Then consider this a two-fer." He typed something into his phone and then slid it into the cell phone holder she had on her dashboard so she could see the new directions.

They drove for another hour, chatting about nothing special, when the computerized voice instructed her to take the next right, then a quick left, which put them on a much-smaller road in a more remote area.

There were a few houses that popped up here and there, but they were mostly surrounded by undeveloped land. After driving about fifteen minutes, they crossed over a long bridge to what appeared to be a small barrier island. From the looks of it, it was uninhabited.

"You've reached your destination," the GPS announced.

"We have?" Molly asked, looking around. In the predawn darkness, it was hard to see much, but there didn't seem to be anything around except sand dunes, sea grass, and a few scraggly-looking trees. She switched her headlights to the bright setting.

"Not quite yet." Grant took his phone and stopped the directions. "The place we're going doesn't have a technical address, but it's at the end of this road."

Road seemed like a bold word for the trail they were on. Gravel crunched under her tires as they crept forward, and with all the overgrowth, it was hard to tell where the "road" ended and nature began. "What exactly is waiting for us at the end?"

"A lighthouse." As soon as he said it, she could make out a large shadowy structure looming in the distance. "One of the oldest lighthouses in this part of Florida, to be exact."

She leaned closer to the windshield to get a better view of the tall brick structure. "Is that it?"

"That's her." He tilted his head, looking at it through the passenger side window. "The original lighthouse in this location was built in the mid-1800s. That one was knocked down by a storm, and they replaced it with this one close to the turn of the century."

"Fascinating." Molly pulled to the side of the "road" so she could get a better look at it, although she wished it was lighter out. The darkness made it hard to see the details.

"Want to check it out?"

"Yes, please." She shifted the car into park and killed the engine.

It was quiet outside. The chirping and buzzing of the nocturnal insects had already faded away, and the songs of the birds hadn't started yet. Even the constant sea breeze was reduced to a soft whisper. The entire world seemed to be asleep, which added to the mystery of the towering giant in front of them. Molly walked across the sandy soil to examine the bricks that made up the exterior.

"A lot of lighthouses were built to warn sailors of hazards in the oceans. Jagged coastlines, unexpected islands, that sort of thing." Grant stepped up next to her and laid a hand on the century-old bricks. "But this one was commissioned to guide sailors home. It marked the entrance to the river that led to a harbor."

"Lighting the way home. I like that." She tipped her head as far back as she could to stare up at the massive structure. It had to be close to a hundred feet tall, and from this position, it was impossible to see the top. "I've never been this close to a lighthouse before."

"I figured they didn't have a lot of lighthouses in Kansas."

"Nope. The cows don't usually have trouble steering clear of the corn." She took a step forward and rested her hand on the weathered brick exterior, feeling the warmth it'd held onto from yesterday's sun. "It's beautiful."

This was exactly the kind of excursion she'd had in mind when she made this deal. Well, maybe not a lighthouse specifically, but experiencing something new and different. A sense of satisfaction flowed through her.

"If you think it's pretty down here, you should check out the view from up there." Grant's voice interrupted her peaceful moment, and she glanced over at him. Even in the darkness she could see the twinkle in his eye.

"Like, at the top?" Her calming cascade of satisfaction stalled, and she pointed her finger at the sky as if there were any question about which direction "up" would be.

"That's the spot." He pulled two headlamp flashlights from his pocket and handed one to her before slipping the other over his forehead. "And we'd better get started if we want to catch the sunrise. We've got roughly nine floors of rickety spiral staircase to get to the top." He headed around the side, where there was an old wooden door secured closed with a padlock.

Molly followed, tugging her own headlamp over her head. "Are we allowed?"

"Allowed?" He twisted his mouth to the side and bobbed his head back and forth as if considering the meaning of the word. "Let's just say it's probably better if we don't get caught."

Without further explanation, he reached down and spun the dial on the rusty old lock. It made a grinding sound as he turned it first to the left, then right, then left again before it popped open. He pushed the door open and a stale, musty odor drifted out.

"Come on." He stepped inside, disappearing into the darkness.

Molly eyed the opening then looked to her right and left to make sure no one was around. "Here goes nothing," she whispered, and stepped over the threshold into the lighthouse.

The inside was dark and dank. She switched on her headlamp and stood just inside the doorway to get her bearings. Whatever calm feelings she'd harnessed outside had now officially been replaced by a galloping pulse and a hefty dose of trepidation.

"Hanging out with you is turning into a dangerous hobby." She gripped the handrail and stared at the seemingly endless stairs that twisted up into the darkness.

"I think the word you're looking for is 'adventurous.'" He waggled his eyebrows. "And weren't you the one who commissioned this excursion?"

"I'm not sure trespassing qualifies as an excursion."

He shrugged, climbing up the first steps of the spiral staircase that wrapped around the inside of the structure. "Potato, patahdo." He glanced over his shoulder. "Trust me, the view at the top is worth it."

Carefully, she stepped on the first step, testing it to see if it would hold her weight. She wouldn't have stamped it with the sturdy label, but she didn't fall through, which seemed positive. "*Carpe diem,*" she muttered to herself.

They climbed for a while in silence as Molly focused on step after worn wooden step. It didn't take long until she was out of breath and starting to get dizzy.

She paused to catch her breath and gauge how far they'd gone. "I can't believe the lightkeepers used to do this climb a couple of times a day. They must've been in great shape."

"It was the original StairMaster." Grant sounded much less winded than she was, and she wondered what kind of workout he did to stay in such good shape. Also, she wanted to tell her old spin instructor that he had nothing on lighthouse stairs.

"How did you know the code to get in this place?" Molly was partly curious and partly trying to distract herself from the vigor of the climb.

"I have a buddy who works for the parks department. They haven't changed it in years. We used to come out here right after they stopped the restoration."

"Why did they stop?" Molly had noticed that the stairs were in decent condition. They certainly weren't original, but not much else looked like it'd been touched in many, many years.

"About twenty years ago, they started the process. They repainted it, fixed the broken glass at the top, and put in new stairs. But there were budget cuts before they could get it up to code, and they never finished."

"And now it sits here? Empty?"

"Pretty much."

"That's kind of sad, really." The interior was getting lighter, which made Molly think they were getting close to the top. But she trudged step after step without looking up, not wanting to be depressed by how far they still had to go. "It's like a piece of history forgotten."

"Not today."

It only took two more turns around the cylindrical lighthouse before the platform at the top came into view.

Grant stepped on it first and stood to the side to wait for Molly to join him. "It's a bit of a tight squeeze up here, but it looks like we made it in time." He led her on the catwalk around the giant light in the center to where there was a small part of the window that could be opened. Grant pulled the hatch, revealing an opening to the outside that was just big enough to crawl through. "After you."

Molly eyed the opening. She wanted to ask if it was safe, but let it go. She'd come this far, hadn't she? "*Hakuna matata*," she whispered to herself and crawled through.

She stepped out onto the narrow walkway that surrounded the light and clenched the old metal railing with both hands. Grant followed, stepping close to her in his gentle, protective way. A soft breeze skimmed her skin and ruffled her hair as she took in the scene before them.

"Breathtaking" didn't seem to do it justice. The Gulf stretched out to the golden horizon, where the tip of the sun was starting to peek out above the ocean. Long clouds painted in deep magentas and violets highlighted the sky, and their colors pooled in the glassy water below. It was nothing short of a masterpiece.

"Amazing," Molly breathed out, trying her best to soak it all in. "This view is totally worth all those stairs."

"Agreed."

They stood there in silence for the moment as the sun rose, its rays slowly drenching the world with light. Grant's shoulder gently grazed hers, allowing some of his strength and confidence to seep in, and Molly let the beauty of the moment wash over her.

She had always liked sunrises, but this one felt different. It was bigger, resonating somewhere deep in her chest, like it wasn't simply the start of a new day. This sunrise felt like the start of a whole new hope-filled beginning.

"Thank you for bringing me here," Molly said eventually, well aware that the man beside her was turning out to play a major role in her new beginning. Being here was special, but being here with him conjured up a whole lot of feels that she wasn't sure she wanted to dive into yet. This morning was too perfect to ruin it with thinking.

"You're welcome," Grant said simply.

"I don't know how many laws we broke…" Molly kept her eyes on the beautiful watercolor that painted the early morning sky. "But this view was worth it."

Grant chuckled. "I'll have you know, there were no felonies committed in this morning's adventure. Your conscience can rest at ease."

"Good to know. Going to jail might put a damper on my current mood."

"Tell me about it." He glanced at his watch. "Although, we should probably start moving, or we really are going to have trouble getting there on time."

"If we must." She closed her eyes and tried to burn the image into her memory, letting the golden colors seep into her soul. She considered taking her phone out of her pocket and snapping a picture, but there wasn't a camera in the world that could fully capture the essence of this view. After one more deep breath of calm, morning air, she blinked her eyes opened. "Okay, I'm ready."

"Great. So to get down, we're going to tie a rope to this rail and rappel down the side. Nothing to it."

Molly could feel the golden color drain out of her toes. "We're going to what?"

Grant's grin widened, causing little crinkles around his eyes. "I'm kidding. We're going down the same way we came up."

Molly gave him a playful nudge with her shoulder. "I seriously think my heart stopped."

"Sorry. I couldn't help myself." He pushed the window open and held it for her. "But you have to admit, rappelling off the side would be an adventure."

"Learning new surgery techniques is an adventure, too. Let's make scientific lectures be our next adventure."

"We'll see." He winked. "But I make no promises."

Grant spent the majority of the morning lecture thinking about new adventures for Molly. Naturally, they all had a coastal theme and there was no shortage of ideas, some of them more realistic than others. Kite surfing, for example, qualified for the list, but he felt fairly confident he wouldn't be able to convince her to strap her feet to a board and be pulled out to sea by a giant kite. At least, not yet.

But standing on the top of the lighthouse had made it clear that this little deal they had was going to be a good thing. Maybe even a great thing. He was excited to get to work with her at the clinic, and he couldn't wait to take her on more adventures. In fact, he was a little concerned this deal might be a little one-sided, slanted way more in his direction.

To be clear, his eagerness to spend time with her was on a fellow-human level. This was in no way romantic. He had no desire to be tied down in a relationship, especially right now. In fact, that might've been one of the reasons he liked the idea of hanging out with Molly. Since her assignment in Emerald Cove only lasted three months, she wouldn't be around long enough for things to get serious. But she'd be there long enough to have some fun. Plus, he liked the way she smiled when she experienced the joy of something new.

"Please tell me you know someplace close for lunch because I'm starving. But I don't want to be even a little bit late to the afternoon session." Molly's voice broke his trance, and he looked up from the list he was working on to notice that everyone was standing and milling around. He must've been so distracted that he'd missed the announcement that they were breaking for lunch.

He snapped his journal shut, trying to focus on the present. "Lucky for you, I have the perfect lunch plans, and I guarantee we won't get back after the presenter." A zing shot through him, which was entirely because she was going to love this next surprise and had absolutely nothing to do with any sort of feelings for her. Okay, fine. There was a chance a small portion of it had something to do with his feelings for her. "Follow me." He stood, but instead of heading for the doors like the rest of the crowd, he fought his way against the flow of traffic to the front of the room with Molly following behind.

"I'd ask you where we're going, but I've decided it's a useless question that I probably don't want to know the answer to anyway."

Grant chuckled. "I promise, our lunch plans don't involve safety gear."

"I'm not sure your lack of safety gear gives me any more reassurance."

When they got to the front, they waited a second for Dr. Simmons to finish up the polite conversation he was having before he walked over to them.

"Grant!" Dr. Simmons, a tall man with salt-and-pepper hair and a lingering hint of a German accent, held out his hand.

Grant took it and pulled his old friend in for a hug. "It's good to see you, Oscar. It's been far too long."

"I know. What happened to that promise to take me out on your boat?"

"Pretty sure you canceled because of research."

Oscar stroked his jaw thoughtfully. "Oh, right. That pesky job keeps getting in the way."

"Tell me about it." He turned to Molly. "I want you to meet my colleague, Dr. Molly Lawrence. She's acting as the interim veterinarian at Turtle Rehab."

Oscar extended his hand. "A fellow turtle enthusiast. It's a pleasure to meet you."

"New turtle enthusiast. I'm by no means on the same level as most of the people here, but I'm eager to learn. I've very much enjoyed your workshop today. Thanks for allowing me to come."

"Any friend of Grant's is a friend of mine. Especially one who's so flattering to my ego." He pushed his glasses up on his nose before he picked up the folder with his lecture notes and tucked it under his arm. "Now, what do you say we get out of here before anyone else stops me for questions? Talking for three hours always leaves me famished."

"Listening to you talk for three hours leaves me famished," Grant joked. "And I just got a text from Jonathan that they're there and lunch is ready."

Oscar turned for the door, and Molly leaned into Grant. "We're eating lunch with Dr. Simmons?"

"I hope you don't mind. Some of the old university gang had made plans to eat lunch together. I added you to the reservation when I found out you were coming."

"Mind? I hope they don't mind that I'm crashing

your reunion. Also, there's a good chance I'm going to ask a ton of questions." She tapped her chin. "Will they kick me out for too many questions? And what would that threshold be?"

Grant chuckled. "As long as your questions are related to their research, your bigger concern will be getting them to shut up."

They walked down the short hall and into the small conference room the hotel had set up for their catered lunch. Grant spent the next few minutes introducing Molly to his friends in the room. She fit right in with the group of animal lovers, and it only took a matter of minutes before she was engrossed in a conversation with another one of the university's vets. As everyone found a seat for lunch, she managed to snag herself a spot between Dr. Simmons and her new friend, Dr. Lana Krolik.

Is this okay? she mouthed across the table as she slid into her chair.

He gave her a nod of approval and took a seat at the other end of the table next to Jonathan.

"You didn't mention you were seeing someone when we had dinner the other night." Johnathan's gaze darted in Molly's direction as he took a sip of his iced tea.

"Who, Molly?" Grant glanced across the table at Molly and their eyes met. She shot him the kind of wide-eyed grin of a kid on Christmas morning. And, right on cue, the familiar flutter kicked in.

He quickly looked away. So maybe it was fair to say he was crushing on Gulfview's new locum vet, but who could blame him? She was the most interesting woman he'd met in a long time, and the more time he spent with her, the more captivating she became. But it wasn't serious. It couldn't be serious. "Nah, she's just a colleague. She's doing some contract vet work for the rehab center while our normal vet is out on medical leave." Of course, he had every intention of spending as much time as he could with her while she was still in town.

"Well, that's good. It's one less thing to consider in taking this job." He put his napkin on his lap and pulled his plated salad toward him. "Have you given it any more thought?"

Grant picked up a fork and speared some of the lettuce leaves on his own plate as his thoughts switched from Molly to the position Jonathan had offered a couple of weeks ago. "Some."

And by some, he meant a lot. Over the past couple of weeks, he'd thought about it from every angle. Of course he wanted the job. As director of research, he'd get to oversee an entire team of researchers dedicated to making a difference in marine life everywhere. The reach of this job was inspiring. But if that wasn't enough, the current project was one he'd dreamed up. For the next five years, the entire team would be dedicated to studying the intricacies of marine habitats. The information they gathered would help with how to better focus conservation efforts and allow zoos and aquariums to create healthier, more authentic environments for their residents. Plus, they were even willing to let him finish his PhD while he was working on it. To put it simply, it was the perfect job offer. Those only come around once in a lifetime.

"It's an intriguing offer." He pushed the salad around his plate as a vision of the job danced through his mind. "The combination of spending small spurts at sea between longer stints in the lab is especially appealing. The best of both worlds, really."

"It's almost as if the job was designed specifically for you by you." Johnathan speared a large clump of salad. "Oh, wait. It was." He grinned as he shoveled the bite into his mouth.

"*Touché.*" He thought back to the days when he'd worked on the proposal for this very study. Life had looked so different then. But wasn't life always changing? Every time he thought about this job, he kept coming back to the same thought: maybe it was time for life to change again. "The new director needs to start at the end of the summer?" His sister's wedding was scheduled for the beginning of August. There was no way he could leave before that, but after…?

"We're aiming for middle of August. We'd like to have the new director in place for the start of the fall semester. Tell me you're saying yes."

Grant popped a cherry tomato in his mouth and chewed slowly, giving him time to think.

On the one hand, how could he leave Emerald Cove? His sister, Turtle Rehab, everything else he'd moved home for. Were they at a place where he could walk away?

Then he glanced at the familiar faces gathered around the table. Some were laughing with each other; others were in the middle of deep conversations, all of them enjoying being together. There was no denying he loved it here. These were his people. And this work? It was what he was born to do.

It was a difficult decision, but saying yes to Jonathan wasn't saying yes to the job. It only moved him to the next step of the process. Anything could happen when the board got involved. But if he let this opportunity pass him by, he would always wonder.

"Alright, I'm officially throwing my hat in the ring." There was a hitch of hesitation in his voice, but who would blame him? This was a big decision with a lot on the line.

"Yes!" Jonathan, apparently oblivious to the hesitation, leaned back in his chair and pumped his fist in the air. "I told Dr. Ford this was the job that would get you back."

"Don't get too excited yet. I'm only agreeing to be interviewed. I still have to convince the board of directors to choose me." He'd looked up the other two candidates, and they both were highly qualified and excellent choices. There was a decent chance that deciding if he was ready to leave Emerald Cove was a moot point.

"I like your odds," Jonathan said. He lifted his iced tea glass for a toast. "Here's to you being back where you belong."

Grant picked up his glass and clinked it with Jonathan's. "To being where I belong."

He just hoped fate knew where that was and he wasn't making a giant mistake.

Chapter Seven

THE SUN HAD ARCHED ALL the way across the sky and was starting its descent into the opposite side of the ocean by the time Molly and Grant were getting close to Emerald Cove. Molly was aware she'd talked nonstop since they'd gotten in the car, but she couldn't help it. It had been one incredible day.

"Thank you again for taking me with you. I don't know what kind of strings you had to pull, but they were worth it." She hadn't been this energized about her career in a long time. "And your friends are amazing. Did you know Dr. Simmons said he'd be happy to Zoom with me for Shelley's entire surgery to talk me through the process? What a generous offer."

"So that means you're going to do the surgery?"

Molly stared at the road in front of her, thinking about the things she'd need to do to prepare herself for that kind of procedure. "I think so." She said the words slowly, as if stepping on an unsteady rock. She felt moderately confident it would hold her, but she still needed to proceed with caution.

"If we do it now, there's a good chance she could be back in the ocean by Christmas," Grant added.

"What a great Christmas gift for her." Molly's mind drifted to imagining the release of the turtle. "I wonder where I'll be in December?" The idea that she wouldn't be here came as a bit of a shock, but it shouldn't have. A short stay was the whole reason she'd taken this job, wasn't it?

Grant shifted in his seat. A look of concern flashed across his face, which caught her off guard, and he quickly changed the subject. "How about we focus on something more pressing for tonight, like dinner."

Molly glanced at the clock. She'd been so caught up in the fun of the day, she hadn't even noticed how late it had gotten. And now that he'd mentioned it, her stomach rumbled in agreement. "Dinner sounds good. Do you have a place in mind?" One thing she'd noticed about these small beach towns that lined Florida's panhandle was there were a lot of fantastic locally owned restaurants. But since they were usually tucked into strip centers or had names she didn't recognize, trying to spot one from the highway while driving proved to be a challenge.

"Maybe," Grant answered. "How do you feel about hamburgers hot off the grill?"

"I like hamburgers."

"Claire's having a backyard barbeque tonight. Just a small family thing, but she's insisting we stop by. Do you mind?"

Socializing at a backyard barbeque wouldn't have been her first choice after a day of meeting a ton of new people. But she was still energized by the success of the day and she really liked Claire. Plus, she didn't hate the idea of a homecooked hamburger. "Sure."

"Thanks. We don't have to stay long, I promise."

He typed a message into his phone. "I'll tell her we're on our way."

She followed his directions to the neighborhood and parked on the street. Molly's first clue that she and Grant had different definitions of "a small family thing" should've been the number of cars lining the street. But for some reason, she let that detail slide when they parked three houses away from where they were going. She didn't catch on until they walked through the gate into a backyard full of people.

"Exactly how many people are at this small family function?" Molly asked, trying to take it all in.

"Not everyone. I have a lot of cousins." He pulled a concerned face. "But maybe more than I thought."

Molly didn't even have the chance to let her nerves swirl all the way through her before Claire bounced over to the fence to greet them. "Hey! I'm glad you could make it." She gave Molly a hug. It was a quick one, the familiar kind that were shared between close friends, and it made Molly feel like family. Like she belonged in this backyard full of people.

"Thanks for having me," Molly said, pushing the thought away. She liked feeling comfortable in her surroundings, but she didn't belong. This place was only temporary, after all.

Claire waved over Mateo, the rehab director she'd met at Turtle Rehab, and the other guy who was manning the grill with him. "Molly, I don't think you've met my fiancé yet. This is Lance."

Lance was tall and thin and had the pale complexion of someone who spent more time inside than next to the tanks at Turtle Rehab. He shifted the long metal spatula to his other hand before wiping his hand on his grilling apron and offering it to Molly. "It's great to meet you. Grant and Claire can't say enough good things about you."

She shook his hand. "Thanks. Let's hope some of them are true."

"Hope y'all are hungry. We've got some of everything on the grill right now. Burgers, brats, chicken. What's your— Whoa!"

Flames shot up from the grill. Hissing sounds filled the air as grease from the cooking foods fueled the fire. The people standing close to it took a few steps back.

"We should probably get that under control first." Lance jogged toward the grill.

"I'll help. You've gotta tame the flames without ruining the meat," Grant instructed as he followed behind him.

"This is not going to end well." Claire shook her head. "Please excuse me." Before they could answer, she'd already caught up to the boys.

Mateo studied the action for a second before he turned back to her. "While they're busy searing our dinner, can I get you a drink? Or, maybe more accurately, can I show you to the cooler and let you choose one for yourself?"

"That would be awesome." It was nice to have a familiar face in this backyard full of strangers, and Molly felt her confidence build as she followed Mateo to a row of coolers along the fence near a fire pit.

"How was the conference?" he asked.

She opened one of the coolers and selected a bottle of water. "It was amazing. I learned a ton. Grant has some pretty impressive friends."

"Grant's as impressive as the rest of them. He was on the same trajectory of becoming an industry expert when he put his career on hold."

His career on hold? Molly had assumed his career ambition was what he was doing, running the family business. Did this paused career have anything to do with the PhD he hadn't finished? "What career?"

"Technically, I think he's what's called a marine habitat specialist," Mateo said.

Molly unscrewed her water and took a quick sip. "I want to sound like I know what that is, but the truth is I have no idea."

"Basically, he does a whole lot of research on animals in their natural habitats. That research helps with designing exhibits in zoos and aquariums that are more beneficial to the animal, as well as knowing where to focus conservation efforts."

"You mean like the tank at Turtle Rehab?"

"Exactly." Mateo nodded once. "That was the kind of thing he was designing before he left."

So, the tank wasn't just a hobby. It was his passion.

She glanced over at the grill where the flames were still raging. "Why did he quit?"

"Because of Claire," Mateo said simply.

"Claire?"

"Yeah, she was still in high school when their dad got sick. Their mom had died two years earlier, so he didn't want Claire to be alone. He left the university in the middle of the year to come home and take care of everything."

Molly watched Grant interact with his sister as they battled the flames, and her throat tightened with a mixture of sympathy and admiration. She couldn't imagine how hard it would be to lose both of your parents. But on top of that, he'd left his passion behind to come home and take care of his family. "That must've been tough."

"It was a sacrifice for sure, but that's the kind of guy Grant is. He does what it takes for family."

His compassion didn't surprise her. From what she'd seen over the past week, he was one of the kindest, most caring people she'd ever met. But realizing its depth caused a whole different type of admiration.

Mateo turned and watched the action going on at the grill, too. "Although, he's a lot like a sea turtle. He'll always be able to find home, but he was never meant to stay here. Not like the rest of us. Not when there's a whole wide world for him to explore."

Molly could see that. His love for the ocean, his need for adventure, his passion for helping.

The grill flared again, causing the three flamefighters to jump back.

"I think it's time for me to show those three how to take care of business." Mateo set his drink down on one of the coolers and marched across the backyard, giving orders to the trio at the grill. Molly stood there and watched.

What kind of guy gave up his dream to come home and take care of his sister? There was a warmth spreading through her that she wanted to blame on the balmy Florida air, but she knew, deep down, that it had much more to do with the air in this backyard.

Hadley was right about the people here. Molly thought she knew small towns since she was from one, but where she came from wasn't like this.

Since she'd left, the only people who'd checked in on her were her parents, not that it surprised her. In the aftermath of The Great Breakup, the people she'd thought were her friends had slowly started to drift away. Of course, they'd all been sympathetic in the beginning, but as time had faded on and the shock had worn off, she'd found she'd been the one getting excluded from the invitations under the pretense of "we didn't want to make things awkward for you." What they really meant was they didn't want to make their own parties awkward by filling them with the tension of the new happy couple and their ex-fiancée/best friend.

But the people of Emerald Cove seemed different. Seeing the way they took care of each other and had each other's backs was refreshing. Of course, it still didn't make her want to start laying down roots or get a hundred percent invested. The sting from that sort of commitment was still too fresh. But it was encouraging, and as she watched it, she could feel a tiny piece of her broken heart start to mend.

Claire, who'd disappeared in the house, returned with two pitchers of water and dumped them over the grill. A puff of steam rose up as water streamed out the bottom. Molly was pretty sure everything that'd been cooking, along with any shot of using the grill again tonight, had been destroyed. But at least the flames were out. Grant, Lance, and Mateo all stared half longingly, half horrified at the drenched barbeque as if they'd just watched a bag of diamonds get flushed down the toilet.

After some discussion, Claire went into the house

and came out with a package of hotdogs and metal coat hangers.

Grant grabbed a couple of each and headed in her direction. “So, change of plans. How do you feel about fire-roasted hotdogs?”

Molly grinned. Just because she wasn’t laying down roots didn’t mean she couldn’t like it here. “Who doesn’t love a good weenie roast?”

“Let me get this straight. You guys can save the world one turtle at a time, but you can’t handle a couple of burgers on the grill?” Molly teased.

Grant chuckled and held his hotdog on a stick over the flames of the firepit. “We let that one get away from us, didn’t we?”

“Little bit.” Molly shot him a sidelong glance.

Grant took a seat on the stone bench and spun his hotdog over the flame. “And what about you, Ms. High-and-Mighty? Are you a master griller?”

“Who me?” Molly claimed the spot next to him, sharing the small space with him as she leaned forward enough to hold her stick in the fire. “No way. I should never be trusted with open flames. I’m more of a keep-you-company-while-you-cook-my-food kind of girl.”

“So I shouldn’t be expecting an invitation to dinner anytime soon?”

She shrugged. “Not unless you want brownies. I make some pretty good brownies. And, I hate to brag, but I can scoop ice cream like a champ.”

"I like ice cream and I've never said no to a brownie." Grant pulled his hotdog away from the heat and examined it, not that it mattered what it looked like. At this point, he was so hungry he would eat anything. He grabbed one of the buns he'd brought over and took a bite. "Kinda wishing I had a brownie *à la mode* to top off this meal."

Molly laughed. "I'm afraid I can't help you out tonight, but next time, for sure."

"I'll hold you to it." He liked the thought of next time when it came to Molly. He found himself hoping there were a lot of next times.

Molly kept her attention on the hotdog she was roasting. She pressed her lips together as if she was trying to decide something. A couple beats of silence passed before she spoke again. "Why didn't you tell me that your doctorate was in animal habitat research?"

Grant paused mid-chew. "What?"

She pulled her hotdog off the flame and looked over at him. "When I asked what you studied, you said marine biology. But you left off the part where your focus was on research and habitat design."

Normally, Grant would've carefully sidestepped that question. What he studied didn't have anything to do with his job here. What mattered here was that he knew turtles, and he could keep Turtle Rehab operating in the black.

But now things had the potential of changing.

"I..." Grant scratched his head, trying to think of a way to simplify the last six years and all the decisions that had gone into it. "Would you accept that it's a nickname for an overly wordy field of study?"

She shot him a look that said she wasn't buying any of the fluff he was selling.

He let out a sigh and shoved a hand through his hair. "To be technical about it, my degree is in marine biology, which is an umbrella term. My specialty is habitats of marine life with a focus on research."

Molly turned all of her focus to him and leaned in, her eyes lit up with genuine interest. "That sounds fascinating. Tell me more."

Her attention filtered through, making him feel valued and seen and, for the first time since he'd found out about the job, Grant felt the urge to share the news that had been weighing on him. And it wasn't lost on him that he didn't want to share this with just anyone. He wanted to share it with her.

The realization left him slightly off-kilter. He took the hotdog stick out of her hand and held it over the flame to finish cooking it for her as an excuse to focus on something else as he voiced his secret. "I was recently approached about a job that would put me back in that world."

She sat straight up; joy resonated from her. "Grant, that's great!"

Was it? He watched the flames dance, thinking through the positives and negatives of the university director position. Or maybe he should say positives and negative, in the singular. "First of all, I wasn't offered the job. Only the chance to interview for it."

"Still, it's a big deal. Congratulations." There was a genuine excitement for him in her voice that somehow boosted his confidence.

"It's a pretty great opportunity." He allowed himself to envision himself in that role, being among his friends and doing research that could affect not just one turtle at a time, but hundreds of turtles, along with a lot of other ocean animals. But before he let himself get carried away, he shut it down. "But deciding whether to take it or not gets a bit complicated." He glanced around the backyard. This place, much like the room at lunch, was also full of people he loved, and loved working with. His being here was important as well.

"Because of family?"

He nodded. "Like I said, though, it's a long shot. Right now, I've only agreed to be interviewed along with an impressive list of candidates." He pulled her hotdog off the fire and passed the stick to her.

"I'm still happy for you. And whatever happens, I hope you get what you want." She took her stick and started fixing her hotdog.

"Thanks." If only what he wanted could coincide with what he needed to do. "Anyway, I haven't told anyone about it. I don't want to cause a stir if I don't have to. You know how it is."

"Your secret's safe with me." She clamped her lips together and mimed locking it with a key.

She had just finished throwing away her imaginary key when Claire joined them. "Sorry about that. I hope you both got enough to eat."

"The hot dogs are perfect." Molly smiled up at her and took a big bite as if to illustrate her point.

"We'll have to plan a do-over," Claire said, sitting next to Molly and holding her own stick over the firepit. "Lance is looking for a chance to redeem his grilling skills."

"Sounds great," Molly agreed. She'd been here just

over a week, but she already seemed to fit right in with his family. "I'll bring the brownies."

She was only going to be here for a few months, Grant reminded himself. On top of that, she was simply a coworker. Did he enjoy spending time with her? Sure. Who wouldn't? But her temporary presence in his life made her a safe choice to share his secret with. She wasn't a factor in his decision to stay or go.

Although, he had to admit, now that she was here, it was hard to imagine a life without her in it.

Chapter Eight

GRANT WAS ABOUT READY TO call it a day on Wednesday when Mateo came into his office and dropped a file on his desk.

"The babies are all set up. Molly did a quick initial exam and put them on a feed-and-grow treatment plan. But she said she wanted to wait to do the comprehensive exam until they had some time to rest."

"Molly's here?" That probably shouldn't have been his take-away. The important part of the report was the update on the two turtle hatchlings that'd been brought in that morning, but for some reason, he couldn't get past Molly. "She's only supposed to come in on Tuesdays and Thursdays." He tried his best to sound nonchalant about it.

Mateo shrugged. "Either she doesn't know that or she doesn't care, because she showed up about forty-five minutes ago."

"Huh." And she hadn't stopped by his office? A ripple of something that felt a whole lot like disappointment floated through him, but he tried to push it away. She was well oriented with the facility now, and most of her day-to-day dealings were with the turtle caretakers and not him. Still, he hated missing any chance to see her.

"Regardless, it's nice she was here and those little guys got their exam already," Mateo said.

"Right. Exactly." Because she wasn't here to visit him. She was here to do her job, like the amazing, talented professional she was. "Sounds like they're all set up."

Mateo studied him for a second, then jerked his thumb at the door. "You know, she's still out there by their tanks."

The news seemed to fill his office with sunshine, and Grant's pulse kicked it up a gear. "Great. I have a question I was going to call her about. But since she's here..." His voice might've had a tad more excitement in it than he'd intended.

His cousin, who'd also been his best friend since birth, gave him the accusatory look of someone who could actually see his nose growing as he talked. "Right. Anyway, I'm outta here. You go ask Molly your question, and I'll see ya in the morning."

Grant followed Mateo out of his office, but while Mateo turned right to head out to the parking lot, Grant headed toward the Turtle Zone.

Sure enough, there was Molly, standing at the small square tanks midway between the Care Floor and the Discovery Lagoon, in a part of their facility that was officially called Head Start.

He strolled toward her, admiring the look of wonder on her face as she peered over one of the tanks. When he got closer, she turned in his direction.

"Grant! We've got babies!" She clasped her hands together in front of her chest, and he could almost see little cartoon hearts floating out of her head, which made him smile. Her passion for animals was endearing and left him feeling...hopeful. In fact, the whole world felt a little brighter when she was around.

"I heard." He'd actually been the one who'd taken the call from the wildlife rescue center that'd found the hatchlings. They'd been spotted only a couple of feet apart but more than two hundred yards from their suspected nest, which was rather uncommon. Occasionally a new hatchling would get disoriented and wander in the wrong direction, but they didn't usually go off in pairs. Their best guess was that a greedy bird had tried to snatch what he'd thought would be a big meal, but couldn't hold onto both.

He stepped up next to her and looked down at the tiny green turtles. They were smaller than the palm of his hand. Each of their tanks had been portioned off to make it a more suitable size, but they still looked tiny in comparison.

"They're the most adorable things I've seen in a long time. I can't make myself walk away," Molly said.

"The good news is, they might be sticking around for a while." He watched the tiny hatchling on the left lift his head out of the water for a breath. They were the kind of precious that forced a smile even on the gloomiest of days, and he found himself wanting to wrap his arm around Molly's shoulders and pull her close as they experienced this moment together.

"Longer than it'll take them to get their strength up?" She looked up at him with her bright, caring eyes, only intensifying whatever feelings were already stirring in his chest.

But since they were only colleagues, he shoved his

hands in his pockets instead. "It appears so. I just got off a call with Florida Parks and Wildlife, and they think these two little adventurers would be perfect candidates for the head start program."

"What does that mean?"

"Only about one in a thousand baby sea turtles survive their first two years. So occasionally we hang onto hatchlings we rescue until their second birthday. They can grow and get strong here. Then when we release them, they've already beaten the odds, helping the overall turtle population."

"And I get a daily dose of cuteness." She opened the chart she was holding and scribbled a note in the margin. "Looks like the bird's greediness turned out to be the turtles' good fortune."

"Exactly right. I always like a story with a happy ending."

She gazed into the tank and let out a contented sigh. "Me too."

"While we're on the subject of happy endings, I need your professional recommendation."

She turned, focusing her attention on him. "Sure."

"We need to pick a candidate for The Great Turtle Race."

"Is that the event where they put trackers on a bunch of different turtles and see how far they go?"

"Yes. Different rehab facilities all over the state enter a turtle they're ready to release. We get to see not just how far they go, but where they head once they're back in the wild."

"That's so fun. How do they pick a winner?"

"Technically it's the turtle who logs the most miles in their first thirty days. But it's not really about winners or losers. The main focus is raising awareness while also getting valuable research."

She gave him a sidelong glance. "You haven't won recently, have you?"

"Dead last three years in a row."

She chuckled. "Who are you considering entering this year?"

"It has to be a loggerhead, and the only one who might be close to the required release date is Hope. You think she'll be ready?"

Molly twisted her mouth to the side in consideration and started walking up the three steps to the Care Floor. "When's the race?"

"The turtle has to be released some time during the first two weeks of August."

"That's about the same time I'll be leaving," she mused.

There was a pang somewhere deep in his chest at the thought of her leaving, which only annoyed him. Of course she'd be leaving. Just like with the turtles that came into the clinic, he'd known from the beginning that her stay here wasn't permanent. In fact, there was a chance he'd be leaving around that same time too. Perhaps August was the perfect time for new starts all around.

"I'd love to see her released before I go," Molly continued. She stopped in front of Hope's tank and rested her hands on the side. "I never want to rush the healing process, but she seems to be doing great." She gazed down at the turtle. "What do you think, Hope? You want to be the official race turtle?"

The loggerhead turtle, who'd already gotten comfortable in her new surroundings, lazily paddled around her space, popping her head up for a breath right in front of Molly.

"I think that's a yes."

"Great. I'll submit her bio as our contestant." Grant's grin widened, which seemed to be becoming a habit anytime Molly was around. "What do you think? Does she look like she's from Key West?"

"Key West?"

"Or maybe even farther, like the Bahamas. I hear there's great foraging in the Bahamas."

Molly gave him a playful shove. "Stop. You'll give her a complex. Maybe she's happy right here in the emerald waters of the Gulf."

"All of our turtles seem to be happy in the Gulf. That's our problem. Last year's winner is currently hanging out off the coast of Cuba. I'm just saying, maybe she wants to check it out. See what all the fuss is about."

Molly rolled her eyes. "You go wherever you want, little mama. Don't listen to Mr. Competitive over here."

"What are you two laughing about?" Claire walked up behind them, wiping her hands on the towel slung over her shoulder.

"I'm trying to convince your brother that the gorgeous waters of the panhandle are just as good as, if not better than, the Bahamas."

Claire nodded. "Agreed. Does that mean you were able to talk her into going snorkeling?"

"Wait, what?" Molly's eyes got large and she turned to him.

A dash of nervousness shot through his veins. That was another question he'd had for her, but he'd hoped to present it to her a little more gently to let her warm up to the idea. But this had all the gentleness of being pegged with a giant water balloon. "We were actually talking about entering Hope in The Great Turtle Race," he explained to his sister while keeping his gaze locked with Molly's, trying to gauge her reaction.

"Oh." Claire made a face that showed she realized she'd spilled the beans. Then she tiptoed around them to put Hope's food in her tank, as if trying to not step in the mess she'd made.

"What's this about snorkeling?" Molly asked, her pointed gazed burning into him.

"I was thinking it'd be fun for your next excursion. You can't come to our gorgeous coast and not admire the ocean life."

"Snorkeling means swimming in the middle of the ocean, right?" She propped her hands on her hips. "I thought we agreed on no more swimming in the middle of the ocean."

"Is it still considered the middle of the ocean if you can see land?" Claire chimed in from the far side of the tank.

Grant jerked his thumb in her direction. "What she said."

"Tag-teamed by the siblings? This is hardly fair." Molly gave him a pointed look that was part serious but mostly playful.

"I've gotta finish up getting everyone fed so I can get out of here." Claire pulled a face that was the visual representation of "oops" as she set the empty stainless-steel bowl on the cart. She pulled off another containing a combination of leafy greens, which she shoved into Grant's hand. "Plus, I'm gonna excuse myself from this awkward conversation I inadvertently created." She pushed the cart onto the main path, heading the direction of the Discovery Lagoon. "It'll be fun," she called over her shoulder.

"She's not wrong." Grant leaned against the tank and focused on Molly, adding a bit more compassion to his voice. "It is swimming in the middle of the ocean, but you can see the bottom and the boat will be nearby. I think you'll love it."

Molly snagged her bottom lip as she considered the activity, a healthy dose of anxiousness swirling in her eyes. But then she shook her head slightly as if shaking off whatever fear was holding her back. "No, you're right." She drew in a breath, and her eyes met his. "Let's do it."

"So that's a yes?" Excitement for Saturday started to build up inside.

"Yes," she said eventually. "But you don't have to take me to do things every weekend. The deal was for once or twice a month, remember? I think you've more than met your quota for this month."

Grant shrugged, scattering a few pieces of lettuce around Hope's tank. "True. But that was when you said you were only coming on Tuesdays and Thursdays. Seeing as how it's Wednesday, we're going to have to up our excursion quota."

Molly playfully shook her head and snagged a few pieces of greens from the bowl, dropping them on the other side of the tank. "I'm here because I want to be. Plus, you've got baby turtles, so now it's going to be hard to keep me away."

Grant strolled around the tank, scattering more of

the greens for Hope. "The truth is, you're an important part of our team. Look at all the turtles you're helping while you're here. Hope, Shelley, those new little guys who don't have names yet."

"Buzz and Woody."

"What?"

"The hatchlings' names are Buzz and Woody. I guess the wildlife expert who brought them in named them. Something about them being found on the way to 'infinity and beyond.'"

"Cute. Visitors are going to love that." He dumped the last of the bowl's contents into the tank. "The fact that you know all the turtles' names is proof that a single ride on my boat and a trip to a self-serving turtle vet conference isn't enough payment."

Molly leaned against the tank next to him. "As long as you're sure it's not putting you out."

"Are you kidding? This is the kind of stuff I live for. I'm never going to pass up the chance to spend the day on the water." Especially when that day included his new favorite veterinarian.

"In that case, it's kind of like I'm doing you a favor," she joked, a cute little snarky grin tugging at the corner of her mouth.

"Exactly. So we'll see you at ten on Saturday for the snorkeling trip?"

"I'll be there with bells on." She shrugged. "And my lifejacket and floaties, and I might even bring my noodle again."

Grant could feel his grin throughout his entire body. "I wouldn't expect anything less."

Chapter Nine

"I've been meaning to ask..." Molly tried to sound casual as she sipped her latte on the balcony Friday morning. "Do either of you have snorkeling gear I can borrow?"

"When are you going snorkeling?" Ellyn asked.

"Tomorrow, I guess." She blew on her coffee as she tried to dampen the hesitation building up in her. "You know, as long as the weather stays clear."

"I'm guessing this is part of your Turtle Rehab excursion-payment?" Hadley asked.

"Uh-huh." Molly stared out at the ocean that stretched out in front of them. The clear, green-blue water that sparkled under the morning sun was stunning. But even as beautiful as it was, the thought of swimming in the middle of it, far from any sort of land, still caused her stomach to tie into knots. "Although, I gotta be honest, in my head, this kind of stuff was supposed to get easier."

Hadley reached across the balcony and squeezed her hand. "Change takes time. Be easy on yourself."

"Agreed." Ellyn nodded. "So where are you going?""

Molly shrugged, trying to recall the details Grant

and Claire had given her. “Some artificial reef that’s not too far from here and close to shore.” At least, she was pretty sure that’s what they’d said. She had to admit the details had started to get a little fuzzy when they’d mentioned the open-water swimming portion of the trip.

“I bet you’re going to Starfish Reef.” There was a sunny element to Ellyn’s voice that made it evident she was more than fond of the reef in question. “It’s great for beginners. It’s only about twenty feet deep and so close, you can see the beach. Some people even paddle out there in kayaks.”

“After jumping in the literal middle of the Gulf to rescue a turtle, you’ll be fine. You’ve got this,” Hadley added.

“I hope so.” The sound of the distant waves drifted past her as she let her friends’ encouragement build her confidence. “I’ve become someone who sails and snorkels on the weekend. Who am I?”

“We’re turning you into a true Floridian.” Ellyn beamed. “It’s part of our diabolical plan to keep you here so you can pass the coffee.”

“Ahhh, it’s your caffeine addiction that’s fueling all this,” Molly joked.

“Don’t judge.” Ellyn took a sip from the mug she had clutched between her hands. “But back to the snorkeling trip. I have a mask and fin set you’re welcome to borrow.”

“And today’s Friday. Don’t we all get off work early?” Hadley said. “Why don’t we meet on our beach after work for a quick snorkeling lesson? You can practice in the shallow water before you brave the deep water tomorrow.”

Ellyn brightened, sitting straight up on the edge of her chair. “That’s a perfect idea! I’ve been wanting a girls’ night!”

“You two don’t have to do that.” Molly glanced at her friends sitting on either side of her. “But I have to admit, a girls’ night sounds amazing.”

“Then it’s a date,” Hadley said.

“Absolutely.” Ellyn gave an animated nod. “I’ll grab sandwiches on my way home from work.”

“And I’ll whip up my herby avocado hummus. It’s perfect for the beach,” Hadley offered.

“I can bring something sweet. The café next to the vet clinic makes these amazing key lime tartlets.” Molly would have to place her order early, because they tended to sell out by lunchtime on a normal day. A beautiful Friday with the promise of a gorgeous weekend threatened to bring more tourists than normal.

Ellyn beamed. “Should we say five o’clock?”

“Perfect.” Hadley nodded once.

“Seriously, you two are the best.” Molly felt the warmth of true friendship flow through her, causing another tiny crack in her heart to mend. “I’ll be there.”

The rest of the day seemed to speed by in anticipation of the beachy girls’ night. Molly even finished up all her paperwork early for the first time ever and left work on time for a change.

It didn’t take her long to change into her swimsuit and toss a few things into her beach bag, and she managed to make it out the door at exactly five o’clock. She trudged across the sand with her towel rolled under one arm, a folding beach chair she’d found in the closet hanging from the other shoulder, and the box of key lime tartlets balanced on her hand.

The closer she got to the water, the more she started to question if this was a good idea. Not the tartlets. She felt quite confident in her choice of desserts. In fact, it'd taken all her willpower to not sneak one before now. No, what was giving her pause was the snorkeling bit. When had she become a person who swam with the fishes? She was pretty sure, according to some iconic movies, that phrase had a pretty unpleasant ending.

Hadley was already chilling in her chair when Molly walked up, sipping some fruity drink that probably should've had an umbrella sticking out of it.

"Let the girls' night festivities commence." Molly propped her chair open and sank down next to Hadley, wiggling her toes in the soft, powdery sand.

"After the day I've had, the timing couldn't be more perfect." She pulled a Thermos and a stack of reusable plastic cups from her bag. "Can I pour you a Mango Passion?"

"Yes, please. And then you can tell me all about your bad day."

"Ugh. It was a menagerie of unfortunate events. Two of the boxes of the tiles we special-ordered from Italy arrived damaged. They're rushing us a replacement, but it's still going to put us at least a week behind. And there's some sort of electrical wiring issue I don't fully understand that has to be redone." Hadley poured the drink and passed it to her, drawing in a long, cleansing breath. "But it's the weekend now, and I don't have to think about all that mess again until Monday morning."

Molly accepted the drink. "Plus we're on the beach, which makes everything better." The rhythmic sound of the waves rolling into shore seemed to back up her claim.

"Exactly." She held up her cup. "To girls' night."

"Cheers." Molly tapped her cup against Hadley's and took a sip of the frozen concoction. Yep, she was right. The combination of mango, coconut, and lime, combined with a hint of spice, definitely needed a little paper umbrella sticking out of it. It was one of the best drinks she'd had in a long time. "Mmm. This is delicious."

"Thanks. I got the recipe from a friend who used to call it summer in a cup."

"That's exactly what it tastes like. It's the perfect complement to a night like tonight." She took a second sip and savored the frosty drink and the spectacular view. She and Hadley chatted for several more minutes before Ellyn's voice interrupted them.

"I'm not late yet," she called from behind them. "I have to be more than fifteen minutes past the meetup time to be considered late."

Hadley and Molly exchanged a look. "She's never less than fifteen minutes late," Hadley joked.

"I heard that!" Ellyn said from halfway up the beach. It took another minute for her to reach them. She handed the tray of sandwiches to Molly before dropping her bag and chair in the sand. With her arms now free, she looked out over the water and let out a loud exhale. "I made it."

"Mango Passion?" Hadley offered.

"Please." She accepted it and took a sip before

opening her chair and collapsing in it. "Now, this is much more relaxing."

"Rough day at the gallery?" Molly asked.

"Just busy. We're a couple of weeks away from opening the biggest show we've done in a long time with the biggest artist I've ever worked with, and there are a lot more loose ends to tie up than I was anticipating." She made her eyes wide before she took another sip.

"First of all, it's going to be great, and we believe in you. But if you need any help, let us know," Hadley said. Molly nodded in agreement.

"Thanks. Y'all are going to be at the opening, right? Two weeks from tonight?"

Molly grinned. "Wouldn't miss it. I already have a dress picked out especially for the occasion."

"Me too," Hadley added. "Not the dress-picked-out part. I'm not nearly that well planned. But I'll be there."

"Speaking of timelines, let's focus on a much more pressing decision." She leaned forward and paused for dramatic effect. "Should we eat first or snorkel first?"

"Eat first," Hadley said without so much as a second thought. "I missed lunch and I'm starving." She reached over and snagged a sandwich from the tray of mini sandwiches and fruit kabobs Ellyn brought.

"I'm not going to argue with that. These look amazing." Molly considered all the yummy choices before selecting a chicken salad on croissant.

"Eating first it is." Ellyn selected her own sandwich then re-covered the tray and set it on the beach blanket laid out in front of them. "Plus that'll give us plenty of energy for our little snorkeling adventure."

Molly nibbled on the buttery croissant as she looked out at the Gulf, considering their next activity. "I know fear has played a factor in preventing me from doing this before now, but I'm thirty. I feel like snorkeling is a skill I should've already acquired."

"Why?" Ellyn licked her fingers. "I hope I'm still acquiring new skills at ninety."

Hadley nodded. "Breaking out of your comfort zone is brave no matter what age."

Molly examined her sandwich, considering that. "I guess so. But right now, I don't feel brave. Right now, I feel like a wimp."

"That's because you haven't gotten in the water yet. You'll be singing a different tune after our lesson." Ellyn took a bite of her mini turkey wrap.

"You know what I want to do that's outside of my comfort zone?" Hadley asked, pulling out her famous hummus dip and a container of cut veggies. "Climb Mt. Kilimanjaro."

"That sounds fun. I've always wanted to go on an African safari, where you get to see lions and elephants roaming around in their natural habitat." Ellyn scooped up dip with a carrot stick. "How far up are we climbing?"

"To the top, of course." Hadley flashed them a look that said even considering anything less would be ridiculous. "I'm not flying all the way to Tanzania to stare at the peak from halfway up."

"Wow. Okay. Just for the record, I'm going to need lots of time to train." Ellyn's brow wrinkled with concern.

Molly nodded. "Same. Plus, I might need a little head start to be able to fully wrap my mind around how high we'll be. The world's third tallest mountain? That's no joke."

Hadley shrugged, unconcerned. "Go big or go home, ladies."

Molly and Ellyn exchanged a look that said that trip was going to take a whole lot more prep work than repeating a clichéd catchphrase.

"Well, my step out of my comfort zone doesn't require a plane ticket to a location halfway around the world, but it does stick with the conquering-heights theme." Ellyn paused and confidently sipped her drink. "I want to ride in a hot air balloon."

Hadley pressed her lips together, considering it. "Interesting. I could get on board with that."

Simply hearing the idea made Molly's stomach tumble like a barrel over a waterfall, but she was pleasantly surprised to realize that she didn't automatically shut it down like she might've before. Maybe her personal growth plan was working after all. "I bet the views are amazing, but y'all might have to remind me to look down from time to time."

"That can be arranged." Ellyn grinned.

"But before we can tackle any of those adventures, we have to cross 'learning to snorkel' off your bucket list," Hadley said with a healthy dose of determination. She popped the last bit of sandwich in her mouth. "I say it's time to take this party to the water."

"Let's do it." Molly stared out at the gentle waves rolling onto the shore, digging deep to build up her courage. "Watch out, fish. Here I come."

Chapter Ten

THANKS TO THEIR GIRLS' NIGHT beach party, Molly walked into Turtle Rehab Saturday morning feeling confident. She had Ellyn's snorkel gear in her bag and she was ready for a day at sea. At least, as ready as she could be. The fears of running into Jaws or living out the rest of her days like Robinson Crusoe weren't easily shed. Baby steps.

On her way to Grant's boat, Molly strolled through the gift shop and past a group getting a tour of their facility. She was running a few minutes behind, thanks to an unusually long line to get a bagel and traffic moving at the pace of a Galapagos tortoise. This must be what Grant kept warning her about. A bike would've been a faster mode of transportation today.

However, even though she was late, she couldn't resist stopping by to visit Hope.

It was amazing how much stronger the loggerhead had gotten since she'd arrived. Her wounds were starting to heal and she was already back to an almost normal activity level. She was strong and a fighter, and watching her healing process was an inspiration. Molly liked all the turtles here, but there was something about Hope that she connected with on a different level. Visiting her was like therapy for her soul.

"Wish me luck, Hope. I'm off to brave the ocean for the first time since we did it together."

Hope chose that moment to dive down and curve to the left in one fluid movement.

"Fancy move. Keep getting strong and pretty soon, you'll be pulling that stunt out in the big, blue sea too."

The turtle swooped up to the surface and raised her head for a breath right in front of Molly. And Molly couldn't be totally sure, but she felt pretty certain Hope was telling her she had this.

"Thanks for the encouragement." She blew Hope a kiss and hurried the rest of the way down to the boat.

"Hey there, sailor." Grant strolled over as soon as she got close. He looked like an ad for some sort of boating lifestyle company. His dark brown hair was perfectly windswept, and he wore a long-sleeved shirt with a vintage beachy scene on it and a sun visor. His signature polarized sunglasses were secured with a cord around his neck, and his leather flip-flops had that naturally-worn-but-not-worn-out look.

But the part that got her every time was his smile. It was warm, authentic, and joyful. Plus, it showed off his dimples. The combination hit her square in the chest, which always took her by surprise. Yes, it was a great smile, but after a few weeks of knowing this man, she should be used to it, right?

He nodded his head at *Dream Catcher*. "You ready for this?"

"I think so. Check this out." She pulled Ellyn's snorkel and mask far enough out of her bag so he could see it.

Grant whistled. "Look at you with your own fancy equipment."

"And I even know how to use it." Molly waggled her eyebrows. "Although, in full disclosure, it's not mine. I borrowed it from my neighbor. But who knows? Maybe I'm one trip away from becoming an avid snorkeler."

"Or a diver. If you like this reef, you should see the underwater art museum that's a little farther out."

Molly held up both hands to stop him. "Let's not get ahead of ourselves here. I can only conquer one adventure at a time."

"Right. We'll save that conversation for after you fall in love with the reef." He winked, which delivered a second punch to that same part of her chest. Maybe Molly needed to stop looking at his face altogether.

"Then I'd better get on board so we can get to it." She gripped the rail of the boat and stepped off the solid dock onto the gently rocking catamaran.

"Claire and Lance are already here. We're just waiting for Mateo before we take off."

"That should give me plenty of time to make sure my life jacket is properly buckled and snug," she joked. She headed down the narrow side of the boat to the deck and into the salon, where she found Claire putting drinks in a bucket of ice.

"Hey! You made it."

Molly set her bag on the banquette. "I did. How did your dress fitting go this morning?" The question was equal parts interest and trying to keep her mind off being nervous.

This morning's early dress fitting was the first time Claire had seen her wedding gown since the day of the disastrous ordered-the-wrong-size incident. Which, Molly mused, happened to be the last time she'd been on this boat.

"The seamstress is incredible. Unless you hold it up to the original, you'd never notice the differences. And, more importantly, it fits perfectly." She flopped down in one of the chairs, looking content. "Crisis averted."

"What crisis?" Mateo asked from the doorway.

Molly turned to greet him. "We were talking about Claire's wedding."

"Ugh, more wedding talk." He wrinkled his nose and grabbed a drink from the bucket of ice. "Just kidding, cuz. I can't wait for the big day." He leaned down and brushed a kiss across Claire's cheek.

"You thought you were invited?" Claire joked. "Well, this is going to be an awkward conversation."

Mateo chuckled. "As if you could keep me away from my favorite cousin's wedding." He grinned at her before opening his coconut-flavored sparkling water and downing half of it.

"Who's ready for a gorgeous day on the water?" Lance, who'd been helping Grant with the ropes, walked into the salon. Claire seemed to brighten at the sight of him, and he walked over and perched on the side of the chair she was sitting in, casually draping his arm around her. "Grant says to get comfy, because we're about to take off."

As if to prove his point, the faint sound of the engines turning on hummed in the background.

"Right. I guess we should head outside." Claire snuggled into her fiancé. "Unless you'd prefer to hang out in here while we cruise."

"Sit in here when there's a perfectly good view out there? No way. I'm headed to the front. Who's with me?" Mateo stepped out on the aft deck without waiting for anyone to answer.

"It is a gorgeous day. What do you say, love?" Lance leaned down and sweetly kissed her lips.

"The front sounds great." She stood and took his hand, gazing up at him with a look of pure loving adoration. It was exactly the kind of expression Molly would've expected from a couple only weeks away from tying the knot. She found it endearing. Watching a couple on the verge of entering into forever reminded her that real love stories existed. There was something encouraging about knowing that happily-ever-afters weren't only in fairy tales.

True, her own romance had ended in a flaming disaster, and she had no intention of getting anywhere near the L-word again, but that didn't mean she didn't cheer for love. In fact, it was the opposite. For some reason, her own disaster made her more desperate to see success stories. She needed to live in a world where love won.

Also, now that there was some distance between her and her failed attempt at forever, she was starting to wonder if she'd ever had that look. But today was much too pretty to focus on such a deep, soul-searching topic.

Claire turned to Molly. "You coming? It's a great view from up there."

Molly shook her head. "Y'all go ahead. I'm going to see if Grant needs company." She followed the lovebirds walking hand-in-hand out of the salon, but when they turned right, she turned left. Gripping the railing tightly, she climbed the four steps to Grant.

"You forgot to tell me you were running *The Love Boat* today," she said as he came into view.

"It's the only boat-related show you hadn't mentioned yet, so I thought it was time to shake things up." He glanced over at her with a twinkle in his eyes.

"How considerate of you."

He chuckled. "You ready?"

Molly tightened her grip around the rail and widened her stance to maintain her balance. "As ready as I'll ever be." Although, she had to admit that she was starting to feel more comfortable on a boat, and it did not escape her that a large part of that was due to the fact that Grant made her feel comfortable.

"Then let's do it." He focused his attention on the sea in front of them and they pulled away from the dock.

They puttered slowly at first, the wide, flat catamaran gently rocking over the waves. Then, as they got a little farther away from shore, he picked up the speed. The wind blew against her face and every once in a while, a mist from the boat's spray would dust her skin. The sky in front of them was a deep shade of clear blue that begged people to come outside and enjoy it, and the sunlight danced on the water, making it sparkle.

Molly drank in the scene, letting its beauty fill her. "It's the perfect day to be on the water."

"I one hundred percent agree." Grant stood next to her with his sunglasses on and his hair being ruffled by the breeze, looking like there was no place in the world he'd rather be. "Although, as far as I'm concerned, almost any day is the perfect day to be on the water."

One thing she admired about Grant was that he approached every situation with confidence, but his confidence when he was at the helm of his boat was on a whole other level. It was as if he was born to be at sea. As if standing on a ship in the ocean was where he was most at home, and she loved getting a chance to witness him doing the thing he loved.

"Who taught you to sail?" She wanted to know more about this passion that brought him to life. Really, she just wanted to know more about him.

"My dad." A fond, reminiscent smile tugged on one corner of his mouth. "I don't think I've ever seen anyone love to be on the water more than he did."

"I'm sorry I didn't get a chance to meet him." Although, she was pretty sure she had a good idea of what Mr. Torres' love for the ocean looked like. She had a feeling it was the same passion she was admiring on the man next to her.

"Me too. He was an amazing man. There's not a creature that'll be on this reef today that he wouldn't have known. There wasn't a shell he couldn't identify or a plant he couldn't name."

"I bet he was really proud of you."

"I hope so." Grant pressed his lips together as if thinking about a memory of his father. Molly stood quietly next to him, not wanting to interrupt his moment. After a few silent seconds ticked by, his easy grin returned. "Did you know that a quarter of all marine life live on a coral reef? To put it in perspective, that's more than four thousand different species."

"I did not know that."

"And luckily for you, you're about to get to experience a little slice of that first-hand. There's the reef." He pointed to an area in front of them where several boats were tied up to buoys and dozens of people were face-down, snorkels-up in the water.

The boat slowed, and he and Mateo worked to get *Dream Catcher* tied up to the buoy. Almost as soon as Grant killed the engine, the other three jumped in the water and swam off in different directions.

Molly waited on the deck, enjoying the warm sun on her skin, and took in her surroundings while Grant put up the dive flag and set a couple of other things. As promised, the coast wasn't far away. And to make it even more picturesque, this particular part of the beach was part of the state park. Instead of the beach being lined with houses and condos, the natural grass-covered sand dunes went back as far as she could see.

"So did you bring that fancy gear just for show, or are you going to put it to use?" Grant joked as he joined her on the deck.

"I was just waiting for my swim buddy who was being rather pokey," Molly teased.

"Well, the wait is over." He pulled his T-shirt over his head and tossed it on the bench, then opened one of the storage bins and pulled out a set of snorkeling equipment. "The water's calling, swim buddy."

"Lead the way." She put her hand in his and a

thrill streaked through her like a bolt of lightning. It was so powerful and also so unexpected that it almost knocked her backward.

She followed him down the five steps that led to the water, trying desperately to push away the sensation. Friends. They were just friends. Absolutely nothing more.

He stood on the bottom step that bobbed below the surface every time the boat rocked and pointed to the step she was standing on. "If you don't want to put your fins on in the water, you can sit here to do it."

"Okay." She let go of his hand and sank down, carefully stacking all her gear next to her. Grant, meanwhile, jumped into the clear, shimmering water. He swam up to the surface and gave his head one big shake to get rid of the water.

"You're such a pro, you can put on all your stuff in the water?" Molly eyed him as he floated on his back and slipped on his fins with the same ease as slipping on a pair of flip-flops on land. She, on the other hand, was still trying to jam her foot into the tight rubber that she was convinced was a couple of sizes too small, even though Ellyn had assured her otherwise.

"Don't worry, by next time, all this will feel like second nature."

"I'm going to have to take your word for it." She gave a small grunt as she wiggled her foot and tugged at the fin to get it on.

With his fins already on, he pulled on his mask, resting it on his forehead while he waited. "By the way, I should probably warn you. The ocean is addictive. Once you get a taste of snorkeling and get salt water in your blood, it's hard to stay away."

"That's what you keep telling me." She managed to get her first fin on and stopped to catch her breath.

Although, she had to admit, she'd already started to see his point. She'd only been here a little over two weeks, and already she loved this place more than she'd ever imagined she would. But she'd walk away when her assignment was finished because that was her whole reason for taking this job. She didn't want roots.

"That's because it's true." He clasped his hands behind his head and lazily floated on his back, as if to prove his point. "Hey, by the way, I already have your next excursion planned."

She picked up the second fin, hoping this one would be easier. "Shouldn't I at least master getting my snorkeling gear on before we start talking about our next adventure?" She tugged at the fin.

"Trust me, you're going to like this one. It doesn't involve flippers or snorkels or climbing tons of stairs. But it does involve an early wakeup call. Like, really early."

"And what exactly is this really-early-but-on-the-ground excursion?"

Grant shook his head. "Nope. It's a surprise. I just wanted you to save the date on your calendar."

She supposed it didn't hurt to have a full calendar while she was here. She was making the most of her time, which was very different than laying down roots. "Date saved." She finally slipped her second foot into the fin and held her flippered feet out in front of her to wiggle her toes.

"But enough delaying. Put your mask on, and let's do this already."

She pulled the mask over her head and secured it on her face, the way she'd practiced last night. "Like dis?" Her voice had the nasal sound of her nose being plugged.

"Perfect."

"More importantly, dough, how do I look?" She gritted her teeth together and gave her best attempt at an exaggerated toothy smile with the mask pressing down on her top lip and scrunching her face.

Grant's eyes widened in a look of mock fear. "Don't do that underwater. You'll scare away all the fish."

Molly giggled, dissipating whatever nerves were left. "All right, here goes nofing." She drew in a deep breath and held it as she pushed herself off the last step into the water. Between the extra force of the fins and her lifejacket, the only part of her face that got wet was her chin. She let out her breath as she adjusted to the water. "This isn't so bad," she said, feeling far more confident than she thought she would when floating in the middle of the ocean. "Now, where are these fish you keep talking about?"

Grant jerked his thumb in the direction where several people were sprinkled throughout the water. "This way. Follow me." In one smooth motion, he pulled his mask over his eyes and kicked off toward the reef.

Molly kicked after him. The world seemed to fade away as the underwater sanctuary came into focus, and a sort of calm swept over her.

It was different than she'd thought it would be. Quieter. More peaceful. The only sounds were the slight crackle of the water and her own rhythmic breathing. Even floating on the surface seemed effortless.

She followed the trail of bubbles caused by Grant's fins moving through the water. At first, there wasn't much to look at except the sandy bottom. But after a few kicks, she spotted a crab.

Well, to be honest, she wasn't sure it was a crab. It didn't look anything like Sebastian from *The Little Mermaid* or those things they pulled out of the water on *Deadliest Catch.* But this little guy was definitely a crustacean of some sort, scuttering across the bottom with his antennae going every which direction.

It was fascinating to watch. She could've floated right there for a while, quietly spying on this creature in his natural habitat, but in order to keep up with her snorkel buddy, she had to keep swimming. And she was glad she did, because as fascinating as the crab was, what came into focus in front of her was breathtaking.

"Oh, wow," she breathed out through her snorkel, releasing a round of bubbles around her.

A large structure rose out of the sand. Grant had told her these artificial reefs were made up of a series of towers made from recycled concrete and limestone. While that might've been a technical definition, it didn't do justice to the beauty in front of her.

The tiered stone structure was covered in colorful coral and purple sea fans that swayed in the ocean's current. Hundreds of fish of all shapes, sizes, and colors darted in and out, like a group of kids at a playground. Watching the underwater world was fascinating, calming, and inspiring all at the same time.

As she slowly kicked around, taking it in from every angle, she couldn't help but think of Grant learning about each one of these creatures from his dad. She took mental pictures of her favorites so she could ask him about them when they got back on the boat.

Molly wasn't sure how much time had passed when she felt Grant gently tug on her hand. She lifted her head up, reentering the noise and brightness of the above-water world.

"What do you think?" he asked.

"I think there's definitely going to be a next time."

"So you like it?"

"It's like nothing I've ever experienced before."

"This is only the first tower. You know, there are about thirty more." He motioned to the sprawling space dotted with other snorkelers. It had to be a hundred yards wide.

At the moment, Molly couldn't imagine swimming that far, let alone taking in all the underwater towers. "That's a lot of ground to cover."

"How about one more for today? My favorite's over here. There's usually an octopus who hangs out there."

Molly raised an eyebrow. "An octopus, huh?" It wasn't exactly on her list of adorable sea creatures she wanted to encounter, but perhaps, like the rest of her time here, it would surprise her.

"They tend to be shy, but today might be our lucky day." He held out his hand. "Shall we?"

She stared at it for a second, not sure if she wanted to take it again. It wasn't that she didn't want to follow him. So far, she'd loved every place they'd gone together. Grant was easily her favorite person in Emerald Cove. Their friendship was natural.

But a friendship was all it could be.

There were a million reasons why there could never be anything more than a simple friendship between her and Grant, starting with the fact that serious relationships were strictly out of the question for her and ending with the fact that they'd both be going their separate ways in two months.

Was he the kind of guy she might've been interested in if things were different? Maybe. But that didn't matter. Things weren't different, and as it stood, any sort of a romantic relationship simply didn't make sense. He knew it, she knew it, everyone knew it. She didn't need tingles from her hand, which didn't get the friend-only memo, messing up her vibe every time they touched.

But that problem had been fixed, right? Memo received?

"Let's do it." She hesitantly reached out to take his hand again. As a friend. Completely neutral. Ready to follow her *tour guide* to their next destination.

But apparently her hand didn't read memos.

Grant was one hundred percent content as he started the engines to head home. Every last detail of their day had been perfect. The weather had been fantastic, his boat was full of the people he loved having a good time, and he and Molly had even seen a spotted ray, an octopus, and two happy, healthy green sea turtles. He'd classify the day as a success.

"Thought you might want some company," Mateo said as he climbed up the steps to join him at the helm. He handed Grant one of the icy cans of sparkling water with a lime wedge sticking out of the top.

"Thanks."

"What a day, huh?" Mateo stood next to him and took a long pull from his own drink.

"Can't beat it."

They both were quiet for a moment as Grant marinated in the perfection of the day.

"Molly has been a great addition to our crew," Mateo said eventually.

Just hearing her name caused Grant's heart to flutter and he glanced down at where Molly was sitting on the bow with Claire and Lance. She was gaining confidence on the boat. And she looked happy.

"We've been lucky to have her." He could think of a lot of reasons to back up that statement, but he decided to focus on the professional. "She's done some great things, like Shelley's surgery. Oscar said he hadn't seen a surgeon that gifted in a long time."

"A vet who loves sea turtles and gets along with your sister. If I didn't know any better, I'd say she was a unicorn. Too good to be true." And, whether he wanted to or not, his cousin was diving head first into the personal.

The truth was, though, Mateo wasn't wrong. Grant glanced again at the source of the laughter that floated their direction. Molly and Claire were sitting together, laughing the way friends would. This wasn't the first time he'd seen it. He'd often find Molly and

Claire chatting and hanging out at Turtle Rehab. Their friendship had been easy.

It was no secret that Grant's exes hadn't always had the greatest relationship with his sister. Sure, they'd all been civil, but they hadn't clicked. The biggest example would've been his most recent ex. Claire had never liked her, and Jen hadn't seemed motivated to try to foster a friendship. It was the first sign that their relationship might not work. Family was important.

Molly, on the other hand, seemed to effortlessly fit in with his family. She seemed to effortlessly fit in with his life.

"Too bad she's not sticking around. But then again, you might not be, either." There was a hint of question in Mateo's statement.

He was the only other person besides Molly whom he'd told about the opportunity at the university. Technically, he hadn't as much told him as Mateo had started to catch whispers of it in the community and had point-blank asked him. It was hard to keep secrets in the turtle world.

"Like I said before, it's far from a done deal. Getting the job requires the board of directors to be convinced that the most underqualified candidate is best for the position."

"Underqualified? Because you're missing a few letters at the end of your name? Your qualifications come from knowledge and experience, which you have hand-over-fist over those other two."

Grant smirked. He wasn't usually one to engage in the "yay-me" game, but he had to agree with Mateo on this one. Their other two choices seemed rather underqualified in the experience department. Still, they both had very impressive education backgrounds. "We'll see if the board feels the same way."

"And the timing couldn't be better. Turtle Rehab is in a great place, and Claire's all grown up. You did good here, my friend."

"The timing does seem right." His gaze flickered again to Molly and the familiar feeling soared. A talented vet who loved turtles, got along with his sister, and was ready for an adventure. She was perfect.

"And what about her?" Mateo asked.

"Who? Molly?"

"Yeah, Molly. The one you can't stop making eyes at."

Grant took another drink and refocused on the water in front of him. "First of all, I'm not making eyes at anyone." He shot his cousin a pointed look that was meant just as much for himself. "And secondly, she'll be gone before I am." Which meant that whatever was going on here would be over before it even started.

"Great. Then it sounds like there's nothing standing in your way."

"Except getting the job."

"Minor detail."

"So that's it? I should start packing my bags."

Mateo shrugged. "You said it, not me."

"Are you trying to kick me out so you can steal my job?" It was no secret that if Grant left, Mateo would be the natural choice to take over as director. He too had grown up there and he'd been head of rehab almost as long as Grant had been working as director.

"I've already started measuring your office to see if

my stuff will fit," Mateo joked, then turned more serious. "But mostly, we all want to see you back where you belong. Don't get me wrong. We love having you here, but this isn't your dream. This was your dad's dream, Claire's dream. Shoot, even my dream. Your dream, what you were built to do, is research. It's time for you to get back out there."

Grant let the words marinate for a moment. There was a lot of truth there, and some of it stung a little. Turtle Rehab had been his dad's passion, the legacy he'd left to the world. Grant wanted nothing more than to see it thrive. He wanted it to be a living, breathing memorial to the incredible husband, father, and man his dad had been. And there was this tiny nagging voice in his head that kept asking, what kind of son would he be if he walked away?

On the other hand, while he truly loved this place with all his heart, Mateo was right. Turtle Rehab had never been his passion. His passion, the thing that made him feel alive, was research.

Stay here and preserve the family legacy, or start a new adventure by following his own dream? It was the million-dollar question.

Grant held up his can for a toast. "To everyone getting the job they deserve."

"To everyone getting the job they want." Mateo clicked his can against Grant's.

Today had been perfect, but Grant had a feeling change was in the forecast.

Chapter Eleven

The following Saturday, Molly, once again, pulled into the parking lot of Turtle Rehab well before the sun came up. She would've classified herself as a morning person, but these predawn excursions Grant planned were painfully early even for her.

She shifted into park next to the turtle ambo and took a long pull of the hot coffee in her travel mug before she got out of the car. She hadn't even finished closing her door when Grant stepped out of the dimly lit gift shop, looking bright-eyed and bushy-tailed.

"Morning, sunshine. You ready for this?"

Molly locked her car and strolled over to him, his perkiness causing her own to grow. "I'd say yes, but then again, I have no idea what we're doing."

"Fair enough." He turned and locked the front doors of the gift shop before he motioned for her to follow him around the side of the building. "But for the record, it's going to be great."

"And let me guess—I'm going to love it?"

"Have I ever steered you wrong?"

No. He hadn't. And the truth was, the more adventures he took her on, the more time she wanted to spend with him. She found herself counting down the days until their Saturday excursions and hoping each one would last longer than the one before.

Where did that leave her? She didn't know. And frankly, she didn't want to mess this morning up by thinking too hard about it. She'd come up with a plan later, but for now, she wanted to enjoy whatever it was that he thought was worth getting out of bed at an unspeakable hour. "In that case, let's stop blabbing so we can get to it."

His chuckle rang through the cool morning air. "Fair enough. Although, in full disclosure, this next part can be tricky in the dark. Watch your step."

He led her on what appeared to be a narrow path over the dunes, and he wasn't kidding. Between the loose sand, the descent, and the darkness, it required her full concentration to keep from stumbling. Silence filled the air, and she focused on the last hundred or so feet to the beach below.

An ATV was parked near where their path through the dunes met the flat beach. Grant walked over to it and picked up one of the helmets resting on the seat. "Your chariot awaits, my lady."

She took the helmet and studied the ATV. "We're going four-wheeling on the beach?" She had to admit, it was something she'd never done before, but it didn't seem like an activity that demanded such an early wake-up call.

"If by four-wheeling on the beach, you mean driving the ATV in the sand, then yes." He patted the beefy-looking vehicle. "But it's only a mode of transportation. We're on Turtle Patrol, and we have five miles of beach to cover before sunrise. This big guy is going to get us there."

That sounded slightly more intriguing. "What does that mean?"

"Every morning during nesting season, the beach is monitored for any new nests that were laid overnight. Then on the way back, we'll check on the nest we already know about." He picked up the second helmet and held it up. "I even broke out the safety gear just for you."

She grinned. "I feel so seen." So, Grant had been right again. She was going to love this.

"But we need to finish up before sunrise, so we should probably get started." He climbed on the ATV and motioned to the seat behind him. "You coming?"

She stared at the seat. While her over-zealous apprehension was starting to mellow, she was far from being fearless. "Here goes nothing." She slid on her helmet, tightened the chin strap, and climbed on behind him.

"To be clear, we don't always spot new nests. There are plenty of mornings where this is nothing more than an early ride."

"Don't get my hopes up. Got it."

"That being said, it's prime season, and there has been a lot of activity lately, so the odds are in our favor." He flipped on the tiny headlight and started the engine. "Your job is to spot the turtle tracks. They'll come out of the water toward the dunes."

"Okay." She gave him a double thumbs-up, eager to help even though she wasn't entirely sure what she was looking for.

Before she got a chance to ask any more questions, Grant shifted into gear. "Here we go. Hold on."

She slid her hands around his waist, holding onto him for support as the ATV lurched forward in the deep sand. A thrill rolled through her, which was becoming a regular occurrence anytime she hung out with Grant. She could try to explain it away, but this morning she wanted to enjoy the moment.

"See? Not so bad, huh?"

It wasn't bad at all. In fact, Molly would've gone so far as to say it was pleasant. The early morning air was cool with a slight hint of the day's coastal humidity already lingering, and gentle ripples replaced what were usually rolling waves. It was a different beach than during the day, or even during those quiet, dark hours that followed sunset. It was calm and still and sleepy and peaceful, and she drank in the uniqueness of the predawn scene.

"I'm going to pick up our pace; otherwise, we'll be out here all day. You okay with that?" Grant called over his shoulder.

Molly tightened her hold on his waist. "Let's do it."

The surprising part was that she meant it which, she realized, was almost entirely due to her ever-growing trust in Grant. It was a deep-seated trust, the kind that grew out of respect. The kind of trust that made her daring enough to step outside of her comfort zone, confident enough to tackle things that once had seemed outside of her reach, and valued enough to be vulnerable about her feelings along the way. With him by her side, she was able to take risks she never would've considered before.

Not that riding on the back of an ATV was much of a risk. All things considered, this was one of the tamer adventures he'd taken her on. But then again, because of him, her comfort zone was quite a bit wider than it had been before. Especially when he was there with her.

She scanned the soft, white sand that shimmered under the fading light of the moon as they made their way down the beach, not entirely sure what she was looking for. So far, she'd only spotted the remains of what must've been a pretty big sand castle that had lost the battle with high tide and an impressive sand sculpture of a sea turtle that used pieces of shells to make up the mosaic on his back. While both were great finds, they weren't what they'd gotten up at zero dark thirty for.

"Tell me again what they look like." She had to shout to be heard over the combined noise of the engine and the wind. "Will it be obvious?"

"They sort of resemble a tire track with a comma-shaped tread. Some are more obvious than others," he shouted over his shoulder. "But trust me, you'll know it when you see it."

"I'll have to take your word for it."

They drove for a few more minutes. The sun was still a ways from coming up, but the sky was starting to lighten. It casted a faint glow over the whole beach, giving everything a blue tint, which seemed to add to the calm, peaceful vibe. She still wasn't sure about the turtle tracks, but she could get used to these predawn beach strolls.

She closed her eyes and drew in a deep breath of salty, morning air when she felt the ATV slow to a stop. "Well, look at that," Grant said.

She quickly blinked her eyes opened and scanned the sand. In front of them was what indeed looked like a wonky tire track leading from the seaweed line up the beach.

"Turtle tracks?" Excitement sparked inside her and she sat a little straighter.

"Looks like it. Let's park the ATV by the dunes, and we'll take a closer look." He turned and headed toward the dunes, making sure he left plenty of room between them and the tracks. When he found a spot out of the way, he killed the engine and climbed off. Leaving his helmet on the seat, he walked around and slung the heavy canvas duffel that was attached to the rack on the back over one shoulder, then grabbed a long metal pole that was shaped like a T with his other hand. "I'm assuming Mama has already headed out to sea. But we should approach silently until we know for sure."

Molly nodded, unbuckling her helmet and setting it next to his. As quietly as possible, they stepped through the soft sand toward the tracks. When they reached them, Grant squatted. She followed his lead, taking the opportunity to get a closer look at the flipper prints in the sand.

"Yep, it was definitely a green sea turtle. This set right here is headed toward the dunes, and that set on the other side is headed back to the water."

Seeing his enthusiasm caused her own to grow. "You're telling me we're in the vicinity of soon-to-be baby turtles?"

One side of Grant's mouth pulled up in a lopsided grin. "It would appear so. Want to check it out?"

"Are you kidding? Of course." She felt like she was on the cusp of discovering buried treasure, making her playful and giddy. "I can't believe you get to do this all the time."

"Not all the time. I'm only on Turtle Patrol once every ten days. Four a.m. comes awfully early. And like I said, we don't always spot new nests." He stood and followed the tracks to the dunes. "But it's pretty thrilling when we do." The excitement that radiated from his rugged features seemed to mirror her own, and she couldn't imagine anyone in the world she'd rather share this discovery with.

"Totally thrilling." Her eyes locked with his, and for a moment she wasn't sure if she was talking about the turtle nest discovery or standing here with him.

Turtle nests. It was definitely the turtle nests. She shook her head slightly to refocus on the task at hand.

"Shall we?" he asked.

"Lead the way."

She followed him into the dunes. Once they got to the sea grass, it became harder to tell where the tracks went. Grant carefully stepped through the vegetation, his gaze focused on the ground. Molly did her best to follow, trying not to let her footsteps damage anything.

After a couple of minutes, Grant stopped, setting the duffel on the ground. "Looks like it's right around here." He motioned to the sand in front of them. "Want to do the honors?" He held out the T-bar to her.

"Of course." The automatic answer leaped out of her mouth before she'd even had a chance to think about it, which was completely uncharacteristic. She couldn't decide if she should blame it on the excitement of the moment or the effects of the man she was with. Apparently, trust was a powerful emotion.

It wasn't until she had the metal rod in her hand that she stopped to considered the task.

"What exactly are the honors? And what am I supposed to do with this?" She held up the tool she'd never seen.

"We use it to figure out exactly where the nest is

located. Hold onto the handle at the top, and push it into the sand."

She adjusted her grip. "Like this?"

"Perfect. We're looking for soft sand that gives way when you push into it. That's how we know where Mama has been digging."

"How far down should I go? I don't want to hurt the eggs." Hesitation crept in. This was why she needed to stop and think before jumping into a new situation.

"You don't want to go too far, but far enough to know if it's part of the hole. You just have to feel it."

She eyed him skeptically. "Just feel it? That's your best direction?"

He gave her a sheepish grin. "Not helpful, huh?"

She shook her head. "Not at all."

"Maybe it would be easier to show you."

"Please."

But instead of taking the T-bar from her to demonstrate, he stepped up behind her and wrapped his arms around her, gently closing his hands over hers. Electricity buzzed through her. Of course, they had touched before, but never like this. Never had she felt his warmth so closely or experienced his bold confidence flowing through her as it did right now. The effect was dizzying.

"You just press down, like this." His breath skimmed across her neck, and she had to force herself to concentrate instead of melting into him.

With his strong hands over hers, they pushed the metal pole into the sand. She hadn't needed to worry about pushing too deep into the sand, because they barely got a few inches down before it felt like they hit rock bottom.

"I'm guessing this isn't it." She tried to keep the moment light to counterbalance the intense emotions that were flowing through her. This wasn't supposed to be happening. They were supposed to only be looking for turtles. In fact, her whole reason for being in this town was to avoid any sort of close, personal connection like the one flowing through her at this very moment.

"See? I told you you'd be able to feel it," he said. And just when she thought his touch was going to overtake her, he stepped away, leaving her feeling cold and alone.

Scratch that. Not alone. On her own, which was a very different thing. In fact, it was what she wanted, wasn't it? And as for the cold, well, she should've brought a jacket to combat the brisk morning breeze.

"Now move it a few inches to the left, and try again."

She did so, hitting the same hard sand only inches below the surface. She repeated the process four or five more times, each time with the same result.

It was on the sixth time that the pole went deeper, like a hot spoon plunging into a bucket of ice cream. She felt the difference instantly and a zing shot through her, bringing with it a smile that stretched all the way across her face.

"That was it, wasn't it?" Grant asked.

"Soft sand." It was a glorious feeling, and what made the moment even sweeter was that he hadn't done it for her. Instead, he'd trusted her to do it herself.

"I think we found ourselves a nest." He grinned, showing off his deep dimples and causing those same feelings to dance in her chest again. “What do you say we make it official?”

It was barely six o’clock in the morning, but Grant was pretty sure he’d already reached the highlight of his day. Finding a new turtle nest was always a treat, however finding one with Molly had been especially invigorating.

It’d taken about thirty minutes to record all the information they needed for the new nest. Once that part was done, they roped it off with wooden stakes and orange tape, attaching an official warning to not disturb it, along with the date it’d been discovered. Molly had blown the nest a kiss as they’d walked away, already convinced this particular group of soon-to-be hatchlings was special. And Grant, for the first time in his life, was jealous of a pile of eggs.

They climbed on the ATV and drove the remainder of the five miles he was responsible for patrolling, Molly happily chattering the entire way. The rest of the beach seemed to be untouched overnight, and when they got to the spot where a second set of tire tracks started, signaling the start of someone else’s patrol, he pulled closer to the water’s edge.

He killed the engine and pulled his helmet off. “Want to watch the sunrise?”

“I’d love to.” She removed her own helmet and stared out at the horizon. “But you should know, you’re now in the running for the person I’ve watched the most sunrises with.”

“A title I’ll gladly claim.” He climbed off the four-wheeler and leaned against the front, folding his arms over his chest. The sky was already a soft shade of pink with wispy clouds that looked as if they'd been brushed on with lavender paint. It was the perfect conclusion to an already exceptional morning. "I have to admit, I'm a sucker for a good sunrise. There's something that makes everything feel..."

"Hopeful?" Molly swung her legs around so she was sitting sideways on the seat, facing the ocean. She had a look of wonder on her face that drew him to her, because it was the exact same wonder he felt in his soul.

"Yeah." It took all of his effort to pull his gaze from the beauty in front of him and focus on the beauty in the sky. "Sunrises are the biggest benefit of living on a boat at sea. Without any of life's distractions getting in the way, they're inspiring."

"I could use a couple of those." There was a hint of sadness in her voice that caught him off guard. It was the same whisper of lingering hurt that he'd caught a few times. He could've ignored it. In fact, maybe he should've ignored it. But for some reason, he didn't.

"Why did you really move here?" He was aware it was a bold question. One he wasn't sure he'd earned the right to ask, but the success of the morning made him feel bold. Or, if he wanted to be completely honest with himself, staring at their second sunrise and sharing the same sense of wonder made him feel closer to her than when she'd been sitting behind him with her arms wrapped around him on the ATV. And that closeness made him want to know her story. It made him want to know *her*.

She drew in a deep breath, her gaze fixed on the golden horizon. "Heartbreak," she said simply. "The kind that derails life. At least, it derailed my life. I guess I was looking for a new track."

His own heart ached for her, but he didn't ask any more questions. Instead, he just waited for her to share when she was ready.

Hurt flickered in her eyes, followed by resolve and strength, which added to his growing admiration of her. "I thought I had life all figured out and was on my way to the altar. But, as it turned out, my fiancé was actually in love with my best friend. And, according to the few reports I've gotten from home, they're now the epitome of a happy couple."

Grant's heart lurched to the point that he could no longer ignore it. He reached over and wrapped his arm around her shoulders, pulling her in to himself. "Oh, Molly. I'm so sorry." He gently kissed the top of her head, hoping his touch could take away even an ounce of her pain. "For the record, he sounds like the biggest fool who ever lived."

Molly scoffed. "You might not be wrong." Instead of pulling away from his embrace, she rested her head against his shoulder and he wrapped his other arm around her. "But to be fair, I think he probably did us both a favor. Marrying him would've been a total mistake."

Grant held her, marveling at how good it felt to have her nestled against him. How right she felt in his arms. And all while his disdain for a man he'd never met grew. "Still, he sounds like a jerk. If you want us to name a disgusting task after him, say the word, and I'll do it. There's currently a very smelly algae that crops up from time to time that we're looking to nickname."

He could feel Molly's body shake from the soft chuckle. "Thanks. I'll think about it."

"So, that was it? You called off the wedding and packed your bags for greener pastures."

"If by greener pastures you mean white sand, then yes." Molly sat up, pulling free from his embrace, and stared out at the pinkening sky. "Although, it wasn't quite that quick. I stuck around town for a couple of miserable months before it became clear that to move on, I needed to start over."

"I'm sorry that things went down the way they did, but their loss has been Emerald Cove's great gain."

She grinned at him, causing a golden glow to spread through his chest. "Thanks."

"Do you miss home?"

She twisted her mouth to the side as if considering the question. "Surprisingly? No. I mean, there are a few things I miss, like my mom's famous pork tenderloin and not having to pull up a map every time I want to drive anywhere. But even then, I haven't regretted leaving for a single second."

"I'm not sure we have anything that can compare to your mom's pork, but we've got some amazing seafood that can try to make up for it."

"I'll agree with you on that front. Plus, the sunrises are pretty great." She motioned to the scene in front of them.

Grant shifted his attention to the beautiful display. "It almost makes up for waking up early on a Saturday, doesn't it?"

"More than makes up for it, I'd say." Molly sighed. "Of course, the nap I have planned for this afternoon doesn't hurt, either."

"I like the way you think." He was starting to like

a lot more than just that, although he stopped himself before he could fall too far down that rabbit hole. "But, for the sake of options, you're always welcome to swing by and help us clean out tanks. Nothing says 'happy Saturday' like scrubbing algae off the bottom of a pool."

"Tempting. The thing is, I've already committed to the nap and I'd hate to cancel last-minute." She gave him a faux-apologetic shrug. "But check in again next weekend. Maybe my schedule will be freer."

Grant chuckled. "I'll make a note on my calendar."

He knew Molly's presence here wasn't permanent. For that matter, neither was his. But at the moment, he had no intention of letting her go anywhere.

Chapter Twelve

The following Friday night, Molly was full of anticipation as she and Hadley drove the half mile from their condos to Ellyn's art gallery for the invitation-only opening of her big show.

"I've never been to a gallery opening. This is so exciting." Molly climbed out of the passenger seat of Hadley's car and was greeted by a blast of warm, humid air. She'd been here just over a month now, and while she wasn't sure there'd ever be a point when she was totally used to the heavy humidity of the Florida beach town, she didn't find it as oppressive as when she'd first arrived. In fact, she'd even be willing to go so far as to say she now found it endearing, like the charming quirk of a best friend.

Hadley clicked the lock button on her key fob and tossed her keys in her purse. "One advantage of living in a tourist town is you get all the benefits of small-town living with a few big-city type attractions thrown in." She shot Molly a mischievous grin as they walked through the parking lot to the sidewalk that led around to the store fronts. "It also doesn't hurt when the gallery owner is your best friend."

"It certainly has its perks," Molly admitted. While she would've helped Ellyn with any project, she'd thoroughly enjoyed her early peek at the show last night when she and Hadley had come to set up. The artist on display was a photographer and sculptor with a coastal theme, and she found his work inspiring. She couldn't wait for a second chance to admire the art tonight.

"And one of those perks is getting to go to the party early. We're there to mix and mingle before the party starts to make it look like the hottest ticket in town, but we also get first dibs at the best appetizers. A word to the wise, go for the mini crab cakes."

Molly's mouth watered. Crab cakes had always been one of her favorite foods. "Good tip."

They reached the front of Emerald Gallery, and despite the "closed" sign that hung in the window, Molly could see several people already walking around inside. Hadley lightly knocked on the door, and Ellyn hurried over to open it for them.

"Y'all are here!" She hugged each of them as she ushered them into the gallery.

"We wouldn't miss it," Molly said.

Hadley glanced around the room, beaming with pride. "And I have to say, everything looks perfect."

Ellyn was glowing. "I'm really pleased with how it turned out. Let's hope the general public is as impressed with Landon's work as I am."

"I have a feeling it's going to be a complete success," Hadley said. "We'll get out of your way so you can do what you do best. But if you need anything tonight, we're here for you."

"I second that," Molly agreed.

Ellyn beamed. Then her animated expression changed to the wide-eyed surprise of someone who'd just discovered a hidden treasure. "Oh, I almost forgot. Guess what I heard today?" Before either of them could respond, she glanced over at Hadley with a knowing look. "The contract on the empty store next to mine fell through. That space is available again, and the owner of the building is offering a nice little signing bonus to use toward the buildout."

Molly didn't know why Ellyn needed to share that news, but based on the way she looked at Hadley—almost like she was daring her to do something, with a hefty dose of friendly encouragement behind the dare—Molly guessed there was more to this story.

Hadley, on the other hand, rolled her eyes. "I'll pass that tip along if I hear of anyone interested."

Ellyn shrugged, looking awfully proud of herself. "Just saying." The artist motioned to Ellyn from the other side of the room. She started off in his direction, tossing them an apologetic glance over her shoulder. "Sorry, ladies. Excuse me?"

They both watched Ellyn for a second before Molly broached the new rental subject. "An empty store? What was that all about?"

Hadley shrugged as if it wasn't important. "Ellyn has this idea that I should open my own coffee shop there." Her tone might've been dismissive, but Molly wasn't dismissing it.

"What about you? Do you want to open a coffee shop?"

Hadley waited a beat before answering. "It's something I've considered on a dreaming kind of day. A little coffee-slash-book shop by the beach with the quaint and charming feel that's the perfect antidote to those rough workdays."

"It sounds amazing," Molly agreed.

Hadley's enthusiasm grew. "Right? Maybe comfy conversation areas for gathering with friends, and cozy spots for those who need to escape from everything. And of course, there would be some tables outside with brightly colored umbrellas and plenty of sea breezes."

Molly raised an eyebrow. "It sounds like you've considered this more than once."

"Maybe I've thought about it a few times." Hadley flicked her wrist as if erasing the whole idea. "But it's just a romantic dream. The reality is, quitting what I know to start a business I know nothing about is far too big of a leap to make sense."

Molly shrugged. "Maybe. But as someone who's opened herself up to taking more risks lately, I'm here to tell you, you can't let the fear of the leap stand in your way. Pretty great things can come from those giant leaps."

Hadley paused, as if the comment struck a nerve. Molly could see the fear lurking just under the surface, something she was all too acquainted with.

She reached over and gave Hadley's hand a gentle squeeze. "All I'm saying is, don't let the size of the leap keep you from considering something you really want."

"Valid point. I promise I'll think about it." She drew in a deep breath that seemed to chase some of the fear away. "But for now, what do you say we consider finding those crab cakes?"

"I'd say that's a leap worth taking, for sure." They

both giggled and managed to grab a couple of the delicious *hors d'oeuvres* from a passing waiter.

A few minutes later, the doors officially opened. It didn't take long before the entire gallery was filled with residents and guests of Emerald Cove. Molly was amazed at how many of the guests she knew, even though she'd only been here a month.

She hadn't even been able to flag down a second crab cake when Lydia, a client she'd seen earlier in the week at Gulfview Animal Clinic, greeted her. "Lydia, it's great to see you! How is Homer recovering?" She pictured the frisky Great Pyrenees puppy who'd been in for a standard procedure.

"Great. He doesn't seem to be bothered by the surgery site at all and he recouped all his energy. The hardest part is going to be keeping him out of the water for the two weeks while his incision heals. I've never seen a dog who loves the ocean as much as Homer does."

Molly's heart went out to the playful pup, who probably didn't understand why he was being kept from doing all the things he loved. "Poor guy. But two weeks will go by in a flash. And if he needs an outing, feel free to bring him up to the clinic. I'd love to get my fill of puppy rubs between appointments."

Lydia smiled. "Thanks. I might take you up on that."

Molly continued to circulate around the gallery, admiring art and chatting with locals she'd met since she'd been here. She'd been making small talk for about forty-five minutes when she glanced up and noticed Grant walking through the door.

Even though she was on the complete other side

of the room and he hadn't even stepped all the way into the building yet, their eyes met. It was a warm, personal connection. Friendly. The kind that sparked delight, as if the person she'd been waiting for had finally arrived.

That was ridiculous, of course, because she hadn't been waiting for him. Sure, they'd shared a moment last weekend over the turtle nest, but that didn't mean they had to spend every moment together. In fact, she'd never even asked him if he was coming tonight.

Of course, she assumed he'd been invited, and there was a part of her that hoped he'd show up. But she'd been totally content to circulate the room on her own. After all, tonight was about supporting Ellyn. Or at least that was her story until he'd walked through the doors.

He didn't even make it two steps inside before he was stopped by someone he knew. He chatted with the man but kept glancing up so his gaze locked with hers. His dimple-producing grin set off a round of sparkles, making her feel warm and floaty. She could no longer deny the draw between them. Yes, it was a stronger draw than any she'd felt in a long time, but that was because she hadn't met anyone like him in a long time. Maybe ever. Why wouldn't she want to spend time with him?

She started across the room, weaving her way through the crowd to reach him, keeping her focus on him. She greeted a couple people she'd seen Ellyn talking with earlier. He moved on to shake hands with someone she recognized from the backyard barbeque at Claire's house. The whole time, they kept eye contact as if there was an invisible link connecting them.

After several minutes and multiple conversations, anticipation sizzled through her as they were finally about to meet. She could feel her grin widen and her mood brighten. But before she could take the final step to him, Lottie Jenkins, the head of the local animal rescue organization, stepped in her path.

"Dr. Lawrence! I was hoping I'd run into you."

There was a fizzle of disappointment which caused her wide grin to waver. She was fully aware it was a ridiculous reaction. She liked Lottie and loved the work she did. She shouldn't be disappointed to have to talk with her.

She refreshed her smile, although it took a bit more work this time. Hopefully Lottie didn't notice. "Hello, Lottie. It's good to see you."

Behind her, Grant finished up his latest conversation and made a playful wide-eyed face that poked fun at how hard it was for them to make it to each other. The expression made her want to laugh, but instead she swallowed it, and focused on the woman in front of her. But, on the bright side, at least her smile wasn't as forced anymore.

"I have some excellent news." Lottie leaned in to share it with Molly. "All but one of the feral kittens we found have forever homes."

"How wonderful!"

Lottie nodded, looking pleased. "The last one, the gray-striped, is as sweet as banana pudding, so I'm not concerned about finding him a family. In fact, I already have a place in mind." She looked thoughtful for a second, then waved her hand in front of her.

"Anywho, I wanted to let you know the good news, since you connected with the kittens at their appointment."

Molly pictured the sweet little furballs she'd nuzzled during their final kitten exam. Two of them in particular had the loudest purr she'd heard in a long time. They were going to make great companions. "I'm glad you did. I love hearing updates. And maybe I'll see a couple of them again when their new owners bring them in."

"You should. I gave each of their new owners your card. Be on the lookout for them!" Lottie said a quick goodbye as she hopped off to chat with someone else, and Molly finally stepped up to the person she'd been waiting all evening to reach.

"That felt much more complicated than it needed to be," Grant joked.

"Right?" She reached up and gave him a hug. It was meant to be a quick greeting, the friendly type she'd give to Ellyn or Hadley or Claire. But as his arm slid around her waist and he pulled her into his embrace, the connection that had drawn her to him from across the room intensified. She wanted to linger there, to stay in his arms.

The thought made her jump back. He was a friend, which was all circumstances dictated he could be. And since her time with him was limited, she didn't want anything to complicate the relationship with her favorite person in Emerald Cove. Especially not tonight.

She pushed her hair out of her face and reharnessed the friendly excitement she had about seeing him. "I was hoping you'd show up tonight. I have a surprise for you."

Amusement danced in his warm brown eyes. "Fun. What's the occasion?" He tucked his hands into the pockets of his jeans.

"You always have things planned for me. I figured it was my turn to do something for you." Molly couldn't contain her grin. In fact, there was a good chance it was bordering on goofy, but she couldn't help it. If she knew Grant like she thought she did, he was going to love this. She couldn't wait to show it to him. "Come on, this way."

Grant stuck close to Molly as they wove their way through the crowd. "You look nice tonight, by the way."

"Nice" might've been an understatement. She was stunning. She wore a short, black dress and heels, which accented her long legs. And instead of the usual ponytail, her hair was down tonight, flowing over her shoulders like a cascading, golden waterfall. He picked up whiffs of her floral shampoo as he trailed behind her.

"Thanks," she said. "It's kind of fun to get dressed up for a change."

They passed the makeshift bar and slipped into the quieter back hallway, where the bathroom was located. He followed her to a door at the end with a PRIVATE sign.

Grant raised a questioning eyebrow. “Now look which one of us is breaking into restricted areas.”

“Apparently you’re a bad influence.” She shot him a playful look that ignited something inside him. Doing a quick check of the hallway behind them, she twisted the knob and led him inside.

The space seemed to be some sort of supply closet and was a stark contrast to the clean, crisp look of the rest of the gallery. The walls didn’t have the same pure, white gleam. In fact, with all the paint-splattered tables, wooden crates, and utility shelves full of supplies, it was hard to see the walls at all.

Molly wandered into the room. “I was helping Ellyn and the artist set up yesterday. They were making the final decision on which pieces to put on display, and there was a whole series of pictures they decided against that I thought you’d enjoy.”

“And you decided to sneak me into the storage closet for a private viewing?”

Molly grinned one of her hypnotic grins. “Something like that.”

“I’m intrigued.”

She turned a corner in the L-shaped room and stopped in front of a table holding six different framed photographs. “May I present to you, for the first time on semi-public display, the collection entitled ‘Beautiful Beginnings.’”

There were six different shots of ocean sunrises, each of them taken from a boat offshore. The beauty of the dawn was unobstructed, making it a different kind of touching.

“They reminded me of the sunrises from your boat that you described. The ones you said that were the most inspiring," Molly explained, staring at the photographs.

They reminded *him* of those sunrises, which was hard to do. It was impossible to capture the essence and grandness of an inspirational sunrise in a photograph, but this photographer had gotten as close as anyone he'd ever seen. The images moved him.

He stepped up to the first piece to examine it more closely. "Why would they not use them?"

"A whole lot of artsy reasons I can't even pretend to understand. Something about the feel of the space and the story of the show." Molly leaned against the table opposite of the art. "But, to be fair, I didn't understand most of the conversation that went on last night. Have you ever heard art people talk about lighting?"

He didn't know a thing about art-related lighting, but what he did know was that he connected with these pieces. "I didn't get to see everything on display, but it's a shame a room full of people won't get to enjoy these." He moved to examine the second one.

"You like them, then?"

He turned to her, his gaze meeting hers, and a thrill reverberated through him. "Very much." And what made the moment even more special was that she'd known he'd enjoy it and had set it up for him. "And I'm guessing we didn't break any laws or copyright infringements by being in here?"

Molly grinned, hoisting herself up to sit on the table, as if she planned on sitting there to admire the pieces for a while. "I have full permission from Ellyn and Landon. Ellyn said you should be honored, because she doesn't let just anyone in here. And also, please ignore her mess."

"Clearly she hasn't seen the supply closet at Turtle Rehab." He pushed himself up on the table next to her. His thigh grazed hers in the process, sending a zing racing through him. "But you can tell her that with these impressive works in here, it was impossible to see anything else."

Molly looked pleased. "What are you doing next weekend? The photos should still be here. I could pack us a picnic brunch and we could enjoy another sunrise together. At the perfectly reasonable hour of noon this time."

"Tempting." Grant let his legs swing as he pictured the supply room midday-sunrise picnic with Molly. "Unfortunately, I won't be here next weekend. I have my interview."

"Oh, right." Molly brightened, looking as stunning as the morning sky. "How could I forget that? Are you nervous?"

He considered the question for a moment. "A form of nervous, maybe. There was a time when I would've given anything for this job. At Turtle Rehab, we can save one turtle at a time, but the studies and research done at universities can help hundreds, even thousands of turtles."

"Sounds inspiring."

Grant nodded, trying to figure out how to put into words the job that moved him. "It is. Plus, I love the discovery. And getting to interact with nature. And the adventure of it all. Really, I enjoy the whole package."

Molly's understanding gaze was focused on him

in a way that allowed him to feel her sympathy. "It must've been a big sacrifice to give that up and come home."

He thought back to the day he'd packed his car, sparking a ping of sadness from all the loss that had followed. He shifted, as if a more comfortable sitting position would somehow ease some of the ache of the past. "A sacrifice, yes, but I love my family more. It was an easy choice." If he had it to do over again, he'd still make the same choice every time.

"And going back there?" Molly gently prodded.

The same inner conflict he'd been dealing with since he'd first heard of the opportunity pawed at him. "The decision's not as clear-cut this time."

Molly nodded as if she understood, and he got the feeling she could probably relate more than most. "Well, from what I've heard, there's no way they'll say no. It sounds like you're the perfect person for the job."

There was something about her words that sparked confidence in him. Or maybe it was her faith in him in general. Either way, it left him feeling more optimistic about the future than he'd felt since he'd found out about the job. "There are a lot of ways they could say no, but I appreciate your vote of confidence."

"When is the big interview?"

"Friday."

"Well, I wish you all the luck in the world. Unless you decide you don't want it, in which case, I hope you totally bomb."

Grant laughed. It was the legit, all-the-way-from-the-belly kind of laugh that chased away any of the residual nerves. “I appreciate your support.”

Molly grinned, looking quite pleased with herself. “That’s what friends are for, right? Anyway, when do you leave?”

“Thursday afternoon. And since I’m in town, I’m going to stay the weekend to hang out with some friends. I’ll be back on Monday.”

“Whatever will we do without you?” she joked.

“It’s hard to imagine, but I’m sure you’ll stumble through somehow.” Although he had to admit, deep down, he was starting to have the exact same thought about her.

Chapter Thirteen

The one thing Molly couldn't get used to was how quickly the weather could change on the coast. Right now, for example, the sun was shining where she was, but way out at sea, close to the horizon, dark, brooding storm clouds were building. And, judging by the wind, the storm was headed this direction.

It was a lazy Sunday afternoon a week after the gallery show, and Molly sat on her balcony, sipping tea and watching the calm waves start to pick up, and the wide, blue sky swallowed little by little by the dark clouds. This was her first quiet weekend since she'd been here. She hadn't realized how many friends she'd made and how entertained they'd kept her until they were all out of town.

Hadley was gone on a short vacation to meet a few of her friends from Texas. Ellyn was working all weekend. Claire had gone to the town where her fiancé was from for a bridal shower. And Grant was out of town for his interview.

For someone who'd moved here with the distinct purpose of making no connections, she'd made a lot of connections. It was an interesting turn of events. The one thing she'd been running from had turned out to be the one thing she ran into. True, it might make it a little harder to leave once her time was up, but she wouldn't trade any of the friendships she'd made here for the world. Hadley and Ellyn. Claire and the staff at Turtle Rehab. Grant. Each one of them had played a part in helping her learn to trust again, and she had every intention of soaking it in as long as she could.

She was distracted by the sound of the sliding door opening on the balcony next to her. She stood up from the chair and peeked around the divider to Ellyn's balcony.

"What are you doing home?" Molly asked.

Ellyn was pulling one of the large potted plants inside. "I was taking a lunch break and thought I'd bring in some of these. That doesn't look good." She waved her hand at the distance, where the stormy clouds seemed to be getting darker by the second.

Molly was from Kansas. She was no stranger to big storms, but she'd never been in a big storm on the beach before. "Should I be nervous?"

Ellyn shook her head. "It won't last long. But it looks like there will be lightning, and the wind can pack quite a punch. It's been known to blow the furniture across the patio."

"Thanks for the head's up. Sounds like a good night to order takeout and stay in."

"Exactly. But word to the wise, make sure to order well before the storm hits. Delivery people won't drive in the heavy rain, and our streets have the tendency to flood in a downpour."

"I take it that's a tip from experience?"

Ellyn flashed a guilty grin. "Sadly, from more than one occasion. There's nothing like craving pad thai and having to settle for a frozen pizza."

"Order early. Got it." Molly sipped her tea. "How's packing up the show going?"

"Almost done. Did I tell you we sold all but two pieces? It was the most successful special exhibit we've ever had." She let out a weary sigh. "But that's a lot of pieces to crate to be shipped in the morning. All I can say is I'm going to sleep well tonight. Assuming I can finish it up."

"You can do it. I believe in you." Molly pumped her fist in the air, cheerleader style. "And if you need help, I'm happy to lend a hand."

"Thanks, friend." Ellyn beamed. "I think I got this one. But I might take you up on the offer next time I'm trying to get ready for one of our junior art classes."

"Just say the word, and I'm there."

"I appreciate it." Ellyn motioned toward the storm clouds. "Don't stay out here too long. These kinds of storms always sneak up faster than you think."

Ellyn wasn't kidding. Molly sat out there for a few more minutes before she got up to take in some of the smaller objects on her balcony. When she came back, every last bit of blue sky had disappeared, and the sun had been blotted out by the charcoal clouds. A cold, strong wind whipped past her when she opened the door, pushing her back. At the same time, a bright streak of lightning flashed across the sky.

"Whoa." Molly had barely finished whispering the word before a deafening clap of thunder shook the windows, causing her to jump. “So much for ordering takeout.”

She scurried inside and slid the door closed, making sure to lock it. She wasn’t sure why she’d locked it. It wasn’t like the wind was going to blow her sliding glass door open, but it made her feel safer.

She stood there and watched for a minute as the rain over the ocean inched its way closer and closer until huge drops splattered across her balcony. About thirty seconds later, those huge drops turned to a solid sheet of rain. It was coming down so hard and fast that she couldn’t see past her railing. The wind howled, and the thunder crashed.

Molly backed away from the window, finding a cozy place on her couch under a blanket, and turned on a movie. She could see why delivery people wouldn’t go out in this. There was no way anyone could drive even if the streets didn’t flood. The rain was blinding.

She’d just gotten past the opening credits when the electricity flickered. She froze, as if her movement might trigger a power outage, but her gaze darted around the room. Several slow seconds ticked by, but nothing else happened. The lights stayed on.

“That was close.” She returned to her movie, turning the volume up so she could hear it over the constant rumbling of thunder and the sounds of the rain pelting the door.

Then there was a blinding flash. It was so bright it flooded the room like a search light. Almost simultaneously, there was an ear-shattering crack, louder than anything she’d ever heard before. The entire room shook, and the hairs on Molly’s arms stood straight up. Molly’s heart pounded in her chest as she pulled the blanket up to her eyes. That was close. Too close.

The lights flickered again and then went out completely. The storm continued to rage outside, but inside was eerily quiet. Molly sat there in the darkness for a moment with her eyes peeking out just above the top of her blanket, willing the power to come back on. It didn't.

"It's fine. I'm fine. Everything's fine," she whispered into the darkness. It was just a storm. Sure, it was the worst storm she'd seen in possibly forever and she was all alone in a fourth-story condo with nothing but sand between her building and the raging ocean, but storms passed. She was safe. Everything was going to turn out okay. Hopefully.

Maybe what she needed was a little light to chase away the darkness. Light always helped, and she was pretty sure she'd seen a large lantern-type flashlight under the sink.

Another clap of thunder rattled the windows as she stood from the couch. She wrapped the blanket around her shoulders for protection—not that she knew what she needed protection from inside her own, safe condo. Or what the fuzzy blanket was going to do about it even if a problem did arise. But the cape thing seemed to work for superheroes, so she figured it wouldn't hurt.

She fumbled her way through the darkness into the kitchen. Holding the counter as a guide, she made her way to the sink and squatted down. It was pitch black inside the cabinet, but a well-timed lightning strike lit up the room enough to catch a glimpse of the lantern. The lightning was good for something, after all. She reached for the lantern and switched it on.

Light filled the room. "Better," she said out loud. Now that she had some light, she felt more confident about her safety, and headed into her bedroom to get her phone that had been on the charger.

The first text message was from Ellyn.

You ok? Lightning hit a transformer. Electric company estimates power back in five hours.

Five hours, huh? Looked like it was going to be a quieter evening than Molly had thought. She typed a quick reply to tell her friend that all was well there, then headed over to the bookcase. If she remembered correctly, there was a jigsaw puzzle that someone had left. A night without electricity seemed like the perfect time to get it out and put it together.

She held the lantern up to view the items on the shelves until she found it, a tropical scene of a sea turtle swimming over a reef.

Sea turtles!

Molly had almost forgotten about the turtles. Grant had explained to her on one of the more in-depth tours of the facility that the turtles were fine in most storms. They were animals used to living in the wild and instinctively knew what to do to stay safe. The only real concern was if there was a storm surge from a hurricane that came up higher than the tanks, or...

"A power outage that stops the pumping system," she said out loud. According to Grant, the turtles would be fine in a short outage, but anything longer than half an hour required the generator to be turned on. It was one of the reasons they always had someone living on the property. But Grant was out of town until tomorrow.

Concern swirled through her as she stared at the picture of the sea turtle on the box and then looked out the window. The storm was still raging with no sign of letting up soon. She grabbed her phone and typed a quick message about the power outage to the only other person she knew was in town: Mateo. His reply dinged almost immediately.

I got the alarm but I'm in Seagrove.

Seagrove? That was a twenty-minute drive in good conditions. Even if he could do the drive in these treacherous conditions, there was no way he'd make it in time.

Molly, on the other hand, lived just over a mile from Turtle Rehab. The roads might have water building up on them, but she doubted there'd be anyone else out. Who else would want to drive in this? If she drove slowly and in the middle of the road to avoid the water pooling, she'd be okay. Besides, what other choice did she have?

Stay there. I'll go. I'm much closer.

Driving on the dark roads through a sheet of rain didn't sound like a great idea, and there was a healthy dose of icy nervousness flowing through her veins, but what other choice did she have? There was no way she could sit here and let something happen to Hope or Shelley or Buzz or Woody.

She tossed the blanket on the couch and grabbed her raincoat from the rack. "Let's do it." With new resolve, she marched out the front door with her keys in one hand and the lantern in the other.

As she predicted, there wasn't anyone else on 30A,

which was probably a good thing. Molly drove in the middle of the street to avoid the growing puddles as she crept down the highway at fifteen miles per hour. Even with her windshield wipers going full speed, there was no keeping up with the rainfall. The normal five-minute drive felt like it'd taken forever when she finally pulled into the empty Turtle Rehab parking lot. Her shoulders were one solid knot and her jaw hurt from clenching her teeth, but she'd made it. Step one: check. Now all she had to do was get through the building to the generator outside.

That, of course, required her to run from her car to the door in the raging storm. Making sure she had her keys ready, she grabbed the lantern, took a deep breath, and dashed for the entrance. It was only a three-second trek, maybe four at the most, but by the time she got inside and pulled the door closed, water poured off her raincoat. She was pretty sure her clothes underneath were damp too. How could that much water fall from the sky at the same time?

She leaned against the door, letting out a long exhale. Her heart thumped in her chest, and she held her lantern up to survey the room in front of her.

She'd walked through the gift shop dozens of times and was very familiar with the facility as a whole, but in the darkness it looked different. The lantern cast eerie shadows on the walls and floor, and the continuous flashes of lightning and crashes of thunder added an extra layer of fear.

"It's fine. I'm fine. Everything's fine," she repeated as she slowly made her way through the space. Once on the other side, she opened the door and eased down the long, dark hallway. If she remembered correctly, the switch for the generator was next to the control panel, which was located against the outside wall. Of course, first she had to figure out how to get through the automatic sliding doors which, at the moment, weren't automatic. There had to be a way to open it manually, right?

"They really should teach us this kind of stuff in school," she said to no one in particular. Holding the lantern close to the door, she moved it along the parameter. Once she'd found how to unlock it, she used both hands to pull the doors apart from each other. A gust of wind blew in the narrow opening, bringing a spray of cold rain with it. Outside, Molly could hear the flapping of tarps and the crash of the waves against the dock. With the doors opened wide enough, she pulled her hood over her head and plunged outside.

She clung close to the wall as she headed to the control panel on the far end. Rain dripped in her eyes, and she had to wipe it away before she could open the metal door. Labels along the side indicated what each switch controlled. Molly ran her finger down the row until she found the one she was looking for.

"Emergency generator for tanks," she read aloud. "There you are."

She flipped it to the left and looked around for some sign that it had worked. There was some sort of motor-ish sound that she felt fairly certain wasn't there before, but between the wind, rain, and darkness it was hard to tell for sure. The only way she could think of to verify that the generator had turned on was to see if the pumps were working in the tanks.

And since she'd come this far, she wasn't going inside until she was sure the job was done.

On the plus side, the walkways were covered. In theory, she was somewhat protected from the raging lightning storm. On the negative side, the narrow covering seemed to do little, if anything, to shield her from the rain. She pulled her rain jacket tighter as she neared Hope's tank.

She hurried to it and peered over the edge. Hope was swimming around toward the bottom, not nearly as concerned about the monsoon happening around them as she was. And better than that, Molly could see that the pump was indeed working.

She breathed a sigh of relief. "All's well that ends well, right, Hope?"

Another crash of thunder reminded her that all hadn't ended quite yet. Standing outside in the thunderstorm wasn't smart, but Molly wanted to check one more thing before she headed back to ride out the rest of the storm inside the gift shop.

"Don't worry, Hope. This should all be over soon." That comment was probably more for herself than the seemingly unfazed turtle, but she didn't care. She was putting the positivity into the world.

After blowing Hope a kiss, she scurried down the wet path as fast as she could without slipping on the slick concrete. She needed to check on the hatchlings. Since they were the smallest and had the least amount of water in their tanks, they faced the greatest risk if something went wrong with the water system. The pumps running properly was imperative for all the tanks, but it was even more so for the hatchlings. Plus, she wanted to make sure they were staying safe in the storm.

Rain pelted her face, making it hard to see, and her feet squished in what felt like an inch of water inside her rainboots. Her gear didn't seem to be any match for the storm. She skidded to a halt on the sidewalk next to the small square tanks.

Unlike Hope, who had more life experience, these two were both hiding in the bottom corner of their tank. Molly's heart lurched and she wished she could pick them up and comfort them. "Don't worry, fellas, it should be over soon."

She held her lantern up to the tanks to assure herself the pumps were working correctly. Relief flowed through her as she noted that all looked good.

"All right, you two, I've gotta get outta here. But I'll come check on you as soon as the storm ends." She gave the side of their tanks a squeeze, hoping some of the warm embrace would seep down to them. After one last look, she turned to run back to the building.

Although as soon as she turned, she saw something that scared her more than lightning striking all around her. A large hooded figure was coming right for her.

Molly screamed.

Her heart pounded like a kettle drum and the sound of her racing pulse reverberated in her ears, drowning out the sounds of the storm. She wanted to run; in fact, she was pretty sure she told her feet to run, which felt like the safer option here. But as her fight-or-flight reflexes kicked in, she learned that her internal default was to fight, something she'd be sure to consult with herself about later.

But for the moment, she stood there, holding her ground in her soggy rainboots, and grabbed the long-handled net attached to the tanks next to her. "Don't come any closer! You need to leave this property right now before I call the police."

The figure didn't stop. Molly took one bold step forward, using all her strength to slice the pool net through the air the way a samurai would swing a sword.

"Molly!"

At least she thought that was the word that swirled through the wind and rain, which was enough to make her pause. Still holding the pole out in front of her, she tried to blink the rain out of her eyes.

The form reached up and pushed his hood back. Lightning flashed behind them, causing her to jump, but it also gave enough light to see that the hooded figure wasn't an intruder at all.

"Grant?" She dropped the net to her side as rain dripped off her face. "What are you doing here?" She had to shout to be heard over the storm, adrenaline still pulsing through her veins.

"I could ask you the same thing, Warrior Princess." He smirked and pointed to the net hanging at her side. "Did you decide you needed to get in a little fencing practice in the middle of a rainstorm?"

Molly stared at the net in her hand as if it would help her put the pieces together. "Aren't you supposed to be in Tampa?"

"I decided to come home early to beat the storm." He motioned to the rain falling around them. "I don't think I made it."

It was a lame attempt at a joke, but still enough

to make her laugh. All the tension she'd been holding onto melted away, and she threw her arms around him. "It's so good to see you."

Another crash of thunder hit at almost the exact same moment.

He pulled her in with a protective arm, and even though they were standing in the middle of a raging storm, she finally felt safe. "It's good to see you too, but how about we take this reunion inside?"

"Great idea!" She grabbed the lantern she'd dropped and they both dashed to the building. Once inside, Grant pulled the sliding doors closed, muffling the sounds of the storm. They stood there in the empty hallway in the dim light of her lantern. Water dripped off them and pooled on the tile floor by their feet.

"Okay, let's try this again." He slipped off the long, dark-green rain slicker and ran his hands through his wavy hair. "What are you doing here?"

"I came to turn on the generator." She peeled off her own rain jacket, although she seemed to be just as wet underneath. The cool air hit her skin, and she shivered. "I knew you and Claire were out of town, and Mateo was too far away. Ellyn told me the power will be off for a while. I didn't want anything to happen to the turtles." Water dripped off her ponytail and she tried to position it so it ran onto her shirt instead of adding to the puddle on the floor.

"You drove through the storm to check on the turtles?" Even in the darkness, she could see something sparkle in his eyes. Respect, maybe? Or appreciation? He paused for a second as if considering something. "You, Dr. Lawrence, are a unicorn."

A unicorn? "I'm taking that as a compliment...?" Her forehead wrinkled as she considered the phrase.

"Yes, it's a compliment. We..." he made a sweeping motion to include all of the turtles outside the glass, "are lucky to have you."

Heat flared in her cheeks and in order to avoid Grant seeing her blush, she looked down to brush the water off her shorts. "What about you? Why are you here?" Remembering the heart palpitations he'd caused when he'd arrived, she looked up and planted her fists on her hips. "You know you almost scared me to death."

"Yeah, sorry about that, but I admire your ninja skills. No one's going to mess with the turtles with you around." One side of his mouth pulled up in an amused smirk.

Molly giggled. "I've got skills you don't even know about."

"Apparently." He paused. "I came back for the same reason you did. I heard there might be big storms today, and I didn't want to risk a power outage with no one here. But I guess I didn't leave early enough."

"It came fast."

"Thanks for standing in the gap for us. I really appreciate it." He stared into her eyes, and the sincerity of his words flowed through her.

"You're welcome." Her job here and her relationship with Grant were professional, but there was something in his statement, something in the pull between them that felt more personal. It was almost as if the air between them crackled.

Molly looked away. She didn't want there to be any

pulling or crackling. Making friends in this town was one thing, but letting herself fall for someone? That was a different game altogether. And it didn't matter how much trust her new friends had helped her restore, she had no intention of going near that kind of relationship, no matter how strong the pull or how audible the crackle.

"Oh, goodness. Look at what a mess we're making." She motioned to the puddle on the floor, changing the subject.

"I'm more worried about you. You're completely soaked." He stroked his jaw. "You know, I think Claire usually keeps a change of clothes in her desk in case she gets dirty working with a turtle. You're close to the same size." He motioned for her to follow him through the dark hallway into the even darker offices.

He used the light on his phone to make his way over to Claire's desk, where a clean and dry T-shirt and pair of shorts were neatly folded in the bottom drawer. He pulled them out and handed them to Molly.

"Dry clothes will help," Molly said. She knew it would start getting stuffy inside without the air conditioner running, but for now she couldn't stop shivering from the chill against her damp skin.

"I'm going to get towels from the clinic to dry the hallway." He disappeared from the office, and Molly changed out of her wet clothes. Feeling much better, she walked out to where Grant was standing by the sliding doors. He held out a dry towel. "I thought this might help too."

"Thanks." She took the towel and used it to dry her hair, staring out the window as she did. "It looks like it's finally starting to let up. Maybe I can make it home."

Grant shook his head. "The highway has high water on it. The police were setting up barricades right past Turtle Rehab when I pulled in. It will take at least a couple of hours for it to drain off."

"Oh." Apparently, it was a good thing she'd come when she had, although she'd never even considered not being able to get home. "Guess I'm hanging out here for a while. Got any good board games?"

Grant's eyebrows raised with a look of mischief. "Actually, I got a better idea."

Molly eyed him. She knew that look. It usually ended with her at the top of a lighthouse or swimming in the middle of the Gulf. "To be clear, driving through that typhoon to turn on the generator was more than enough adventure for one day."

Grant motioned toward the outside. "That? We call that a summer shower," he joked.

Molly rolled her eyes, and Grant's expression melted into a reassuring smile.

"What I have planned is much tamer. I have a cooler full of shrimp my buddy caught yesterday and a grill that's itching to be fired up. What are your thoughts about dinner?"

"Dinner I can handle. I'm a big fan of dinner."

Grant's stomach rumbled as the succulent scent of shrimp and veggies brushed with his secret spicy garlic sauce wafted up from the grill. The combination of skipping lunch on the drive home and the delicious food cooking over the fire made him hungrier than he'd thought he was.

"Five minutes, and we'll be ready to eat," he called to Molly.

"Perfect, because we're almost ready over here."

It had stopped raining, but since the water was still rough, he thought it'd be more comfortable to eat on stable ground instead of the rocking deck of his boat. He'd left Molly on the dock with a folding table and all the candles he could scrounge up while he quickly assembled the kabobs and cooked them on the built-in grill on his boat.

When the Gulf shrimp were cooked to perfection, he pulled them off and stacked them on the waiting platter. Holding the platter in one hand and a bottle of wine in the other, he made his way around to the deck side for their make-shift picnic. "Food's ready." He rounded the corner, and the scene that came into view caused him to pause.

The candles he'd given her sat in creative clusters in the middle of the table, then more were along the edge of the deck in a neatly spaced-out row. Between the light from the candles and their reflection in the water, the space glowed. And Molly, who was standing in the middle, seemed to glow right along with it.

"Amazing." He felt pretty sure at least part of that word was meant for the setting. As for the woman standing in the middle of it, she never stopped amazing him. "If this is what you can do with a folding table and a handful of half-burned candles, you're officially part of the decorating committee for our next gala."

Molly's giggle drifted into the velvety sky as she reached for the platter. "Between the candlelight and the starry night, it does look pretty fancy, huh?"

He made the wide step from the boat to the dock and stopped to look up at the twinkling sky. "It's hard to believe the sky is clear now after that storm. Welcome to Florida weather."

Molly set the platter on the table and sank into the folding chair at the far end, tipping her head back to look up at the stars. "I like it. It's a great reminder that storms don't last forever. And sometimes, what comes after them is beautiful."

"That's pretty deep for a barefoot, paper-plate kind of night." He took his own seat on the other side of the table.

"What can I say? Candlelight makes me philosophical." She picked up two kabobs and placed them on her plate.

"So, tonight's dinner conversation will revolve around solving life's greatest conundrums?" He held up the bottle of wine to offer it to her.

"At least until the candles burn out." She nodded and held out her cup. "And up first is your new job opportunity. How'd the interview go?"

Grant poured her a drink before serving himself. Then settling in his chair, he thought back to his meeting with the board of directors. Bits and pieces of their lengthy but encouraging conversation floated through his mind. "Good."

"Good?" She shot him an accusatory look. "You're gone all weekend for a meeting that could literally change what your life looks like, and all I get is 'good?'"

The question caused something inside him to move. Molly wasn't afraid to challenge him. She didn't let him sidestep hard questions, but she did it in a way that made him feel safe. It was one of the things he liked about her. "Fine, it was great. Better than I could've hoped for." The familiar internal struggle pulled at him, and he let out a sigh. "And that's where the problem lies."

"Great is a problem? We really are getting philosophical tonight." She took a bite of a shrimp. Her eyes closed and she chewed slowly. After she swallowed, she blinked her eyes open and looked over the candlelight at him, motioning at the plate with her fork. "I don't want to minimize your thing, but this is amazing. I think it's the best meal I've eaten since I've been in Florida."

"Glad you like it. It's a recipe that's been famously passed around the marine biology department at the university. Once you get a spot on the faculty, they give you the recipe." He speared a piece of pepper. "They say it's a rite of passage, but I really think they're looking for new people to cook for them."

She laughed and ate another shrimp. "You're making their recipes and your interview was great. I'm having a hard time seeing where the problem is."

Grant slumped in his chair and waved his hand at the area around him. "This." In the dark, moonless night, it was hard to see much, but he could make out the outline of the Discovery Lagoon and hear the hum of the pumps behind them.

Of course he wanted the job. It was the job he'd dreamed about for years. It was the exact position he pictured when someone asked where he wanted to be in five years. But this place was family.

"How do I walk away from a legacy?"

Molly glanced around too, wonder written all over her candle-lit face. "That's a hard call. I guess the question you have to ask yourself is, is this your legacy?" She refocused on him. "Because if it's not, it doesn't matter how magnificent it is, you're still in the wrong place."

The truth of her words hit him like a gale-force wind. He gazed out at the dark ocean. "How do I know?"

Molly reached across the table and rested her hand over his. Her touch was soft and gentle but wrapped around him like an encouraging hug. "You're the only one who can answer that question. But I think when the time comes, deep in your heart, you'll know."

Her words hung in the air between them like a beautifully wrapped gift. The promise of what was inside excited him.

Or was it the promise of what sat before him?

Molly herself had been a gift. One he wasn't expecting and, frankly, didn't even know he'd wanted. But now that she was here, she'd turned out to be his favorite.

"But if you're only worried about what will happen to this place once you're gone..." She jerked her thumb in the direction of the turtle tanks. "I gotta say, Claire and Mateo run a tight ship. Not a lot of funny business going on with those two in charge." Molly's playful smirk glowed in the flickering candle light, lightening the mood.

"Are you saying I'm replaceable?"

"Not entirely replaceable. I mean, you are the one with the boat." She speared a shrimp and held it up. "And you grill a mean shrimp kabob."

He scoffed. "Thanks for the vote of confidence." Yup, she was a gift, all right. The realization prompted him to ask the question he'd been toying around with all weekend. "That reminds me, I've come up with an idea for our next excursion."

"Let me guess." She tapped her chin, feigning a look of deep contemplation. "Parasailing off the back of your boat."

"No, although that's an interesting idea."

"Surfing lessons in twenty-foot barrel waves."

"First of all, we don't have twenty-foot waves around here. And second, I'm not a great surfer."

Molly pretended to look shocked. "What? There's something beach-related that the mighty Grant Torres can't do?"

"Hold up a second." Grant held up his hand. "I said I'm not great at it. I never said I couldn't do it."

Molly let out a sigh, her shoulders sagging as if she was thoroughly disappointed. "Since we can't go surfing, what's your next proposed activity?"

"Be my date to my sister's wedding." As soon as the words left his mouth, a flurry of nerves scurried through him like a high school freshman who'd just asked the most beautiful senior out on a date, which he wasn't expecting. They were friends—he'd even venture to say good friends—and they did things together all the time.

But the truth was, this ask felt different. It felt bigger. He wasn't asking her to hang out with him on his boat or go to a turtle conference. He was asking her to stand by his side at the most significant event he would attend all year. And he was asking her because there was no one he'd rather have with him than her.

Molly hesitated more than a few beats longer than he felt was normal. "Oh. I, um..." An expression flashed across her face. He didn't know quite how to describe it, but it was the same one she'd had when she'd boarded his boat for the first time, and then again when she'd stood at the base of the lighthouse. It was vulnerable and hesitant and determined and strong all rolled into one. And he got it. He tried to avoid relationships too. There was way too much risk with not enough reward. But this...this was different. This felt right.

"The thing is—" He started to dive a little deeper into his feelings, but before he could get out anything else, the entire world instantly lit up like someone had suddenly transported them to the surface of the sun. The sudden brightness against the unusually dark night was shocking. Disoriented, he looked up, drawing his attention away from Molly as he searched for the source of the light. "What in the world?"

The floodlight over the dock gleamed with the intensity of a supernova. He'd never liked that light. It'd been installed many, many years ago for the rare occasions they needed to do something with a boat or at the dock at night. They used it so infrequently, he'd often forgotten it was there.

"Good grief, that's bright." Molly shielded her eyes with her hand.

Grant couldn't have agreed more. He jumped out of his chair, squinting against the light, to look for the off switch. Most of the time the floodlight stayed on manual mode, which allowed it to remain off until they needed it. But when the power was out for extended periods of time, it always reverted to its default setting. Which apparently was to light up the night with the vigor of the sun. "I guess the good news is the electricity's back on."

The bad news was that the light changed everything. Whatever magic had been hovering somewhere between the glow of the candlelight and the twinkling stars had vanished. What had seemed like a cozy dinner spot was now an old dock littered with storm debris and a beat-up card table. And where romance had once been swirling now sat a friend. A friend, he reminded himself, who would disappear from his life in a matter of weeks.

He found the manual switch for the floodlight and cut it off, making a mental note to reprogram the settings later. "Sorry about that." He returned to his seat, letting his eyes adjust to the darkness. "Where were we?"

"Something about your sister's wedding."

"Right." He picked up his fork to finish off his dinner, which didn't seem quite as flavorful as before. "I was saying, for your next adventure, would you care to join me as my non-date plus-one to my sister's wedding? If you're up for it, of course."

A pang of regret stabbed at him, but he disregarded it. It might not have been the question he'd wanted to ask, but it was the right question. Since she was leaving soon, it was safer this way. Less chance for either of them to get hurt. With the limited time they had left, the last thing he wanted to do was ruin the great thing they had going with a bunch of complicated relationship titles.

"If I'm up for it, huh?" Almost instantly, the hesitation he'd seen creep up a moment ago faded away, and her playful grin returned.

"Not that it's much of a decision. For starters, I'll be there, which could be enough enticement on its own. Plus, you'll already know most of the people."

"And there will be cake," Molly added.

"Exactly. And since I helped pick it out, it's guaranteed to be great."

"Cake and your company. How can I say no to that?" she joked.

"You can't." He switched to a more serious tone. "Claire would love for you to be there, and I'd be honored to have you accompany me. What do you say?"

"I'd love to."

Chapter Fourteen

"You're going with him to his sister's wedding, but it's not a date?" Hadley asked as she laid on Molly's bed, watching her get ready for Claire's wedding.

"Yup." Molly held up two dresses. "Which one?"

Hadley examined both and pointed to the one on the left. "That one. The teal color looks great on you, plus that flowy skirt will be fun for a beach wedding."

Molly held up the maxi dress and looked at her reflection in the mirror. This dress with its high neck, low back, and long, flowing skirt had always been one of her favorites. "Good choice." She hung the other dress in her closet and tossed the chosen one on the bed next to Hadley, heading into the bathroom to finish her makeup.

"You'll sit next to him at dinner?"

"Yes."

"And dance with him."

"Yes."

"And co-mingle with all of his family and closest friends?"

Molly brushed mascara on her lashes. “I’m starting to wonder if you understand how weddings work.”

“The wedding bit I got. It’s the friends bit I’m checking on.”

“Friends can’t dance together?” Molly tossed her mascara back in her bag and picked up her brush, working on her hair.

Hadley appeared in the doorway. “I’m sure they can, but they don’t have that look in their eyes.”

“What look?”

“That one you got when you saw your reflection in the mirror and imagined yourself dancing with him in that dress.” Hadley met her gaze, a knowing glint in her eyes.

Guilt pricked at Molly. She immediately pushed it away and distracted herself by searching for bobby pins on the counter. She’d only pictured dancing with him for a second. For the briefest of moments, she’d allowed herself to imagine what a romance with Grant might’ve been like, what could’ve been if things were different, before she’d shut it down. And Hadley had caught that?

“We’re just friends.” Molly wasn’t sure if she was reiterating it for Hadley’s sake or her own. It was the truth, wasn’t it? Was he a great guy she loved spending time with? Absolutely. In fact, in the two weeks since their candlelight conversation, she’d spent a decent chunk of her free time with him doing everything from going on runs on the beach to helping him scrub algae off the bottom of a tank. But that didn’t change anything.

“That’s good.” Hadley selected a tube of lipstick from Molly’s makeup bag and twisted it up to examine the color. "There are definite benefits of being a... what was it you called it again?"

"A non-date plus-one."

"Right. A non-date plus-one." It sounded a lot lamer when Hadley said it.

"That's a thing, you know." Or it should be a thing if it wasn't one already.

Hadley recapped the lipstick and tossed it in the bag, choosing another one. "Sure. All the benefits of having a plus-one without the hassles of a date."

"Exactly. Less pressure on everyone." Feeling slightly more justified in her plan, she stuck a couple of bobby pins in her hair.

"Like, if there's no attraction whatsoever, you don't have to worry about having something stuck in your teeth. Your non-date will have your back." Hadley picked up a third lipstick tube.

"Right. And no need to worry about awkward silence. We can talk, not talk, doesn't matter."

"There's no need to analyze his dance moves and consider if you could really let someone who danced that badly be the father of your children."

Molly paused and glanced at her friend. "Now that's a bad date story I want to hear." They both giggled.

"Girl, you don't even know." Hadley shook her head as if contemplating the absurdity of it all. "I have enough bad-date stories that I could start my own podcast. I'm going to call it *The Chronicles of the Never-Afters.*"

"I have a couple of episodes I could add. Starting with 'The Wedding that Never Was.'"

What a disaster that had been, but now that there was a little space between her and her engagement's demise, she was able to see a few things that she'd missed at the time. The most notable revelation was that she'd never been in love with her ex at all.

That was probably something she should've caught during the first year of their relationship—or even when he'd proposed—but she'd been too busy looking in the wrong direction. She loved the idea of him. He was the exact type of handsome, successful man, committed to living in their small town, whom she'd always dreamed about marrying. And she'd loved what their life could've looked like. Could it get any cuter than husband and wife vets who ran their own neighborhood clinic and drove to work together every morning in matching scrubs with their dogs riding along in the backseat?

But somewhere in the middle of all that, she'd never noticed the most important thing—that she hadn't actually loved him.

Hadley wrapped her arm around Molly's shoulders and gave her a squeeze. "I'm sorry, honey. You deserve so much better."

Molly rested her head on her friend's shoulder. "Thanks. I don't love how it went down, but it all worked out for the best. And now it's time to leave the past in the past and focus on the future."

"Absolutely. Your perfect forever is out there."

"For sure," she agreed. Only, she had no intention of finding him.

The truth was, she didn't trust herself. She'd come dangerously close to marrying a man she hadn't loved because she'd been so blinded by matching scrubs that she couldn't see the truth that'd been sitting in front of her the whole time. Who's to say she wouldn't do it again?

Nope. The only way to make sure she didn't repeat that mistake was to take herself out of the game. From here on out, the biggest commitment she'd be making was as a non-date plus-one.

Hadley let go of her shoulders and picked up the abandoned tube of lipstick. "For the record, I've been at a wedding with Grant before. He's an excellent dancer. There would've been no need to question his moves." She leaned toward the mirror as she applied the lipstick.

"Is that so? You want me to get you his phone number? Because I happen to know he's single," Molly joked.

Hadley rolled her eyes. "Just remember that a non-date plus-one doesn't mean you can't enjoy yourself. Have fun."

Molly grinned as excitement pulsed through her. Regardless of what she wanted to call it, she always loved spending time with Grant, no matter what they were doing. "I'm sure that can be arranged."

Grant bounced on his toes as he stood under the porte cochere of Seashell Inn. There was so much anticipation in the air that the day seemed electric, and the one person he wanted to share it with was Molly. He'd been waiting for her all day, and now, according to her text, his wait was almost over. She was due to pull up any minute.

If he really stopped and thought about it, he'd been waiting for Molly his whole life. He'd seen great examples of beautiful couples, like his parents and his aunt and uncle, that defined what real love looked like. They laughed together, had fun together, conquered life's problems together. They didn't just stand side by side, they had each other's backs. Always.

Of course he wanted that. Who didn't? But after a few failed attempts, he'd been starting to wonder if maybe that kind of relationship didn't exist for everyone. Maybe, like Mateo said, he was looking for a unicorn.

And then Molly had shown up.

She'd only been around for a couple of months, but she'd quickly become his first person. If he had good news, she was the first person he wanted to tell. If there was an adventure waiting, she was the first person he wanted to come with him. And if she was doing something great, he wanted to be the first person to cheer her on. He wasn't ready to call that love. At least not yet. Love seemed much too big and much too scary. Maybe a better description would be allure. He'd even go so far as to say like. He liked Molly.

Her black SUV pulled into the drive, and a wide grin spread across his face. It seemed to be automatic anytime she stepped into the room lately, and he was powerless to do anything about it. He was going to have to come to grips with the fact that if Molly was around, he was one of those guys who had a big, permanent goofy grin.

The valet walked to the driver side and opened her door. They traded spots, and Grant waited for the car to move out of the way to be able to see her. After what seemed like forever, the valet shifted the SUV into gear and slowly pulled forward, like the big reveal on one of those home-makeover shows, until he could finally see Molly standing on the other side.

He'd heard of people being described as breathtaking before, but never had he had his breath taken away by someone until now.

She was stunning.

He didn't know anything about hairstyles, but he knew the way hers was pulled up showed off her sparkling sapphire eyes. And he couldn't tell you the style of her dress, but he could tell you it was the same color as the deep ocean and the long skirt billowed in the coastal breeze like a wispy cloud on a clear summer day. It was as if he was looking at a vision from a dream, and a powerful, all-consuming feeling swirled inside him.

"Wow." He was aware it was a clichéd response, but uttering it was a completely involuntary reaction. He hadn't realized, probably because it'd never happened before, that being rendered breathless also left you speechless.

Molly grinned as she crossed the driveway toward him. "Wow, yourself. You clean up nicely."

He glanced down at his tux. "I was going to wear shorts, but since they were all dirty, I figured this would have to do." He shrugged. "Guess I need to stay on top of the laundry situation."

She laughed. He loved her laugh. It was as if joy had become tangible, and he found himself wanting to be the one who made her laugh more often.

"You look gorgeous, by the way."

Pink tinged her cheeks, but she still held his gaze. "Thanks."

"Also, before we head in there, I have some news to tell you."

"What?"

"I got the job."

Molly's eyes widened with delight. "You did?"

He nodded as the excitement he'd tried to keep contained all day bubbled to the surface. "Dr. Ford called this morning to officially offer it to me. He said the board didn't hesitate with their decision and I can pick up my doctoral studies right where I left off. The job's mine if I want it."

"That's fabulous!" She threw her arms around his neck. Her touch was like the cherry on top of an excellent day. It filtered through him, intensifying his already jubilant emotions.

He wrapped his arms around her waist and, picking her up, spun her around. Her flowy dress flared around them as they twirled, and the only thing Grant could think was how right she felt in his arms. How right it felt to be here, with her.

He set her on the ground, trying to refocus on the conversation at hand.

"Did you accept? Have you told your sister yet? When do you start? What did Mateo say?" She peppered him with a round of questions, hardly taking a breath in between.

Grant held up his hands to slow her down, although her enthusiasm was contagious. "Slow down, Speed Racer. One question at a time."

She drew in a deep breath, making a display of calming herself, but her smile still stretched from ear to ear. "Okay, one question at a time, starting with, what happens now?"

Grant glanced at the entrance of the boutique hotel. "Right now, we have a few other non-job-related things going on."

"Oh, right. How're the wedding day festivities going?"

"I'm about to walk my baby sister down the aisle to marry some man. I gotta say, I'm a little more emotional than I thought I'd be."

"Not some man." Molly linked her arm through his and started walking toward the entrance. "Lance is a great guy and they both seem very happy. But I get the emotion."

He knew she'd get it. She got him. And now that he had her support to lean on, the underlying sadness he'd managed to keep tucked behind all of the other intense emotions floated to the surface. He stopped in front of the doors and stared at them. "I keep thinking I wish my parents were here to see this. My mom would've loved it." Tears stung his eyes.

"I bet."

She pulled closer to him and rested her head on his shoulder. They stood there, just outside the doors, in a comfortable silence for several moments as the surging emotions played through him. Once again, he kept coming back to the fact that out of all the people here, out of all the people in his life, Molly was the first person, the main person, he wanted by his side to walk through this today.

Finally, he drew in a cleansing breath and wiped his eyes. "To be clear, those will likely not be the last tears I shed today."

"Lucky for you, I packed extra tissues in my clutch." Molly gave him a squeeze.

Like he said, she got him.

His confidence returning, he opened the hotel door. "You want to come say hi to Claire before the ceremony?"

"I'd love to."

With her hand still tucked in the crook of his arm,

he took the final step over the threshold and into the place where his sister would be married. They walked through the hotel to the guest room Claire was using to get ready. He knocked on the door then used his keycard to open it.

Claire, dressed in her wedding gown, stood in front of the full-length mirror on the opposite side of the room. Even though he'd seen her multiple times today, it was still a surreal experience to look at his baby sister dressed in a wedding gown. She was the one he'd given piggyback rides to. The one who couldn't say "spaghetti" right. The one he'd have to help find Mr. Panda so she could go to sleep. When had she turned into this beautiful, amazing adult? He had to blink back the fresh wave of emotion that stung his eyes.

"Look who I found lurking around the parking lot."

Claire's face lit up when she saw Molly's reflection in the mirror. "Molly!"

Molly let go of him and crossed the room to his sister and hugged her. "You are radiant," she gushed. She stepped out of the hug and admired the dress. Claire spun to show it off. "You're right. I can't even tell where the seams were. The seamstress did a fantastic job. Did she sew all these beads on by hand?"

He watched as the two women discussed the dress and the shoes, the flowers in Claire's hair, and giggled about wedding stuff. Other bridesmaids joined in the conversation until the room was full of happy chatter and laughter. And Molly was in the middle of it, as if she'd always belonged there.

As if she belonged here with him.

The wedding coordinator knocked on the door and

stuck her head inside. “About ten minutes, and we'll head down.”

“Oh, gosh. Already?” For the first time today, he saw a flicker of doubt flash across Claire's face.

Molly must have seen it too, because she grabbed both of Claire's hands and stared into her eyes. “You look amazing, everything is in place, and you're ready for this. Time to say those ‘I dos.’”

Claire beamed. “You're right. Regardless of what else happens today, at the end of the night I'll be married to my best friend.”

“Exactly. And I'd better skedaddle so I don't miss it.” She turned to him.

“Can I walk you down?” Grant offered her his elbow.

“Please.” Once again, she slipped her hand into the crook of his arm.

He turned to his sister over his shoulder. “I'll be back in a flash.” And they headed out the door. “Thanks for that.”

“For what?”

“Stopping by, encouraging my sister, being here. Take your pick.” They started down the stairs that led to the main level. More guests were walking in, and he could see through the window that the chairs set up outside were almost full.

“There's nowhere else I'd rather be.”

“That's good, because I'm about to parade you all the way down the aisle to sit on the front row.”

She cocked an eyebrow. “The family row?”

“Yep. But since I'll be the only one on that row, I was hoping you'd join me so I don't have to sit alone. Do you mind?”

“Not at all. In fact, I'd be honored.” She tucked a

stray piece of hair behind her ear. "But I should've gone down earlier. You realize everyone will be looking at me as we walk all the way down the aisle, right?"

"In that dress, everyone would've been looking at you anyway." He waggled his eyebrows and pushed the door to the outside ceremony area.

Yup, it was official. She was his first person. And since big changes were on the horizon, he had a feeling things were about to get complicated.

Chapter Fifteen

MOLLY HAD BEEN NERVOUS ABOUT coming to the wedding, which had nothing to do with Grant. In fact, probably the opposite was true. He'd become one of the people she most wanted to spend time with, even more than Hope or the baby turtles, which was saying a lot.

She'd been nervous about tonight's event because she'd thought being at a wedding would be tough. This was the first time she'd sat through someone else's nuptials since she'd canceled her own. It had potential to trigger some wounds.

"Well, look who it is. The Mollster's holding down the front row." Mateo slid into the second row among other people Molly knew to be Grant's cousins. He held his fist out for a knuckle bump.

"I heard they were seating people according to how fabulous they were and naturally assumed this row was reserved for me." She tapped her fist against his.

Mateo chuckled as he settled into the chair directly behind her. "You're here with Grant?"

She nodded. "He's up with Claire."

"Right." A look flashed across his face, which she

didn't quite know how to interpret. Curiosity with a hint of concern, maybe? Or perhaps it was the other way around. Either way, it vanished almost as soon as it appeared, and she dismissed it. "Just make sure you stay down in front. I don't want anyone obstructing my view of my favorite cousin getting hitched," he teased.

"I'll do my best but I make no promises."

The music changed, and Molly turned her attention to the back of the ceremony space. Lance stepped in the aisle, escorting his mother. She watched as he kissed his mom and joined his groomsmen in the front, then turned her attention to the procession of bridesmaids.

The music changed again, and the guests stood. A collective gasp rose as Claire stepped up to the end of the aisle, escorted by her brother. She was glowing, the perfect picture of a bride in love. Molly's hand flew to her heart and unshed tears pricked her eyes as she took in the elation that filled the air.

And that was the moment Molly realized two very important things.

First, and probably most important, celebrating someone else's happiness was always a joyous occasion. It didn't matter that her own attempt at happily-ever-after had ended in a dumpster fire. Today, love won. Today, Claire got to say "I do" to the one her heart desired, and Molly got the great privilege of witnessing it. It was a truly happy occasion worth celebrating, and the wounds from her past, no matter how deep they cut, didn't stand in the way of her wholeheartedly rejoicing with them. In fact, she was pretty sure she could feel part of her heart healing as the sounds of the wedding march filled the air.

Which brought her to her second realization.

While calling off her wedding and breaking up with her fiancé had left her heart shattered in a thousand pieces, her time in Emerald Cove had started to put it back together. It was a phenomenon she hadn't expected. In fact, if she was being totally honest, she hadn't been sure it was even possible.

Of course, she hadn't expected to find in Emerald Cove what she had. She'd found friends who were honest and real, a job that was rewarding and fun, a mission with the turtles that was life-giving to all who were involved...

And Grant.

The pair started down the aisle, and Molly's gaze shifted to Grant. Seriously, it should be illegal to look that good in a tux. It wasn't that it was perfectly fitted, although clearly the tailor in Emerald Cove was just this side of a magician. Most of what made Grant irresistible was the way he wore it—with confidence and charm and kindness.

The fact that she found him irresistible was a whole conversation for another day. Non-date plus-ones who were zoned for the friend category were not supposed to be irresistible, even if they had played an important role in her heart-mending process. Her heart needed to get on board with what her head had already decided before this got out of control, but she didn't want to ruin this beautiful moment with that sort of stern self-talking-to.

They made it to the front and stopped next to Lance. Instead of the usual kiss on the cheek, Grant shook his sister's hand, both of them looking serious and formal. But right before their hands should've broken, mischievous grins spread across their faces.

Still holding right hands, they grasped each other's left hand, doing two over-exaggerated shakes. They let go, their arms windmilling over their head. Both jumped around so they were back-to-back. In a choreographed moved, they wiggled their hips with their hands in the air, first to the right and then to the left. They hopped around to give each other double high-fives and ended with a hip bump.

Laughter drifted up from the guests at the fun brother-sister display. As soon as the handshake routine was over, Grant engulfed his sister in a giant, protective bear hug. He whispered something in her ear, turned to shake Lance's hand, and stepped out from in between them.

Molly could see tears glistening in his eyes as he made his way over to take his seat next to her. "Well done, big brother," she whispered, rubbing his back.

He swiped at his eyes. "I'm not crying, you're crying."

She quietly chuckled and pulled a tissue from the pack in her clutch, handing it to him. "How about we cry together?"

He let out a soft sigh, beaming with pride. "They make a beautiful couple. It's a happy day," he whispered.

"Yes, it is." She slipped her arm through his and settled in to watch the start of their promise of forever.

His sister was married. It was a weird thought. Sure, he was happy for them. Claire and Lance had the kind of relationship that reminded him of their parents', but it was still weird. His baby sister was now someone's wife.

"I think that does it for the family photos," the photographer announced after what felt like a thousand shots with every different combination of people imaginable. "Everyone but the bride and groom are free to go."

Unbuttoning his jacket, he stepped away from the group and made his way to where Molly was waiting. "My jaw is officially sore from all the smiling." He rubbed his hand along his jawline.

"One day you'll be glad to have the photos that captured these moments." Molly handed him one of the glasses of champagne she was holding.

"Lucky for me, we took so many, I'll be able to choose the exact moment I want to remember."

They walked over to the split-rail fence that ran along the edge of the bluff to watch Claire, Lance, and the photographer make their way down the long wooden staircase to the beach below for more pictures. The crowd of family members who'd hung around the ceremony space for the photo shoot started to dissipate as most people headed for the pool area, where the cocktail hour and reception were located. Before long, Molly and Grant were left standing there alone.

It was a beautiful summer evening. The soft light from the low-slung sun made the colors of nature more vibrant. The rich green of the grass they were standing on, the vivid blue of the sky, the jewel-like teal of the water, the pure white of the sand. This view, the view of home, had always resonated with him, but tonight it seemed even more impactful.

"While there's a break in your official brotherly duties, I wanted to take the moment to propose a toast."

"Smiling that much is hard on the cheek muscles, but I'm not sure it's toast-worthy."

Molly didn't even dignify the joke with a laugh. "I'm sure Claire is exceedingly grateful for your sacrifice. But this isn't wedding-related."

Her gaze swept through him like a breeze, filling him with an odd combination of exuberance mixed with peace. It was that feeling of knowing he was exactly where he wanted to be. "So, what non-wedding related topic are we toasting?"

"You," she said simply, holding up her glass.

"Me?"

"Well, not just you. To your new job."

"I told you I haven't accepted it yet, right?"

She waved a dismissive hand in the air. "Details. What we're toasting tonight is the pursuit of your dream, and that the board of directors decided what the rest of us already knew, that you're amazing and talented and anyone would be lucky to have you as the director of their team."

"That's a really long sentence."

She shot him a warning look. "Are you going to take the compliment or not?"

He bowed slightly as a sort of apology. "Please continue."

"As I was saying..." She drawled the last word out with an exaggerated eyeroll. Then she held her glass up and switched to an authentic tone. "I'm really proud of you, Grant. Congrats."

He clinked his glass against hers and a mixed bag of emotions filtered through him. "Thanks." He took a sip of the sparkling champagne and turned, looking out toward the water, where Claire and Lance were still taking pictures. "I didn't realize how much I wanted it until they called to offer it to me." He got quiet for a moment, thinking through what getting the job actually meant. There were so many questions about taking the position, and he'd charged forward under the presumption that when the time came, the answer would be clear.

Well, the time was here, and the answer was still as hazy as the day he'd first found out about the job.

"If it's her you're worried about, you don't have to be," Molly said gently. "She's got it all under control."

He watched his sister, splashing in the surf with her new husband. She'd been just a kid when he'd come home, but she wasn't a kid any more. She'd grown into a beautiful, talented, responsible woman. "I know."

"And between her and Mateo, Turtle Rehab is in great hands. They won't have you, which will be different, but they'll be fine."

They'd probably be more than fine. Mateo had great ideas and strong leadership, and Claire was the heart and soul of the place, much as their mother had been. "They'll both be great."

"Then there's nothing standing in your way." Molly's cheerful voice had a note of decisiveness in it.

He propped his arm on the rail, turning to her. She was beautiful. Not just in a pretty way that one might notice when passing a stranger on the street, although she was very much that too. But Molly was the whole package who personified beauty in every definition of the word, and her presence consistently took his breath away. "I guess not."

Although, that wasn't entirely true. The biggest thing standing in his way was right in front of him.

The day he'd found out about this position, she hadn't been anywhere on his radar, and now he couldn't consider the job without considering her. The problem he kept coming up against was he wasn't quite sure what to consider. He didn't know how to define whatever this was between them, but he knew he wasn't ready to let her go. And with both of them getting ready to leave, he wasn't sure where that left him. Or where that left them.

"I know it's not an easy choice. It takes courage to go after what you want. But I'm proud of you for not backing down."

Courage. That word kept tumbling through his mind for the rest of cocktail hour and into dinner. Courage wasn't something he'd ever thought of himself lacking. He was willing to sail to the ends of the earth and dive to the bottom of the sea. He wasn't afraid to blaze new trails or summit new mountains. But when it came to relationships, did he have the courage it took?

It wasn't until Molly was out on the dance floor

with Claire and some of the other women that the topic resurfaced.

He sat next to Mateo at the empty table, watching the action on the dance floor.

"You hear anything about the job yet?" Mateo asked.

Grant eyed his cousin. "Are you asking out of curiosity, or because you know something?"

Mateo crossed his arms over his chest and settled in his chair. "I might've heard the board was making a decision today."

"And?" Grant egged him on.

Mateo shrugged. "All I know is that a decision was forthcoming." He shot a knowing look at Grant. "And I wondered if it forth-came to you."

Grant refocused his attention on the dance floor. He'd wanted to tell Claire before the rest of the world knew, but that didn't seem to be in the cards. Even if he played coy with Mateo, one call to his sources was all it would take for him to find out the truth. "As a matter of fact, I got the call this morning."

"You're in?" There was an excitement in his voice that could only be found in a true best friend who felt Grant's successes like his own.

"I'm in."

Mateo slapped him on the back, becoming his normal, fully animated self. "That's great news."

"Yeah." His gaze flickered to Molly.

Mateo's eyes narrowed and he studied Grant. "You sound rather subdued for a man who got what he's waited seven years for." That was the problem with best friends. They celebrated your successes like they were their own, but they also knew when you were lying to them.

"I'm excited. It's just complicated."

Mateo looked out at the dance floor too. "Claire? We talked about this before. She's not a kid anymore. She's probably more equipped than either of us to run that place."

"I know, it's…"

"Molly?"

He watched her bobbing in the middle of the dance floor among his sister and all her friends. "I'm just trying to figure out where she fits in all this."

Mateo studied him with the sort of serious expression of a psychologist during a session. "Where does she think she fits?"

Grant shifted in his seat. This line of questions was starting to venture out of his comfort zone. "We haven't exactly talked about that."

"Where do you want her to fit?"

And with that, they had officially catapulted past any question he felt like answering. At least not on a night as perfect as this one. Grant shot his cousin a look. "Am I paying for this session? Should we find a couch for me to lay on?"

Mateo held up his hands innocently. "Can I help it if I'm trying to kick your sorry keister out of this place to greener pastures?" he joked.

Grant chuckled, letting go of some of his tension with it. "Fair enough, but the only place this keister is going tonight is to the dance floor." He pushed his chair away from the table as the music switched to a slower song. "Excuse me."

He wove his way through the tables, deliberately

avoiding anyone who might try to stop him, until he got to Molly.

He extended his hand, that automatic goofy smile returning to his already tired cheek muscles. “May I have this dance?”

She placed her hand in his. “I thought you’d never ask.”

He spun her once and pulled her into him. The rest of the world, along with all the problems and internal debates, faded away as they glided around the wooden floor under the café lights strung overhead.

Having her in his arms felt right. It felt like here, with her, was where he belonged.

“Hadley was right about you,” Molly said.

Grant raised an eyebrow. “You and Hadley talk about me?”

“Consider it your vetting process. I have to know what I’m signing up for, after all.” She glanced up at him from under her lashes with a sort of flirty sass that sent heat racing through him.

“Fair enough.” He spun her again. “And what valuable information did you find out from your official source?”

He pulled her in, and she rested her hand on his shoulder, standing closer to him this time. “That you’re a great dancer.”

He placed his hand on the middle of her back and, holding her close, he stepped around and around, spinning together, making the world blur around them. “You had doubts?”

“Simply making sure I wore the right shoes.”

He slowed their spin, putting them on the far edge of the dance floor. “And? Did I live up to the hype?”

She gazed into his eyes as they glided in perfect rhythm not just with the music, but with each other. "Exceedingly."

It might've only been one word, but it was all he needed. Right then, in the blurred light of the dance floor, everything became crystal clear.

Chapter Sixteen

EXCEEDINGLY. IT WAS THE FIRST word that popped into her mind any time Molly thought about Grant. He was exceedingly gifted at working with the turtles, exceedingly intelligent, exceedingly fun to be around, exceedingly kind.

This wasn't supposed to happen. He was supposed to be a colleague. When it was clear their relationship had slipped right past being professional, she'd been willing to settle for a friend. She'd even go so far as to say he was a good friend. But he was never meant to be *exceedingly*.

Although right here, in his arms on the dance floor as reality swirled around her, "exceedingly" was the only word that fit.

"You know, my mom always told me the key to being a good dancer isn't mastering the moves." His eyes locked with hers. "It's finding the ideal partner." There was a huskiness in his voice that swept through her, taking her breath with it. As if proving his point, he once again held her close as they twirled in tight circles, their feet making the steps in perfect unison.

Molly was pretty sure there was still music playing and she felt certain other people were still on the dance floor, but all of that had fallen away. At the moment, the only person in her existence was Grant. Her heart thumped in her chest as she focused on his warm, brown eyes. "Is that so?"

He gave a slight shrug, his charming half grin pulling at the corner of his mouth. "Well, my mom said it, so it must be true."

Man, she loved his grin. "In that case, what you're saying is it's my dance moves that are ideal."

"No." His playful tone fell away, replaced with one full of passion. He let go of her hand and his thumb caressed her cheek. Even though they'd stopped spinning, the world still twirled around them. She felt effervescent, as if everything inside her was sparkling. It was quite possible that she was sparkling on the outside too, although she wasn't sure. At the moment, she wasn't sure about anything except the magnetic pull between her and the man who held her in his arms. "What I'm saying," he continued, his adoring gaze fixed on her, "is that you, Molly Lawrence, are ideal."

The words swirled around her before they settled in her chest, setting off a mini explosion that sent tingles racing through her body. She might've been engaged before, but Molly knew for a fact that she'd never felt like this.

The music stopped, but the magnetic force pulled her closer to Grant. She was acutely aware of his touch, the way his thumb gently skimmed the surface of her cheek and how his hand felt on her back. He leaned closer, and she closed her eyes, anticipating his lips meeting hers. She honestly had never considered kissing him until right this moment, but now she couldn't think of anything she'd rather do. Or why she'd waited so long to do it.

"Ahem." The sound of someone clearing her throat broke the trance, and Molly's eyes popped open. She stood there, still in Grant's embrace, as whatever world they'd been in fell away and reality reemerged around them.

Grant's face, which was only inches from hers, turned to the wedding coordinator, who was standing several feet away, her eyes looking anywhere but at them.

"Excuse me, Mr. Torres. It's, uh, time for the brother-sister dance. We need you at the front when you're, um, ready."

Grant nodded once, his face lit up with the guilty grin of a school boy. "I'll be right there." Laughter danced in his eyes, and he pulled a face that was a combination of oops and amusement. Molly giggled. It'd been a long time since she'd been caught in an almost-kiss, and somehow it made her feel even closer to him. "I guess I gotta go. But hold that thought. We can finish this conversation later." The unmistakable note of disappointment in his voice matched the yearning that tugged on her chest.

He brushed a gentle kiss across her forehead, which was a painfully lacking consolation prize for what she'd been anticipating. Reluctantly, she dropped her hands to her side, and he took a step back.

She watched him make his way to the front as

she drew in a deep breath, trying to calm the fluttery emotions that were doing a conga line through her.

She had almost kissed Grant Torres.

The thought wasn't quite as shocking as the fact that she still wanted to kiss Grant Torres. And she wanted that kiss to be the beginning of something special. What was happening here?

She'd spent the last two months fighting it, but the truth was, the draw between them was undeniable. He had captivated her from the very first time he'd walked into her clinic, and for good reason. The man was incredible on so many different levels. But where did that leave them? She slowly strolled to the edge of the dance floor, contemplating it.

Like she'd said before, this wasn't supposed to happen. She came here with the specific purpose of not making connections. She certainly wasn't supposed to fall in love—not that what was happening here was love. This was far from being the L-word.

But, hypothetically speaking, if she was willing to give love another try, Grant would be the kind of guy she'd be looking for. He was smart, funny, compassionate, and caring, not to mention easy on the eyes. He encouraged her in ways she'd never thought possible, gave her the confidence to become the person she wanted to be, the person she'd somehow lost along the way.

Of course, she wasn't ready to go anywhere near forever, but she was no longer willing to settle for this undefined thing they had going on now. She wanted something more than a simple friendship. She wanted a them.

Yes, she was fully aware it got a bit complicated

because they were both about to leave, but that was only logistics. They could figure it out. A weekend here, a couple days there. The fact they'd be keeping it casual with no long-term commitments would help with the long-distance thing.

She accepted a glass of champagne from a passing waiter for the toast that would follow the dance and watched Grant chat with Claire as they waited for the band to start their song. It felt as if she were floating, which was different than how she'd expected to feel tonight. In fact, her whole experience in Emerald Cove had been different than what she'd expected when she'd pulled into town. But it was a good different. The kind of different that made the future seem bright for the first time in a long time.

"You ready for the big performance?" Mateo stepped up to her, holding his own champagne. "I hear they've been working on this dance. Should be entertaining."

"Is it anything like the handshake?"

"That handshake was one hundred percent authentic. They've been doing it since they were kids." He held his drink out in the direction of the dance floor in a gesture to the dance. "This is a new routine. I caught them practicing in the vet suite when no one was there, but got shooed out before I could see any of it."

"So that's what y'all use the vet suite for when I'm not there."

"You didn't know it doubled as a dance studio?" Mateo joked.

Molly sipped her drink and they stood there for a

second in a somewhat awkward silence as they both stared at the dance floor in front of them.

"I hear Grant got the research director position at the university," Mateo said, breaking the silence.

A fresh round of excitement fluttered through Molly. "I know. He's going to be awesome at it."

"He was made for the position," Mateo agreed. "I only hope he can get over all his hesitations that are holding him back."

Molly waved a dismissive hand in the air. "He's worried about walking away from Turtle Rehab and you guys, but he knows you have things under control."

He pulled his gaze away from the action on the dance floor and looked at her. She wouldn't have necessarily classified it as accusatory, but it was significantly south of friendly. "I don't think Claire and I are the only ones he's worried about leaving."

The comment stung a bit, stealing some of her bubbly joy. "Who, me?" Molly pressed her hand against her chest as she tried to figure out why Grant would turn down the job because of her. "I'm leaving Emerald Cove too. There'd be no reason for him to stick around for me."

Mateo slowly nodded, as if considering that information. "What happens when you leave? Between the two of you, I mean."

Heat flared in her cheeks, which she wanted to blame on anger, but she had a feeling it was more closely related to embarrassment. His best friend, his number-one wingman, was questioning her about her intentions. Suddenly the answer she'd thought was perfect a moment ago didn't seem good enough. She swallowed hard. "He's become a really good friend. Someone who's special to me. I don't see that changing."

Mateo's eyes narrowed like a detective evaluating the suspect's interrogation. "A friend, huh?"

Clearly that was the wrong answer, but she didn't know what else to tell him. She didn't think calling him her non-date plus-one was going to help her case. "It might get more complicated when we're both in different places, but we'll figure it out. That's the benefit of keeping things casual."

"And what if he's not looking for casual?"

In theory, she loved the idea of the best friend making sure the love interest was worthy. Everyone deserved someone who had their back like that. In reality, though, she wasn't sure she liked being the one answering all the questions. Especially when she knew those answers didn't measure up. "We're just friends, Mateo. Casual is the only option there is." There was an edge of annoyance to her voice, but she didn't care. For starters, Grant had only found out a few hours ago that he'd gotten the job. It was perfectly reasonable for them to not have the answers yet. They would get to that part if people would stop interrupting them.

But there was also the possibility that Mateo's truthful words had struck a nerve. Casual was all Molly had to offer. Forever was not an option for her. If that wasn't what Grant was looking for...

"The thing is," Mateo continued, his gaze back on the dance floor, "Grant has a big heart. For better or for worse, the guy goes all in or not at all. He's gotten his heart broken a few times because of it."

And suddenly, Molly realized what was happening here. Mateo wasn't asking Molly questions to get to the truth. He was asking questions so Molly would get to the truth. "It's not like… I mean, we're not…" She fumbled over the words, looking for some way to justify her side, but she couldn't find any. Mateo was right, and she knew it.

"He's put his own life on hold to help everyone else. And now that he's getting a shot at living his dream, I'd hate to see him jeopardize it because he's holding out for something that doesn't exist."

Molly watched Grant perform the goofy dance next to his sister, a broad, joyful smile lighting up his handsome face, and what was left of the effervescent sparkles drained out of her. "I'd hate to see that as well," she said quietly.

In other words, Mateo was telling her she had a choice to make. When it came to Grant, she either needed to go all in…

Or she needed to walk away before someone got hurt.

Chapter Seventeen

THE FIRST THING GRANT WANTED to do after finishing his brotherly dancing and toasting duties was find Molly. Now that he knew how he felt about her and what he wanted their relationship to look like, he didn't want to waste any time not being around her. Plus, if he was reading the signals right, she was feeling the same way.

"What did you think of my toast?" he asked her. "Perfect combination of heart and humor, right?" She wasn't holding her glass up, but he clinked his against it anyway. "I hate to brag, but I pretty much nailed it."

He was energized. The day had been a complete success. The wedding had been great, Claire was happy, Molly was amazing, he'd gotten the job he wanted, and he was in love. Fine, maybe "love" was a bit bold, but he was solidly in like and cruising in that direction.

"It was great." She flashed one of her dazzling grins, but the gesture didn't come anywhere close to reaching her eyes.

Concern crept in, causing his euphoric wave to mellow. “Are you okay?”

She waited a beat before answering. “Of course.”

It might’ve been a positive answer, but something was off. He searched her eyes for a moment, looking for any sign of what could be bothering her.

The concern must’ve been evident on his face because she laid a hand on his forearm and her voice softened a bit. “I’m fine. I just have a headache.”

“You want to take a walk? Maybe a stroll on the beach will help.” Plus, there was something he wanted to tell her and he’d rather do it where there wasn’t the chance of getting interrupted again.

She visibly relaxed. “That sounds nice.”

They set their glasses on a nearby table and headed down the serpentine, torch-lit path that ran along the edge of the property. They strolled a bit until they got to the long wooden staircase that led from the bluff to the beach. The brightness of the twinkle lights began to dissipate as they descended the steps, and the music from the band faded into the sounds of the waves washing up on the beach.

“I don’t think you could ask for a more beautiful night,” Molly said as she sank down on the bottom step and started to unbuckle the ankle straps of her stiletto sandals.

Grant looked out over the water. A perfect half-moon hung in the velvet sky, and its reflection danced on the ocean’s surface. “I’m pretty sure we paid for that as part of the deposit.”

She chuckled, and part of his good mood returned—not quite to the level it had been during their dance, but it was close. Most of that was because being with her, especially on the beach, felt right. It felt like where he belonged.

With both sandals hanging from her finger, she stepped off the final step. They walked across the soft sand to the spot just above where the waves rolled to a stop.

"I'm going to miss this when I'm gone. Way more than I thought I would." She wiggled her toes in the sand.

"There are very few things that beat standing at the edge of the ocean."

"Is one of them standing on the deck of your boat in the middle of it?"

"On a clear day? Absolutely." And the other was standing next to her, wherever next to her took him.

He knew things were changing. That part didn't bother him. He actually liked change. It might've been a product of his love for the sea, where the only constant was there was change. It kept things new and exciting.

It didn't even bother him that those changes included putting distance between them. Relationships were like sailing. The wind kept shifting, but as long as you adjusted the sail, you would get to where you were going. Was he going to miss her not stopping by his facility on a daily basis or working with her? Sure. But part of the adventure would be figuring out what the next chapter looked like.

The thing he found slightly worrisome was that he didn't know exactly where they stood. Up until now, it hadn't been a problem. They'd been enough on the same page that there wasn't anything that needed to be said. Status quo had been working for them.

But status quo was about to shift. For the first time in whatever this thing between them was, they were going to have to talk about where it was going. And that was where he started to run into a problem. Feeling, he was pretty good at. Talking about feelings? Not so much.

He dug his toe in the sand, searching for the right words to breech the subject. “So listen, about—”

“Are you going to take the job?” she jumped in over him.

He paused, taken aback by the conversation switch. “The job?” He shrugged. “Probably.”

“What would stop you?”

Hadn’t they already talked about this? At length? “I don’t know. I guess I’m taking a moment to make sure it’s right. You know, ‘fools rush in’ and all that.”

She snagged her lip with her teeth. “That’s smart.”

“Plus, I feel like I should at least tell Claire about it before I accept it. She deserves to give her blessing before I start filling out the change-of-address forms.”

Molly raised an eyebrow. “Do you really need a change-of-address form when your address itself goes wherever you go?”

The tension that’d been hanging in the air between them started to ease, giving him more confidence. “Valid point.” He relaxed. “Why the sudden interest in my job decision?”

“I want to see you live out your dream.” She pulled her gaze away from the water and focused on him. There was something about the way she looked at him that felt like she could see all the way into his soul, confirming everything he wanted to tell her. “You deserve this.”

"About that..." He cleared his throat, once again searching for the right words to bring up the conversation he'd tried earlier. Really, it shouldn't be this hard to find the words for what he needed to say. In fact, three popular ones came to mind. "There's something I've been wanting to talk to you about." So it wasn't the most romantic start, but it was a start, which he counted as a win. "It has to do with the, uh, dance."

She gathered her wind-blown hair into a sort of ponytail and draped it over her shoulder. "I say we blame it on the wedding. All that lovey-dovey romance starts to cast a spell after a while."

"There certainly was something in the air." He wasn't sure he wanted to call it love yet, but he was definitely hoping that was the final destination. "The thing is, Molly..."

I like you. I might be falling in love with you. I'm pretty sure I want to spend the rest of my life with you. There were a thousand choices of how he could finish that sentence. Why couldn't he get one out?

Molly didn't wait on him to find the right words. Instead, she placed her hand gently on the center of his chest. "I hate to do this, but this headache is getting the better of me. Would you mind if we finished this conversation later? I think I'm going to slip out early."

Once again, the sudden turn of the conversation caught him off guard, and it took him a second to get his bearings before he could answer. "Absolutely. Are you okay?" He wrapped his hand around hers, holding it against his heart. Disappointment comingled with concern.

She offered him a weak smile. "It's nothing a little rest won't cure."

"Of course." The elation of the night seeped out of him. He let go of her hand and shoved his own hands in his pockets, taking a step back. This wasn't at all how he'd seen this conversation going, but he knew as well as anyone that life didn't always go according to plan. Reluctantly, he tucked away his confession for another time. "Can I drive you home?"

She shook her head. "No, thanks. You should stay. Enjoy the rest of the party."

A dull ache started to rise up deep in his chest. Yes, it was just a conversation, but there was something about this moment that he hated to let pass. "Right. I'll catch up with you tomorrow." Besides, there were still things that needed to be said.

"For sure." She stared at her toes in the sand for a long moment as the waves rolled in and out. Finally, she looked up into his eyes. "For the record, I really enjoyed tonight."

"Enjoy" wasn't nearly strong enough to describe the way he'd felt about the evening. Maybe it didn't end the way he'd wanted, but he wouldn't have traded the rest of it for the world. "Me too."

She turned and headed for the stairs, slowly trudging through the warm sand.

"Molly," he called. She paused on the bottom step and turned back to him, her beautiful features lit by the soft moonlight. "I hope you feel better."

"Thanks."

He could've sworn a hint of sadness flickered under her smile, but he dismissed it. He was probably projecting his own disappointment. Tomorrow. They'd have this talk again tomorrow, when she was feeling better and all would be right with the world again.

"A headache?" Hadley asked the next morning as she, Molly, and Ellyn walked down the sidewalk to Ellyn's art studio to help her set up for the kids' painting class that afternoon.

"Yes. A throbbing one right behind my eyes." She massaged her temples for emphasis.

"And you left him there? On the beach?" Ellyn asked, taking as sip of one of Hadley's coffee creations from her travel mug.

"I mean, technically he was still standing on the beach when I walked away, but it's not like I deserted him. He went back to the party." At least, she assumed that's what he'd done. She hadn't dared look back. She hadn't trusted herself to keep going if she looked into his eyes even one more time. And she'd needed to go.

She took a sip of her own coffee, savoring the energizing velvety mocha. Coffee wasn't going to solve all her problems, but it sure wasn't going to hurt.

"But the rest of the wedding, the pre-headache part, was good?" Ellyn asked.

"It was really lovely. Claire was a glowing bride, and it was the perfect evening."

A better description of the night would've been "magical," but she kept that word to herself. She didn't want to think about how enchanting it had felt to be held in his arms or how the air around them had seemed to sparkle with wonder, and she certainly didn't want to try to explain it to anyone else.

"But did you dance with him?" Hadley shot her a knowing side-glance.

The same sparkles from last night rained through her like a tickertape parade at the mere mention of the dance, but she worked to keep her face neutral. "It was a wedding, wasn't it?" She took a sip of her coffee and pretended not to notice the look Hadley and Ellyn exchanged across her.

"That sounds like a story we need to hear," Ellyn said.

"Nope. There's no story." At least, not one they needed to hear, and certainly not one she wanted to tell. "We shared one dance. A single spin around the floor. That was it." She held up one finger in case they needed more clarification.

Of course, that dance had been enough to change everything.

In the course of one song, everything had shifted. Suddenly, as they'd spun in time to the music, she'd realized she didn't want to be friends with Grant. She wanted so, so much more.

She wanted to be his someone. She wanted to be the one who was there for the big moments. And the small moments. And all the moments in between.

And, for the love of all things holy, she wanted to finish that kiss.

She had no idea how it would work when they both went their separate ways at the end of the month, and for one glorious second, she hadn't even cared. The world had just shifted, and she didn't have to have all the answers yet.

"Only one dance?" Hadley said. "Too bad you couldn't stick around for more."

Molly sipped her coffee instead of commenting. It was because of the one dance that she'd had to leave. If she'd stayed, she would've kissed him. Even right now, everything inside her ached to be back in his arms and have him look at her the way he had on the dance floor. But that couldn't happen.

Mateo had brought up a valid point. The last thing she wanted was to hurt Grant. She was much too familiar with the pain of heartbreak and would do anything in her power to protect him from having to experience that. Which was where she found herself in a pickle.

Molly wanted to continue seeing Grant. That had become crystal clear last night. But Grant deserved to have what his heart desired. If he wanted forever, she wanted to see him get his happily ever after.

The only problem was, Molly wasn't interested in forever. In fact, she wasn't sure she'd ever be up for that kind of commitment again. Sure, they could dive into something casual now—after all, kissing the man didn't require a marriage proposal—but what happened down the road when he was ready for the kind of future she wasn't able to give him?

"But you're feeling better today?" Ellyn asked.

Molly offered the cheeriest smile she could muster. "Two Advil and a good night's sleep always do the trick." She only wished that prescription worked on matters of the heart too.

"Good to hear." They stopped in front of the gallery, and Ellyn pulled her keys from her pocket. "You two wait here, and I'll run around to the back door to turn off the alarm, then let you in."

Ellyn jogged off around the corner, and Molly stepped closer to the window to admire the new sailboat sculpture on display. It was an interesting combination of whimsy and detail. Yes, any sort of sailboat triggered thoughts of Grant, and at the moment, those thoughts caused a small pang in her chest. But Molly pushed it aside and focused on the interesting aspect of the creation in front of her.

"I haven't seen this piece before. It's stunning." She turned over her shoulder to gauge Hadley's reaction, welcoming any excuse to focus on something other than her own personal drama.

But Hadley wasn't looking at the window. Her gaze was on the empty store next door. There was a hint of yearning in her eyes

Molly stepped next to her friend, trying to imagine a busy coffee shop full of café tables and casual conversations. And Hadley in the middle of it. "You know, being the project manager of your own project might be a welcome change, and that's not much of a leap. Maybe it's time to create something you'll get to enjoy instead of handing over the keys at the end of the project."

Hadley hesitated, twisting her mouth to the side.

Before she could respond, Ellyn pushed open the door. "Come in, come in. And you'll probably want to put these on, since we'll be squirting paint onto little plates. I don't want anyone painting their clothes." Ellyn tossed them each a canvas apron before heading back into her shop, in full go-mode.

Molly eyed Hadley as she slipped her apron over

her head, following Ellyn into the gallery. "Don't think you were saved by the bell. This conversation isn't over."

"I wouldn't dream of it. Although, it might be a short conversation, since there's nothing to talk about."

"Promise me you'll at least think about it."

"I will." She wrapped the long strings of the apron around her then tied them in a bow in the front. "But what about you? You sure you're okay?" Genuine concern was written across her face.

"I'm okay." Molly was aware her words lacked the authenticity needed to sell them.

The truth was, her soul ached. She was facing an impossible decision. She either needed to figure out if forever was somewhere she was willing to go, or she needed to get off before someone got hurt.

It reminded her of what the train conductor at the amusement park she'd gone to as a kid would say when they'd pulled into the station: "*Stay on or get off, but you can't do both and you can't do neither, either.*"

But what happened if she couldn't stay on but had no desire to get off?

"You know, these kinds of things always have a way of working themselves out." Hadley squeezed her hand. "You've got this."

"Thanks." Although at the moment, Molly wasn't sure she agreed.

Chapter Eighteen

By the time Tuesday rolled around, it had felt like an eternity had passed since Grant had last seen Molly, and he found himself counting down the minutes until she showed up at Turtle Rehab.

Their conversation on the beach hadn't gone exactly how he'd envisioned it. There was so much he wanted to tell her, and he couldn't seem to get any of it out. Although, maybe delaying the conversation wasn't a total loss. He'd realized a couple of things in the past few days that might change what he had to say. Most notable would be that he wasn't falling in love with Molly. He'd already fallen.

What did that look like? He wasn't sure. In fact, he was far from having it all figured out, but that didn't mean they couldn't make it work. The important thing was being with her. Everything else was just details.

She was scheduled to show up any minute to do Hope's final exam, and since Claire was still on her honeymoon, he was the one scheduled to help her. He was hoping she'd stick around afterward to have dinner with him. He'd bought a couple of steaks to throw on the grill, thinking they could celebrate, and this time he wasn't going to fumble the words he wanted to say.

Excitement of what lay ahead welled in his chest and he found himself whistling as he walked out to the supply locker to prepare for what would hopefully be Hope's last ride to the vet suite.

"Someone's in a good mood today." Mateo stood inside the cabinet, drawing up the injectable medicine for one of their patients.

Grant grabbed a big black bin they used to transport the turtles from the stack of sanitized supplies. "Releasing turtles always puts me in a good mood."

"How about accepting new jobs? Does that put you in a good mood too?"

Grant felt the start of a guilty grin pull at his mouth and he plopped the bin on top of a rolling cart, locking it in place.

He'd waited until Monday to disturb Claire on her honeymoon, but after a quick phone call, she'd told him what he'd thought she'd say. She was thrilled for him and was already planning his goodbye party.

Perhaps he should've been offended that everyone in his life seemed quick to push him out of town, but instead it gave him confidence that what he was doing was the right choice. And his first call that morning had been to the university to officially accept the job.

"Apparently news travels fast."

"In this industry? It's like a bunch of gossipy old biddies. I bet you hadn't even ended the call before the rumor mill started."

Grant chuckled. "Very true." So much for holding off on making the official announcement to his crew so he could tell Molly first.

"Don't get me wrong. We're going to miss you, but it's high time you beat it out of here."

"I'm touched by your sentiment."

Mateo set the dose of medicine on the silver tray in front of him and held out his hand. "Don't be a stranger."

"I couldn't stay away even if I tried." Grant grasped his handshake and pulled his cousin and lifelong best buddy in for a hug. "Now, you going to help me get this turtle out of her tank, or am I going to have to do it all on my own?"

"On the other hand," Mateo said, closing the medicine cabinet and sliding the tray of meds onto the lower rack of Grant's cart, "maybe I'm not going to miss you after you leave."

They strolled over to Hope's tank and gently lifted the turtle into her transport container before Mateo grabbed the tray of meds and headed off to treat the thriving Shelley. In fact, all of their turtles were thriving at the moment, and a big part of that was due to a certain talented Dr. Lawrence.

"Big day for you, Hope, my girl. Last check-up before we declare you seaworthy. This time next week, you'll be well on your way to the Bahamas." He pushed the cart through the sliding glass doors and pivoted in the hall to back through the swinging doors of the clinic. "Or, I hear the Virgin Islands are quite lovely this time of year."

"Still scheming to win this year's Great Turtle Race?" Molly grinned at him from the sink where she was washing her hands, and his already sunny mood brightened.

"Options. I'm giving her options."

"The only option I'm worried about is getting her back into the ocean." Molly dried her hands on a paper towel and grabbed a pair of latex gloves. "Aren't you the one who's always telling me the reefs around here are incredible?" She joined him at the cart and helped him lift the turtle onto the exam table.

"I think the word you're looking for is showing, not telling. I'm always showing you how awesome our reefs are."

"My mistake." Molly kneeled down next to the turtle. "And how is my favorite lady today?" The turtle wiggled her front fins in response.

"She's the perfect picture of a healthy loggerhead. Her appetite is great, she has tons of energy, and her wounds have all healed. From our end, it doesn't look like there's anything holding her back." Grant gave her the official caretaker report, even though he was fully aware that Molly knew everything there was to know about this turtle.

Molly gently ran her finger along the spot on her leg where one of the cuts had been. "Honey is my new favorite medicine. Who knew it worked so well?"

"How do you know it wasn't my charming personality that was the key to her speedy recovery?"

She glanced up at him with a disparaging look.

"Fine." He leaned against the counter and crossed his arms in front of his chest, watching her do what she did best. "We'll give all the credit to the honey."

Although, it was no secret that a main contributor to her perfect bill of health was a certain locum vet.

Locum. A Latin word that meant a temporary place-holder, but nothing about her effect on this place was temporary. Her presence here had changed everything. A warmth spread through him.

Molly crossed to the other side of the turtle, examining the other healed wounds. "I don't even think this one is going to leave a scar. Hope, sweetheart, you're looking great."

"Sounds like the kind of good news that's worth celebrating with a big trip to the Caribbean, don't you think?"

Molly rolled her eyes and grabbed the doppler monitor to check the turtle's heartbeat. She slid the monitor against the turtle's neck just under the shell, and the familiar whooshing sound filled the room. Grant didn't care how many times he heard that sound, it never got old. Hearing the unique heartbeat of any creature inspired him. It reminded him that life was precious and worth fighting for. It reminded him that what they did mattered.

Molly glanced at him, the smile on her own face seeming to echo his feelings. "It sounds strong."

"Very strong," he agreed.

She pulled the monitor off and set it on the counter. "It's official. She has a clean bill of health. All I need is a weight and I can sign off on her release."

Grant helped Molly carry the turtle to the scale and they gently set her down.

Molly stepped back, hands on hips, to examine the readout. "One hundred sixty point two. I'd say her appetite has improved."

"That's a twentyish-pound gain, isn't it?" Grant grabbed her chart and flipped through the screens to find her weight track.

"Twenty-four point five to be precise," Molly said.

Grant finally found the page he was looking for and did the quick math in his head. Molly was exactly right, which didn't surprise him. When it came to these turtles, she didn't miss a thing.

She turned to Grant. "That's it, then? She's ready for her big release day?"

Grant handed her the chart. "Your signature will make it official."

Molly pressed some buttons on the digital form, then used her finger to sign the bottom. "I've never been so happy to sign a release in my whole life." She handed the tablet to Grant. "What happens now?"

"Now she switches to an all-live diet to get her in the habit of catching her own food again, and we'll fit her with her shiny new tracker on Friday. In the meantime, we celebrate."

"After we get her back in her tank, of course."

"Right. Walk with me to help lift her?"

"I'd love to." They lifted her from the scale into her transport cart and he pushed it out of the vet suite into the hall, with Molly walking along next to him.

"With any luck, this will be the last time Hope ever sets a flipper inside a building."

"It's an incredible feeling, watching a situation that seemed bleak turn into a celebration. Is this first-timer emotion, or do they all feel this way?"

Grant stopped in front of Hope's tank, his own spirit soaring. "They pretty much all feel this way. But you think this is emotional? Wait until the moment we put her back in the ocean." They set the giant turtle in the tank and stood there for a second, watching her flippers paddle through the clear water. "Be prepared for ugly crying. I'd say I'd bring a hanky for you, but since we'll be chest-deep in the water, I don't think hankies will be of much use."

Molly looked taken aback. "We'll be in the water?"

"Of course—how else do you think we'll get Hope out to sea? We usually wade at least waist-deep before we let her go. We want her path to be as clear as possible."

"We? As in me?" She pointed a finger at herself. "I get to carry her into the water on release day?"

"You pulled her out of the ocean and have cared for her the entire time she's been here. It's only fitting that you're the one to carry her back in, don't you think?"

Her hand covered her mouth as tears glistened in her eyes. "Oh gosh, cue the ugly crying already." She waved her hand in front of her face in an attempt to dry her eyes before she pressed it back to her mouth. "I'm so honored." Tears spilled down her cheeks.

Grant wrapped his arms around her and pulled her into a hug. "These are happy tears, right?"

He could feel Molly's head nod against his chest. "Perfectly happy. Exuberant, even."

"How about we take these happy tears and celebrate over dinner?" A gush of excitement mixed with nervousness rushed through him. But it was the good kind of nervousness. The anticipatory kind that circled back to excitement. "I was thinking about grilling, and I have an oceanside table reserved for the occasion."

Molly seemed to stiffen in his arms. Then she stepped back from his embrace, swiping at the moisture on her cheeks. "Dinner?"

"Yes. I thought maybe we'd celebrate my official

acceptance of the new job too. Or the beginning of my one-month countdown, whichever way you want to look at it."

"You took the job." Her words were airy, as if she were saying them to herself instead of him, but he answered anyway.

"I accepted this morning." The theme of the day seemed to be new beginnings, and he was hoping to add one more to the tally over dinner—the beginning of a new relationship. The thought sent excitement buzzing through him. "Join me for dinner?"

"Oh... I, um..." Molly nibbled her bottom lip, and the mood between them seemed to shift. "It's just that I have a lot I need to get done tonight."

His own good mood stuttered. "Sure. Everything okay?"

She waved a dismissive hand. "Of course. My time here is coming to a close too, and you know how it is. A lot of loose ends to tie up before I head off to my next assignment. Plus, I told Hadley and Ellyn I'd try to join them for a late dinner." Her smile returned, although it looked a lot more forced than natural. "Raincheck?"

"Absolutely." He tried to shake the feeling that something was off. "Is there anything I can help with?"

"Nah. It's nothing I can't handle." She jerked her thumb toward the building. "But I'm going to finish up that paperwork. I don't want anything to keep Hope from having her big day. And I wanted to check on Shelley's incision site and get a weight on the hatchlings before it gets too dark."

"Right. I need to get started on feeding everyone.

I'm covering for Claire, since she's on her honeymoon. But I gotta say, feeding this crew is one stinky job."

Molly giggled, some of the spark he loved returning to her eyes. "Let me know if I need to find you a clothespin for your nose."

"You laugh, but the stank of squid is no joke. Think of me as you're doing your non-smelly tasks."

"May the force be with you." There was laughter in her voice as she looked into his eyes, then it was as if everything froze and the two of them were suspended in time.

He wasn't sure what had triggered the progression, but something must've. The laughter dancing in her eyes flickered and was replaced by a flash of sadness. And just like a wave that rolled up on the beach, he felt her slowly slipping away.

"I'm outta here. Is there anything you need before I leave?" Mateo called, breaking up the moment.

Grant looked up at his friend, who was standing at the sliding door with his backpack slung over one shoulder. "Nope. We got it from here. See you tomorrow."

Mateo held up a hand in a wave and disappeared through the door, and when Grant looked back, Molly was already walking away. "I'd better get started on my stuff too, if there's any hope of me getting out of here at a decent hour."

"Right," Grant said, trying to wrap his mind around what had just happened. "Well, I'm here if you need anything."

She paused, halfway to the building, and turned to him. "Thanks. You're a great friend, Grant."

Friend. There was that word again. While he loved

being Molly's friend, that wasn't where he'd seen tonight going.

Molly sat on a stool in the vet suite, staring at the same page of Hope's chart that'd been on the screen, for the last fifteen minutes. What was she doing?

There was absolutely nowhere else in the world she'd rather be than on the deck of Grant's boat, laughing under the stars as the waves provided the background music. Really, there were few places in the world she wouldn't want to be as long as Grant was there with her.

The problem wasn't the company or the location, it was the words that would be said. Yes, she was well aware that their relationship had flown right past friends and had settled somewhere in romance-land. It wasn't where she thought they'd end up when she'd walked into his rehab center two months ago, but now that she was here, she wasn't overly opposed to it. In fact, she kind of liked the place where she'd landed. If everything could stay exactly as it was, she wouldn't have a problem with dinner now or any night in the future.

But it couldn't stay the same. That night on the dance floor, the thing that had shifted was awareness. One almost-kiss had made her achingly aware of where this was heading. This wasn't the casual train. This train was headed toward forever. Wedding bells and picket fences were on this route. Okay, maybe not picket fences. Grant seemed more like the-world-is-my-backyard kind of guy, but same difference.

And while she wasn't fundamentally against those things—in fact, the opposite was true—she wasn't sure that was *her* final destination.

She'd taken that train before, and it had ended in a near-fatal blow to her heart. She felt certain she wouldn't be able to last a second blow. Of course she didn't think that was where this was going, but no one anticipated heartbreak. Love was always a risk. If you let yourself fall, there's always the chance you'd hit the ground.

And that was precisely why she had to say no to dinner. Until she'd figured out what she wanted, she couldn't go any farther. As much as she wanted to be with him, it wasn't fair to Grant for her to stay on this train with no intention of going where he wanted to end up. That's how people got hurt, and the one thing she wasn't willing to risk was Grant getting hurt.

"*Stay on or get off.*" It was a simple enough choice, but considering how opposed she was to either option, she wasn't sure how she'd make the decision.

Chapter Nineteen

"TODAY'S THE DAY!" HADLEY HERALDED the words as she passed Molly the first latte Saturday morning.

"Are you so excited? I mean, I know it's thrilling for all of us who get to cheer on this turtle, who's like our town mascot. But I can't imagine how you feel." Ellyn accepted the mug with both hands and took a sip.

"Honestly, it's a little bittersweet." Molly took her cup from Hadley. "I couldn't be happier to see her go home, but I'm going to miss her more than I thought I would."

That seemed to be a theme running through her life at the moment. Her stop here was always meant to be temporary. There was literally an end date before she'd ever shown up. But knowing a goodbye was coming didn't make it any easier.

"Send-off is at two, right?" Ellyn asked.

"Yup. As long as everything goes according to plan, the turtle should be in the water at two o'clock."

"What kind of things wouldn't go according to plan?" Hadley asked.

"No idea. I thought we just put the turtle in the water, but apparently there's a lot more to it than that." Molly shrugged and sipped her coffee. Normally she could linger on Saturday mornings, but today she had to be at Turtle Rehab in thirty minutes for the release briefing, the first in a very tight schedule of meetings and final checks before Hope's send-off.

"Before you go, I have to give you the surprise we've been working on." Ellyn set her mug on the table next to her and clapped her hands together. "Hang on. Let me grab it." She disappeared from sight, and Molly heard her sliding door open.

"Do you know what this is about?" she asked Hadley.

Hadley shrugged and blew on her coffee with the guilty look of someone who was involved up to her eyeballs.

Molly didn't have time to press her on the subject before Ellyn reappeared with a package wrapped in brightly colored paper. She handed it around the partition to Molly.

"This is from both of us in honor of your big day."

"You two really shouldn't have." She tore off the paper and pulled out a teal T-shirt. The small logo on the front and the larger logo on the back were the same. Both said Team Hope with a picture of a sea turtle. Tear stung her eyes as she took in one of the most thoughtful gifts anyone had ever given her.

Molly held it in front of her and examined it. "Y'all! It's perfect!" She pulled it in and hugged it close to her chest.

"We're glad you like it, because today we're all Team Hope." Hadley untied her robe and pulled it off to reveal a Team Hope shirt underneath.

Ellyn had apparently done the same, because when Molly looked to the right, in the place of her signature zip-up hoodie, Ellyn was sporting a matching teal T-shirt.

"You two are too much."

"I tried to tell her that, but Ellyn's middle name is Too Much," Hadley said, casually sipping her coffee.

Ellyn rolled her eyes at her friend. "We want you to know that your legacy to this town and to the turtles and to us won't be forgotten."

Molly slipped the shirt over her head, the thoughtfulness of her sweet friends causing a lump to form in her throat. "Let's not talk about goodbyes yet. I can only handle one send-off at a time."

"Plus, you have a few more weeks before you leave, right?" Ellyn asked.

"Right." Although, it sounded like the clock was already ticking down, which caused her chest to tighten. How was she going to say goodbye to the two people who restored her faith in friendship? For that matter, how was she going to say goodbye to this place in general?

Before she could dive too deep into that topic, she pushed it away. She would have to figure that out another day. Today was about Hope.

She reached around the partition to give Ellyn a hug. "Thanks for this. It means a lot." She walked to the other side of her balcony and gave Hadley a hug. "And I'm still holding two spots for you in the VIP tent. Your names are on the list."

"We'll be there," Hadley said.

She glanced at her watch. "Yikes. I'd better run or I'm going to be late."

"Good luck, and go, Team Hope!" Ellyn cheered.

Molly waved to her friends and headed inside long enough to grab the bag she'd need for the day and her keys. She headed out to her car, but summer traffic made the short trip slower than she'd been expecting, and she pulled into an already full Turtle Rehab parking lot only five minutes before the briefing meeting.

"Hey, Kya!" Her voice was cheerful as she rushed through the giftshop to the Care Floor, where the meeting was taking place.

Kya picked up a two-way radio. "Molly just walked in," she said into the speaker before returning the greeting.

"Am I late?" She checked her watch again, but according to the schedule she'd been given, she was still a solid three minutes early.

"Send her straight back," Mateo's voice came over the radio.

Kya shrugged innocently. "They started asking if you were here almost an hour ago. But don't take it personally. They're always like this on release day." She held up the walkie-talkie. "But I get to play with this, so it's not all bad."

Molly chuckled. "Silver linings. Tell them I'm on my way."

It wasn't a necessary message, since she'd be walking out the back door about the same time Kya finished delivering it, but it would put all those jittery nerves to good use.

Molly broke into a jog when she got to the hallway and was out the sliding door in record time. But, if the crowd of staffers assembled in the staging area was any indication, she was the last to get there.

Claire and Mateo were standing on either side of a white board with a detailed schedule of how the next few hours would go and a diagram of the release site. Every rehab tech on staff, along with a few volunteers, were there with clipboards in hand, ready to take notes. Grant stood on the far edge of the group, leaning against a pole.

Molly slowed her jog and sidled up to him, hoping to not draw attention to herself. “You failed to mention that being five minutes early was ten minutes late on release days,” she whispered.

Grant handed her a clipboard and grinned, showing off the charming dimples she loved—liked. She meant liked. “First of all, you were considered ten minutes late ten minutes ago,” he whispered. “And second, I would’ve mentioned it, but you left without saying goodbye the other day.”

Ouch. So he’d noticed that she’d been avoiding him all week. “Sorry about that.” The familiar angst that had pulled at her for the past week swirled inside her.

Luckily, she didn’t have time to focus on it because Mateo’s gaze burned into her, keeping her focus on the task at hand.

“Now that we’re all assembled, our meeting can finally commence.”

She pulled a face to show she felt bad. “Sorry about that.”

Mateo didn’t acknowledge her apology. Instead, he launched into an explanation of the detailed schedule that was written out in large, bold letters on the white board in front and also on everyone’s individual clipboard.

“Commence?” Molly whispered to Grant. There

might've been a smidge of judgment in her raised eyebrow.

Grant leaned his head toward her. "He uses big words when he's stressed. He just told Claire they didn't have time for *superfluous* questions."

Molly held her clipboard over her mouth to hide her giggle. "High school English teachers everywhere are so proud."

"Right? He'll relax. He's extra stressed because this is the first time he's run point on a release."

That made sense. Since Grant was less than a month from leaving, he'd started the process of handing the reins over to Mateo. But she could only imagine that this release, one that was a huge media event with the backing of the national Great Turtle Race and live internet coverage, was more complicated than most. No wonder he was breaking out the big words.

"Plus, there's been some speculation that his sudden switch to decaf so he wouldn't be jittery today is making him extra grumpy. I was going to have Kya swap out his cup with a double espresso, but now that you're here, maybe you could start an IV and streamline some caffeine to his system?"

"I'll get right on that." It always took her by surprise how easy it was to be with Grant, not to mention fun. Their relationship was effortless, which was exactly the reason she'd been avoiding him. It was hard to contemplate walking away when being here felt so right.

Mateo paused his speech and turned his attention to the two of them, narrowing his gaze. "Is there a question?"

Grant shook his head. "Nope. Just filling Molly in on what she missed."

"Right." Mateo didn't look like he thought it was right at all, but he returned his attention to the white board. "As I was saying. After a final visual check from the vet at T-minus two hours, the turtle will be loaded into the turtle ambo and transported to the release location."

Molly raised her hand.

Mateo turned to her, all business. "Yes, Dr. Lawrence."

Wow, so official. She wasn't sure she'd ever heard Mateo call her Dr. Lawrence, and it took her aback. "Sorry, what kind of visual check will I be doing?"

"Just a quick visual exam," Grant explained. "You've already signed off on her health, but we like to do a final look to make sure nothing has changed since you last saw her. I'll walk you through it."

Molly nodded once. "Great, thanks."

"As I was saying..." Mateo went back to walking through the day, down to the tiniest detail. It appeared they'd carefully planned for every factor, but since Molly was new to this, she kept getting lost in the verbiage. Mateo was three bullet points down explaining the positions of the various jobs in the pre-release activities when Molly's hand shot up again.

"Yes, Dr. Lawrence?"

"Transporters and carriers are not the same job, correct? And which one am I?"

"You can find a detailed list of who is assigned to each position on page three of your packet. It might be helpful to acquaint yourself with that information."

Molly gave him a thumbs-up. "Oh, right. Thanks. I'll do that."

Grant leaned his head toward hers. "That would be a superfluous question."

Molly gave him a playful nudge with her shoulder before she flipped to page three. "Excuse me, sir, I'm trying to acquaint myself with the information," she whispered.

As a carrier, her entire job was to carry Hope from the turtle ambo to the water. Of course, there was more to it than simply walking, but knowing the different job titles gave her clarification as to what parts of Mateo's walk-through she needed to pay the most attention to and which parts didn't involve her.

"The final go/no-go will come from our offshore boats when the carriers are in position. No-go at that point will be restricted to an imminent wildlife threat."

Molly's head popped up at the word threat. She raised her hand again.

"Yes, Dr. Lawrence." He still had the patient look of a kindergarten teacher talking to a child, but she could tell constant interruptions were starting to wear on him.

"What qualifies as eminent wildlife threats?"

"Sharks. The no-go will come if there are sharks within two hundred yards of the turtle."

"Hold up. So you're going to wait until I'm about ready to walk in the ocean to decide if it's a shark free zone or not?"

"No," Mateo said. "We're going to make that call when you're already in position, which, if you check your sheet, means you're hip deep in the water with the turtle."

Molly's eyes got so large she thought they might

pop out of their sockets. She'd come a long way getting more comfortable with ocean adventures, but she was far from the comfort level that would include swimming among sharks while holding their favorite snack. She turned to Grant. "We're going to walk into water with sharks and just hang out to see if they swim closer to us?"

Grant chuckled. "In all the years we've done this, we've only had a shark in the vicinity once, and he didn't come near us."

"That's not making me feel better."

"I told you today was going to be an adventure." Grant slid his arm around her shoulder. "You're going to be fine. I promise."

Almost as soon as his arm settled around her, his comfort seeped in, and she got that feeling she often had around him. It was the feeling that gave her confidence, that made her try new things, that told her together, they could do almost anything. It was enough to give her a tiny nudge in the direction of forever.

"When we get the final go from the offshore boats, I will give the command to the carriers, who will release the turtle," Mateo finished, and Molly pushed the internal debate out of her mind. Right now wasn't the time to think about forever verses *adios*. Her entire focus needed to be about Hope and her homecoming. "On that command, the tracker will go live on the big screen, video coverage is switched to the underwater feed, and the celebration ensues."

Grant shot her a look at the additional use of a fancy word.

"Grant, do you have anything to add?"

He straightened up and turned more serious as he addressed the group. "I think you covered everything. How about a hand for Mateo and his well-orchestrated plan for the biggest release we've had this year? Well done, Mateo." Everyone clapped, and Grant's gaze shifted to the entire group. "It is an exciting day for me to get to pass the torch not just on heading up the releases, but for director of Emerald Cove Turtle Rescue and Rehab. Most of you know by now that I have accepted a new position at the university, and Friday will be my last day. I leave knowing that the turtles and this place are in excellent hands with director Mateo Torres and head of rehabilitation, Claire Price."

Grant kept talking, but Molly couldn't comprehend anything else he said. Friday? This wasn't supposed to be his last week. Hadn't he told her when he'd accepted the position that it started in a month? He was supposed to leave after she did.

She stood there stunned as he finished speaking and everyone rose from their chairs and headed in different directions. Some went to discuss different points with Claire or Mateo, some went off to start their first assignments, and others came over to wish Grant congratulations. Molly, on the other hand, remained in her same spot as if her tennis shoes were glued to the ground.

When the final person drifted away, she turned to Grant. "Friday?"

Perhaps there should've been more to her question, but unlike Mateo, she used fewer words when she got flustered.

"The timeline got moved up, and the university

asked if I could come sooner." He slid his hands in his pockets and looked at her, regret lingering in his eyes. "Since this place is in good hands and I don't have much to pack, I didn't have much of a reason to say no."

"Sure, yeah. Makes total sense." Thoughts swirled around her head. "When do you actually leave town?"

"My last day here will be Friday. I set sail on Saturday."

"Wow, that's..." She let her words trail off, because "soon" didn't seem to cover it. "Rushed" seemed more appropriate. "Expeditious," even. She'd thought she had more time to figure out what she wanted.

"I wanted to talk to you about it, but I know you've been busy this week."

Guilt pinged her as she realized that could also be translated as, *"I would've told you, but you've been avoiding me."* "Sorry about that."

"No worries. But maybe we could meet up after the celebration this afternoon. There's one last excursion to take you on before we fulfill our contract."

Something fluttered in her gut but she couldn't tell if it was apprehension or anticipation. "Sure. Of course."

"Great," he said, his expression was more serious than she'd seen in a long time. "Plus, there are things that...need to be said."

Apprehension. It was definitely apprehension. "Right."

There was no denying that things needed to be said. The only problem was that Molly had between now and then to figure out what those things were.

Grant would be lying if he said he wasn't nervous

about what would go down at their sunset rendezvous. "I was saving this excursion for last, since I think you'll really like it. But with the timeline moving up, I guess last is now."

"I can't wait." Her smile looked stiff, which seemed to be par for the course as of late.

A week ago, he'd been confident about their relationship. And while the tides were turning, he'd had no doubt they could turn with them. But now that Molly had been ghosting him for the past seven days, he wasn't so sure. "I'll text you the address. Should we say seven thirty?"

"Seven thirty's great. I'll be there."

"Dr. Lawrence, can we get your expertise over here?" Mateo called from his location next to Hope's tank.

Molly nodded her head in his direction. "Duty calls." A sassy grin lit her face. "Or maybe I should say my vocational expertise is required."

And there it was. The Molly he'd fallen in love with. The one he wanted to be a permanent fixture in his life. "Don't let me impede you."

The fluttery heart he'd become so accustomed to in her presence twisted with a blast of chilly anxiousness. He wasn't sure what would happen tonight, but there was one thing he knew for certain. He'd finally gotten a glimpse of forever. And even though he wasn't sure it would last, what a sight it had been to behold.

Chapter Twenty

At the exact time written on the detailed schedule, Molly stepped into the cabin of the turtle ambo. "As a girl who loves a good schedule, Mateo's ability to keep us on his exact timeline is impressive," she said to Claire, who climbed in behind her.

"Right?" Claire pulled the doors closed and took a seat on the built-in bench next to Molly. "I think he's trying hard to prove to Grant that he has nothing to worry about."

"Is that why you came home from your honeymoon early?"

"Yes and no. Grant's leaving so soon was a factor. But I also decided I didn't want to miss Hope's release. I'm going to miss this turtle."

"Me too." Molly stared at the covered crate on the floor in front of them. "I knew today would be emotional, but I wasn't expecting to be sad."

Claire nodded. "It's bittersweet, for sure. Even though they come to us with the sole goal of sending them home, it's impossible to not get attached."

"Oh good, I was starting to think I did it wrong."

"Not at all. I tend to think if you're sad to see them go, you did your job right."

"At least she has a tracker on her so we can keep up with her." Molly pulled out her phone to make sure she already had the site plugged in.

"Agreed. And between the location of her rescue and the time of year, there's a strong chance she nests around here. I wouldn't be surprised if she headed back this direction at some point." Claire leaned closer to the crate. "Not that we want to see you again, little missy. Stay away from those hazards."

"I second that."

Claire shifted her focus to the clipboard in her lap. "Once we arrive, I'll hop out and start the go/no-go procedures."

"It sounds so official."

Claire held up her two-way radio. "I have a clipboard and a walkie. It must be official."

"Well, you go be official, and I'll hold down my post here—hanging out in the air-conditioned ambo with Hope and fighting off any obsessed fans who try to come hang out with us."

"You laugh, but at big send-offs like this, there is always at least one person who tries to slip in to snag a selfie with the turtle."

"Don't worry, Hope. I've been practicing my ninja skills." Molly did a fancy punching sequence to demonstrate.

Claire laughed. "We clearly assigned the right person to this job."

The turtle ambo slowed to a stop, and the back doors opened to reveal Mateo. There was a small crowd behind him, craning to get a look at Hope. Behind that was a scene that was nothing short of a celebration. From Molly's limited vantage point, she was able to make out brightly colored banners and the large screen with a digital clock counting down until the release. Music blared from speakers she couldn't see, and the mood of the crowd was electric.

"Right on time," Mateo said, still as serious and stony-faced as when he'd left the facility.

"Everything's all good here," Claire said, hopping out of the truck. "Let's get started." She held her radio up to her mouth and started talking.

Mateo drew in a breath. "You two sit tight, and we'll be back. T-minus twenty-nine minutes and counting."

Before she could respond, he closed the doors, and the sounds of the activity outside faded into a muffled murmur.

Molly sat perfectly still in the silence for a moment, straining to hear what was going on outside. There were no windows back here, no way for her to see the party that was in full swing all around her. It was a weird feeling, but she could see how this quiet, closed-in space would be less stressful for the turtle who had no idea what was going on. Being cocooned in their own little space was oddly peaceful.

This was also the first chance she'd had to slow down since she'd shown up to the facility this morning. From the moment she'd stepped into the gift shop until she'd been loaded into the turtle ambo, time had seemed to move at warp speed. To be honest, it felt like time had been moving in warp speed ever since she'd pulled into Emerald Cove. It was nice to have a moment to sit down and take it all in.

Molly leaned over and pulled back the cover to peer down at Hope, sitting snugly in her transport crate. "It seems somewhat poetic that it started with just the two of us, and it's ending with just the two of us."

The loggerhead blinked, which Molly took as her way of agreeing.

"I guess this is goodbye, then." She pushed herself off the bench and sat cross-legged on the floor next to the crate. She knew touching the turtle excessively this close to returning her to the wild was discouraged. Wild turtles shouldn't be sensitized to humans. They were meant to be free and alone, exploring the depths of the ocean. Molly probably shouldn't even be talking to her at this point, but this turtle had been a major factor in her healing process. Somewhere on her own road to recovery, Hope had been the one to help Molly recover.

"I'll be forever grateful to you," Molly continued. "I came here with a broken heart I thought was unrepairable, and you played a big part in putting it back together again. You reminded me what it meant to hope."

The turtle moved her head closer to Molly as if urging her to go on.

"Fine, it wasn't just you. Turtle Rehab reminded me why I got into animal medicine in the first place, Hadley and Ellyn reminded me what true friendship looks like, and Grant..."

His name got stuck in her throat.

Grant.

It was hard to put into words the role Grant played during her time in Emerald Cove. She closed her eyes and leaned her head against the bench behind her, sucking in a deep breath. Grant had been responsible for reminding her of all the L-words.

How to live, how to laugh, how to listen and be listened to. How to linger and to learn.

How to love.

The word swirled around in her chest like the colors of a kaleidoscope. Was she in love with Grant? Possibly. Or maybe it'd be more accurate to say probably. What she felt for Grant was unlike anything she'd ever felt before, mostly because he was unlike anyone she'd ever met before.

No, the problem wasn't if she loved him or not. The problem was if love was enough.

The truth was, as much as her time in Emerald Cove had healed her shattered heart, there were still scars that went deeper than time could repair. The question she had to figure out before she met up with Grant later tonight was, could she go all in? Or would those scars cause her to hold back forever?

"What do you think, Hope? Stay on or get off?"

Hope moved both her front flippers as if trying to paddle forward.

"Stay on, huh?" It wasn't a surprising choice. Hope had been the poster child for hope since the first weekend Molly had arrived in Emerald Cove. She'd hung on long enough to get rescued. She'd worked through all of her rehabilitation goals in record time, and she hadn't hesitated to meet her release criteria the day they'd been set. Hope didn't give up. "And you'll do great once you're home. The whole wide ocean is waiting for you, my friend."

But Molly wasn't sure the same was true for her.

Her heart sank as she considered there were some scars that seemed too big to overcome.

The disappointment of her own situation and the heartache from the impending goodbye overcame her, and tears slid down her cheeks. "I couldn't be happier for you, but that doesn't mean I'm going to miss you any less. Why do goodbyes have to be so hard?"

She had a feeling this was going to be the theme of the next two weeks, which felt a little ironic for the chapter in her life whose sole purpose was to be able to walk away unscathed.

"The best-laid plans and all that," she said to Hope as she brushed the tears off her cheeks. She sucked in a cleansing breath and refocused her outlook. Saying goodbye might be hard, but if anyone was going to reclaim beauty out of ashes, it was Hope. "It's timc to get you home, my love. And, as Mateo would say, it's going to happen in T-minus fifty-nine seconds."

She watched the second hand on her watch tick down the exact time on the schedule. It ticked only one too many before the double doors of the ambo swung open. Molly had to blink against the blinding light of the mid-afternoon sun. But when her eyes adjusted, Grant's face came into focus.

"Let's do this." Excitement lit his handsome features, and she couldn't help but let it trickle all the way through her, as well. Like she'd said, the question wasn't if she loved him.

Molly slid to the edge of the ambo and, once on the ground, she reached in and pulled the crate toward them. With the help of a couple of volunteers, they lifted it to the ground.

"Tell me about the imminent wildlife threat," Molly asked Grant.

"Nada. Claire is on one of the offshore boats watching the radar, and other than a school of medium-sized fish and a gorgeous eagle ray about five hundred yards offshore, there's nothing out there."

Molly breathed a sigh of relief. "Hope feels so much better knowing that."

Grant chuckled. "Good to know. Now, what do you say we send her home."

"Let's do it." They pounded knuckles across the top of the crate before they both kneeled to grasp either side of Hope's sturdy exterior shell.

There was a rope running from either side of the turtle ambo down to the water's edge, creating a walkway. Two Turtle Rehab technicians led the way, and Grant and Molly followed behind, carrying the star of the show. People, lots and lots of cheering people, lined either side all the way from the truck to the sea.

The noise was almost deafening. The cheers and whistles and celebrations rang out all around them. Somewhere in the distance, Molly was vaguely aware of a familiar microphoned voice giving a play-by-play of what was happening, but all she could focus on were the turtle in her hands, the man at her side, and the steps in front of them.

They walked into the cool water and continued on until the hem of her Team Hope shirt was wet and Grant slowed. They were still holding Hope above the waves, but by the way her front flippers had started moving, she knew exactly where she was.

"We're waiting for the go/no-go call, then we'll walk four more steps and set her on top of the water."

"Oh, right. This is the part where I'm waiting to see if I'm going to be some shark's midafternoon snack or not," Molly joked.

Grant grinned. "Exactly." He looked around, as if taking in the surroundings for the first time. "There are a few more people here now than when the three of us were last in the ocean."

"It's probably a good thing because if there was even one more person, I wouldn't have gotten in the water that day."

"And aren't you glad you did?"

Molly nodded. "Glad" didn't even cover it.

"Grant, you're a go!" The words rang out over the speaker system.

Grant gazed into her eyes. "You ready for this?"

Molly shook her head. "Not at all. But let's do it anyway."

They took four more slow steps, until the surf was washing against Molly's ribcage and it was getting hard to hold the turtle above the water.

"On three," Grant said.

"Okay," Molly agreed. Delight, pride, sadness, and a whole lot of other feels she couldn't quite identify overtook her and she had to blink back the tears as the cheers from the crowd behind them rose to a fever pitch.

"One, two…"

"Three," Molly said and lowered the turtle to the water. "Be free, my friend."

"Godspeed, Hope."

Hope didn't falter. The second her flippers hit the water, she took off, diving under the surf and heading straight for sea.

Grant threw his arms around her, and they bounced together in the water, cheering as they watched the turtle they'd both grown to love return to the place she belonged. Molly couldn't be sure, but she could've sworn Hope paused for a fraction of a second and looked back at them before she dove deeper into the emerald waters of her home and out of sight.

The noise of the crowd shifted directions as they turned from watching the live action in the ocean to the computer tracker being displayed on the big screen behind them. But Molly and Grant stood there, still holding each other and staring out toward the horizon.

"I don't think I've ever felt more inspired in my whole life while also completely sad at the same time."

Grant pulled her close to his chest, rubbing her back. "Spoken like a true turtle rehabber."

It felt good to be in his arms, and for a moment the thought that she wouldn't want to be anywhere else or with anyone else flashed through her mind. But as soon as she realized what she was thinking, she stepped back, using both of her hands to wipe the tears from her cheeks.

He held his hand out to her, a mist in his own eyes. "What do you say we celebrate?"

"As long as you don't mind if I spontaneously burst into tears, I'm all in." She took his hand. The hand of the one person who knew exactly how she was feeling. The hand of the man who encouraged her more than anyone else in the world. And together they trudged through the waves toward the shore.

They stepped onto the dry sand, and Mateo held out a towel for each of them. "Well done, you two. According to the GPS tracker, Hope is almost a kilometer offshore already."

Grant accepted the towel and wiped his face. "A kilometer out? I'd say she's in the clear." He turned to Molly to see if she agreed, but she was engulfed in a sort of hug sandwich by her two neighbors, who were wearing shirts that matched hers.

Molly wrapped the towel around her as her friends swept her up the beach to where the party was in full swing. Grant watched her walk away. A faint ache started to edge in somewhere deep in his chest and he wondered if Hope wasn't the only one he'd let go today.

"I'd say it was a hundred percent success. The media coverage we've gotten is outstanding. We have two local news stations, two influencers streaming live, and our own live video feed," Mateo chattered, looking more animated than he had since Grant had informed him he'd be running point.

"It has been a perfect release," Grant agreed, although he was only partially invested in the conversation. He was having a hard time keeping his eyes off Molly, who was now halfway up the beach talking with a group of people he didn't recognize.

"There's a reporter waiting for an interview. I thought you'd be the best person to do it. Do you mind?"

"Mm-hmm. Okay," Grant agreed, gaze still following Molly. He was confident she felt the same thing he did, so why was she pulling away?

"Grant," Mateo said, more forceful this time.

"Yes?"

"Will you do the interview?"

Grant shook his head, clearing the internal Molly discussion, and focused on the task at hand. "The interview. Right. Who am I looking for?"

Mateo pointed to a local news anchor dressed in a sport coat standing next to a camera person.

"And for the record, you did great. Good job, buddy." He clapped Mateo on the shoulder as he walked away. "You're not even going to miss me when I'm gone."

A relieved grin replaced the worry lines and serious scowl Mateo had been wearing all day. "Isn't that what we've all been telling you?"

He was going to miss a lot of things about this place, but it had never been clearer that it was time for him to go.

He just had one more meeting to see if he was taking something with him, or leaving everything behind.

Chapter Twenty One

AFTER A DAY FULL OF excitement and a quick shower, Molly pulled into the parking lot that matched the address Grant had sent her. To be technical, he hadn't actually sent her an address. It was a pin-drop location, and she might've questioned the otherwise abandoned parking lot in the middle of a state park being the right place if the bright green turtle ambo wasn't also parked there. There was no sign of Grant, though.

She stepped out of her car and took in her surroundings. The state park ran along the coast about fifteen miles outside of Emerald Cove. It was beautiful in a natural seashore way, full of dense tropical plants highlighted by tall pine trees. Molly had been meaning to check out this place since she'd gotten to town. She'd heard it had great hiking trails and beautiful beaches untouched by development, but nine weeks had flown by faster than she'd thought it would.

Oh, well. She was here now. Except, she wasn't exactly sure where "here" was supposed to be. There were three trails leading in three different directions away from the parking lot. One had an arrow pointing to beach access, and the other two were the starts of different hiking trails. Molly pulled out her phone to check the directions Grant had sent her.

"Take the Sandpiper Loop Trailhead," she read aloud and looked up to see which of the signs claimed to be the Sandpiper Loop. "There you are." She headed toward the trailhead on her right and stepped off the asphalt onto the narrow sandy path.

The park felt secluded at this early evening hour. Most hikers and beach-goers had already called it a day and packed up, leaving the parking lots and trails empty. The sun seemed to have the same idea as it slid slowly toward the horizon, casting long shadows in the forest. It was quiet and peaceful and, after the active day, Molly let the calm wash over her. She walked for a couple of minutes, enjoying the sound of silence.

But then a couple of minutes turned into a few, which turned into several, and she still hadn't seen anyone. Not even Grant. Peaceful silence started to slide into concern. She was on the right trail, wasn't she?

Just when she was about to pull out her phone to text him, she rounded a bend, and he came into view.

"You made it."

"I did." The joy of seeing his inspiring smile was quickly overshadowed by an apprehension that prickled in her gut. But instead of focusing on what was to come, she decided to focus on their unique coastal surroundings. "Where exactly are we?"

"This is my favorite place in all of Emerald Cove."

Her brow furrowed in confusion. "Right here?" She didn't want to seem judgy, but he'd taken her to some pretty amazing places over the past two months. This random spot in the middle of the woods was nice, but was it favorite-spot worthy?

"Not so much here..." he pointed to the ground where they were standing, "as up there." He turned and pointed to a metal structure about twenty yards off the path that she hadn't noticed yet.

She tipped her head back to take in the whole thing. There was some sort of small hut on a larger platform, suspended fortyish feet in the air by four thick metal posts painted brown to blend in with the surroundings. "What is it?"

"A treetop ranger observation station. Want to check it out?" There was a note of scandal in his voice that she was starting to get used to.

"I'm guessing by 'check it out' you mean we're going up there. And even though it says no trespassing, you have some sort of maybe-legal connection that's getting us in."

His Cheshire grin widened. "You know me so well."

Molly propped her hands on her hips, sizing up the task in front of her. "How do we get up there?" There was a ladder built into the side of one of the large metal posts, but it didn't start until at least ten feet above the ground.

Grant walked a little farther off the trail and picked up a ladder that had been propped against the far side of a tree. "We climb."

"Of course we do." Molly followed him. She'd come a long way from the girl who'd rolled into town three months ago and had been hesitant about everything.

This adventure stuff wasn't quite second nature yet, but she'd gotten better at stepping out of her comfort zone. Plus, she was learning that the view at the top was usually worth it.

Grant extended the telescoping ladder with hooks at one end and connected them to the bottom rung of the built-in ladder. Once he'd made sure it was sturdy, he stepped back and held his hand out. "After you."

She started up before she could talk herself out of it, keeping her gaze cemented on the spot above her as she climbed. She might've gotten better about going on adventures, but that didn't mean staring at a ground that was rapidly getting farther and farther away was something she was up for.

"What exactly is a treetop observation station?" she asked as they climbed. The second trick she'd discovered was to keep her mind off the scary tasks while in the middle of doing them. It helped her to not rethink decisions she should probably be rethinking.

"It's mainly used for things like research and park management. There were several of them built across the state as a joint effort between the parks department, a few universities, and some wildlife conservation organizations."

"And let me guess, you know the guy who's in charge of it?"

Grant chuckled below her. "I do know most of the rangers around here, but my access to this is based on my own work. I've been involved in a few different research projects that used it."

Molly got to the top and stepped off the metal rungs to the more stable platform, breathing a sigh of relief. She scooted to the side and waited for Grant to reach the top.

When he got to the platform, he put his fists on his hips like an explorer who'd summitted a new peak, and drew in a deep breath. A look that Molly could only describe as the overwhelming peace of finally coming home washed over him. Molly switched her focus from the magnificent man in front of her to the magnificent view around them. The climb was definitely worth it. This view was nothing short of breathtaking.

"Welcome to Treetop Research Outpost Number Three." He breathed the words with an air of reverence.

Molly couldn't help the chuckle that escaped her. "Research Outpost Number Three? That's the best you could come up with for a place as great as this?"

Grant dropped his hands to his side with a little shrug, his own amused grin pulling on his lips. "Right? We researchers tend to not be the most original." He strolled around the outside of the platform to the other side of the hut, his hand casually sliding along the railing. "Maybe we needed to contact the English department to help us come up with a better name to capture her beauty. Or those marketing kids."

Molly hugged as close to the hut as possible and followed, forcing herself to take in the view. "Beauty" didn't seem like a big enough word to describe this. They weren't quite as high as the lighthouse, or even her condo, but the perspective was different. Those were on the beach, offering an unobstructed view of the ocean, which was impressive. But the outpost was roughly the same height as the trees that surrounded it. It seemed to blend into nature to offer a bird's eye view of the ocean, the beach, and the natural protected land that led up to it. And especially at this sunset hour, it was nothing short of dazzling.

"They might've tried," she said, fully immersed in the scene. "But I don't think there are words that can do it justice."

"I agree." Grant came to a stop on the side that faced out to the ocean. "Being a fellow animal lover, I thought you might appreciate this place. There's no better seat for watching wildlife in its native habitat than right here."

He sank down on the platform and let his legs dangle off the side. Molly took a seat next to him. But instead of letting her legs dangle over the side, she opted to pull her knees into her chest. While she'd made a lot of growth this summer, she still had limits.

A broad, mighty hawk, much bigger than what she was expecting, swooped by, catching her off guard. His beauty was majestic and powerful, and she watched him dive and soar to the symphony of song birds.

"It's beautiful." A pair of squirrels at eye level played on the branch of a nearby tree, and the clouds lazily drifted by overhead. "How many more of these amazing spots do you have up your sleeve?"

Grant gave her a mysterious grin. "I'm a man of all kinds of surprises."

Didn't Molly know. That was the main reason for the current predicament she was in.

"Actually..." He popped up and took the two broad steps required to get to the hut. He punched a number in the keypad on the door and disappeared inside. A few seconds later, he returned, holding two sets of high-powered binoculars. He handed one to Molly. "For your viewing pleasure. But I recommend you put the strap around your neck. I happen to know from a very unfortunate experience that they do not fare well if dropped from this height."

Molly was already slipping the strap over her head. "You dropped one of these?"

Grant held his set up to his eyes and pointed them toward the ocean. "Not me, a buddy I was up here with. And if we're to be technical about it, the fault really lay with a certain squirrel who'd been nicknamed Mr. Naughty Pants."

Molly giggled, looking through her own binoculars. "Who said researchers couldn't be original?"

"Trust me, the title was spot on. That squirrel caused all kinds of problems."

"Everyone's always blaming the squirrels," Molly joked.

"Don't feel too sorry for the little guy. He has a pretty great life. But he had the skills of Houdini. It didn't matter how many ways we tried to keep him out of the hut—for his own safety, I might add—he could always find a way in."

"What happened to him?"

"Not sure. I haven't seen him in a while." Grant shrugged, his binoculars still pressed to his eyes and gaze focused over the trees. "He's probably out there in the forest, living his best life. Maybe tormenting the lifeguard stand for a change of pace."

Molly chuckled.

"Pod of dolphins at one o'clock," Grant reported.

She swung her binoculars to what she thought would be one o'clock and searched the water. "Ahh, there you are."

She focused on the group of three—or was it four?—dolphins swimming parallel to the shore in a westward direction, as though they were chasing the sunset. One jumped, making a perfect arc through the sky before reentering the water. Then another one followed suit as if proving he could do it better.

She watched them for a second through the binoculars, admiring all the details she was able to see with the enhanced vision. Then she dropped the binoculars to her lap and took in the whole, big picture. The setting sun splashed puddles of red and gold across the surface of the ocean. The calm of pre-twilight seemed to draw out all sorts of animals. Besides the dolphins, a couple of what must've been really large rays glided just below the surface in a sort of choreographed dance. Birds lazily drifted over head as squirrels scampered through the trees. She could here an owl hoot off in the distance somewhere, just waking up from what she assumed was a long nap. It was completely alive and active and completely peaceful at the same time. It would've been noteworthy on its own, but sitting here, shoulder to shoulder with the man she'd grown to admire, elevated it a notch. This moment was inspired, and if she had the ability to freeze time, she'd freeze it right here, sitting next to Grant, fully immersed in the nature they both loved.

"So, Saturday. I'm moving on Saturday."

Or they could do that.

He lowered his binoculars, focusing his warm chocolate gaze on hers. Seriously, why did he have to be so attractive? Or charming? If they were venturing into the why-abyss, why did he, out of all the people in all the world, have to be the one to walk into her clinic on that hectic Friday afternoon?

"I know it's a little faster than anticipated," he continued.

A little faster? If they wanted to get technical about it, this was a lot faster than she'd been anticipating. Light years faster. She was supposed to have at least three more weeks to figure this out, not seven days.

"But the timing feels right, you know? Things are in a good place."

Some things, she supposed. "If today was any indication, Mateo and Claire are more than ready to take over the Turtle Rehab. Shelley, Buzz, Woody, and the rest of the turtles are in expert hands." Other things, though...

Grant rested his chin on the wire that made up part of the protective railing and stared into the distance. "Claire was born for this role, and Mateo is probably far more qualified to be the director than I ever was. I have complete faith in both of them."

"And we have two more releases coming up. Mateo asked me today if I could do the final exam for Taylor Swifty sometime this week, and they're looking at scheduling Little Bear for the week after that."

"Seems like it's time for everyone to move on."

Yup. Change was definitely in the air, which brought her back to the decision that'd been running through her mind since the wedding. *Stay on or get off.*

"The thing is—" Grant started, but Molly cut him off before he could get any farther.

"The last couple of months have been really fun." She needed to stay in front of this conversation before it headed in a direction she wasn't ready for.

"Right." He shifted, looking a bit nervous. "Part of the reason for that, or at least some of the reason for that..." He paused. His lips pressed together as if he was searching for the right words to say. A second ticked by, and then something seemed to click. His confidence returned, fueled by the strength and courage that she admired, and he turned to her.

To be more specific, he gazed into her eyes.

Honestly, up until this exact moment, she'd thought gazing in someone's eyes was a symbolic phrase used in stories, kind of like love at first sight. It wasn't the kind of thing that happened in real life. But apparently, she'd been wrong.

The way Grant looked at her went so deep and was filled with such adoration that it resonated in her soul. It caused a physical reaction that literally drew her to him. She felt herself leaning toward him with a gravity she was powerless to stop. A gravity she didn't want to stop.

She knew what words were going to follow. She could almost hear them resonate in her mind, taste their sweetness, feel them engulf her like an embrace. They were the words she equal parts longed to hear and couldn't let him say. Maybe if they weren't uttered into the universe, what she was about to do—what she had to do—wouldn't be as excruciating.

Because, as long as she was being honest, her decision had been made long before they'd ever gotten to this moment.

"The last couple of months have been so great because of what great friends we've become? I feel the same way." She was proud of herself that the words didn't get clogged in her throat.

Grant's eyebrows knitted together. "Friends?"

She plastered the best fake smile on her face. A pain stabbed at her chest, but she pushed past it and wagged her finger, trying desperately to keep the moment playful and light. "Not friends. Great friends. And really, in my opinion, that's the best kind of relationship."

The words hung there between them.

Eventually, a resigned smile crept across Grant's charming, handsome face. "Right." Even though neither of them moved, it felt like the space between them ballooned. It left her with a bit of a chill, which was to be expected, right? Being too close was suffocating, which meant this newfound space was…

She pushed that thought aside too, because it didn't matter what it was now. What mattered was this was the right call for the long-term. She wanted to tell him that she was doing this for him. That maybe if things were different or if she'd met him four years ago instead of now, this story would have a different ending. But she swallowed those words. For starters, they didn't change anything. Also, there were some things, like whatever she'd stopped him from saying, that were better left unsaid.

Her heart ached to the point that she almost changed her mind, but this wasn't about her. This was about sparing him from the kind of hurt she knew all too intimately. She turned away, not trusting herself if she continued to look at him. The sun was starting to slip into the sea, leaving only a perfect half circle peeking out above the horizon. Its light bathed the world in a golden glow that made everything seem too good to be true. Kind of like this thing she had going with Grant.

"Wasn't it you who said the best thing about saying goodbye is knowing they're finally heading to where they belong?" She clutched her hands together in her lap and stared at them.

"It does sound like something I would say."

"And that the whole wide world is waiting?"

He drew in a deep breath and nodded. "True, for sure."

She knew this moment was going to hurt, but she had vastly underestimated the severity of that pain. This was by far the hardest goodbye she'd ever had to say, and it took every ounce of strength she had to keep herself composed and not reverse her decision. But, since she didn't know how much longer that strength was going to hold out, it was time to go. She got to her knees and rocked back on her heels in anticipation of leaving.

She forced herself to look into his compassionate eyes one last time. "You, Grant Torres, are amazing. And it has been my great honor to get to know you." She leaned forward and brushed a kiss across his cheek. "Time for you to change the world," she whispered.

And before she could talk herself out of it, she stood and made her way to the long ladder without looking back.

Grant sat on the platform and watched her walk away. So that was it, huh?

Yes, he'd had girlfriends before. He'd even claimed to be in love before. But never had he come close to feeling anything like he did for Molly.

He watched her until she disappeared in the trees. Sure, he could've stopped her. He could've said the words that had been building up inside of him since the moment they'd met. The better question was, *should* he?

Clearly, Molly wasn't in the same place as he was. She had her own goals. Her own dreams. Her own views about relationships. Maybe he could've pressed the issue. Maybe he could've even convinced her to give it a chance, but at what cost? He loved her for who she was. He'd never ask her to be anything other than that. Even if that meant he couldn't be with her.

So that was it, then. From here on out, he could honestly say he'd fallen in love once. It was the all-consuming kind of love that rocked him to his core and made him believe in words like "forever." He knew what it was like to be with the person who made him the man he wanted to be, who completed him.

Of course, the only one he'd ever truly loved also happened to be the one he couldn't be with.

Chapter Twenty Two

"IT'S OFFICIAL," MOLLY SAID AFTER she took her first sip of coffee on the balcony Tuesday morning. "Dr. Lacey comes back on Monday." She had to work to keep the note of cheerfulness in her voice. After all, this was what she'd wanted, wasn't it? For her job here to come to an end and be able to move on to the next adventure? Then why did her heart feel so heavy?

"Really?" Ellyn cradled her coffee mug between her hands, her bouncy morning expression turning somber. "I'd kinda started thinking maybe she wouldn't come back and you could stay here forever."

"Does that mean this is your last week?" Hadley's brow was furrowed with a look of concern and disappointment.

Molly had to admit their reactions were a small-scale version of her own. How had the time gone so fast? "No, thank goodness. She asked if I could stay on for two additional weeks to help her transition."

"Well, I'm sad there's an official end date," Ellyn

said. "But three weeks is better than three days, so I'll take it."

"Me, too." Hadley took a sip of her coffee. "Any idea where you'll go next?"

Molly shrugged, running through the list of available positions. "There are a few options I'm considering." And one location that was a hard pass, but she kept that tidbit to herself.

"Are any of those options close?" Ellyn gestured out to the ocean. "I'm just saying, a view like this can make a drive worth it."

"Sadly, short of trading my car for a plane, none of them are anywhere close to commuting distance." That had been the first thing she'd checked.

"Have you completely ruled out the plane thing?" Hadley asked. "Because I think you could make that work."

"I wish." Molly let out a sigh. The three of them were quiet for a moment, letting the distant sounds of waves filter through the morning air. "I was kind of holding off on committing to the next job until I had a firm end date for this one. But now that it's official, I guess it's time to get serious about making a final decision." Although a big chunk of her indecision had less to do about not knowing her end date and more to do with the fact that deep down she didn't want to leave.

Man, she was going to miss this place. It wasn't just the sweeping ocean views and the refreshing sea breezes that she was sad to leave behind, although walking away from this view would be hard. The part that she was going to miss the most, the part that made leaving so difficult, was the sense of community, the incredible people, and the life-giving friendships. And at the top of that list were the two dear friends standing on either side of her.

"And what about Grant?" Hadley gently lobbed the question in the air as if tossing a practice Wiffle Ball to a timid toddler. Ellyn shot her a warning look, to which Hadley played innocent.

Yes, Molly had been doing her best to avoid thinking about Grant since their sunset rendezvous, but that didn't mean he was a taboo subject. She was happy to answer her friends' questions. It was just that it was...well...complicated. "He leaves on Saturday." Molly tried to keep her voice as neutral as possible, as if she was a news reporter delivering the facts. She took a sip of her coffee to cover any residual emotion that might've popped up on her face.

"Saturday? Like, this Saturday?" Ellyn, on the other hand, didn't bother to mask her shock.

"The timeline for his new project moved up." Molly traced an imaginary design on the railing. Facts. She was simply reporting the facts. "But it's a good thing. This is a great opportunity for him."

Both Hadley and Ellyn stared at her for a second, neither of them bothering to hide the concern or questions that seemed to be brewing in their head.

"How long have you known?" Hadley asked, taking the first bold step into a conversation that promised to go deeper than Molly had any intention of going.

"He told me on Saturday." Once again, it was a simple fact, as if she was stating that the current temperature was eighty-one degrees. Perhaps it was a little balmier than appreciated, but it was what it was, right?

"And you're okay with this?" Ellyn lobbed from her other side.

Molly blew on her coffee, more as a stalling technique than any real need to cool it off. Of course she wasn't okay with it. Her person, the one she wanted to be with more than anyone in the world, was leaving in a handful of days. But what other choice did she have than to let him go when their expectation of where this thing was heading was in totally different directions? "I'll be leaving soon too. It's the season for new adventures."

They both continued to stare at her, wide-eyed and expectant, quietly not allowing her to get away with her vague non-answer and careful sidesteps of their questions.

After three long seconds of waiting them out, Molly lowered her cup to her lap and let out a defeated sigh. "This assignment was meant to be temporary. Goodbye was always part of this story."

The ache that had started in her chest the moment she'd climbed down that ladder on Saturday night now radiated throughout her entire body. It wasn't as much of a question of if she was okay with it as it was about doing the right thing.

And she was doing the right thing, wasn't she?

"It's for the best." Molly nodded once to confirm the truth of her statement. She just hadn't expected this decision to cause her heart to hurt the way it did.

Molly spent the rest of the day trying to push aside the aching heart and focus on enjoying what was left of her time in Emerald Cove. There was still a lot to enjoy, wasn't there? Three more weeks of getting to hang out with her neighbors. Lots of cuddles and snuggles as she treated Emerald Cove's cutest furry friends. And extra time with the turtles, including at least two of her favorite kind of appointments—the final exam.

Of course, the thought of today's final exam caused her stomach to do a strange sort of flip-flop. Grant would be there. Grant was part of all the final exams. And while she was quite clear on how she felt about him—she loved him but had to walk away—she wasn't at all clear on how she felt about *seeing* him.

Awkwardness was a guarantee. While technically she hadn't broken up with him, shutting down any sort of future between them might as well have been the same thing. And nothing was more awkward than seeing your ex for the first time after a split.

There was also a better-than-decent chance that the encounter would be hard. Her heart was still tender from letting him go. The squeeze of staring into the eyes of what could've been would only intensify the ache.

But, buried deep under all the other emotions, there was a tiny part of her that was looking forward to seeing him because, even after how everything had gone down, there was no one in the world she'd rather spend time with than Grant Torres.

She pulled into the ECTRR parking lot after a long day at the clinic trying to come up with a game plan of how to tackle the encounter with her kind-of ex. So far, the best thing she'd come up with was to act like nothing had ever happened, which seemed like a sorely lacking plan.

"Good afternoon." Kya had her normal cheerful

smile when Molly walked into the giftshop. "I've been told to tell you to head to the vet suite when you get here. They're about to bring Taylor Swifty in."

"Perfect." A flurry of nerves skittered through her, but she did her best to keep them under control.

"I hear she's being released next week," Kya said.

"That's the plan." Molly took the opportunity to shift her focus, letting her happiness for the turtle knock down any lingering hesitation. "Today's her final exam. I wore my turtle scrubs to celebrate the occasion." She struck a pose to show off her blue-and-green scrubs covered with tiny sea turtles.

"I love it! Fingers crossed the exam goes well." She crossed the fingers on both hands. "But a heads up, a tour just went through those doors. You might have to weave through the crowd to get to the vet suite."

"Thanks for the warning." Molly cautiously opened the door to the hallway, peeking through to make sure she didn't hit anyone.

Like Kya said, a group on a guided tour of the facility crowded the hall as the volunteer guide told them the specifics about the turtle hospital and how it worked.

"And here is one of our fearless vets now. Everyone give a big hello to Dr. Lawrence," Joslyn, the tour guide, announced.

All eyes turned to look at her. Molly gave a smile and a wave before she ducked into the quiet of the vet suite to start getting set up for the exam.

She had finished washing her hands and was drying them with a paper towel when she heard the cart being wheeled down the hall. Her heart lurched, which was unexpected but not necessarily unpleasant. Being excited to see Grant was a good sign, wasn't it? Maybe it meant they really could be friends, even after they went their separate ways. After all, it was their easy, natural friendship that had drawn her to him in the first place.

She snapped on her gloves and turned to the door as it started to open.

"Wow, that was one inquisitive group. I thought I'd never get past them."

It was times like these when Molly wished she had a better poker face. She could actually feel her expression fall as Claire backed through the doorway with the cart.

It wasn't that she was disappointed to see Claire. She loved Claire. Working with her was always fun. It just wasn't who Molly was expecting.

She hurried to hold the swinging door for Claire, fixing her face on the way. She peeked out in the hall to see if Grant was following along behind, but all she saw was the tail end of the tour heading through the sliding doors.

"That was a big group," Molly said.

"I heard it was a family reunion. And judging from the amount of questions, I'd say they all got the talkative gene. Poor Joslyn's going to be hoarse when she's finished."

Molly glanced the other way to make sure Grant wasn't coming from the office or the giftshop. The last of the tour made it outside, and still the hallway remained empty. "Is it just us today?"

Claire wheeled the cart next to the exam table and locked the brakes. "Yep. The new girl is orienting outside today. I didn't want to disrupt her flow by bringing her into this yet."

"Right." Molly tried to push the disappointment aside. Doing the exam with Claire was probably better anyway, since she'd be the one at the release. Plus, it would be a lot less awkward. Still, she was caught off guard by how much she missed Grant being there. But that was natural, right? It didn't mean walking away had been a mistake.

She shook her head to clear her mind and focused on the task at hand. After all, that was the real reason she was here, wasn't it? "And how is our patient today?" She helped Claire lift the green turtle to the exam table.

"Looking good. She's finished her treatments, hit all of her rehab goals, and has a healthy, appropriate appetite. She's swimming in a full tank with a high level of activity. I'd say she presents like a turtle in great health."

Molly bent over to examine Swifty. "Then what do you say we make it official and get you out of here."

After the comprehensive exam, Molly confirmed that Taylor Swifty was indeed in great health and ready to be sent home. The official release was scheduled for the following Thursday.

"You'll be there, right?" Claire asked as they loaded the turtle onto the transport cart. "Even though this release is technically public, it'll be much smaller than the last one. I have to say, I kind of like the smaller send-offs because they feel more personal, you know?"

Molly nodded. "I have to check the schedule at the vet clinic, but I'll do everything in my power to not miss it."

Claire disappeared from the room, and Molly stood next to the counter, finishing up all the notes she needed to put in the chart. After she signed the official release, that would be the last time she touched that chart, which was a good thing. Her entire goal for being here was to help more turtles return to the ocean faster. With two turtles back where they belonged and two more following close behind, Molly would say her time here had been a success. Grant and his persuasive, charming grin could be thanked for that.

She headed across the hall to his office with the finished chart in her hand, to let him know. Plus, if he wasn't going to come see her after their conversation, the least she could do was go see him.

Weaving through the desks in the open main space, she made her way to Grant's office. As she rounded the last corner and caught sight of the interior, she paused mid-step. Grant wasn't sitting behind his desk. Mateo was.

Or maybe it would be more accurate to say Mateo was sitting behind his own desk.

"Hey." She had to force herself to casually walk the last few steps into the office, doing her best to keep the surprise out of her voice. "Look at you behind the big desk."

Mateo looked up from his work and waved her in. "This chair is a lot more comfortable than my old one, but spending this much time inside is going to take some getting used to."

"I bet." She held up the tablet in her hand. "I'm dropping off Taylor Swifty's chart. Do I give this to you or Grant?" She made it a point to stare straight ahead and not glance over her shoulder to look for him. Where was he?

"Grant's already left for the day. Besides, all of this technically falls to me now, since I officially took over the position yesterday." He held out his hand to accept the tablet, an air of formalness surrounding him. "Sit, tell me about the exam."

Molly tentatively perched on the edge of the chair across from his desk. Even though she'd sat in this same spot many times before, it felt different now. "I didn't realize Grant ever left early." Once again, disappointment and perhaps a tinge of guilt pulled on her.

Mateo absentmindedly nodded as he tapped on the screen to review the chart. "It used to be a rare occurrence. But he had a few things to take care of before the move."

On the same night she was here? "Oh." Molly hadn't meant for the word to sound as disappointed as it had. She quickly changed the subject, hoping Mateo wouldn't notice. "Swifty's exam was perfect. She appears to be in great health. I don't see any reason she can't be released."

"Good." Mateo finished reading the chart. Finally, apparently satisfied with what he read, he pushed the tablet back and looked up at Molly. "I haven't said this before, but your help over the last few months has been invaluable. We really do appreciate you."

"Thanks, Mateo. That means a lot." She had to

swallow the lump that formed in her throat at the thought of leaving. And the thought of other people leaving. "I gotta say, this job looks good on you."

He leaned back in his chair, looking the most comfortable and the most like his old, joking self since he'd taken over the new role. "You think? Because a couple of these computer programs seem to disagree."

Molly motioned to the two computer screens in front of him. "Keep reminding them who's the boss. They'll come around."

Mateo chuckled. "Is that formal IT advice?"

"Consider it a free tidbit from one recent newbie to another."

Mateo paused, his playful demeanor turning more serious. "Listen, what I said the other night at the wedding..." He rubbed his jaw thoughtfully. "I might have overstepped."

Molly waved her hand to dismiss the thought. "You were looking out for your friend. I respect that."

"Yeah. I might've gotten a little caught up making sure he got what he wanted. But for the record, we all like you. And Grant is a great guy. Literally, the best."

"And like I said before, he's just a friend." No matter how much her heart disagreed. She pushed away the nagging feeling and focused on Mateo. Besides, he'd been right, hadn't he? "No hard feelings."

Mateo flashed a guilty grin, looking relieved. "Still, I know I can come off a little intense sometimes."

She held up her thumb and finger an inch apart. "Little bit. But we love you anyway."

"That reminds me. I have something for you." He reached down and pulled open a drawer of the big wooden desk.

"For me?"

He pulled out a rectangular package wrapped in plain brown paper. "Just a little something to say thanks for last weekend and all your help with Hope."

She took the package from him, the thoughtfulness brightening her mood. "Thanks." She stared at it for a moment, letting the warm glow of being appreciated wash over her before she flipped it over to unwrap it at the seam.

"Excuse me, Mateo. Do you have a second? I think we found the problem with that pump. You want to come see while we're able to replicate it?"

"Yes." Mateo popped out of his chair and headed for the door. "The big-boy job strikes again. Do you mind?"

"Not at all. I was heading out anyway." She held up the package. "Thanks again for this."

After he disappeared, she sat there in the quiet office for a second. It felt different without Grant in it. The framed family picture of him, Claire, and their parents that had sat on top of the filing cabinet was gone. The ballcap with his college logo that had always hung around the armrest of his chair wasn't there. The wrappers from whatever lunch he'd eaten at his desk had been cleared away.

And, as if to rub it in, he hadn't even been here for the exam.

She hugged the brown-paper-wrapped gift to her chest. "Time to get off," she said aloud and stood.

She drew in a deep breath and took one more luxurious moment to burn every last detail of this place, of her time here, into her memory. And then she turned and walked away.

Chapter Twenty Three

TWO MORE DAYS. THAT'S ALL Grant could think when he pulled into the nearly empty parking lot Thursday evening. He turned off the engine and sat there for a second, staring at the entrance to the place he'd worked and lived for the past seven years. The place he'd considered his second home since the day he'd been born. It was strange to think he'd be leaving it in two days.

Of course, he'd left this place before. Plus, he'd come back with every intention of leaving again. He knew in his gut that this was not where he was meant to spend his forever. But he couldn't get past the feeling that he was leaving more behind this time.

Regardless, it was time to go. He grabbed the bag of supplies he'd gotten in case he had to make any emergency repairs during the three-day sailing trip he and *Dream Catcher* would be taking from Emerald Cove to St. Pete, and climbed out of the truck.

Don't get him wrong. He was beyond excited about the new job and all of the possibilities that lay ahead. This was the right decision. He knew it. But that didn't mean that he was going to miss this place any less.

Feeling nostalgic, he decided to walk through the dark gift shop and office area to get to his boat instead of the faster route of walking through the side gate that led directly to the dock. He wanted to soak in every last second.

As expected, the gift shop was dark and empty, with only the fish in the tank on the wall making any sort of movement. He strolled through it, taking in the interactive displays they'd installed a couple of years ago and the new, revamped merch section they'd redone last spring. Molly was right. The plain front exterior didn't do justice to the thriving education and rehabilitation experience that happened inside these walls. Perhaps they should earmark funds to do something about that.

Correction: perhaps *Claire* and *Mateo* should do that.

He made a mental note to mention it tomorrow and sped up his pace. He pushed through the door from the gift shop into what he was expecting to be the dark hall of the business side of the building. Only, to his surprise, the hall wasn't completely dark. There was a thin ribbon of light coming from the office side. Either all the lights hadn't been turned off, or someone was working well past quitting time.

He pushed the door open to check it out and instantly heard voices coming from his old office. Not just any voices, two familiar voices, and he strolled through the cubicles toward them.

"It's after eight. What are you two still doing here?" He leaned against the door frame and crossed his arms over his chest, giving his father-knows-best look to Mateo and Claire.

Claire glanced up from the folders in her lap, tiredness pulling on her features. "You forgot to tell us how long all this stuff would take." She motioned to all the papers in her lap and spread out on the desk in front of her.

"Rule number one, it always gets easier on the other side of the learning curve." He knew something about that from his own experience. "And rule number two, all of this will be here in the morning. Go home."

"I know, but—" Mateo started, but Grant held up a hand to stop him.

"No buts. There will always be one more thing. If you don't find a place to stop, you'll never leave." He reached over and closed a couple of the file folders that were open on the desk. "You two have got this. There's nothing here you haven't done before. It's time to call it a day."

Mateo leaned back in his chair and rubbed his temples. "All the numbers were starting to run together."

Claire pulled out her phone and let her thumbs fly across the keyboard. "And Lance texted me not long ago that he made dinner. If I leave now, maybe it'll still be reheatable."

"Mmm. Food sounds nice." Mateo gestured at the sack in Grant's hand. "Whatcha got there?"

Grant held it up and stared at it as if he could see through the canvas bag. "Extra engine oil, batteries, and a couple of spare engine parts the boat place advised I have on hand."

Mateo made a face. "You're no help."

"That's where you've been?" Claire asked, a hint of questioning in her eyes. "Buying spare boat parts?"

Grant shrugged. "Among other places, yeah."

Her head bobbed in what looked like a nod but he knew was judgment.

"What?" Buying boat supplies was something that needed to be done before the store closed. He had a trip to prepare for.

"Claire seems to think you're avoiding a certain vet who only comes around on Tuesdays and Thursdays," Mateo offered.

"I don't think. I know," Claire added. "Every time she's scheduled to come, you disappear about thirty minutes before and get back long after everyone else is supposed to leave."

Grant fiddled with the bag, doing his best to not make eye contact with his sister. "I had a couple of errands to run."

"Why are you avoiding Molly?" Claire asked, a little more sympathetic this time.

"I—" He started to argue with her assessment but let his voice trail off. The truth was, that was exactly what he'd been doing. And clearly he hadn't been stealthy about it. "It's better this way."

Claire cocked an eyebrow. "Better for whom?"

Him, her, everyone else involved. "She was a great locum vet. If the need ever arises, I hope Dr. Lacey uses her again. But it's time for her to move on to her next assignment."

Claire narrowed her eyes. "She has two more weeks. And what happened to the whole 'distance doesn't change anything among true friends' speech you gave me the other day?"

"I'm pretty sure that speech was about family, not friends." Grant did his best to sidestep the question.

"Is she the one?" Mateo asked.

The question caught Grant off guard, and he pulled his focus off his sister to stare at his friend. "What?"

"I know you two were vibing, but it's more serious than that, isn't it?"

The thought of Molly caused a wave of complex emotions to ripple through him. Was she the one? No. It took both parties being on the same page to be the one.

But could she have been the one? If things were different? That question was where things got a little complicated.

"We were friends. I enjoyed working with her. That's all." He hadn't exactly answered the question, but it was the truth.

Mateo continued to study him. "So that's it?"

Grant held his hands up to stop the rapid questions coming from the firing squad. "First of all, her plan was always to leave when her job was finished. As was mine. According to the plan, we're both right where we should be."

Claire's brow knitted together with concern. "And you're okay with that?"

No, he wasn't okay with that. But what choice did he have? It was what it was.

"Plus," Claire continued. "When has life ever followed through on any sort of plan? Isn't it you who always says 'plans were made to be changed?'"

Mateo nodded his head at her. “She has a point.”

Grant let out a sharp exhale. What did they want him to say? That this story could have a different ending? That he believed things like distance could be overcome, and when it came to them, “forever” was an achievable word?

That he finally had fallen in love?

Those things might all be true for him, but it wasn’t true for Molly. She wanted to be “great friends.” She’d made it clear her intention was to move on when her job here was done. And if that’s what was going to make her happy, he wasn’t going to be the one to stand in the way. No matter how badly it hurt to watch her go.

“Of course,” he lied. “All good things must come to an end. Much like today’s work. Like I said before, time to go home.” He reached down and took the folders from Claire’s lap.

Claire reluctantly stood and gave his arm a gentle squeeze. “And sometimes, one ending is the beginning of an even better chapter.” She neatly stacked the pile that was on the desk in front of her and picked it up to leave.

Grant appreciated her encouragement, but at the moment, his broken heart didn’t agree.

Molly woke up early Saturday morning feeling restless. She had an idea of why, but she didn’t want to think about it. In fact, she thought it best if she pushed it as far out of her mind as possible. And to help with that, she decided to focus all her energy on cleaning her already tidy condo until it was time to meet Hadley and Ellyn on the balcony. Besides, nothing said productivity like having a shining, piney-fresh bathroom before seven a.m.

Since the condo was so small, the cleaning process didn't take long. She'd finished her bedroom and bathroom and still had time to spare. She headed into the main living space like a girl on a mission. She fluffed pillows, refolded throw blankets, and wiped down counters. There wasn't so much as a hair out of place. In fact, the only thing out at all were the two tote bags she kept hanging on the hooks by the front door. Maybe, for the sake of making the space super clean, she should put those away too. She could easily grab them from her closet when she needed them.

She swooped into the entryway and grabbed the bags. There was a decent amount of weight to one of the bags that she wasn't anticipating, and the force she'd used to pull them off the hook sent it swinging wider than expected. It bumped into the wall with a muffled thud.

"Oops," she said aloud. She examined the wall. It didn't appear to leave a ding, but she used her finger to rub the spot for good measure. Then she pulled the handles apart and peered into the bag to see what was responsible for the wall thump.

There at the bottom was the metal water bottle she'd taken to work with her on Tuesday and a brown paper-wrapped package. The gift Mateo had given her. She'd forgotten all about it.

She pulled it out and sat down on the couch, staring at the gift. She'd meant to open it that night, but had gotten distracted because...

She shook her head to clear the thought from her mind. Why she hadn't opened it didn't matter. The important part was that she open it now. She gently slid her finger under the seam and pulled the paper back from the neatly wrapped package.

Underneath was the back of what looked like a picture frame. A smile creeped across her face as snapshots of her time at Turtle Rehab flashed through her mind. Maybe it was a picture of Hope. She hated to play favorites, but the loggerhead she'd helped rescue would always have a special place in her heart, and she hadn't been able to get a great picture of the turtle with her phone.

Anticipation building, she pulled the paper away and flipped the frame over. All at once, the world around her froze. The picture staring back at her had captured her time at Turtle Rehab, all right. It just wasn't the aspect she'd been expecting it to capture.

Of course, Hope was in the center of the picture. The turtle seemed to be smiling at the camera, poised over the crystal-clear waters of the Gulf on the day of her release. But Hope wasn't the only one in the picture. She and Grant, who were holding the turtle on either side, were also smiling at the camera.

Molly had no recollection of taking this picture as they'd carried Hope into the water, which wasn't all that surprising. There'd been photographers and camera crews all over the place that day. It wasn't even surprising that the composition of the action shot was so perfect it could've been staged. She'd learned long ago that wildlife photographers were amazing at what they did.

What caught her off guard was how this one photograph, which was meant to capture the beauty of a specific loggerhead, seemed to instead capture the essence of her relationship with Grant.

They were both beaming at the camera, their heads tilted together and their smiles radiating joy. But there was so much more to them than that. Their easy comradery was evident by the way their steps, even in the photo, were in unison. Their natural teamwork and how they brought out the best in one another was obvious by the way they effortlessly carried the one-hundred-sixty-pound turtle through the shifting sands of the surf. And their love for each other...

Even if she wanted to, she couldn't deny the obvious passion that pulled them together.

But that didn't change anything, did it? She'd always known their easy friendship was a rare gift. She might've denied it in the beginning, but she was willing to admit now that, against all effort to stop it, she'd somehow fallen in love with him.

But what was happening in the picture wasn't the problem. It was what would happen down the road that had her pumping the breaks. Or, perhaps more accurately, shutting it down altogether. She wasn't walking away because there wasn't anything there. She was walking away because—

Her spinning mind was interrupted by the incessant pinging of new text messages coming in one after the other. Feeling like she was under some sort of a trance, she picked up the phone from the coffee table in front of her.

Hadley had texted,

Where are you? Your coffee's ready.

And getting cold

And then Ellyn had chimed again.

And so is mine. Xoxo

But we still love you

Molly glanced at the clock. She'd been sitting here staring at this picture for longer than she'd thought. She stood, still clutching the frame, and made her way to the sliding door.

"There you are. I was about to send a search party to check on you." Hadley picked up a mug and passed it around to her.

Molly felt like she was in a haze, but she set the picture on her high-top patio table and dutifully passed the coffee over to Ellyn anyway.

"What's that?" Ellyn eyed the frame as she took her first sip.

"A thank-you gift from Mateo." Molly avoided looking at it as she took the second mug from Hadley.

"Oh, fun! May I see?" Ellyn asked.

"Sure." She stared at it. Two, possibly three silent seconds ticked by with her not making any move to touch it.

"You might have to, I don't know, show it to us for us to see it." Hadley eyed the picture then eyed Molly.

"You okay, sweetie?" Ellyn asked from her other side.

"I think I'm in love with Grant." It felt strange to say those words out loud. She'd thought them, sure, but she hadn't let herself say them before. There was something oddly freeing about uttering them now, like a weight had been lifted.

"Oh, we don't think. We know. You're totally in love with him," Ellyn agreed.

"And please let the record show that I called that match on day one." Hadley had a confident glow.

"I'm in love with Grant," Molly said again slowly, this time considering the ramifications of the words.

"I'm guessing you still haven't talked to him?" Ellyn asked gently.

Panic started to rise inside of her like the foam of a soda that had been poured too quickly. "The man I love is leaving today, and I'm going to let him go." Which was the right decision, wasn't it? There were too many risks. Too many unknowns. Too many opportunities for someone to get hurt.

"Or you don't," Hadley said with an air of finality. She fixed her gaze on Molly. "The Molly I know, the one who's taken Emerald Cove by storm, isn't afraid of a challenge. She doesn't let the unknown scare her off."

"No sirree," Ellyn added from the other side. "The Molly I know isn't afraid to jump into the deep end when the need arises."

"I can confidently tell you that Molly is afraid of those things. Very afraid, in fact," Molly said. The memory of the day her life as she knew it came crashing down around her skidded to the front of her mind. She couldn't let that happen again. She *wouldn't* let that happen again.

"But the Molly we know doesn't back down. Not when the right thing is on the line." Hadley held her hand out, and Molly took it. She gave her a gentle squeeze. "You've got this, my friend."

"But do I?" It was one thing to jump into the middle of the ocean while wearing a life jacket to save a turtle, or step out on to the platform of a lighthouse with someone there to help her. Risking it all on love was something else entirely. And in case anyone was wondering, there was no safety gear when it came to falling in love.

"You do," Ellyn said with all the confidence of someone betting on a one-person race. "And you have your friends behind you, backing you up the entire way."

"No matter how far away you are."

The foamy panic started to subside, disappearing until there was nothing left but the truth.

And suddenly, in the morning light of what promised to be a beautiful summer day, everything became clear.

"You guys, I have to go." She popped out of her chair, sloshing some of the lukewarm coffee onto her hand. There was an urgency as a plan started to form in her mind. She tossed back the rest of the cup o'caffeine and handed Hadley the empty mug. "Thanks for the mocha. And the pep talk." She blew kisses to each of her friends and headed for the door to her apartment. She only hoped she hadn't waited too long.

"Go get him." Hadley beamed as Molly pulled open the sliding glass door and stepped in to her apartment.

"And don't worry," Ellyn called after her. "You can show us the picture another time."

Chapter Twenty Four

Grant was ready to go. He'd already said goodbye to his sister, had taken one last lap around the turtle tanks, and had done a final check of his boat. His course was plotted, his gas tank was topped off, and his fridge was full. The only thing left was to untie from the dock and push away from Emerald Cove.

He put a few bottles of water and a couple of snacks for his trip in a small cooler and secured it by the helm. He ignored the feeling that he was forgetting something, or leaving something behind. He'd tied up all the loose ends, hadn't he? Everything else he was setting free, which was the right thing to do. He was sure of it. Fine, maybe not sure. Maybe it was more accurate to say he was moderately confident.

Or maybe it was better if he didn't think about it at all.

He trotted down the steps to the deck then wove his way through it, stopping to tighten one of the latches. It was time to focus on what was ahead. As if to prove it to himself, he mentally reviewed the path he'd plotted. His mind was completely consumed with all things trip-related by the time he got to the spot where his boat met the dock.

"Were you going to leave without saying goodbye?"

He paused mid-step at the sound of her voice. That tiny flame he'd been trying to squash all morning flared in his chest, and he looked up to see Molly standing on the dock.

"I—" To be honest, leaving without saying goodbye was exactly his plan. He'd chalked the idea up to being the best thing for her, but truth be told, the decision was more about him. He'd already watched her walk away once. He wasn't sure if he could handle having to go through that a second time. "Goodbye seemed so final. I thought we could save it for later." At least, that had been the plan. He'd never said it was a good plan.

"Smart." She nodded as if she agreed with his half-hearted excuse. "Let's put a pin in the goodbye thing and we can circle back." She took two, slow sauntering steps toward his boat, her warm, expectant gaze fixed on him. "But first, I thought I'd tell you about my new assignment. Want to take a guess on where it is?"

He paused, his eyes darting from side to side as if somewhere there would be cue cards feeding him his next line. "Somewhere on the coast?" Seriously, did she have to look so kissable while they were having this conversation? It was hard to stand here and think when all he wanted to do was hold her in his arms.

She took another slow step toward him. "Bingo! From what I hear, it's a charming beachy town with tons to offer." There was a peppiness to her voice, a cheekiness that said she knew a secret. It caused the flame to grow inside him. What was she up to?

"And where is this charming beach town that will be lucky to have you?"

Her gazed locked with his, her eyes twinkling. "Sarasota."

"Sarasota?" The shock of the news caused him to sway, stealing his train of thought. "That's only forty-five minutes from where I'll be."

"That's what I hear." Her cheeky grin widened. "And as a semi-local, I was hoping you could show me around. Maybe we could try out some of your favorite places to eat."

Confusion twisted through him, and he shifted. "You want us to grab dinner?" He treaded carefully, not exactly sure of where this was going.

"I do." She grasped the railing and stepped aboard his boat; hcr eyes twinkled with the sort of playfulness he loved. Of course, if he were being technical about it, there was a long list of things he loved about her, and it seemed to grow every time he was around her. "But just to be clear, I'm not looking for a friend. And I'm no longer interested in being your non-date plus-one."

He could feel his own wide smile spread across his face as this conversation took a turn. "No? So what exactly are you looking for?" He took a step toward her.

Her passionate gaze burned into him. "Us."

The word washed through him, causing the flame in his chest to spread with the speed of a wildfire. "Now there's a word I can solidly get behind."

Molly glowed as she took one last step, closing the

gap between them. "I'm only there for a six-month assignment, but it's a start. And we can figure the rest out as we go." She slid her arms around his waist. "As long as you're up for it, that is."

Her grin, her look, the culmination of the past ten weeks overtook him, and suddenly he could no longer hold back the truth he'd been wanting to tell her. The truth that had been building inside him since the first moment he'd seen her in the vet clinic. "I'm in love with you, Molly." The world seemed to brighten as he said the words. He slid his hand behind her head, letting his thumb graze her cheek, and cherished getting to hold her without anything holding him back. "Fully, deeply, helplessly in love with you."

She swayed as if his words were more powerful than she'd been expecting. A dreamy look washed over her. "I'm pretty sure that was supposed to be my line."

Grant chuckled, confidence surging in him. "Was it, now? Sorry, I didn't mean to steal your thunder."

She huffed with playful annoyance. "So, I'm guessing that's a yes to the 'us' idea."

"That's a yes to all of it as long as we get to be together."

"That's good to hear." She gazed into his eyes with a look of pure adoration that said more than words ever could. "Because, as it turns out, I'm in love with you too."

The words blew through him like an invigorating wind, fanning the flames and making him feel more alive than he'd ever felt before. He wrapped his arm around her, pulling her close. "You are, huh?"

"I am. Fully, deeply, helplessly."

"Now who's the one stealing lines?" he teased.

"Borrowing—although, to be fair, I have every intention of using them again."

"I'd like that." He leaned in and kissed her. It was the kind of soft, passionate kiss that had been building up since the night of his sister's wedding. And much like the charming girl in his arms, it was perfect. "Why the change of heart?" he asked eventually.

"I've been wanting to add more adventure to my life. As long as those adventures are with you."

"I think that can be arranged." He gently tucked a flyaway lock of her hair behind her ear. "So what's next?"

She shrugged. "I don't know. I have two more weeks here, then I'll head that direction. Maybe you can help me look for an apartment. It'll be hard to beat my setup here. But maybe someplace nice with a view."

"Or you could come with me."

She cocked her head to the side, looking baffled. "I am. We just covered that."

"No, I mean sail this first leg with me today. I'll have someone pick you up at the town where I'm planning on anchoring tonight."

She looked at him with the same hesitant look she'd had the first day she climbed aboard his boat. "Come sailing with you, all day, on the open water?" He started to backpedal, thinking maybe he'd pushed too far, too fast. But before he could even complete the thought, her concerned look melted into an energetic smile. "I'm kidding. I'd love to."

He pulled her closer to him. "'Love.' That word

sounds good coming from you." He playfully kissed her lips.

"After trying to keep it in for so long, it feels really good to say."

"Then what do you say we get out of here? There are adventures to be had."

"Sounds ideal."

He hopped down to the dock and untied the ropes, tossing them on board. He gave the dock a strong shove before he climbed back onto the boat to join Molly. "Next stop, forever."

She grinned. "Forever. I like the sound of that."

So did he. Even more than he'd thought he would. "I almost forgot to ask. Do you want a life jacket? Or two?" He started to grab one from the storage bin where he kept them.

"No." She laced her fingers through his and they walked up to the helm. "Today, I think I'll risk it."

Epilogue

One Year Later

MOLLY BLINKED AGAINST THE GLARE of the headlights as she stood, clutching her coffee mug in the parking lot of her old condo building. It was early. Really early.

Grant's jeep pulled to a stop next to her, and she stepped forward to open the passenger door.

"This had better be good," she grumped as she slid into the seat and fastened her seatbelt. They'd come back to Emerald Cove for a visit, and she'd stayed up far too late with Ellyn and Hadley.

True, they came for regular visits, but this time, she'd been telling them all about her new, permanent job as a staff vet at the local zoo and aquarium. It took her back to her first passion and, so far, she loved it. And, of course, she'd had to hear about Ellyn's new artist and Hadley's new adventures as the owner of The Beach Read coffee and bookshop. And there was laughing. Lots and lots of laughing.

Then, as she'd been heading to bed—well past

midnight—Grant had called to say he had a surprise for her. One that required him to pick her up at four a.m.

"It's going to be great. You're going to love it." He flashed her one of his charming grins before he leaned across the seat and gave her a quick kiss.

"Where have I heard that before?" She let the sweetness of his good-morning kiss flow through her. But she had to admit, with the amount of sleep she was missing, this needed to be better than great.

They drove for about twenty minutes before Grant pulled into a vacant beach access parking lot along a stretch of the coast that didn't seem to be inhabited. They got out of the car and she peered through the darkness, searching for something recognizable.

"Where are we?"

"You'll see." He handed her a flashlight that emitted a faint red glow. "Follow me."

Molly sighed, draining off the rest of her coffee before she left the empty cup in the car. In the year they'd been together, she'd learned that it was useless to ask too many questions on one of these surprise adventures. He never gave up the details.

Also, though she wouldn't admit this to Grant for fear of it going to his head, his surprise destinations were always great.

She used the red light to illuminate her path as they walked down a wooden staircase to the beach and turned left, sticking close to the dunes.

"We have a short walk to get to where we're going. But it's a nice morning for a stroll, don't you think?" He kept his voice at a low whisper.

Molly glanced around at the empty beach as the

chill from the pre-dawn breeze blew past them. "Is it fair to call this morning? Or are we technically still in night territory?"

Grant chuckled. "Point taken. But trust me, this is worth it."

They walked for a few more minutes in easy silence before Grant slowed. He turned off his flashlight and crept forward, studying the dunes as if looking for something. Molly followed his lead, although she had no idea what she was searching for or why they couldn't use their flashlights to find it.

Then she caught sight of movement from somewhere in front of them. It was just a flurry, and she only caught it out of the corners of her eyes. She turned that direction, but she couldn't make out anything other than sand. What had caused it?

She started to take a step closer to get a better look, but Grant stuck his arm out to stop her. He was focused on the vicinity of where the flurry had been and a look of wonder lit his face.

She was used to nature causing this reaction in the man who had a heart bigger than any she'd ever known. He had a passion for the outdoors that she found inspiring. But this look was different. It was bigger, full of admiration with a hint of something she wanted to call pride.

"There it is." His tone echoed the wonderous look on his face and he crouched down, taking four slow, deliberate steps. He motioned for Molly to follow. She did, although no matter how hard she concentrated on the dark sand, she couldn't find the source of the movement. Or what had caught Grant's attention. "Do you see it? Right there." He pointed at a spot in front of them.

Molly searched again, willing her eyes to adjust. "Is that..." Her breath caught as it came into focus.

"A turtle hatchling? Yep," Grant confirmed. As the clouds moved and the moon became brighter, she could just make out the tiny turtle hatchling clumsily making his way through the sand to the water.

Molly was captivated. As much time as she'd spent working with turtles, she had yet to see brand-new hatchlings emerge from their nest and make their way to the ocean. "Wow," she breathed out. "What a treat."

"Exactly. But it gets better," Grant whispered, his grin widening with anticipation. "He isn't just any turtle. That little guy is one of Hope's babies."

It took a second for the words to register, then Molly's jaw almost hit the sand. "Hope? As in, our Hope?"

He nodded. "Our Hope."

The wonder that had lit up Grant's face now welled up inside her, leaving her speechless. She was staring at one of Hope's hatchlings? "How do you know?"

"Do you remember us talking about how we thought she might nest somewhere around here?"

"Maybe." It sounded vaguely familiar, but a lot of life had happened between now and that passing conversation. Plus, it was hard to recall year-old details on three hours of sleep.

"Well, about two months ago, her tracker showed her making her way this direction, so I started watching." Grant took a seat on the sand, looking like he was settling in to watch the hatchlings from a safe distance for as long as time would allow. Molly sank to her knees next to him, still wonder-struck. "One day, her tracker had her unusually close to the beach.

In fact, it looked to me like she came on shore. I had a couple buddies of mine check it out. Sure enough, there was a brand-new loggerhead nest right where her coordinates had been." He pointed at the dunes in front of them, where a second tiny, dark figure flopped its way through the soft sand. "Look. There's another one."

Pride bubbled inside her as a third and then a fourth hatchling emerged and followed the other two. "Her legacy lives on." An overpowering combination of joy mixed with pride flooded her as she watched the offspring of the one turtle that had touched her more than any other.

"Not only her legacy. Your legacy. You played a part in this."

"We," Molly corrected. "We played a part in this."

They watched for a few more minutes until the first turtle toddled into the waves and was carried out into the inky sea.

"Well done, Hope," she whispered, doing her best to burn the scene into her memory. "Looks like this story got its happy ending."

"Actually..." Grant cleared his throat, and she could sense his movement. "I was kind of hoping this was just the beginning." She turned to find him on one knee, holding out a ring. "Molly Grace Lawrence, will you marry me?"

Both hands flew to her mouth as, for the second time before the sun had even risen, she found herself stunned speechless.

"There's no one I'd rather tackle adventures with. No one I'd rather be great friends with. No one I'd rather spend my forever with. I love you, Molly."

Molly's gaze flickered from the ring to the face of the man holding it.

The man who believed in her when she had trouble believing in herself.

The man who showed her how to trust and reminded her how to hope.

The man who loved her.

The man she loved with her whole heart.

"Did she say yes? I didn't hear her answer." Ellyn's loud whisper came from the darkness behind them.

"I don't know. I can't see," Claire responded in a hushed voice. "We should move closer."

"Seriously, let the man propose already," Mateo jumped in.

Grant grinned, his eyes still locked with Molly's, and nodded in the direction of the motley crew. "Sorry, a few people tagged along. They insisted I couldn't do this without them."

Molly looked over her shoulder. Ellyn, Hadley, Mateo, Claire, and Lance were huddled in the dunes about fifty feet behind them, apparently doing a bad job of staying out of sight. Ellyn gave a little wave, and Claire did a discreet thumbs-up.

"Of course not," she said. Because what was life if you didn't have your friends and family backing you up? And, she had to admit, they had a pretty great group of friends and family.

"But they bring up a valid point. You haven't given me an answer yet." He wiggled the sparkling vintage-inspired engagement ring.

"Yes! Absolutely, yes." She leaned over, put her hands on either side of his face, and kissed him.

"She said yes!" Ellyn cheered in her not-so-hushed whisper.

"Are you sure we can't take a picture of this?" Hadley asked.

"No flash. But since she already said yes, we can go see the turtles," Claire answered.

Grant sat down next to Molly and slid the ring on her finger as the rest of the crew crept over and sat on the sand around them to watch the hatchlings. "You still think it's okay they came?" he whispered, wrapping his arm around her shoulders.

She snuggled into him, rested her head on his shoulder, and held her hand out to examine the ring. "I wouldn't have it any other way."

The End

Tequila Lime Grilled Shrimp

A Hallmark Original Recipe

In *The Beach Escape*, Grant and Molly are alone at the sea turtle facility during a blackout caused by a huge storm. Since they both haven't had a chance to eat, Grant fires up the grill and cooks up a dinner of shrimp with his super-secret sauce—that quickly turns romantic over candlelight. Our recipe for Tequila Lime Grilled Shrimp is so delicious, it's no secret they'll make any meal special.

Prep Time: 1 hour
Cook Time: 4 minutes
Serves: 12

INGREDIENTS

- 1/2 cup tequila
- 1/2 cup fresh squeezed lime juice
- 1/4 cup olive oil
- 1/2 medium-size red onion, sliced
- 4 garlic cloves, crushed

- 2 sprigs fresh cilantro
- 1/2 teaspoon cumin seeds, toasted
- 1/4 teaspoon kosher salt
- 2-pound large shrimp, tail-on, peeled and deveined
- Bamboo skewers, soaked in water
- Fresh lime wedges

PREPARATION

1. Combine tequila, lime juice, olive oil, red onion, garlic, cilantro, cumin and salt in a nonreactive stainless bowl or glass bowl and stir to blend.
2. Add shrimp and marinate for 1 hour, stirring frequently.
3. Remove shrimp from marinade and drain. Discard marinade.
4. Thread 3 to 4 shrimp on each skewer. Grill over medium-high heat for 2 minutes on each side or until shrimp are opaque.
5. Serve shrimp skewers with fresh lime wedges.

About the Author

Rachel wrote her first novel when she was twelve and entered it into a contest for young author/illustrators. Unfortunately, the judges weren't impressed with her stick figures, so she dropped the dream of becoming a world-famous illustrator and stuck to spinning stories. When she's not busy working on her latest book, she loves to travel with her family and friends. By far, her favorite destination is the beach, which tends to work its way into most of her stories. Between vacations, you can find her at home in The Woodlands, TX with her wonderful husband, their two adventurous kids and a couple of spirited pets.

Turn the page for a free sample of

Beach Wedding *Weekend*

RACHEL MAGEE

Chapter One

Paige Westmoreland was on the verge of pulling off the impossible. Most of the wedding planners who came before her swore it couldn't be done, and there had been a few times (two particular flaming disasters came to mind) when she'd also doubted its possibility. But here she was, about to manage the perfect wedding.

Pride swirled inside her as she stood in front of the two-story wall of windows and looked out over the manicured gardens the way a painter stood in front of her masterpiece. Sure, it might be a little premature to claim it yet. The bride hadn't even walked down the aisle, for goodness' sake. But she had a good feeling about this one. After forty-seven attempts, this was the first time she'd ever gotten this far without so much as a hiccup. Every single box on her pre-wedding checklist was marked off, the kitchen was fully staffed and running right on schedule, and the bride and groom, along with everyone they considered important to their wedding, were in excellent health and fantastic moods. From where Paige stood, she could almost see the glittering pot of gold at the end of the proverbial rainbow. And since the bride of this particular wedding was her best friend's cousin, it made the victory that much sweeter.

She drew in a deep breath, letting the joy of the perfect day sparkle through her. In her opinion, especially on days like today, she had the best job in the world. Every weekend, and the occasional weekday, she got to see love win. And, as an added bonus, she had the privilege of doing it in Hilltop, the charming resort town nestled in the heart of the Texas Hill Country.

Paige ran through the timeline for this particular wedding in her mind. Ten minutes until the groom and his men took their spots and the wedding processional started. Twelve and a half minutes until the bride walked down the aisle at exactly five o'clock. Which meant...

"I made it." The jovial voice echoed through the otherwise empty room, but even this didn't surprise her. She typed 8:30 into the timer on her tablet and pressed start before she looked up at the latecomer.

Aiden Pierce strolled across the marble floor of Hilltop Resort's famed wedding pavilion, The Chateau. He had the laidback gait and easy smile of someone for whom life always seemed to work out, and the sight of him brightened Paige's already sunny day.

"Cutting it a little close, aren't you?" She gave Aiden a hard time because that's the kind of friendship they had, but inside her pride beamed with such force she wondered if it made her glow. She'd planned this wedding so perfectly that she'd even anticipated his late arrival. Earlier, she'd caught wind that Aiden's golf game on the resort's course was going to be a close finish, and since he was the bride's cousin, she'd prepared a way to sneak him to the front row where his family was seated with minimal disruption.

Aiden tied his sapphire tie as he walked, not bothering to speed up his lazy pace. "The bride hasn't walked down the aisle yet. Therefore, I'm not late."

There was a twinkle in his eye. The same friendly one that won over almost everyone he spoke with. From what Paige had gathered in the eight years she'd known her best friend Ciera's older brother, it was impossible for anyone to be upset with him. Plus he had the kind of charismatic personality that made him instant friends with everyone in the room.

Paige glanced out the window again at her perfect wedding. Almost all of the two hundred white wooden folding chairs were occupied, but she could see the empty one on the end of the second row she'd saved for him. It just so happened that Aiden's very punctual mama, who was also aware of his tardiness, had chosen the seat right next to it. What could she say? While she could plan for most things, she wasn't a miracle worker.

"I'm afraid I'm not the one you have to convince." Paige pulled a face to show her mock concern.

With his tie in a loose knot, he buttoned the top button of his shirt and ran his hand through his wavy, sandy blond hair in a vain attempt to style it. "Mama talks a big game, but she'll be glad her baby boy's sitting next to her."

Paige tightened his tie for him, smoothing it out against the front of his shirt. This was something she did often because he claimed he liked the way she made it perfectly straight. Perhaps, if he wasn't her best friend's brother, she might've appreciated the way his strong chest felt. But he was, and their relationship, since the day she first visited the Pierce household, was nothing more than friendly.

"Or she'll be wondering why her baby boy couldn't pull himself off the golf course early enough to be here on time."

"Is it that obvious?"

She put her hands on her hips and pretended to examine him with a stern eye. Other than his windblown hair and his sun-kissed face, there was no sign he'd been swinging a golf club until less than five minutes ago. In fact, she found it a little unfair that he could look so great with such little effort. "I suppose you'll pass."

Half of his mouth pulled up into a guilty grin and he motioned outside. "With a day like this, can you blame me? Plus, it was more business than pleasure. I had to be there." He adjusted the sleeves under his jacket.

"You know what they say about excuses."

He gave her an apologetic shrug highlighted by his charming grin. Yep, it was true. It was impossible to stay mad at him. She pointed to the door on the far side of the room.

"If you slip out that door you can walk down the side and slide into your seat without anyone but your mom noticing."

"Thanks for having my back, Westmoreland." He buttoned the top button of his jacket. "On the bright side, at least I'm not as late as that guy." He nodded his head toward the main entrance above them.

For the first time during this wedding, Paige felt the slight flutter of surprise. Now that Aiden was here, she thought everyone had arrived. She followed Aiden's gaze up the grand stone staircase to the mezzanine level lobby until she saw him.

At that very moment everything stood still. It was entirely possible even the world stopped turning. Out of all the things she considered that could've gone wrong today, all the contingencies she prepared for, this one never entered her mind. She stood there, stunned.

"Hey, isn't that..." Aiden broke her trance.

"Brody Paxton," Paige finished. Her voice had a sort of breathless quality to it that she hated, but she couldn't help it.

Brody stepped up to the railing and paused. Perhaps he had a valid reason for stopping in that particular spot, but as far as Paige could tell, it was only to smolder. Which, by the way, he did so well it made her weak in the knees.

His dark hair was perfectly styled in his signature Ivy League haircut, and his well-tailored suit accentuated his lean, athletic frame. The light flooding through the door cast a halo-type glow around him, making him look like a vision out of a dream. The string quartet behind them picked that moment to reach their crescendo, and she couldn't be sure, but she thought she even heard angels singing. After all this time, her ex-boyfriend was still the most beautiful man she'd ever laid her eyes on.

He slipped off his sunglasses and gazed out the massive windows. Even from a short distance, she could see the hypnotic sparkle in his cobalt blue eyes, and something inside her fluttered. Was it her or was there a sudden lack of oxygen in the room?

"Didn't he move to Europe?" Aiden asked.

Paige nodded, trying in vain to get her scattered thoughts under control. "His company transferred him to Luxembourg." At least that's what he'd told her thirteen months and eight days ago, when he'd ended their blissful eleven-month relationship with the news that he was moving overseas. Alone.

The familiar ache pinged in her chest.

"Why is he here?" Aiden whispered.

"I don't know." The same question had been swirling around her mind as well. It had been a while since she'd talked to him, but as far as she knew, he was still living in Europe.

Visions of the dismal day she drove him to the airport trickled to the front of her memory. Watching him walk away was one of the hardest things she'd ever done. She knew the move would be good for his career, but it didn't make the ache in her chest hurt any less.

The one thing that had made it easier was hope and a promise. A faint spark of excitement tingled in the tips of her fingers as the pieces of this puzzle started to come together.

On that dreary day in the busy airport, tears had stung her eyes. Brody had told her it wasn't a breakup, just a pause. They weren't saying goodbye, just see you later. His final goodbye kiss still burned on her lips as his airport promise rung in her ears. *Someday, I'll be back.*

She would adamantly deny it if ever asked, but she'd often daydreamed about what their reunion could be like. Maybe she would meet him at the airport with a welcome home sign and a teary-eyed smile. Or perhaps he would surprise her and show up on her doorstep with a bouquet of flowers and, during some of her more hopeful moments, a ring. The setting might have changed, but the ending was always the same; he'd come back, and they'd be together again.

And here he was.

The fingertip-tingles started to work their way up her arms. She hadn't known if it would really happen. Time had a way of changing things, but what they'd shared was special. She'd been certain then he was *the one*, and seeing him now, all of those feelings came rushing back.

She started to call his name, and the excitement flooding into her threatened to launch her up the stairs and into his waiting arms. But as she took the first step, she caught sight of something else. Or rather, someone else.

Brody turned and offered his elbow to the woman stepping through the door. A smitten smile spread across his face. A smile not made for Paige. She froze in her tracks.

"Whoa. Who's that?" Aiden's words didn't help the sucker punch to the gut reality had just dealt her.

An elegant woman stepped up next to Brody. With one hand she tucked a strand of her long, auburn hair behind her ear, highlighting her delicate features, as she slid the other into the crook of Brody's arm. Suddenly the world started to spin again, a little faster than Paige was anticipating, and she swayed on her feet.

The power couple walked the few steps to the grand staircase and paused, as if displaying their beauty and poise for the whole world to see. All the excitement drained out of Paige's body, leaving her limbs feeling limp and heavy. She considered running away. Not to hide, per se, because that would've been juvenile. She liked to think of it as postponing a conversation until she was fully prepared, which seemed rather responsible. And by fully prepared, she meant the ability to speak without sounding like a blubbering idiot.

But it didn't matter if running was responsible or not: her legs wouldn't cooperate. And even if they had, there was nowhere to escape in this otherwise empty, massive room. So she stood there, with no choice but to face him, scattered thoughts and all.

Brody's gaze landed on her. His polite smile turned up the corners of his mouth, accentuating his strong jaw, before he whispered something to the girl next to him. Her gaze drifted to Paige, then refocused on him. Paige's stomach dropped when his intimate look confirmed their relationship was more than friendly.

The girl smoothed the emerald dress that elegantly hugged her curves and then draped her hand over the railing. Then they started down the wide stone steps in perfect unison.

Brody stepped with his usual steady confidence. The girl moved with the grace of a dancer, each of her footsteps skimming the surface of the stairs. The four-inch stilettos at the end of her toned legs seemed to be an extension of her foot, as if she were made to wear them. Everything about her radiated beauty and poise.

Paige glanced down at her own look in comparison. About the only similarity between them was they'd both chosen to wear almost the exact shade of green. Other than their shared penchant for emerald-colored garments, Paige was the complete opposite of the beauty on Brody's arm.

Paige had chosen her loose-fitting A-line knit dress because it had pockets, something she proudly proclaimed to her friends on staff when she arrived earlier. The fact now seemed childish. Her practical dress was paired with sensible ballet flats, which she wore more for function than fashion, and she'd pulled her hair up in a bun about fifteen minutes after she'd arrived at work to get it out of the way. Even if she hadn't, her mousy brown hair would have been hanging in a stringy mess around her shoulders at this point. It didn't matter how many products she armed her hair with, the Texas humidity always won. And although she'd put on lipstick before she arrived, she was positive there wasn't a trace of it left.

Seeing Brody unannounced at one of her weddings with some knockout on his arm was about as far as possible from any of the reunion daydreams she'd managed to come up with over their thirteen-month absence. Every awe-worthy opening line she'd ever thought up—and, embarrassingly, there were quite a few of them—was invalid. To make matters even worse, at the moment her brain seemed incapable of thinking up something new.

Brody reached the last step and his gaze locked with hers. "Hello, Paige."

The way her name sounded in his smooth voice sent shivers racing down her spine. Although, she had to admit he sounded less surprised to see her than she was to see him, which sent another round of questions swirling through her mind. The girl on his arm smiled.

Paige's mind went blank. She opened her mouth to say something, anything, but nothing came out. Brody either didn't notice or didn't care. The couple glided over and stopped in front of her.

"It's nice to see you." Brody's familiar words caused her heart to skip a beat and his gaze burned into her.

She tried to answer, but since the shock of the situation was still holding her voice captive, she offered a grin instead. Hopefully, it looked more sophisticated-alluring and less lovesick puppy.

An awkward pause filled the air. Aiden cleared his throat and stepped closer to Brody, offering his hand.

"Brody, Aiden Pierce. It's been a while."

Brody held Paige's gaze for another millisecond. Long enough for her to be positive she sensed the air between them crackle. Just like it used to.

Then he grasped Aiden's handshake and shifted his attention. "Good to see you again, Aiden." He let go of Aiden's grasp and held his hand in front of the beauty next to him, as if to put her on display. "Allow me to introduce you both to Sasha Kane."

The bitterness of jealousy mixed with disappointment rose up in Paige's throat, but she tried to appear delighted to meet someone new. When it was clear that was too tall an order, she settled for an expression she hoped looked pleasant-ish.

Sasha extended a graceful hand to Paige first. "I've heard so much about you."

Now was Paige's chance to offer some clever one-liner that would remind Brody of their times together and remind Sasha whose turf she was on. But nothing even remotely clever came to mind. And even if it had, it wouldn't have mattered because her voice still wasn't cooperating.

So Paige just nodded at her. This was not at all how she imagined their first meeting going. Once again, Aiden stepped in.

"Pleasure to meet you, Sasha." He took her outstretched hand and lifted it to his lips. Sasha appeared to be charmed. Brody glared. The whole situation made Paige feel like she might be sick.

The harsh, screeching sound of a digital alarm echoed through the room and broke up the moment. Everyone stared at the tablet in Paige's hand. Everyone, that was, except Paige, who was still trying to figure out what Brody was doing here. And why was he with *her*? And, for that matter, who was she?

Brody pointed to the tablet. "You, uh, want to get that?"

Paige stared at it for another second, trying to comprehend the sound. Since Brody had walked through those doors, she was having a hard time comprehending anything. 0:00 flashed on her screen.

"The bride!" She bobbled the tablet and fumbled with the off button, trying to get the noise to stop. The heat from her cheeks worked its way down her neck. "I gotta go."

She looked up at the newcomers. An expression of cool acceptance crossed Brody's face. Her already sagging spirit plummeted.

Aiden's hand pressed against the small of her back in a gesture she assumed was supposed to calm her frazzled nerves. "We'll catch you after the ceremony."

He winked. Then he looked to Brody and Sasha and held his hand out to the side door. "Shall we?"

The trio crossed the room and exited to the garden. Paige stood frozen in her spot, watching through the windows as Brody and his date claimed the last two empty chairs. Brody undid his jacket and ran his hand through his perfect hair before he settled it on Sasha's knee. Her own knee tingled, remembering exactly how his touch felt.

The string quartet finished their song and silence filled the air. It was the signal for the officiant to lead out the groom. She glanced at her watch, shook her head to try to clear her thoughts, then dashed across the room as fast as her ballet flats could carry her to the bridal suite.

One minute and thirty-eight seconds behind schedule.

So much for pulling off the perfect wedding. Paige plopped down in the empty chair next to her best friend, Ciera Pierce, and let out the long, defeated sigh that had been building up insider her all evening. "I need cake."

Normally she loved wedding receptions, which made her job fun even on the hard days. Being among joyful guests celebrating love was like food for her soul. But right now, a trip to the dentist for a root canal sounded more appealing than being stuck in this room. Too bad she was contractually obligated to be here until the bitter end.

Ciera pushed the plate of half-eaten wedding cake in front of her. "Great job today. The wedding was lovely." She adjusted the strap of her ice-blue dress as she stared dreamily around the room, as if taking in all the decorations.

Paige closed her eyes for a moment and massaged her temples to try to rid herself of the stress headache she'd had since the ceremony. Or, if she was being more accurate, it came on around the same time a certain someone decided to reappear in her life. Blinking her eyes open, she pulled the cake plate closer to her, hoping a sweet treat would help push Brody Paxton out of her mind so she could concentrate on finishing this wedding.

"If you don't count the ceremony starting four minutes late, cueing the wrong song for the first dance or all of the vegetarian meals being cold, then I guess it was okay." She cut off a huge bite of cake and speared it with her fork, perhaps more aggressively than she should have.

Ciera shrugged, causing her tight blonde curls to bounce around her head. "No one noticed those things."

Paige disagreed. She felt sure the seventeen guests trying to force down cold eggplant parmesan noticed, but she didn't argue.

"What everyone did notice were the Longhorn-orange bridesmaids' dresses," Ciera added. She looked out to the dance floor where the bride was dancing among a sea of orange chiffon. "I've never been so thankful to be left out of a wedding party in my whole life."

The thought of Ciera wearing the school colors of her alma mater's number one rival almost elicited a giggle. "They are an unfortunate color. The first time your cousin showed me a picture of them I thought she was joking."

"And you didn't stop her?"

"She said the color signified a time and place that were important to her and her now husband. It's kind of sweet, really." Paige paused and studied the bobbing orange mob. Even with the sweet sentiment behind it, she had to admit the amount of burnt orange when all eight ladies were standing together was a bit much. "I tried to pick flowers that would tone down the color in pictures." Of course, it didn't help when they were on the dance floor without their bouquets.

"Unless you gave them a bush to hide behind, there aren't enough flowers to mute that distraction down."

This time Paige did giggle, just a little, and she shoveled the giant bite of cake into her mouth before the next catastrophe pulled her away and she missed her chance to eat it.

But as soon as the bite hit her tongue she wished she'd been called away first. Whatever cardboard excuse for white cake had been hiding underneath the chalky fondant icing did not deserve to call itself a treat. She considered spitting it out, but since she didn't have a napkin handy, she forced herself to swallow it in one giant gulp.

"Ugh. This is awful."

Ciera glanced at the offending plate. "Oh right. People noticed that, too." She motioned to all the plates with half-eaten cake on their table then pushed her water glass in front of Paige.

It would take a whole pitcher of water to get rid of the taste in her mouth, but Paige settled for a sip from Ciera's glass. She scanned the neighboring tables for more plates of unfinished cake. As far as she could see, not one person had managed to choke down their whole slice anywhere at this reception. Great. Another thing to add to the list of things that went wrong.

Paige pushed the plate away from her and made a mental note to tell the waitstaff to clear them as soon as possible. Maybe if it was out of sight, the guests would forget how bad it was. One could hope, anyway. "I warned her about the cake. I even told her about the bakery everyone raves about, but she insisted on the one from the magazine layout from the expensive place in the city."

As soon as she said it, the music switched to a slow song. The crowd on the dance floor cleared and couples filled the space. Like a moth attracted to light, Paige's gaze went straight to Brody. He stepped onto the dance floor from the far side, looking dapper as always in his dark suit, holding the new girl's hand. After he spun her once, he pulled Sasha into himself and they glided in perfect rhythm around the floor. Paige let out a long, discouraged sigh. "Everyone wants the pretty cake and doesn't seem to care what it's got going on inside."

Ciera shot her a concerned look. "You okay, sweetie?"

"Brody's back in town," she mumbled without taking her eyes off the couple. She and Brody had looked like that when they were together, hadn't they? All happy and in sync?

"Oh." Ciera screwed her mouth to the side and

glanced in the direction of the dance floor, looking more concerned than surprised. "Yeah. I heard that."

"Wait? Heard that?" Paige sat straight up and glared at her best friend. "Like before you watched them walk into the wedding?"

Ciera kept her eyes on the dancing couple and waited a second too long before answering. "Maybe."

"You knew he was in town and you didn't tell me?" Did she have any idea how much humiliation she could've prevented if Paige had a heads-up? The memory of their disastrous meeting in The Chateau caused heat to sear her cheeks. Why would her best friend keep something like this from her?

A pained expression fell over Ciera's face. "We were waiting for the right time to tell you. We didn't want to upset you."

Paige thrust her chin in the direction of the happy couple. Hurt and frustration flanked her already dismal spirit. "Too late."

Ciera squeezed her hand. "I'm so sorry, Paige. I should have told you before tonight, but I honestly thought he wouldn't come. And if he did, I was sure he'd call you first."

Paige watched the happy couple gliding around the floor, and she had an idea of what had been keeping him too busy to pick up the phone. A fresh wave of hurt washed over her. "How long has he been in town?"

"I'm not sure. Georgia told me about it a week ago. I guess his company moved him back to work out of the office here."

"Georgia knows!" Paige shrieked, a little too loud. She glanced around to see if anyone had noticed then lowered her voice. "Am I the last to find out?" Seriously, did any of her friends know how to work a phone? Or drop a text, send a smoke signal, anything? What was wrong with these people?

Ciera took a deep breath. "You're not going to like this next part." She surveyed the room as if looking for help to deliver whatever she was about to say.

"He's one of the groomsmen in Georgia and Lane's wedding. We were trying to figure out how to tell you."

Paige didn't move as she tried to absorb this news. Georgia, Ciera and Paige had been close friends since they met in college, and the two women were bridesmaids in Georgia's upcoming wedding. The one where they would all be spending the weekend at their favorite beach in the Florida panhandle which just so happened to be the very same beach where she and Brody had first gotten together. She could almost taste the iced white chocolate mocha they would sip as they strolled through the cute town, lost in conversation, letting all the other coffees they'd gone to get for their friends go cold.

Sure, she knew Brody was friends with Lane before they started dating. Lane was the reason they met, but she never even considered him being in the wedding. When he went overseas, Paige had assumed he had abandoned all of them.

She watched the happy couple spin around the dance floor as she let Ciera's words settle over her. So, it really was over. Tears pricked her eyes.

This wasn't how their story was supposed to go. Brody's temporary European assignment was supposed to be a speed bump, something to give their perfect story an interesting twist when they told it at their fiftieth wedding anniversary. But here he was, holding some other girl in his arms.

"Who is she?" Paige whispered, afraid that if she used a full voice her tears would spill over her eyelids. And once they started, she didn't know if she'd be able to stop them.

Ciera didn't bother to turn around to look at the girl Paige asked about. "Some actress who's old summer camp friends with Lindy Grant. I guess she's about to start a new TV show that will be filmed in Austin, and she's staying with Lindy while she decides if she wants to get a place there or stay here and make the hour commute."

Actress made sense. She held herself with the kind of confidence and grace which begged people to look at her. And she was annoyingly beautiful. She was the complete opposite of Paige, which somehow felt even more discouraging.

"How'd they meet? They look pretty chummy for two people who just arrived in town."

Ciera shifted, stealing a glance at the couple. "According to Georgia, they actually met in Europe a while back. She was on location for some sort of movie near where he was living, and Lindy set it up so he could show her around on her day off. I guess she was charmed by him and they kept in touch."

"And they just so happened to move to the same place at the same time?"

"She's telling everyone it's fate." Ciera rolled her eyes. "They started dating as soon as he got back in town."

"I don't think I like her."

Ciera laughed. "No? If it makes you feel any better, according to Georgia, neither does Lane."

It did make her feel a little better, in a sad, petty sort of way. She propped her chin on her fist and watched the happy couple. "I should get back to work." Or at the very least, she should stop staring at them. Watching Brody with his new girlfriend was a bad idea, but she couldn't make herself look away.

Someone dropped into the chair on the other side of her and startled her. For the first time since the song had started, she tore her gaze away from Brody to see Aiden's cheerful face. And what was even better than seeing a friend was the delicious sweet scent drifting up from the paper baskets he held in each of his hands. "Food truck's here with the midnight snacks," he said. "Time for some decent desserts."

Paige glanced at her watch. "I didn't realize how late it was. I have to go make sure it's in the right spot."

Aiden and his investment partner owned one of the most popular restaurants in Hilltop. As a wedding gift to his cousin, Aiden had Cedar Break's food truck bring late-night snacks to the wedding partiers. According to her master timeline, she should've been out there five minutes ago to make sure everything was up and running.

"Don't worry, Wedding Boss. I made sure the truck was exactly where you told us it needed to be, and my staff was ready to start pumping out desserts. Your assistant's outside keeping an eye on it." He slid the paper tray holding his famous chocolate lava cake across Paige to his sister. "It's taken care of. And there's already a line." He winked at her and shoveled a forkful of cherry turnover a la mode into his mouth.

Aiden Pierce was more punctual than she was. Tonight was full of surprises. "Thanks." She looked into his eyes, trying to convey how much she appreciated his help.

"My pleasure. Now, what's with the somber mood? What are we talking about?" he asked through a full mouth.

Ciera cut into her cake and the liquid chocolate center oozed out. "Unexpected wedding guests." She nodded her head at the dance floor.

The music had changed to a fast song, but Brody and Sasha were still out there. Even though they weren't touching now, watching them dance to this song was even worse.

Aiden scooped up another forkful of pie and shoveled it into his mouth. "Aww, yes. The European dude." He reached across, snagged Ciera's chocolate cake and slid it to Paige. "Looks like you could use this."

Ciera, whose fork was midway between the cake and her mouth, froze. "Hey. What about me?"

Aiden tipped his chair to look at his sister from behind Paige, held his hand up to block his mouth and pretended to whisper. "Cici, you're not the one whose ex just waltzed back in town with a Hollywood actress on his arm."

"You know I can still hear you." Paige grabbed the fork from Ciera's hand and cut off a hearty-sized bite of her absolute favorite thing on Cedar Break's menu. She hoped the bitter taste of disappointment wouldn't ruin it.

Aiden draped his arm over her shoulder and gave her a gentle squeeze. It had been a crummy night, but the embrace of a good friend brightened her gloomy spirit a bit. Chocolate cake didn't hurt, either.

"If it makes you feel any better, I heard everyone thinks she's not all that," Aiden said.

Paige rolled her eyes. "You've known about her for like five minutes. How do you know what everyone thinks?"

Aiden swallowed the large bite in his mouth. "I've been shooting the breeze with everyone in the room for the past four hours. People talk, and they have a lot of opinions about her."

Ciera took a sip of her drink. "I already told you Lane said she has no personality."

Paige cut off another big bite of the cake and swiped it across the bottom of the bowl to soak up the liquid chocolate. "Is this supposed to make me feel better? Brody's gorgeous new girlfriend is boring?"

"Boring is a big deal," Aiden said. "No one likes boring."

Ciera nodded. "Truth."

It could've been truth to these two, but the fact was, Sasha had Brody and all she had was a growing void where he had once been. "Maybe being devastatingly beautiful trumps boring."

"Occasionally in the short term, but never in the long term." The seasoned voice came from behind them. All three turned around to find Aiden and Ciera's grandmother, lovingly known to all as Gram, standing behind them.

Aiden hopped out of his seat and kissed her on

the cheek. "Gram, here. Take my seat. How are you enjoying the reception so far?"

"I'd be enjoying it more if I were involved in this beautiful versus boring conversation. Sounds scandalous. I need a little scandal in my life." There was a twinkle in Gram's wise eyes as she sank into the seat Aiden had vacated with her gaze glued to Paige.

Ciera leaned across her to fill Gram in. "Paige's ex-boyfriend is back in town and he brought an actress with him." She snagged the fork from Paige and pulled the cake in front of herself.

Gram nodded as if considering the situation. "And how much of a looker is this new girl?"

Ciera shot Aiden a worried look. Paige appreciated her friend trying to spare her feelings, but it wasn't a secret. Anyone with eyes could see what kind of beauty they were dealing with. Paige looked right at Gram and gave her the most honest answer she could think of. "She could launch a thousand ships."

"She's very pretty," Ciera added. Aiden gave Paige's shoulders an encouraging squeeze.

"I see." Gram twisted her mouth to the side in thought. "This reminds me of the time when Lorissa's ex-husband returned with a supermodel who was as dumb as a box of rocks." Gram often lacked a filter. Whatever thought ran through her head came out of her mouth, which Paige loved. It was always entertaining and so different from anything she'd grown up with.

"Are these real friends or soap opera friends?" Aiden asked. Until Paige met Gram, she was unaware soap operas still existed. Apparently they did. And Gram still watched them with diligence.

Gram gave Aiden a stern look. "Soap opera friends are real friends, dear." She turned to Paige. Her weathered hand wrapped around Paige's. The warm, maternal gesture was like a hug to her broken heart. "Did you love him?"

Visions of their year together paraded through her mind. Happy memories of sweet moments when the word forever sparkled with anticipation.

Paige let out a sigh. "Yeah."

Sympathy flashed across Gram's face. "Do you still love him?" Her voice was a little quieter this time, a little more personal. Which seemed appropriate since the question felt personal.

Sure, her heart had broken when he left, which dampened love's euphoric glow, but hope had managed to keep some of the spark alive. In the back of her mind, even on her loneliest days, she clung to the image of him coming back. Someday they could pick up right where they left off, share life together, grow old together. That was love, right?

"I think so," she said.

Gram squeezed her hand, her voice returning to its normal cheerful tone. "Then do what Lorissa did."

Confusion fluttered through her. Gram's sage advice was coming from a soap opera character? "What did she do?"

"She gave him the ole' one-two." Gram let go of Paige's hand and held her fists in front of her face, jabbing the air in dainty punches. "You have to fight for love."

"Fight for love?" Paige asked.

"It's your life, kiddo. You gotta go after what you want." She punched the air again.

Aiden chuckled from behind her and massaged her shoulders. "Easy there, Sugar Ray."

Gram waved him off. "I do Sit Fit every morning. I'm as healthy as a cow."

Aiden's eyes narrowed. "It's 'as healthy as a horse,' Gram."

"Pshaw. At my age it's ridiculous to think I could run as much as a horse. But a cow who stands around and eats all day? That's more realistic. Now, shoo and get me some of that chocolate oozy cake. I need to talk to Paige."

Paige nodded her head at the door leading to where the food truck was parked. "You heard the lady. She needs some cake."

Aiden shook his head. "I get no respect around here."

Paige considered Gram's wise words. "How am I supposed to win him back when she's Helen-of-Troy beautiful?"

"Be Helen-of-Troy beautifuler."

Aiden stuck his head between Gram and Paige. "'Beautifuler' isn't a word, Gram."

Gram wagged a withered finger in his face. "Watch your mouth, young man. And while you're getting my cake, I'd like a glass of milk to go with it." Laughter crinkled her eyes. Aiden shook his head but jogged off in the direction of the door.

"I agree, though." Paige was no stranger to being in the presence of exceptional beauty. Her mother, a supermodel turned fashion designer icon, was known for being a knockout. Paige spent her entire childhood in the middle of the fashion industry among people who turned heads for a living. While Paige considered herself pretty enough, she didn't belong in the same category as they did. "In this case, I'm not sure it's an option."

Gram's mouth twisted to the side as she studied Paige. Everything got quiet for a second. "Sure it is. Being beautifuler isn't about how you look. It's about who you are. Someone may like a pretty face, but we fall in love with a beautiful soul."

Paige tilted her head to the side in confusion. "But he's with Sasha now."

"True. Occasionally people distract themselves with what's around, but when you finally see the one your soul desires, it's impossible to look away." Gram wrapped her warm hand around Paige's. "All you have to do is let the beauty within you shine and the rest will fall into place."

Gram's wisdom swirled around her, breathing life into Paige's deflated spirit. She focused on the memories of their past, the time they had spent together.

"We did have a pretty great thing going." She whispered the words almost to herself.

Ciera wrapped her arm around Paige's shoulders and squeezed. "We simply have to remind him of it."

"Then, go. Fight for love!" Gram cheered.

"But..." A thousand insecurities ran through her mind. *But what if...* Before she could go too far down the rabbit hole, Gram gently rubbed the outside of her arm.

"But nothing. Love is always worth fighting for."

Ciera clapped her hands together, a look of glee spreading over her face. "Operation Get Paige's Man Back commences now."

Thanks so much for reading
The Beach Escape. We hope you enjoyed it!

You might like these other books
from Hallmark Publishing:

Beach Wedding Weekend
South Beach Love
Once Upon a Royal Summer
Love at the Shore
A Simple Wedding

For information about our new releases and exclusive offers, sign up for our free newsletter at hallmarkchannel.com/hallmark-publishing-newsletter

You can also connect with us here:

Facebook.com/HallmarkPublishing

Twitter.com/HallmarkPublish